Wilbur Smith was born in Central Africa in 1933. He became a full-time writer in 1964 following the success of *When the Lion Feeds*, and has since published over fifty global bestsellers, including the Courtney Series, the Ballantyne Series, the Egyptian Series, the Hector Cross Series and many successful standalone novels, all meticulously researched on his numerous expeditions worldwide. An international phenomenon, his readership built up over fifty-five years of writing, establishing him as one of the most successful and impressive brand authors in the world.

The establishment of the Wilbur & Niso Smith Foundation in 2015 cemented Wilbur's passion for empowering writers, promoting literacy and advancing adventure writing as a genre. The foundation's flagship programme is the Wilbur Smith Adventure Writing Prize.

Wilbur Smith died peacefully at home in 2021 with his wife, Niso, by his side, leaving behind him a rich treasure trove of novels and stories that will delight readers for years to come.

For all the latest information on Wilbur Smith's writing visit www.wilbursmithbooks.com or facebook.com/WilburSmith.

Mark Chadbourn is a *Sunday Times* bestselling author of historical fiction novels about the Anglo-Saxon warrior Hereward, published under his pseudonym James Wilde. His *Age of Misrule* books, under his own name, have been translated into many languages. As a screenwriter, he's written for the BBC and is currently developing a series for Lionsgate and several of the streaming networks. He began his career as a journalist reporting from the world's hotspots.

Also by Wilbur Smith

Non-Fiction

On Leopard Rock: A Life of
Adventures

The Courtney Series

When the Lion Feeds
The Sound of Thunder
A Sparrow Falls
The Burning Shore
Power of the Sword
Rage
A Time to Die
Golden Fox
Birds of Prey
Monsoon
Blue Horizon
The Triumph of the Sun
Assegai
Golden Lion
War Cry
The Tiger's Prey
Courtney's War
King of Kings
Ghost Fire
Legacy of War
Storm Tide
Nemesis

The Ballantyne Series

A Falcon Flies
Men of Men
The Angels Weep

The Leopard Hunts in Darkness
The Triumph of the Sun
King of Kings
Call of the Raven

The Egyptian Series

River God
The Seventh Scroll
Warlock
The Quest
Desert God
Pharaoh
The New Kingdom
Titans of War

Hector Cross

Those in Peril
Vicious Circle
Predator

Standalones

The Dark of the Sun
Shout at the Devil
Gold Mine
The Diamond Hunters
The Sunbird
Eagle in the Sky
The Eye of the Tiger
Cry Wolf
Hungry as the Sea
Wild Justice
Elephant Song

WILBUR SMITH

WITH
MARK CHADBOURN

TESTAMENT

ZAFFRE

First published in the United States of America in 2023 by Zaffre,
an imprint of Bonnier Books UK

Typeset by IDSUK (Data Connection) Ltd
Printed in the USA

10 9 8 7 6 5 4 3 2 1

Hardcover ISBN: 978–1–8387–7959–7
Canadian paperback ISBN: 978–1–8387–7960–3
Digital ISBN: 978–1–8387–7961–0

For information, contact
251 Park Avenue South, Floor 12, New York, New York 10010
www.bonnierbooks.co.uk

This book is for my wife

MOKHINISO

I gambled on love and it paid off handsomely
Thank you for being the best bet I've ever made

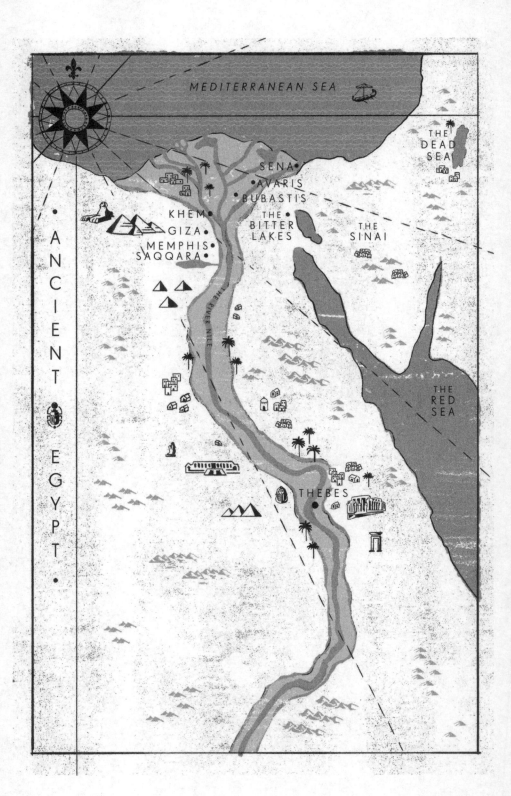

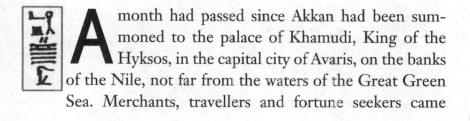

Under the chilly gaze of the glittering stars, in the flickering glow of the flames from the burning farmhouse, Akkan the Child-Killer drew back his curved bronze sword to the fullest extent of his outstretched right arm. He paid little heed to the danger of exposing his chest to the short stabbing spear in the hands of the Egyptian soldier standing in front of him. He had no reason to worry – there was only raw fear in the other man's eyes, no raging defiance, no cool calculation.

The Egyptian had good reason to be afraid. Akkan's torso was so solid and his shoulders so broad and heavily muscled that he fought with the strength of a buffalo, rather than a man. When he pulled his left arm hard behind his back, at the same time twisting his shoulders, swinging his right arm forward and putting the full force of his body behind the sweep of his blade, it sliced through the Egyptian's neck like a farmer's scythe through a sheaf of wheat.

Akkan watched as the head flew sideways. The body to which it had once belonged fell to the ground, blood spurting from the stump of its neck, to lie with the three other Egyptians whose lives Akkan had already taken.

On another night, Akkan might now have ordered one of his men to cut off the right hands of his dead enemies, to be taken to the king's palace in the city of Avaris, where a warrior could expect a reward in gold for every man he slew in battle. But there was no time for that now, and besides, he was hunting something far more valuable.

A month had passed since Akkan had been summoned to the palace of Khamudi, King of the Hyksos, in the capital city of Avaris, on the banks of the Nile, not far from the waters of the Great Green Sea. Merchants, travellers and fortune seekers came there from every corner of the mortal plane. All agreed that there was no city anywhere to compare with the size and magnificence of Avaris.

The royal palace had been constructed high above the ground on a mighty stone pediment, as if to show the Egyptians whose lands the Hyksos now occupied that other men could match the pyramids of which they were so proud. The halls, chambers, galleries and cloisters where the king and his viziers conducted the administration of their lands were arranged on the second tier, alongside the private chambers of the king, the royal family and his majesty's concubines.

The magnificence of the throne room, where the king held his audiences, was of a piece with the rest of the building. The ceiling was higher than any Egyptian temple, the columns supporting it were mightier, the golden decoration more dazzling. This was a fitting chamber for a monarch proclaimed Lord of Strength, by the grace of the Supreme God Re.

Yet when King Khamudi summoned Akkan, this vast chamber, capable of holding many hundreds of people, was virtually empty. The king was accompanied only by a dozen of his palace guards, his chancellor and two of the most eminent and learned priests in the land.

Akkan saw immediately that one of the priests came from the Temple of Re – that much was obvious from his garments and adornments. The other priest, it was equally clear to all those in attendance, represented the Temple of Seth, the Lord of the Red Land and god of storms, disorder and violence. Seth was an Egyptian deity, just as Re was merely another way of naming the Egyptian sun-god Ra. The Hyksos, mindful that the land of the Pharaohs was also the land of the gods who watched over it, and not wanting to provoke divine wrath, had adopted both deities as their own.

Akkan had looked at Khamudi and noted the way his face twitched, and his body shifted and twisted on his gilded throne. He also noticed the urgency with which the priests were conferring with one another and the suddenness with which they fell silent when they heard his approach. They were uneasy, but then, in Akkan's experience, most people were tense in his presence.

This, though, was something else. Akkan felt certain that these people had been apprehensive before the mighty double doors of the chamber had even been opened to allow him into the room. Now, he suspected, they were going to hand whatever it was that troubled them on to him, so that he might worry about it in their stead.

Akkan reached the foot of the step atop which the throne was placed. He got down on his knees and prostrated himself before the king, only rising when his ruler commanded him to do so.

'Lord Chancellor,' King Khamudi said, with a little flick of the hand that served as an order to proceed.

The chancellor was a soft man, as pampered as a temple cat and, Akkan wagered, as apt to run away at the first sign of a fight. When he spoke, his reedy, affected voice bore the accent and intonation of the high-born Egyptians who, though conquered, still clung to their airs and graces, lording their sophistication over mere coarse Hyksos like Akkan.

'Greetings, Akkan, son of Abisha of Uru-Salim, in our father-land of Canaan,' the chancellor began. 'For many years we have held the lands of Lower Egypt. The river delta is under our reign and the coastal lands, too. Memphis, ancient capital of the pharaohs, is ours and the pyramids that rise not far from its walls. Yet still the Pharaoh Tamose – that imposter – clings to Lower Egypt and raises his standard over the city walls of Thebes.

'Now, though, we are ready to finish the conquest that our ancestors began. All the lands of Egypt lie within our grasp. The number of soldiers in the false Pharaoh's armies has diminished day by day, like a storehouse from which grain is constantly taken, but which is never replenished. Our forces are growing mightier each day.

'Soon His Majesty the King – may Re ever guide and strengthen his arm – will order our army to march on Thebes.

We will drive the false Pharaoh and his followers out of the city, all the way south to the kingdom of Kush, to once again beg for sanctuary in those savage lands. Our victory is inevitable – that is beyond any doubt. Thebes will fall back into our hands, just as it did when our ancestors first entered these lands and sent the rulers of Egypt flying away up the Nile, to the furthest cataracts. Our armies are strong, our soldiers brave, our generals possess supreme knowledge and our great king is wise. Above all, our Lord God Re protects us . . .'

But . . . Akkan thought, only just resisting the temptation to speak the word out loud.

'But . . .' the chancellor said. 'There is a new element that will ensure that our victory is even more complete and render our rule over all the lands of the Egyptians both absolute and eternal. It would give us communion with the gods of this land, enable us to harness their divine powers for our own use.'

Akkan's nature was untrusting; he was suspicious of any claims made by other men, but the chancellor's words had gripped his attention.

'Since this is a religious matter, I will let the priests explain it more fully,' the chancellor said. 'I believe that the venerable Mut-Bisir, High Priest of the Temple of Seth, will speak on behalf of both of our priestly guests, since you are yourself a man of Seth, is that correct?'

Mut-Bisir nodded. 'It is so.'

The silver-haired priest stepped forward. Akkan noticed that he was holding a *was*-sceptre – the long staff, with a stylised animal head at one end and a two-pronged fork at the other, that was normally pictured only in the hands of gods and pharaohs. Avaris was evidently now such a powerful city that its priests had become gods themselves.

'Greetings to you, Akkan,' Mut-Bisir said. 'Your devotion to Seth has been proved beyond any possible doubt . . .'

'They call me the Child-Killer,' Akkan said, bluntly, enjoying the discomfort that his words caused the eminent figures in front of him. A man who was willing to do what he had done, in order to quench his desires, was capable of anything. Such a man was very dangerous. But, by the exact same token, he could be very useful.

'Indeed . . . indeed . . .' Mut-Bisir said, before continuing, 'And I gather that you are an initiate to the rites of the blue lotus, one of those whom the orchid transports to the very presence of Seth, the ever-merciful . . .'

It was all that Akkan could do not to laugh. Seth was as merciful as a viper's bite. But then, the priest knew this only too well. Why else would he lie to gain favour with his god?

'I am,' Akkan said, straight-faced, without feeling the need to reveal that the savagery of his sacrifice had enabled him to enter the presence of Seth without the need for the tinctures brewed from the orchid's leaves and seeds.

'Very well, then,' Mut-Bisir said. 'Let me explain why we have summoned you to Avaris. Three months ago, a man arrived at the palace, still caked with dust from his journey, insisting that he had information of great importance to the realm. He said it concerned both mankind and the gods.'

'The wilderness is littered with men like that, all claiming to be prophets,' Akkan said.

'Indeed it is,' Mut-Bisir agreed. 'But this man was Hyksos, a man of some substance and, ah . . . known to His Majesty's advisors. We three broke bread together with him and he told us how he and his men had come across a traveller – a messenger, as it turned out, who had slipped while descending a steep hillside, injured his leg and was unable to walk. The man was covered in tattoos. His arms, his limbs, his chest were thick with strange symbols, and there were black circles of ink around his eyes and his nose too, so that he looked like a living skull.'

Akkan was intrigued. 'What made anyone think he was a messenger?'

'Because he was carrying a small bronze tube, in which was a rolled papyrus.'

'And what was on this papyrus?'

'More symbols. No one has been able to read them. And the injured traveller refused to utter a single word.'

'So, make him talk.'

'Our informant had already tried that, but the man died of his wounds, and, perhaps, from the means used to persuade him to talk. He refused to divulge any information, to even speak . . . except for one thing. With his final breath, the messenger uttered a single sentence – "You will not be the one to solve the Riddle of the Stars."'

'So, what is the riddle?'

'That, too, is unknown to us. But for these past three cycles of the moon, priests from both our temples . . .' Mut-Bisir paused to nod in acknowledgement to the other priest, 'have been searching all the archives and libraries across our conquered territories. We have found fleeting references to this riddle. We have discovered that it dates back centuries. We understand that anyone who solves the riddle will be rewarded with wealth and power beyond any ever seen in this world. And we believe it has a connection with the gods. However . . .'

Mut-Bisir paused, to emphasise the significance of what he was about to say.

'The power of the riddle will surely be bestowed on the wise one that solves it. Therefore, if the Egyptians should somehow learn of its existence and beat us to its solution, then they would be all-powerful, and we would be their conquered slaves. The whole future of our people is in danger. Either we triumph by solving this riddle, or we are destroyed. There will be no in-between.'

'This much we also said to the man who first came to us with his story and his encrypted message,' the chancellor said, re-entering the conversation. 'We told him that if he could find the means to solve the riddle, he would be rewarded with treasures and estates that would make him the envy of all men. But he has not succeeded. So, now we make the same offer to you. Go to Memphis and consult with the scribes and scholars there. Learn all you can of this Riddle of the Stars. Then journey on to Thebes. His Majesty will be in residence there, once the remnants of the false Pharaoh's army have been obliterated. There you can reveal the means by which men will share the power of the gods.'

The chancellor's voice took on an encouraging, even ingratiating tone. 'The task should be well suited to you, Akkan, since you are already a man who talks to gods.'

'There are times when I hear Seth's voice,' Akkan said. 'But I am his servant, not his master. He may or may not choose in his infinite wisdom to assist me, if by doing so I will serve his own, greater purpose. But he will not do my bidding, no matter how I plead. So, with respect to His Majesty the King, and you great men, this appears like a hunt that will never yield its quarry. Why should I waste my time on it?'

The chamberlain smiled, and Akkan realised that he had walked straight into a very carefully laid trap.

'Because the man who came to us was your brother, Khin . . . your younger brother . . . whom you despise . . . So, do you really want to take even the slightest risk that he might become the richest man in all Egypt, because he accepted a challenge that you refused to face?'

The man who was sitting alone in the furthest corner of the tavern had long since forgotten his own name. It had vanished from his mind. Time – and there had been so much of that – had robbed him of many things, but it had also taught him much.

He understood how limited his fellow men were in their perception of the world around them. They only knew what their senses told them, and so were deaf to the sounds that could not be heard and the sights that could not be seen. And when they felt, without knowing quite how, that there was far more to existence than was apparent to them, they told themselves stories to explain the inexplicable.

So, for example, Akkan, son of Abisha, brother of Khin, would have entered the city of Memphis and then proceeded along a certain street, knowing that this was somehow not his idea. And, being the man that he was, with the beliefs that he held, he would, no doubt, be telling himself that it was Seth who was guiding him. And yet it was not so. Akkan was just a piece on a board. And there had been so, so many pieces just like him, over the years that stretched away into the distant past like a river flowing and disappearing into the morning mist.

One day, one of those pieces would survive until the end of the game, and they themselves would become the player. Maybe that piece would be Akkan, or perhaps it would be one of the others who were, though they might not know it yet, embarking upon the age-old quest. Only his old friend, time, would tell.

On entering the bar, the man had offered the innkeeper a small clay jar filled to the brim with salt, in exchange for a cup of beer and a small loaf of bread. It was far too generous – the innkeeper would have settled for a couple of fish or a few bright beads to pass on to his wife – but the man had no desire to haggle.

He had no interest in the food or the drink, either. But they were the price for the seat and table.

The man was tall and dressed from head to toe in a hooded black robe, like a desert tribesman, with the hood up and a black scarf across the lower half of his face. He had made very brief eye contact with the innkeeper and exposed his hand when he put the salt down on the counter. In time, the innkeeper would remember that the skin around the man's eyes had been black, while that of his hands and wrists was unusually pale. But the man would be gone by then and had no plans to return.

A slave approached him, holding his bread and beer. She was a child, no more than nine or ten years old. So, even though the man was sitting at the table and she was standing, she still looked up at him when she placed the cup and the loaf on the table. And as she did that, the scarf slipped from his face. The slave girl's

eyes widened in shock and fear and she let out a little whimper –
too soft, thank goodness, for anyone else to hear.

The man fixed his eyes on hers. 'Ssshhhh . . .' he said, very
softly, raising one of his pale fingers to his tattooed lips.

She had no need to fear him. Yes, he was capable of taking
a life without a second thought, but only when it was strictly
necessary. He had no desire at all to harm an innocent child.

The girl sensed that she was safe with him. She gave him a little
smile, then turned around and trotted back towards the counter.

The man replaced his scarf, wondering what the significance
of it slipping might be, then smiling inwardly as he realised that
he was no better than Akkan – just another mortal seeking to
know the unknowable.

Then, as the name of Akkan entered the man's mind, so the
Child-Killer entered the tavern. The slave girl saw him and
hid behind the counter. The innkeeper asked Akkan what he
required and received no reply. Then Akkan saw the man and
smiled, broadly.

Now he is congratulating himself, the man thought. *He has
decided that it was not his god that led him here but his own astute-
ness. Well . . . wrong on both counts.*

As Akkan walked across the room, his brute physical strength
was evident. So, too, was the sharp, predatory glint in his eye. This
was a very powerful piece in the game, the man thought. One
who might go all the way to the end of the quest. But perhaps his
strength itself, and the degree to which he both took it and the
power of his god for granted, might be his greatest weakness.

Fear could prevent a man from taking unnecessary risks, and a
sense of his own vulnerability would cause him to enlist the help
of others. This man was never afraid; nor were other people
anything to him, apart from tools to be used and thrown away.
But still, Akkan was as powerful as any man he'd ever seen, the
man thought. He was not to be underestimated.

Akkan walked up to the table. He saw the man, and this time,
when the scarf fell away, it was entirely deliberate.

For a second, even the mighty Akkan flinched. His right hand grasped the hilt of his sword. He was about to give an order, accompanied by a threat, but the man saw no need to go through that charade; it would draw too much attention to them both. He simply replaced the scarf, then got to his feet and started walking very calmly past Akkan, towards the door. And beneath the linen fabric that covered his mouth there was the merest hint of a smile.

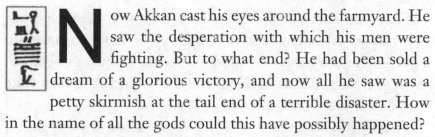

ow Akkan cast his eyes around the farmyard. He saw the desperation with which his men were fighting. But to what end? He had been sold a dream of a glorious victory, and now all he saw was a petty skirmish at the tail end of a terrible disaster. How in the name of all the gods could this have possibly happened?

The Hyksos advance on Thebes had gone perfectly to plan. On the very eve of the final battle came the finest news of all. Pharaoh Tamose, venturing out from his tent to inspect his troops, had strayed too close to the Hyksos lines. A volley of arrows had been loosed and Tamose had been struck by one. Some even said he had died. But whether wounded or slain, his loss seemed like the final blow to Egyptian hopes. The victory of the Hyksos was now a foregone conclusion.

Then the unthinkable had happened. The mighty forces of the Hyksos had clashed with the tattered remnants of Egypt's army, and the battle had gone exactly as King Khamudi had planned. Victory was within the Hyksos' grasp and then, at the very last moment, the cursed Egyptians had suddenly found allies – a whole army of scarlet-cloaked Spartans, and a monstrous troop of huge grey beasts with fearsome curved tusks, who charged through the ranks of the Hyksos, smashing their once-invincible chariots into kindling for Egyptian campfires.

Akkan and his men had played no part in the battle. Their duty was best served by keeping their captive alive and in their hands. They could only watch as triumph became disaster, and with Thebes still firmly in enemy hands, Akkan was forced to close his eyes and seek his master's guidance. Through his divine providence they had been led to this farm, well away from the main line of the Hyksos retreat and the advance of the Egyptians.

The farmer, his family and his slaves had put up no resistance. Akkan had ordered the farmhouse to be set on fire, so that in the unlikely event of any forces from either side passing by, they would assume that it had already been looted and not stop to ravage it themselves.

That task completed, Akkan took his men, their chariots, their horses and their captive to a grove of date palms, out of sight of the track that ran past the farm. They would spend the night there, Akkan decided, and then, when dawn came, he would formulate a new plan of action.

The Egyptians had arrived out of nowhere, a company of them, emerging out of the night and coming directly to the grove.

They found us as easily as I found the tattooed man, Akkan thought.

But he was immediately too busy fighting to take that realisation, and its implications, any further. Now, for all the Egyptians he had killed, and for all his men's skill and bravery, Akkan knew that this little skirmish was about to be lost, just as the great battle had been lost.

Akkan closed his eyes and called to Seth. He knew he was quite safe to lower his guard, for no matter how long he spent with the god, no time ever passed in the land of men.

Each man who could look upon the gods did so in his own unique way. Whenever Akkan gazed upon Seth, the deity came to him with the body, voice and language of a man, but with the head of a jackal. Now Seth spoke in a voice so deep and so powerful that Akkan could feel his very bones vibrate, giving instructions about what would happen and what had to be done, both now and in the days to come.

Akkan gave thanks to Seth, praised him and swore eternal obedience. Then he opened his eyes. Sure enough, it was as if he had done no more than blink. He stepped away from the fighting and walked quickly back to where the captive lay with his hands and legs bound and his head covered by a leather hood. He had not wanted any strangers to see his all-too-memorable face, and Akkan knew that his men preferred it to be hidden, too – they believed that the tattooed man was a demon in human form.

Akkan, however, knew the difference between a demon and a man, and he felt strengthened and reassured by all that Seth had told him. He was quite calm as he squatted down beside the hooded figure.

'I've come to a decision,' Akkan said, pulling out a knife. He put it to the captive's throat, pressing down until a bead of blood appeared at the tip of the blade. 'It's time for me to disappear . . . but I won't be far away. I will be watching you, wherever you go, and I will, in the end, uncover the secret that you are hiding.'

Akkan paused for a second, then in one swift movement he cut the drawstring that secured the hood around the captive's neck. The confident, all-seeing eyes that lived within that death's head looked back at him as he pulled the leather up and over the man's shaven skull. Amid the chaos all around him, the tattooed man seemed absolutely at peace.

Standing, Akkan took one last look around the grove. The Egyptians were on the point of overpowering his men. One or two of the Hyksos were throwing down their swords and pleading for mercy.

Akkan made sure that no eyes were pointed in his direction, then he vanished from the scene, as if he had never existed at all.

Outside the great walls of Thebes, at the furthest, quietest point of the victorious army's encampment, close by the banks of the life-giving Nile, a slender grey cat with cool green eyes was strolling with calm self-assurance between the elephants gathered for the night within a hastily constructed wooden enclosure. The huge animals were exhausted after the battle – the deafening noise, the frantic movement and the war-stench of men's sweat and blood.

The elephants stamped their feet on the ground, flapped their ears and shook their heads, sweeping their tusks, whose creamy ivory was still stained with Hyksos blood, from side to side.

The cat, however, seemed entirely untroubled by the possibility that her slender, sinuous body might at any moment be crushed by the great beasts. She walked with her head held high and her tail proudly erect. And as she passed among the elephants, they seemed to be calmed by her presence and they lowered their heads, one by one, as she went by.

A tall, graceful woman with night-black skin was watching every step of the cat's progress. Her willowy figure was both covered and shown off by the azure dress that hung from a bronze clasp at her shoulder. Now she clapped her hands in delight.

'You see, my darling,' she said, her eyes sparkling as she turned her head to the young Egyptian man who stood by her side. 'I was right, Bast has been blessed by the goddess. Even the elephants bow down in her presence.'

'Ha!' laughed Piay, the spy and adventurer, who loved Myssa the Kushite with all his warrior heart. 'Those elephants are exhausted . . . It's a wonder that they aren't on their knees as she goes past!'

Myssa aimed a playful slap at Piay's chest and he responded by wrapping both arms around her and pulling her closer. He lowered his head towards hers, fully intending to kiss her soft, full lips.

'I've spent the entire day and most of this evening risking my neck,' Piay said, 'first in that battle, and then rescuing you from that evil bastard Sakir. So, now I want a hearty meal, a river of strong drink and . . . above all, my love, my goddess . . . I want you.'

'No,' Myssa said, placing her fingertips on his mouth to stop its advance. 'We have a serious theological matter to settle first . . . And then maybe . . . just maybe . . . you will get all you desire.'

'Very well then, speak.'

'First, that cat bears the name of the lioness goddess, Bast—'

'Only because you named her so.'

'I named her because I could feel her power. And Bast can perform miracles. You can't deny it, because you've seen it yourself. She can leave us one day in one place, and we then go somewhere else, far away, without her . . . and a short while later she'll just reappear and walk up to us as if she'd been with us all the time. How does she do that . . .? Come on, then, answer me that?'

Piay shrugged. 'I admit, I've seen that . . . and I can't explain how she does it.'

'So, I win. And all you have to do to get everything you want tonight . . .' Myssa got up on tiptoes, put her mouth close to Piay's ear and lowered her voice to a soft, deep purr that sent the blood hammering through his entire body. 'Absolutely everything you can imagine and more besides.'

'Yes?' Piay said gruffly, using every last scrap of his willpower to hold himself back from throwing Myssa to the ground and having his way with her there and then. 'What must I do?'

'Just say, "Myssa, you are right, as always. Your cat is touched by the gods."'

Piay hesitated. His lust said, *Speak!* But his pride said, *No!*

'Say it!' Myssa repeated.

Piay gave a great sigh of defeat. 'Myssa, you are right . . . as you are most of the time . . .'

'Be careful now . . . Think what you might be missing.'

'As always . . .' Piay conceded. Then a wicked smile played at the edges of his mouth. His hand began to stroke Myssa's thigh, his fingers going higher and higher, and he leaned forward to whisper in her ear.

Myssa giggled, all pretence at sternness gone, and she might have given herself to him right there, were it not for a rough male voice calling out, 'Give it a break, you two, and get on with saying goodbye. There won't be a drop of beer left in the whole of Thebes if you carry on like this.'

Piay and Myssa reluctantly untangled their bodies.

'Yes, of course, sorry, Hannu,' Myssa said, reaching up to tidy the mass of curly black hair that had sprung from the blue ribbon that exactly matched her dress.

'At last . . .' Hannu muttered. He was a retired soldier, discharged from the elite Blue Crocodile Guards, when the limp he had acquired from a Hyksos sword, slashed across his right leg, had left him unfit for service. He'd been reduced to begging in a dusty street when Piay first met him.

Whenever Piay described what had happened next, he would say that he had taken pity on Hannu's wretched condition and offered him work, food and shelter. Hannu told a different story: that it was he, Hannu, who had taken pity on this raw young man and had decided to guide him on his path in life. Each was happy to let the other persist in his delusion.

The elephants and the Tumisi tribe would be heading south in the morning. For the next few minutes, the humans said their farewells to the men who had been their loyal, courageous companions and the animals they had come to think of as friends. They had travelled together, all the way to Thebes from the furthest depths of the land of Kush, far to the south, beyond even the source of the Nile itself.

Hannu lingered longest with Mero, the senior male of the herd. The elephant was massive. Hannu was short and stocky, with a thick, simian mat of wiry black and grey hair across his back and his chest. They were as unalike physically as two creatures could possibly be, and yet the bond between them was undeniable.

'They're two of a kind,' Myssa said. 'A pair of grumpy old men, who'd rather die than admit that they have sweet, brave, loyal souls underneath all that bad temper.'

'Two grumpy old men that I'd rather have beside me in battle than any other man or beast in the world,' Piay agreed.

'Well, you'd better let Hannu get to his beer if you want him by your side when the next battle comes along.'

'I've had my fill of battles,' Piay said. 'I just want a nice quiet life on a farm with you. I told Taita that, just now. You heard me say it.'

'Yes, and I also heard him say that he wouldn't allow you that life because you'd regret it in the end.'

'What does Taita know?' Piay asked, and then couldn't help laughing at the sheer absurdity of the statement.

'Everything!' Myssa replied, also laughing, for Taita had been Piay's teacher and surrogate father, and was now his commander. Despite being both a slave and a eunuch – neither a free man, nor a complete one – Taita's unmatched gifts of wisdom and insight had made him the indispensable advisor and confidant to a succession of pharaohs. And his skills in both warfare and diplomacy had won Egypt its victory this day.

Piay gave Myssa a kiss, a tender, gentle sign of his love, and she responded in kind, knowing how much more passionate their embrace would be when they finally found their way to their lodgings.

When their lips finally parted, Myssa looked around and asked, 'Where's Hannu?'

'Where do you think?' Piay replied. 'Come on, let's go into the city and have some fun of our own!'

Piay and Myssa made their way, arm in arm, through the camp towards the city's River Gate. Bast was nestled in her owner's arms, contentedly observing all that was going on around them.

Here, the flames came not from burning farmhouses, but crackling fires, surrounded by warriors, who slaked their thirst with flagons of beer and bellowed rousing songs of lives well lived and battles hard fought. Egyptian soldiers, bare-chested, their once-white kilts now filthy with dirt, sweat and blood, moved among their crimson-cloaked Spartan allies, slapping backs and joining in the revelry.

Dotted in between the men were the brightly painted faces and underdressed bodies of Theban courtesans, who had left the city's brothels to ply their trade among men who were only too keen to be their customers. And having settled on their price, neither the women nor the men had any qualms about conducting their business.

'How long, do you think, before the men start fighting over the women?' Myssa asked.

Piay laughed. 'Not long! But don't worry, those girls know just how to deal with drunken soldiers . . . and they'll be very happy when they empty their purses in the morning.'

'Hmm . . .' Myssa murmured in acknowledgement of Piay's words.

They passed through the gateway, with its sturdy guard towers on either side, and into Thebes. The presence of the Hyksos armies to the north and the threat they had posed for so long had cast a deep pall upon the pharaoh's capital. But now a heavy burden had been lifted from the city. She watched a boy, no older than ten, and his mother hugging a soldier as the man kissed the boy on his neck, his forehead and then on the top of his head.

'What's the matter?'

She gave him a gentle smile. 'No . . . I was thinking of us, and the one big thing that you and I both have in common.'

'Apart from wanting to be together all the time?'

'No, I mean, something that has happened separately to each of us in our lives.'

Piay frowned, then sighed as he realised what Myssa meant. 'We're alone in the world. Both of us have lost our families.'

Myssa nodded. 'Yes . . . but at least I was old enough to look after myself when the slavers came to destroy my world. I could understand what was happening. You were so young . . .'

It seemed strange to Piay that he and Myssa should be having a serious conversation at such a moment. He wanted to say, 'Let's talk about this another time', but he knew Myssa well enough to realise that he would be wasting his breath. This was a subject that she wanted to discuss. It would be better and quicker to just let her get it over and done with.

'I was just a normal little boy,' Piay said. 'My parents weren't rich or powerful and we didn't have many possessions, but that didn't matter to me. I didn't know any other sort of life.'

Myssa nodded. 'I was just the same. All I knew was my village.'

'Then one day,' Piay went on, 'my father told me that we were going on a journey, to meet the wisest man in all Egypt. Of course, they were talking about Taita. I thought that we were just visiting and that I'd go home afterwards with my parents. It never crossed my mind that they would leave me there. But then they went away, and they didn't take me with them.'

They were passing a tavern, not far from the pharaoh's palace. It had wooden tables and benches outside. While Myssa found them somewhere to sit, Piay went in and bought a flagon of beer, some bread and a bowl of spicy goat stew. He had not eaten all day, nor drunk anything but brackish water from a leather flask. No sooner had he sat down, and shared out the food between them, than the stew was gone and the flagon empty.

'By Ra, I needed that,' he said, placing the stew bowl on the ground, so that Bast could lick it clean.

'Me too,' Myssa said, and then added, 'So, why did your parents hand you over to Taita, do you think?'

'I wish I knew,' Piay said as Bast hopped back up onto Myssa's lap.

'Maybe they thought they were doing the best thing for you – giving you a life that they could never provide. They were handing over their only child. It must have been a terrible loss for them.'

'That's one way of looking at it. But they might just have reckoned that if Taita raised me up in society, they'd benefit. Or maybe they just wanted one less mouth to feed. One less little person getting in their way. Does it really matter what the reason was? They're gone from my life. They may both be dead by now, for all I know. There's nothing I can do to change the past, so why even think about it?'

'Because I can see it in your eyes – the sadness, the loss. Here you are, this strong, handsome man, with your square jaw and your big muscles, but there is a little boy inside you, who is lost and all alone.'

Piay had been leaning across the table, with Myssa's hand in his. Now he let go and turned his head away, as if her words had hit him like a slap in the face.

'I'm sorry . . .' Missa said, trying to appease him. 'I didn't mean to hurt you—'

'Just to make me feel weak.'

'No, that's not it at all.' As Bast hopped up onto the tabletop, Myssa leaned across and took Piay's hand again. 'I'm saying that I desire you because you are the kind of man that any woman would want. You are a warrior, a leader . . .'

Bast curled her tail neatly around her legs, watching the humans perform their little drama.

Myssa paused to look at Piay's face. He still looked far from happy, but she knew that there was one more form of praise that no man could resist.

'And when we make love,' she said, 'I can feel your strength around me and in me and it makes me feel helpless, but also protected. So, you are a man, have no doubt of that. But when

I see the sadness and loss in you, I know that you have a tender soul, and that I can protect you in the way a woman can, by sheltering and nurturing that part of you. You've saved me . . . but I can save you, too.'

Something beyond the tavern caught Bast's eye. She got up, stretched and walked to the edge of the table and dropped back down onto Myssa's lap.

'And there is one more reason why I love you,' Myssa said. 'You . . . Ow!'

Her words were rudely interrupted as Bast suddenly hissed and stabbed her claws into her owner's dress and the skin beneath its fine cotton fabric. With her footing secure, the little grey cat leaped to the ground and raced away down the street.

Myssa frowned. 'Something's bothered her.'

'Let her go,' Piay said. 'She can look after herself,' he added, contemplating a second round of beer and stew.

'No . . . this is serious.' Myssa looked at Piay and said, 'Trust me, she wants us to follow her.'

Piay reluctantly got to his feet, then had to break into a run to catch up with Myssa and Bast. The cat trotted ahead of her pursuers, and then darted along a narrow alley between two rows of warehouses.

The alley was deserted, the darkness between the buildings broken only by the amber glow of a couple of oil lamps above the doors of one of the warehouses at the far end of the passage.

Bast suddenly stopped in her tracks, arching her back, and spat as if some predator waited just ahead in the shadows. Myssa crouched down beside her pet.

'What's the matter with you, my darling?' she cooed, reaching out to stroke Bast's back.

The cat flinched, rejecting Myssa's touch, still looking down the alley with her teeth bared.

Piay peered into the darkness, wishing he had Bast's feline night-sight. Slowly, his eyes became adjusted to the half-light and he was able to make out a grey shape sprawled on the dusty ground like a dropped sack, a few paces up ahead.

'Oh no . . .' he whispered.

Fearing the worst, Piay drew his sword, his senses alert for whatever dangers might be lurking up ahead.

As he drew closer, he could make out the body of a man, dressed in a white robe. Blood had pooled around the corpse from a slash across the man's throat. His face was contorted in a rictus of fear and pain.

'Stay back,' Piay hissed to Myssa. 'The killer could still be here.'

He wondered who might have committed such a brutal crime on this night of jubilation. Thebes had always been a peaceful city, but in the confusion of the celebrations a thief might have seen an opportunity to rob wealthy folk wandering where they should not. And this victim was no common labourer, Piay could see. Expensive gold thread, embroidered in the shape of the sun god Ra's orb, glinted on the chest of his bloodstained white robe.

'Look,' Myssa breathed, pointing ahead.

Piay glanced in the direction she was indicating and saw what appeared to be four or five figures flitting along the alley, mere smudges amid the gloom. As they neared one of the burning lamps, their steps did not falter, nor could Piay spot a hand reaching up towards the light, and yet it winked out, and the one beyond it, too.

Piay felt a prickle of unease, unsure what he was seeing or how the lights had been extinguished, but, whoever they were, it was too late to pursue them.

Piay crouched beside the body to get a better look.

'I know this man,' he said as he studied the wrinkled features. 'I saw him last night, before the battle, just as the old Pharaoh was dying. There were courtiers gathered to bear witness to his passing. He was one of them . . .' Piay paused, frowning as he tried to picture what he had seen. 'I think he must be a lord of some kind, because I'm sure I saw him at court, years ago, too . . .'

His voice tailed off and he shrugged. As a young man at court, he had paid little attention to the old men who fussed around the Pharaoh. His attention was entirely focused on the female servants, handmaidens and noblemen's daughters that filled the royal halls.

'Poor man,' Myssa said. 'He must have been making his way to the palace and took this path to avoid the crowds.'

'Perhaps,' Piay said again, his attention drawn back to the darkness at the end of the alley, where in his mind's eye he could still see the mysterious figures flitting through the half-light. His mind raced with questions, but no answers came.

Finally, Piay emptied his thoughts of fruitless speculation and got back to practicalities.

'We should alert someone to deal with the remains,' he said.

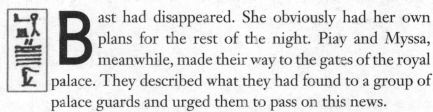

Bast had disappeared. She obviously had her own plans for the rest of the night. Piay and Myssa, meanwhile, made their way to the gates of the royal palace. They described what they had found to a group of palace guards and urged them to pass on this news.

Their task completed, Piay turned to Myssa and said, 'I suppose we might as well get back to the festivities.' But there was more unease than enthusiasm in his voice.

As they pushed through the throng outside the palace, Piay could not turn his thoughts away from the body in the alley and the anonymous figures flitting through the darkness. Breaking through a mass of bodies, he found himself in the middle of a group that had gathered in a square outside one of the city's taverns. They stood motionless amid all the chaos, gripped by the words of a tall, gaunt man, made frail by age, his face a map of his long life. A scribe, by the look of the scroll pressed against his chest, he was standing on an upturned wooden box, his face turned to the heavens, intoning in a thin, clear voice.

'In the time before time the land of Egypt stood as one kingdom. All knew it as an age of peace and prosperity, when men
learned to write and to sing and create great works of art. But
then powerful men struggled for more power, as they always
do, and that unity of purpose crumbled.'

Caught in the scribe's spell, Piay felt his thoughts fly back to
his youth, and the classroom where Taita had first told him of
the Red Pretender. In the years after Egypt had been split into
two, the Pretender had ruled the Lower Kingdom, the territory
to the north where the mighty Nile split into seven tributaries
on its journey to the sea.

Taita had served the Pharaoh Mamose of the Upper Kingdom, which lay upstream on the Nile's southern banks. Mamose
was the sworn enemy of the Red Pretender, and the two men
had hurled their armies into a slew of battles, back and forth
along the line between Upper and Lower Egypt, but for all the
fighting and bloodshed, their forces were too evenly matched
to bring about an endgame.

And then the Hyksos came.

Those warlike barbarians swept out of the east on chariots
as fast as the wind, pulled by powerful horses, a beast that had
never been known in Egypt. The Red Pretender and his army
fell like barley before the sickle. And once the Hyksos ruled the
Lower Kingdom, they turned their eyes to the south.

Piay felt his heart harden. War with the Hyksos was all he
had known. From the moment he became a man, he had choked
on the black smoke of burning fields and tasted the iron tang of
blood on the wind.

Piay was jolted from his thoughts as the tone of the scribe's
voice became darker.

'Yet this is a time of omens,' the man was saying. 'In the
necropolis, monuments have collapsed and graves gape open.
Strange things have been revealed in those pits. Some say the
dead are returning, that the cities of the dead will take over the
cities of the living—'

'Get out of my way, you drunken oaf!' A familiar voice cut through the waking dream the storyteller had cast, and angry faces turned, demanding a hush.

Piay winked at Myssa. 'I think we're needed.'

'If only to stop them turning on our friend,' she whispered back.

Hannu was thrusting his way through the densely packed crowd, his eyes narrowed under heavy brows as he searched the features of those who passed.

'There you are,' he exclaimed when he saw Piay and Myssa. 'The guards said you'd come this way.' He looked around to make sure no one was listening; his face was deadly serious. 'There's some bad things happening.'

'I know,' Piay said.

He was about to tell Hannu of the body they had found, but the old guardsman was already moving away through the throng.

'There's talk of a messenger, rushing to the palace like Apep the snake was after him,' Hannu called back to Piay and Myssa. 'Mark my words, there's trouble on the way.'

As he and Myssa hurried to catch up with Hannu, Piay was thinking about the connection, if there was one, between all these portents of evil and unrest on what should have been a night of celebration.

What remained of the shattered Hyksos army had been put to flight. Could they have regrouped in the north? Might they even now be preparing an attack to recapture what they had lost?

That is not possible, Piay told himself. *There are too few of them left to pose any serious threat.*

So what other threats might there be? Piay could think of none. Over the fifty years since the death of the Red Pretender and the conquest of the Lower Kingdom, Egypt had known no other enemy than the Hyksos.

Myssa hurried alongside him as they ran through the streets. Away from the main thoroughfares, where the festivities were concentrated, it was quieter, and Piay could hear the slap of their footsteps echoing off the walls of the buildings.

They were yards away from the road that ran into the city from the Falcon Gate in the city's northern wall when Piay heard a commotion ahead, saw the revellers pulling each other out of the road.

As they watched, a chariot thundered past, heading from the gate towards the centre of Thebes as if charging into battle. Its frame was edged in gold, in the style that the Hyksos favoured. For a second Piay wondered whether the enemy had after all somehow managed to mount a counter-attack. Perhaps he had been wrong? His body tensed, he pulled Myssa behind him so that he could protect her and drew his sword.

Another chariot and then another swept past – the horses pounding dust high into the air – but now Piay could see that they must have been captured in the battle, for they were being driven by Egyptian soldiers. He relaxed a fraction. He and his companions were in no immediate danger. And yet, Piay could tell from the speed of their approach, the foam that flew from the horses' mouths, the white muck sweat on their flanks, and the intense, almost manic expressions of the charioteers, that it must be bad business that drove them.

As if to underline the point, the soldier standing next to the charioteer in the next chariot to pass, whom Piay took to be the captain of the whole group, was screaming at his driver to go even faster.

Making their way into the road, Piay, Hannu and Myssa pressed themselves against the wall as two more chariots thundered by. And as they passed, Piay saw for the first time that the Egyptians were not alone. These two chariots were carrying additional passengers.

One of them was dressed in a short robe, like a civilian, without any weaponry or armour. But Piay could tell at once by his clothes and the style of his hair and beard that he must be a Hyksos. Though not a very impressive one, he thought, for the man was scrawny. He was bent over, his hands gripping the frame of the chariot for dear life, and his face bore an expression of pure terror at the speed at which they were travelling.

The other passenger was very different. He stood absolutely still, effortlessly keeping his balance, even as the chariot rattled and jumped on the rough road surface. His torso was a mass of tattoos and his entire face and head were covered by a leather hood.

Piay frowned at the sight, wondering why the man's captors had felt obliged to hide his face from public view. What did they not want the world to see?

The chariots crashed on into the heart of the city.

'Looks like they're heading to the palace,' Hannu rumbled.

Piay nodded. 'Then that is where we need to be.'

When they reached the palace compound, Piay informed the guards at the main gate that he was the mighty Taita's closest aide and came bearing news that the great man needed to hear.

'He's a busy man tonight, your master,' the senior guard said, waving Piay, Myssa and Hannu through into the courtyard that lay beyond the gate.

'Look over there,' Myssa said, pointing to the far corner of the yard, where the chariots that had stormed past them stood gleaming under the lamplight. The horses stamped their feet and snorted, abandoned by the soldiers who had brought them in. Of those warriors there was no sign.

'They were driving those horses like madmen. Why would they do that?' Piay wondered aloud. 'And on the night of our victory . . .'

'We'll find out soon enough,' Hannu said. 'But whatever they've got to say, it can't wait.'

Another guard ushered them between the towering pillars of the portico and through the great door. In the days before the Hyksos seized Lower Egypt, robbing the pharaohs of a great portion of their kingdom's wealth, the palace would have been filled with light and perfumed air and the rustle of slaves going about their business. Soon all Egypt would lie under the new Pharaoh's control and the royal court would return to its former glory, but for now only a few lamps glimmered around the vast entrance hall and shadows swallowed the ceiling. The air tasted of sweat.

Piay, Hannu and Myssa strode through the chamber, their footsteps echoing in the emptiness as they made their way towards the great hall of audience where the throne stood. As they neared the entrance, Piay spotted two figures emerging from the interior, their faces drawn. The audience could not have gone well.

One was King Hurotas of Sparta. He was broad-shouldered, with muscles hardened by a lifetime of combat, and the grey hair hanging from his balding scalp was still matted with the sweat of the day's battle. He grinned when he saw Piay walking towards him.

'Thank you, young man!' he called in a cheery voice. 'I'd have missed a fine day's fighting if it hadn't been for you!'

It seemed an age since Piay had stood before Hurotas in his palace in Sparta, pleading with the king to send an army to ally with the Egyptians in their struggle against the Hyksos invaders.

Piay bowed. 'Egypt is forever grateful for your aid.'

The other man was Taita.

Any man might be exhausted by the task of leading an army in battle, but if Taita felt any fatigue, it had no more effect upon his appearance than his age. In sharp contrast to Hurotas, Taita looked as fresh and clean as if he had just stepped from a long, relaxing bath. He wore a pristine white robe that fell to his ankles, the front adorned with delicate stitching and jewels that marked out the wings of Horus spreading across his chest.

His lips were still full, his eyes bright, his skin taut, his cheekbones and jaw clearly defined, and the air around him was sweet with the perfume of the lime and cardamom unguents that he worked into his skin each morning.

It was as if the ravages that afflicted all other men never touched him. Taita always said that the gods had blessed him with an unfeasibly long life. Piay had often wondered if that gift had been bestowed because of the sacrifice his master had made when he became a eunuch: a recompense equal to the magnitude of his loss.

Yet years of experience had taught Piay that Taita's outward appearance was not always a guide to his inner mood. This had been a glorious day, but all was not well. Piay would have to tread carefully.

'Come with me,' Taita said. 'We have much to discuss.'

'You seem troubled,' Piay replied, testing the waters.

'There have been portents in the necropolis. Signs that weigh heavily on me.'

'A scribe in the square was talking of the same . . . He said that the dead were rising.'

'Perhaps, in a way, they are.'

'I'll be going now,' Hurotas said. 'You fellows get on with your business, I'll find my own way out.'

Taita bade the Spartan farewell and thanked him again for his role in the battle. Then he led Piay and the others through a maze of chambers to another large hall where dignitaries from foreign lands had once, in years long past, awaited their audience with the Pharaoh. The hall was as gloomy as everywhere else, with only a few pools of lamplight floating in the dark.

The soldiers whom Piay had first seen racing past him on their chariots were not resting from their journey. Instead they stood with their swords drawn, their bare torsos still streaked with sweat and the dirt of the road, their faces filled with fear, as if they expected an attack to come at any moment.

Piay had not seen hardened Egyptian troops so uneasy before. It was the very last thing he would have expected in the aftermath of such a triumph. He turned his eyes towards the three members of the unit who had taken up a position in the centre of the chamber. They were guarding the two captives, whose hands were tied behind their backs with strips of hide.

Piay saw that he had been right. One of the two bound men was indeed a Hyksos – an emaciated individual with skinny arms and thighs. But there was a shrewdness in his dark eyes as he studied the new arrivals.

He's sizing us up, Piay thought. *He's not as feeble as he wants us to believe.*

The other captive was tall and slim, the black tattoos on his torso a mass of circles, stars and symbols that Piay had never seen before. In the centre of his chest a bull had been etched, its hindquarters raised and the head lowered in a posture that suggested it was about to attack.

He did not move, not a tremor, and if he had been lying on the flags Piay would have thought him dead. The hide hood had been pulled down so tightly that the man must surely have had trouble breathing, yet he showed no sign of distress. His head was tilted slightly back and to one side, as if he were listening intently.

'Put down your weapons,' Piay called. 'We are safe here.'

The captain of the soldiers eyed him with something close to disdain. 'Believe me, no one is safe.'

The captain turned his attention to Taita and bowed. 'Greetings, my lord, I knew we would find you here, preparing the way for Pharaoh.'

Taita clearly knew the man, for he replied, 'Captain Gatas.'

'We thought you would wish to see what we have discovered as soon as possible.'

'Tell me your story, from the beginning, Captain.'

Gatas seemed relieved to unburden himself. He described how he and his men had been tracking the fleeing Hyksos army when he saw smoke rising from a strange quarter of the desert.

'I don't know why, but I just had a sense, almost like someone was whispering in my ear, that I ought to go and find out what was happening, even though it meant losing touch with the main army.'

Taita nodded thoughtfully. Hannu, however, felt the need to come to a fellow warrior's aid.

'That's just an old soldier's instinct, brother,' he said. 'You spend enough time at war, there's things you just know, even if you can't say why.'

'Of course,' Gatas said, though Piay got the feeling that he wasn't entirely convinced by Hannu's argument.

Gatas led his audience to the burning farmhouse, to where the Hyksos troops were waiting for them.

'The rest of their army were running away, it was a rout, but not these ones. They drew their swords and stood their ground.'

'But you and your men defeated these brave Hyksos,' Taita said, breaking his silence.

Gatas drew himself up as straight as a Blue Crocodile guardsman on parade and said, 'Yes, sir, every last one of them. Only these two survived and neither of them is a soldier.'

'So why did you ride back to Thebes as though the worst demons of the underworld were after you?'

'Because they were,' Gatas replied bluntly. 'You see, we prepared the chariots to bring them back to the army . . .'

Piay nodded to himself. The Hyksos had introduced chariots to Egypt. Even now, many years later, their wheeled war-machines were still greatly prized, and Gatas could expect praise and even a handsome reward for capturing so many of them intact. But he neither looked nor sounded like a man who was about to have his pockets filled with gold. And now Piay found out why.

'Then just as we were leaving, we were attacked—'

'By more Hyksos?' Taita asked.

'No, my lord . . . by ghosts, or demons. I can't say what they were, but we never heard or saw a thing. Just . . .' Gatas searched for the right words. 'Just shadows in the darkness.'

'I have seen those ghosts, too,' Piay said. 'Not long ago, here in the city. And they left a dead man behind them.'

'They took four of my men,' Gatas said. 'They'd have killed us all, if we hadn't got out of there as fast as we could. And we didn't let up, either. Didn't want them catching up.'

'I see,' Taita said, apparently untroubled by all this talk of ghosts attacking the living. 'But tell me . . . These Hyksos troops at the farm – do you have any idea of why they were fighting so fiercely?'

'I could not guess,' Gatas said, then jabbed a finger at the tattooed captive and added, 'Until I saw this one.' He nodded to one of his men, who wrenched the hood from the man's head.

'Holy Ra!' Piay gasped as he saw the skull tattoo. There were yet more tattoos on the man's cheeks, his forehead and his shaven scalp.

Myssa put a hand to her face and stared, her sharp wits and strong will giving way to primal, atavistic horror at the sight of the demonic creature in front of her. No wonder Gatas and his men had ridden so hard for fear of what might be following them.

Piay took her hand. The demon stared at Taita without blinking, and Piay thought that such cool aloofness suggested a man used to commanding all who stood before him.

'Did you discover why the Hyksos thought him worth fighting for?' Taita asked, stepping forward to examine the tattoos on the man's head and body.

'He hasn't said a word,' Gatas replied. 'But we did find this on him.'

Gatas dipped into a hide pouch hanging at his side and held out an object of such exquisite craftsmanship that Piay was gripped by the sight of it. He had never seen anything so remarkable before.

It comprised an oval piece of polished translucent rock – quartz, perhaps – so improbably thin it was almost possible to see through it. The stone was held in a gold frame with a golden arm reaching out from one side and another gold band curling from the lower edge. The craftsman had shaped the stone into the form of an eye, but not just any eye. Piay recognised the design instantly, as did every Egyptian there.

It was the Eye of Horus, the symbol of healing and protection, which had its origin in the battle between Horus, the god of kingship and the sky and his uncle, Seth, who ruled over storms, violence and disorder. Seth had torn out Horus' eye, but the orb was magically healed and offered to Osiris, the father of Horus and god of fertility and resurrection, so that its power might sustain him in the afterlife.

Amulets of the Eye of Horus were commonplace, but Piay had not seen one that came close to such exquisite beauty. Taita took the artefact and turned it around so that the lamplight shimmered across its surface.

'Well, well, well . . . It really exists,' he murmured softly, as if he were alone in the vast chamber.

Piay looked around to see the others' reactions. The tattooed man remained impassive, but the Hyksos captive was entranced by what he saw before him. Now it was desire that burned in those dark eyes. The man was even breathing a little more quickly.

He knows exactly what that is! Piay thought.

Taita must have also seen the Hyksos' reaction, too. He looked at him and said, 'Your comrades were fighting for this, weren't they?'

'They were not my comrades, master,' the Hyksos replied. 'Just look at me, I am no soldier. And as for that object you are holding, it is the first time I have seen it.'

'Well, that's a lie for a start,' Gatas said. 'We had no trouble finding it.' He looked at the Hyksos. 'Or are you telling me that you were too scared to search a man with a skull on his face?'

'As far as I know, he was searched. But certainly, that amulet was not found, for if it had been, he would not have been allowed to keep it.'

'And yet we found what you could not,' Taita said, 'and you know what it is, don't you?'

'You flatter me, master. You are Taita the magus. Even in Avaris people speak of your wisdom. How could I, lowly as I am, possibly tell you anything that you do not already know?'

'He knows nothing, my lord,' Gatas said. 'Just give the word and I'll finish him.'

'I'm tempted, I won't deny it,' Taita said. 'But if this "lowly" man were to talk to me, perhaps he might surprise us, and even himself, with the depth of his knowledge.' He looked at the Hyksos. 'What do you think?'

The man shrugged. 'I can try . . .' He grimaced, as if in pain. 'Perhaps if my hands were free, and my wrists and arms were not ablaze with unspeakable agony, I might be able to think more clearly.'

'Or perhaps if you felt my knife on your throat, that might loosen your tongue.'

'If you scare me out of my wits, how then can I reason?'

It was all Piay could do not to laugh. He might be an enemy, but the Hyksos had a way about him that was hard to dislike.

'I will trade whatever I know for my life, Lord Taita,' the Hyksos said. 'And I swear by all the gods that I will tell the truth, for I know you will catch me out if I lie. Please, I implore you, cut me loose.'

Taita nodded and a soldier stepped forward and sawed through the man's bonds.

'Now talk,' Taita said.

'My name is Shamshi of Kadesh. I serve in the Temple of Seth in Avaris, under the command of his holiness, the high priest Mut-Bisir.'

Seth, the god of the desert, of war, of chaos. How many times had his malign and poisonous influence infected Piay's life? How many had died in Seth's name?

'His holiness sent me to be his personal representative and observer on . . . ah . . . an expedition ordered by His Majesty the King, all glory be upon him. He also commanded me to offer any religious guidance that might be required to Akkan, son of Abisha, the leader of our party.'

'And what was this expedition, exactly?'

'Word has reached Avaris of a great mystery,' Shamshi continued. 'I have heard it called the Riddle of the Stars. It is said that whosoever can answer this riddle will gain treasure beyond man's dreams . . .'

Shamshi paused and then, in a voice like a rug trader tempting a passer-by with the quality of the wares inside his shop, said, 'And more than treasure, there will be power . . . power like no human has ever possessed, that only the gods can imagine. Power that can shake the earth . . . that can bring the pyramids crumbling to the ground . . . that could destroy the Egyptian people, every last man and woman, indeed Egypt itself, so that all memory of it sinks beneath the shifting sands, to be lost for all time.'

An awestruck silence fell on the chamber, for it was plain that Shamshi's words were sincere. He truly believed in what he was saying.

Piay could see the intensity in Taita's eyes. Even now, for all the day's success, total victory had not yet been assured. If the Hyksos could somehow find a way to bring new life to their shattered forces, they might yet be able to strike back.

Taita's voice, however, did not betray any of his concerns. He did not ask a single question about this mysterious, all-powerful riddle. He simply asked Shamshi, 'Was this silent man helping you with the search? Are the symbols on his body some kind of treasure map?'

'Please believe me when I tell you, master, that I do not know. No one has been able to find the meaning of the symbols.'

'Nor, apparently, did anyone find the amulet. So, why was he of any significance to your search?'

'Because we had already heard about another man just like him.'

'You are sure that the other man and this one are not in fact the same person?'

'I believe that the other man died.'

'But you do not know?'

Shamshi gave an ingratiating smile. 'As I say, wise one, I am merely a lowly underling. My lord Mut-Bisir only tells me what I need to know.'

'So there are two of these skull-men, and who knows how many more besides. And yet, in all my long years, I have never seen one before. How, then, were you able to acquire one so easily?'

'My lord, I cannot explain it, but the commander of our expedition, Akkan, son of Abisha, felt thirsty as we marched through Memphis, as did we all, for we had been on the road all day. So he allowed us all to enter a tavern, and by chance, this "skull-man", as you call him, was sitting there.'

'In a tavern?'

'Yes, my lord.'

'That you just happened to enter . . .?'

'I know how improbable my story sounds, Lord Taita, but I swear that it is true. If I were telling you a lie, I would surely have made it more convincing.'

Piay noticed that even Taita had to suppress a smile at that example of Shamshi's logic and wit.

'One last question . . .' Taita said. 'Why did you not stay in Memphis, if that was where you found the best – indeed, the only new – clue to your puzzle? Why march south to Thebes?'

'Ah, that I can tell you, master. We were ordered to go to Thebes, for that was where our king, our high priests and all the great men of our nation would be' – he shrugged – 'once we had captured the city.'

'I apologise for spoiling their plans,' said Taita. 'But it seems to me that you should go back to Memphis, accompanied by my most trusted people, to carry out the search that you would have conducted, had you not been sent to Thebes.'

'But, mighty Taita, your underlings are surely Egyptian.'

'Most of them, yes.'

'But Memphis—'

'. . . Is in the hands of the Hyksos?' Taita smiled. 'Tonight, maybe. But I assure you, Shamshi of Kadesh, that won't be the case for much longer.'

For a brief moment all was calm in the great chamber, then Hannu whistled under his breath to catch Piay's attention. When Piay looked around, his comrade was signalling with his eyes and his hand had fallen to the hilt of his sword.

What? Piay mouthed.

Hannu shrugged and shook his head.

The old soldier was obviously unsure about exactly what was concerning him. Yet he, like Gatas and his men, sensed a threat; that was clear.

Piay tried to persuade himself that the soldiers could not be right. The palace was guarded by the Pharoah's finest, most trusted troops. They would surely spot any danger. Then the thought struck him: *Unless there are ways of getting into the palace without being seen.*

Now Piay understood why the nobleman in the alley had been murdered. He must have spent half his life in this building. He would know every nook, cranny, door and window. So, he had not been targeted for his wealth, but for the information he could provide: interrogated first, then killed to ensure his silence.

Before he could alert Taita, Piay blinked. Was the chamber getting darker? The others had noticed it, too.

The flames in the lamps flickered lower. Shadows swelled, pushing back the wavering circles of light.

'Sorcery,' Gatas muttered, his face spectral in the growing gloom.

In the centre of the chamber, the tattooed man was smiling.

Piay lunged and grabbed Taita's arm.

'We're under attack, my lord. You and Myssa had best get away.'

As Myssa ushered Taita from the chamber, Piay snatched out his sword, then turned right around, crouching, peering into every corner, ready to spring forward the moment he saw a foe. Now his nostrils wrinkled at a sour scent, like old wine. It had not been there when they had first entered the chamber, but now it had appeared as if from nowhere and seemed to be getting stronger. Was this what Hannu had smelled earlier? Where was it coming from?

As he glanced round, Piay noticed drifting motes of dust in the yellow lamplight, but more than dust, for they glittered as they hung in the air. He watched the shimmering particles, noting how unusual they were as they gently settled on everyone in the room. Whether those motes were the source of the strange odour, and where they had come from, he could not tell, but unease knotted his stomach.

Hannu slotted in beside him and together they moved in step, still circling, still trying to see who was lurking in the darkness.

'I don't like this,' Hannu said gloomily. 'Don't like it at all.'

Gatas grabbed Shamshi's tunic in his fist and hauled him to the side of the tattooed man.

'One wrong move and I'll gut you where you stand,' the captain snarled. 'Both of you.'

The tattooed man continued to smile.

Piay moistened his lips. His mouth was growing dry and it was not from fear. The dust he was breathing in prickled deep inside him. Could it be poison? He spat.

'Keep your eyes open,' Gatas barked to his men.

'They are ghosts,' one of the soldiers cried back.

'Still your tongue,' the captain commanded. 'If their leader is a man, so are they.'

Piay and Hannu circled in step, their eyes never resting. The chamber was as silent as a tomb.

Then a gurgle erupted near one of the doors and a soldier crumpled to his knees, clutching at his throat. The sound of blood spattering over the stone floor echoed across the chamber.

'Over there!' Gatas yelled.

'Wait,' Piay called.

But it was too late. Confusion erupted as the soldiers scrambled across the hall to where the man had fallen. The lamps guttered lower still. The darkness was almost complete.

A cry rang out. Another soldier fell, this time on the other side of the chamber.

And still Piay could not see the assailants.

'Where are they?'

'They are right here,' Hannu growled. 'It's like they can see in the dark . . .'

Barely had the words left his lips than Piay sensed movement, shapes flashing back and forth like bats flitting among the date palms at dusk. Another cry, another soldier crashing to the flagstones.

'This is impossible!' Piay exclaimed, shocked at the sound of panic in his voice.

A breath of air shifted close to him and he lashed out, driven purely by instinct. He felt the edge of his sword carve through a solid form and he heard something fall to the floor. When he looked down, a hand lay there, clutching a knife with a curved blade. In the gloom, blood from the wound showed up as glossy black on the marble floor.

So, they were men. However silently, invisibly they might move, they were flesh and bone, and when they were wounded, they bled.

And yet they did not cry out, even at the loss of their right hand. What kind of man could bear such agony in silence?

From somewhere on the far side of the room, an Egyptian voice cried out, but was cut short. And the next thing Piay heard was the thud of a body hitting the floor.

'We've got to get the captives away from here,' Piay told Hannu. 'Somewhere we can see what we're fighting.'

'Give me a blade,' Shamshi pleaded, for there was nothing like the threat of death to make a man a warrior. 'Let me defend myself.'

'I'll take off your arm if you so much as touch a sword,' Hannu retorted. 'Now run or die.'

Whirling, Piay snatched the wrist of the tattooed man, yanking him forward. In the last of the lamplight, Piay could see the man's eyes glowing and the ghost of that victorious smile. But as he tried to drag his captive out of the chamber, Piay was suddenly pulled up short. Someone was pulling the man in the opposite direction.

For a second, the tattooed man was motionless, like a donkey being pulled by both its mane and its tail. But whoever was pulling from the other side must have arms and legs and muscle and bone, Piay thought, and none of those things were impervious to a blade.

Still clinging onto the tattooed man's wrist, Piay spun around and lashed out with his sword at where his enemy must be, but the edge of his weapon found nothing but thin air.

Before Piay could brace himself once more, his invisible opponent gave an almighty tug and wrenched the tattooed man from his grasp. The darkness swallowed him.

Piay flew backwards, crashing onto the stone, and as he did he once again felt the breath of air as one of those curved knives slashed by, a finger's width above his head.

Sprawling, he felt a rush of dismay that he had failed to keep hold of the captive. For the briefest moment, he entertained the thought of racing through the gloom to try and recapture him, but he knew that if he did, he would not see another dawn.

As he pushed himself up, a hand hooked under his armpit and hauled him to his feet. It was Gatas.

'Away from here,' the captain croaked. 'Away now or die.'

And then they both were dashing in the direction that Hannu and Shamshi had gone, towards one of the doorways.

When they crashed into the next chamber, the light from the lamps seemed so bright that Piay was momentarily blinded. He realised that his nose and the back of his throat were full of whatever was causing the strange sour wine taste, and he wondered if that was the source of their attackers' seemingly magical abilities: some powder floating in the air that could play games with men's minds? A potion? A spell?

There was no time to dwell on that notion.

'They are following us,' Gatas cried, his voice breaking.

Through a maze of chambers and corridors they raced until they tumbled out into the night. Moonlight flooded the courtyard. Hannu and Shamshi waited ahead and together the four men ran on, out of the palace compound and into the streets.

'They want the Eye that Lord Taita still has,' Shamshi gasped. 'They will not rest until it is back in their hands.'

'And they want you, too,' said Gatas.

Piay had hoped that the crowded streets would make it almost impossible for anyone to follow him and his companions, but most of the revellers seemed to have taken to their beds, and many of those who remained were slumped over tables, or lying in gutters, too intoxicated to move. And the bright, silver-grey moonlight did little to conceal them from their pursuers.

On the other hand, it was at least easier to move more quickly.

Very well, Piay thought. *We're in a race. We have to get to safety before they get to us.*

'Aim for the River Gate,' Piay said breathlessly, as he ran beside Gatas. 'If we reach the camp, we stand a chance. These ghosts can't beat an army.'

Just as he felt his spirits rise, Piay glimpsed movement at the edge of his vision. At the end of a side street, shadows danced by along the road that ran parallel to the one along which they were running.

'They're keeping pace with us, trying to cut us off before we reach the gate.'

'How many are there?' Hannu wheezed.

'Too many to fight,' Gatas barked back. 'Don't even think of engaging them.'

Each time they passed a side street, Piay glanced along it. The shadows were still keeping pace, like a pack of jackals bearing down on wounded prey.

The twin towers of the River Gate soared up ahead, silhouetted against the star-sprinkled sky. With the enemy vanquished and in full retreat, the huge gates had been left open. Piay felt his heart leap. If he and his companions could escape the city, they could seek shelter among the Spartan soldiers still camped outside the city walls.

But the creatures on Piay's tail would surely make the same calculation. They would attack while the odds were still in their favour.

Piay kept his eyes on the final side street before the gate, expecting that that was where the attack would materialise.

'Ready yourselves,' he said.

Then, as swords were pulled from their scabbards, Piay spotted something. Next to one of the warehouses, where merchants had delivered their wares in the days when the city was thriving, there was a wooden scaffold, assembled to repair the crumbling edifice. It had not been used for many a day, but at the top was a platform, still loaded with masonry and the abandoned tools of the stoneworkers.

'Come with me,' Piay called.

Acutely aware that their pursuers were almost upon them, he raced to the foot of the scaffolding and put his shoulder against it. The structure was old, rickety, and he could feel it trembling even with the slight pressure he administered.

The others recognised what he was attempting to do, and without hesitation they slotted in beside him, all heaving as one.

The scaffold wavered, teetered, and then, with one final shove, rolled forward and crashed down. Piay was running again even before it hit the ground. As he passed the end of the side street, he caught a flurry of movement and then the pile of masonry and the scaffold thundered down in a billowing cloud of dust.

Piay prayed the obstacle would slow the cut-throats just enough, and so it proved. He darted through the River Gate, yelling at the guards, in the name of the Pharaoh, to close the gate behind them. Though the sentries must have been bewildered by his request, they did what he said. The trundling of the huge doors rumbled at his back.

Yet the four men didn't slow their step. They careered along the road and sprinted into the heaving mass of celebrating soldiers. Amid the din of the singing and the clouds of smoke from the fires, they finally ground to a halt among the large mauve tents of the Spartan generals.

'Don't know about you, but I've got no intention of going to sleep,' Gatas gasped, resting his hands on his thighs as he heaved in gulps of air. 'Don't care how tired I am, I'm not letting those devils slit my throat in the night.'

'Very wise, my captain,' Shamshi replied. 'This is not done yet, not by a long way.'

Piay knew full well that a set of gates would not prevent the ghost-men who had recaptured the silent, impassive, tattooed captive from climbing over the walls of Thebes and venturing into the camp.

He had little doubt that they had the skill to make their way through it without anyone noticing them. The first he, Gatas, Hannu or Shamshi would know of their presence would be the hands that clasped their mouths shut and the blades that slit their throats.

But time went by, and they were all still alive. It seemed that their invisible enemies were content, for now, to bide their time. They had their man. Soon, no doubt, they would come back for his mysterious amulet. Therefore, a new plan had to be made to foil them, and the Hyksos alike, and there was only one man whom Piay would ever want to devise it.

'I need to talk to Taita,' he said. 'Hannu, you come with me. Captain Gatas, you will have the pleasure of Shamshi's company. Feel free to tie him up. By all means gag him, to silence his blabbering. But I don't think he has any desire to escape.' Piay looked at the Hyksos priest. 'Who knows what might be waiting for him out there in the dark.'

Piay and Hannu walked through the camp, which, like the streets of Thebes, was now much quieter. The excitement of surviving a battle fuelled a man's energy for a while, but fatigue would always catch up with him in the end.

'Lucky sods, getting some rest,' Hannu said enviously as they passed a tent from which the sound of snoring could be heard.

'I also need to sleep,' Piay agreed. 'But not until we've spoken to Taita.'

As they got closer to the tent, Piay saw, to his relief, that there was a ring of soldiers around it, all members of Hannu's old unit, the Blue Crocodile Guards. If they couldn't keep Taita safe, no one could.

Taita must have been expecting them, for the entrance flap was partially open and Piay could see his master in deep conversation with Myssa. She was listening intently, her head slightly bowed, as Taita prowled around her, illuminating his points with hands thrown up or sweeping from side to side. Occasionally, Myssa would nod, signalling she had absorbed the knowledge he had imparted.

Piay stood in the entrance and watched them both, feeling warmed that the two most important people in his life had already formed a deep connection. Indeed, Taita was so intent on what he was telling Myssa that he failed to notice the new arrivals, until Piay gave a discreet cough.

Taita would normally have given Piay and Hannu a friendly greeting, but he just grunted an acknowledgement of their presence and flexed his fingers to direct them to enter the tent. His expression was grim and his mouth was downturned by the weight of his thoughts.

Taita wasted no time before making the reason for his feelings clear.

'The fate of all Egypt hangs in the balance,' he began. 'The one who solves the Riddle of the Stars will wield a power far mightier than even the Hyksos realise. They are right that it will give them the power to destroy us utterly. But that is only the very start of what it offers.'

'So you've heard of it before?' Piay asked, and then, before Taita could answer, he added, 'Which is why you didn't ask Shamshi about it. You didn't want to reveal what you knew.'

'Exactly,' Taita said.

'So, forgive me, master, but what do you know?'

'I know that the riddle begins with Imhotep.' Taita gave Piay the same inquisitorial look that he had used so many times in the classroom, and asked, 'Do you remember who Imhotep was?'

'The High Priest of Ra, the chancellor to the Pharaoh Djoser and the greatest of all architects,' Piay replied, relieved that he had been able to provide an answer.

'And . . .?'

'And he lived a thousand years ago. And . . . ahh . . .' Piay tried to remember what Taita had taught him and, to his great relief, entire sentences came back to him, almost exactly as his master had delivered them. 'And he built a pyramid of steps to serve as Djoser's tomb, the first great monument of its kind. He was the first man to use columns of stone to support a building. He was wise in all things, and now he lives among the gods, as one of their number, for his father was Ptah, the god of craftsmen and architects.'

'Precisely so,' Taita said, and Piay caught sight of Myssa out of the corner of his eye, standing behind Taita and silently applauding. Though whether she meant it, or was teasing him, he wasn't quite sure.

'So . . . I have read hints in the Hall of Records of what the Great Architect sealed away – scraps, rumours, but more than enough to tantalise. The old scrolls speak of Imhotep and his divinations. They say that he could see far into days yet to come, see all that would ever transpire in Egypt. He foretold a great crisis that would decimate the land of the Pharaohs—'

'The invasion of the Hyksos,' Piay said.

'And perhaps those who would be our saviours,' Taita continued. 'But I will get to that in a moment. For now, know that Imhotep, in his great wisdom, was said to have hidden away a mighty force for good that could be used in rebuilding our land, used to bring the two kingdoms back together, a power that would protect Egypt from future harm. But something that could also be used for great ill if it fell into the wrong hands.'

'What sort of power?' Hannu asked.

Taita pursed his lips, letting the gravity of that question and its answer press down upon them before he replied, 'It is said that Imhotep found a way to communicate with the gods themselves. More than that, he could summon them to walk among us and to use their powers here in the realm of men.'

Piay gaped. 'The gods . . . here?'

'That's how it was, way back in time,' Hannu muttered. 'The gods were here, in our world. That's what my father used to say, anyway.'

'He may have been right,' Taita said. 'Even now, the Hyksos claim to be able to speak with Seth and to seek his guidance through their rituals using the blue lotus, the Dream Flower. Imagine, then, if the God of Chaos and War stood with them at all times, unleashing his power in every battle they fought? It is frightening to think of the destruction that could be wrought, the lives that could be wiped away in an instant.'

Silence lay heavy in the tent for a long moment, but then Taita spoke again and the tone of his voice had changed.

'But imagine also what good could be achieved if Osiris walked among us, using his powers to enrich the soil of the Nile Valley so it was more bountiful than ever before, offering the people proof of a life after death. Or Hathor, whose power of renewal could conjure hope from despair, and ensure trade would return to all our cities and bring riches that could forever bind the two kingdoms together.'

'Wonderful things or terrible things, depending on who had the power of summoning,' Piay said.

Taita nodded. 'These spells were too great even for a man like Imhotep, and he took the decision to hide them away until a time when wise men might rise up who could wield them with care, so the accounts say.'

'A wise man like you,' Piay said.

'Thank you.' Taita smiled at the compliment, for he was not without vanity. 'Now come with me,' he said, reverting to his sombre tone of voice. 'There is something you must see.'

Wrapped in a cloak against the growing chill of the night, Taita strode out of the camp into the heart of the necropolis, where the rich and the powerful began their journey into the afterlife. Piay, Myssa and Hannu hurried behind, following the swaying glow of the flaming torch that Taita held high to light the way between the tombs and monuments on either side.

When they reached the oldest part of the necropolis, Piay immediately caught sight of the shattered remains of an ancient obelisk that had crashed across the path. He recalled what the scribe had said in the square about the strange portents that had afflicted the land.

'I did not know the ground had shaken here,' Piay said, noticing for the first time the dry dust that hung in the air.

'It did not,' Taita replied.

'Then what brought the obelisk down?'

His master did not reply. Piay felt a prickle of terror run down his spine. Then Taita said, 'Mark how the obelisk is lying. It is pointing in a particular direction. Now follow that direction.'

They reached a line of graves, on the very edge of the necropolis. Taita paused before a gaping hole, where one of the graves had fallen in. Piay peered inside, but it was too dark to see the bottom.

'In the city tonight, they were saying that the graves were giving up their dead,' he said timorously, stepping back from the edge.

'Yeah, and now here's the proof,' Hannu added.

'I heard those same reports,' Taita said. 'So I came here this evening, before I met you at the palace. And this is what I found.' He offered the torch to Piay. 'Now drop into the grave and tell me what you see.'

'Into the grave?' Piay grasped the torch with hesitance. 'The remains—'

'There are no remains. The grave has always been empty. Now, obey my command. Go in.'

Piay moistened his lips, then scrabbled over the side and dropped a short distance to the shattered rubble that lined the floor of the grave. He swept the torch back and forth and caught sight of a niche carved into the stonework.

'What do you see?' Taita asked.

'A hole cut into one side . . .' Piay leaned in as the shadows vanished. A stone block with a pyramidal head had been set in the niche. He described it, adding, 'There is something carved on it.'

As Piay tried to comprehend what he was seeing, Taita's voice floated down.

'At the top of the block, just beneath the pyramid, look for a square and a compass.'

Piay traced his fingertip along the lines etched into the limestone.

'Yes, it's here.'

'That is the mark of the Master Builder . . . the Great Architect . . . Imhotep himself,' Taita said.

Piay furrowed his brow. 'But we were only talking about him a short while ago – and now we find this. That's quite a coincidence . . .'

He heard Hannu, up above, say, 'And the way the obelisk led us right here. What are the chances of that?'

'It was no matter of luck,' Taita replied. 'Everything was meant to be exactly as it is, at exactly this moment.'

'How can that be?' Piay heard Myssa say.

'If Imhotep could see across the years, as the old stories say, could he not have left this here as a sign – a message to be discovered this night?' Taita asked. 'A message, perhaps, for us.'

Myssa gasped. 'Imhotep could see that clearly?'

'I believe so.' Taita turned his attention back to the grave and called down to Piay, 'What do you find beneath the square and the compass?'

Piay brought the torch closer. 'Two figures. Men. One taller than the other. And there is writing . . .'

'That is the *medu netjer*, the gods' words,' Taita interrupted. 'One figure has the mark of wisdom. The other is the Opener of the Way. Could that be you, Piay, and me?'

'Surely not!'

'When I first saw it earlier, I did not know what it meant, but now I am starting to see a pattern emerging from the sands. Climb back out.'

Once Piay stood with the others, he handed the torch back to his master, asking him, 'What are you thinking, master?'

Piay felt disturbed by all that had happened. The straightforward conflict of a battle between men had given way to something far less tangible. Hannu kept looking around and peering into the dark across the necropolis. He was clearly uneasy, too.

'The foundations beneath that fallen obelisk were not solid,' Taita said. 'When I inspected them, I saw that they had been built in such a way that over time – over many, many seasons – they would weaken. The obelisk would fall and that would draw attention. And that would lead to this grave, that collapsed at the same time, and to the sign it contained.'

For a long moment, there was only the sound of the wind whistling across the graves. Piay dwelled on what he had heard.

'Perhaps the gods themselves spoke to Imhotep, to tell him of what was to come,' he began. 'Perhaps . . . perhaps you, master, are the Imhotep of this age.'

'I think very highly of myself, as you well know, but even I would not raise myself to the heights of Imhotep,' Taita replied. 'But I feel deep in my heart that this has been preordained, and the message the Great Architect has left for us is of the greatest significance. To put these matters in place across a thousand years, how could it not be so?'

'Imhotep is calling on us to find what he has hidden away. Is that what you are saying?'

The torchlight glimmered in Taita's eyes. 'His sign, the square and the compass, has deep meaning. The square represents the world of men, where we all reside. The compass is the world of gods, from where all inspiration springs. The things of men and the things of gods are always separate. But if you had looked closely at that block, you would have seen a line connecting the two elements. Imhotep was able to move between the two worlds. And his message to us, so long after his death, is that if we are to save the soul of Egypt, you will have to do the same.'

Back in his tent, Taita fetched a soft leather pouch and handed it to Piay.

'Open it,' he said.

Piay loosened the drawstring and pulled out a folded piece of pristine cloth, wrapped around something hard. The quartz amulet lay inside.

'Take it,' Taita said.

Piay grasped the Eye of Horus, turning it so that it blazed with reflected lamplight. It was surely the masterwork of one of the greatest craftsmen to have ever lived, he thought, wrought over many years using techniques now lost to the world of men. But there was more. The artefact seemed to throb in his fingers as if it was imbued with some hidden power. He felt sure he could hear it whispering to him deep in his head.

'I pray to great Ra that I am not calling down your death upon you by giving this cursed item to you,' Taita said. 'Find the secret – unlock the spells. And return to Thebes. If it is within my ability, I will then use those spells to reunite the two halves of our great land and make Egypt whole.'

'Yes, master,' Piay said, feeling the weight of the responsibility that Taita had laid upon him.

'But be aware that the ancient writings contain warnings to all who seek to answer the Riddle of the Stars. The secret is guarded by devotees who will go to any lengths to keep it hidden.'

'The tattooed man,' Piay remembered. 'The ghost-warriors . . .'

'Yes. I believe they are the ones of whom the ancients spoke. And no one has yet succeeded in defeating them.'

Piay shook his head. In most circumstances he was blithely confident in his ability to meet any challenge, but now he felt far out of his depth.

'But why entrust this great task to me, master? Why not undertake it yourself? You know so much more than I do.'

'Our new pharaoh has given me an important task that I cannot refuse,' Taita said. 'Khamudi, the king of the Hyksos, has retreated towards Memphis, where he hopes to lick his wounds and gather together his shattered forces. That cannot be allowed. I must set sail tomorrow, with King Hurotas and his men, to crush Khamudi before he can rise up from the ashes of defeat.'

Piay nodded. 'You are the most skilled commander in all Egypt. You won the battle today. You are surely the one who must now finish the war. How would you like me to proceed?'

'You three will follow behind our force, along with a band of the most seasoned warriors in the Blue Crocodile Guards. By the time you reach Memphis, the gods willing, it will be in our hands. You will also be accompanied by Lord Azref, who will supervise the work of making Memphis a truly Egyptian city once again.

'The Hyksos used our people to govern the city – men who forswore their solemn vow of allegiance to Pharaoh and grov-elled before Khamudi in his place. They may provide a little trouble, but Azref is a good man, I chose him myself, and he will protect you while you go about your task.'

The mournful hoot of an owl rolled out across the quiet camp. Piay shuddered – the sound was a portent of death.

'The mission I have been charged with is great indeed, Piay,' Taita continued. 'It may well be the greatest undertaking of my life. Do not imagine it any less. To reunite Egypt and recreate the vast glory of ancient times by bringing the Lower Kingdom together with the Upper. To restore the monuments, the wonders of Egypt, to their age-old beauty, and in so doing, to awaken a long-occupied people to their heritage as heirs to the oldest kingdom in the world. This is my quest – a land united, a land of glory, one Egypt under Pharaoh's rule.'

Piay felt his heart swell with pride.

'And how do you wish me to proceed?' he asked.

'I want you to be two-faced,' Taita replied. 'In public, you will be seen to be conducting a survey of the many monuments, libraries and texts that have been cruelly denied to our priests here in Thebes for fifty years.'

'And behind that we'll secretly be investigating the Riddle of the Stars?'

'Precisely.'

'But forgive me, master, why do you think we will find the solution in Memphis?'

Taita shook his head and sighed. 'Piay . . . Piay . . . do you really need me to answer that? Have you not already done so yourself, this very night? Think, young man – think.'

'Of course!' Piay grinned. 'Imhotep served the Pharaoh Djoser in Memphis. He built Djoser's pyramid in that kingdom and . . .' He frowned, then asked, 'Didn't he also design the Great Pyramid of Khufu and the Sphinx that lies behind it, even though they were built years after he had died and joined the gods?'

'So it is said, yes,' Taita said. 'And remember, Imhotep wanted his secret to be discovered at the time of Egypt's greatest need. So, as with the obelisk and the grave, he must have left clues that the wise can follow to uncover it. Clues that are fiendish enough to deter looters and fortune seekers, but that a thoughtful, inspired seeker can solve.'

Hannu was shaking his head in dismay. 'Then we've got no chance,' he muttered.

'So where do I begin?' Piay protested, ignoring his subordinate's cheek. 'I have none of your knowledge of the Lower Kingdom, and Imhotep—'

'Indeed not,' Taita agreed. 'You have many skills, Piay, and you have learned a little from your lessons over the years, but I would not rely on your wits alone in such a vital matter.'

Piay wasn't sure if he should be offended. Hannu was certainly amused, to judge by the laughter he was hardly even trying to suppress.

'But there is someone else well suited to helping you,' Taita said.

Myssa had been silent up until this point. Whatever Taita had been telling her seemed to be weighing upon her.

'Taita has been passing on what knowledge he feels will be useful,' she said. 'Then, once he is gone, I'll consult the scribes and priests here in Thebes.'

'Myssa has an exceptionally sharp mind,' Taita said. 'I could see that in her from the moment we met. If anyone can follow Imhotep's trail, it is Myssa, I am confident of that. Trust her. Follow her guidance as if it were my own. The barbarian, Shamshi, will accompany you. I am certain he knows more than he has yet told us. I will send Captain Gatas along with you to watch over Shamshi, and to remind him that his survival depends upon his co-operation.'

Piay bowed. 'We will not fail.'

Taita nodded. 'I pray that you will not, for all our days depend upon it. Yet I know, too, that I have sent you into the greatest danger. The ghost-warriors, as you called them, will do everything to stop you solving the riddle. The Hyksos will stop at nothing to use all their cunning and might to beat you to that solution. There will be danger on all sides, and death will be beside you on this journey, every step of the way with each breath you take.'

iay had heard and seen and experienced enough that night to fill his head with a year's worth of nightmares, but his exhaustion was so great, and Myssa's presence beside him so comforting, that when

their lovemaking was done, he fell into a deep, untroubled slumber and awoke to find himself alone in the bed and the sun already high in the sky.

He hurried to Taita's tent, in case his master wished to give him any further instructions, but his master had already left and the servants were packing his possessions to be sent on up the river. Piay was delighted to discover, however, that the table on which Taita's morning meal had been served was still standing.

In accordance with his eminence, every dish that Taita might possibly desire had been prepared for him. But since the ageless sage was extremely proud of his slender physique, only a small amount of the feast had been consumed. It would certainly be a shame to leave all the cooks' hard work to be ruined by the midday sun. So Piay thought it his duty to minimise the waste, by wolfing down sweet baked breads, cheeses and fruits before he set off in search of Myssa and Hannu.

Piay found them on a wharf on the east bank of the Nile, watching the loading of the fleet that would carry the army north to confront the Hyksos. Chariots were being loaded, their wheels rattling against the gangplanks as they were pulled aboard by hastily assembled gangs of soldiers, dock workers and river boatmen.

Myssa greeted Piay with a kiss; Hannu preferred a cheerfully sarcastic, 'How good of you to join us, my lord.'

'Well, if you're going to be like that, you can forget about the thick slice of honey and date cake that I brought with me, in case you were feeling hungry,' Piay said.

'Ah, go on, hand it over.'

Piay grinned. 'I don't think I will now. What kind of a leader would I be if I tolerated cheek and insubordination from my underlings?'

'Haven't a clue, but you'll have one less underling if you don't . . . and if I recall rightly, you don't have any others.'

Piay laughed and threw Hannu the slice.

'Anything for me?' Myssa asked.

'Of course,' Piay said, producing a bunch of black grapes. 'These are sweeter than the honey in Hannu's cake.'

Myssa pecked his cheek. 'Now, go and let Taita know you're here. He said he has one last message for you. And he'll be on a galley and halfway up the river if you don't catch him soon.'

Piay looked around for his master. Then Myssa said, 'He's over there – on that jetty, talking to King Hurotas.'

The Egyptian and Spartan leaders were standing side by side, like the old friends they were. Their hands were folded behind their backs, their heads bowed together, discussing the tactics they would employ once they'd made contact with the enemy. As great as the victory at Thebes had been, King Khamudi would now be rounding up every man he could find to reinforce the remnants of his army. The Hyksos had always been redoubtable warriors and they would fight mercilessly to hang onto the land they had held for half a century.

As he walked towards the two men, Piay muttered a prayer that Taita would survive this bloody struggle. Egypt needed him, now more than ever. Piay needed him.

'Ah, there you are, Piay,' Taita said as he saw his former pupil approach. 'I was wondering what had happened to you.'

'I'm sorry, master . . . and Your Majesty . . . I'm afraid I overslept.'

'No matter, you earned your rest.'

'Quite agree,' Hurotas said. 'You will always be welcome at my table, Piay, should you find yourself in Sparta again.'

'Thank you, sire, that's very kind.'

'Now, if you'll excuse us, Zaras,' Taita said, using the name by which he had first known Hurotas, thirty years earlier, 'I just need a word with Piay.'

'By all means.'

Taita and Piay walked through the hubbub on the riverbank. The Egyptian commanders were shouting at their men to fall into their ranks and prepare to board their vessels. The Spartans, resplendent in their scarlet cloaks, were so disciplined that they barely needed an order – they were already assembled in perfect lines.

But the old man and his pupil were deaf to the sound of the great army all around them; their minds were on more important things.

'No matter what you do, do not leave Thebes until you have received word that we have been successful in defeating Khamudi and freeing Memphis,' Taita cautioned Piay. 'We cannot risk you being captured or killed. Everything hinges on your success.'

'I will do as you say, master,' Piay said. 'But there is one part of all this that puzzles me.'

'Just the one? This whole affair is, by definition, a puzzle from beginning to end. But tell me what in particular troubles you.'

'Well, you said that the tattooed man and the ghost-warriors might be defenders of the Riddle of the Stars, and they're determined to stop anyone getting close to it?'

'I believe that to be the case, yes.'

'But you also said that Imhotep intended the puzzle to be solved.'

'That's right.'

'So why are the ghosts stopping anyone from doing that?'

Taita smiled affectionately. 'You sound like Shamshi, the priest of Seth, trying to confound me with logic.'

'Except that I'm the one who's confounded.'

'Then let me help you . . . I believe that Imhotep set the riddle. And he wanted it to be solved, but only at the right time, by the right person. So the defenders of the riddle are testing all who try to solve it. They kill all who do not come up to the mark. But the searcher who is truly worthy, the one whom Imhotep foresaw . . . That one will defeat the guardians and take Imhotep's great prize.'

'Or perhaps it will be the searcher who has the most powerful god on his side,' Piay said. 'Like Seth, for example.'

'Perhaps . . .' Taita said. 'And perhaps neither you, nor the beautiful, wise Myssa, nor brave, good-hearted Hannu are fated to succeed. But, my boy, for the sake of Egypt, you must still try, with all your heart and might.' Taita laid his hand on Piay's shoulder. 'I am putting my trust, my faith and my hope in you.'

That hand felt to Piay like a leaden weight, pressing a great burden of responsibility onto him. He was no Taita, and never would be. But he told himself to stop feeling sorry for himself.

Taita would never have given you this task if he didn't think you were capable of succeeding. So just get on and do it – for him, for Myssa, and for Egypt.

'I will not let you down,' Piay said, his voice heavy with emotion.

'I know you won't,' Taita replied. Then he smiled and said, 'One moment . . .'

He waved towards a slave, who was standing not far away, holding a parcel wrapped in plain linen.

'I have something for you,' Taita said, handing the parcel to Piay.

Piay frowned. He felt something soft, but there was a hard object, with a familiar shape, lying in the middle of it.

'Two relics that, together, may help you in Memphis,' Taita said.

'Thank you, master,' Piay said, though he still did not know quite what he was thanking Taita for.

The master and his pupil embraced and said their farewells. Taita walked back to Hurotas and the two of them marched together onto the leading galley. They took up a position in the prow, where the whole army and the Thebans who crowded the riverbanks could see them.

As the galley cast off and began its journey downstream, musicians struck up a rousing martial tune. The crowds cheered. The generals waved. Piay watched them go, wondering what the future held for them all, for there seemed to be no half measure between a glorious, eternal victory and crushing, terminal defeat – a defeat that would surely end with his own death.

Piay stood by himself at the river's edge. His eyes were on the water, watching the flow, but his mind was lost in contemplation of the task he had sworn to undertake. He heard a loud cough, and turned his head to see Hannu, standing just a couple of paces away.

'Oh, hello,' Piay said. 'I didn't see you there.'

'I've been standing here for ages . . . but King Khamudi and his army could've marched up to you and you wouldn't have noticed. What's on your mind?'

'What do you reckon?'

'Yeah, well, that bloody riddle, obviously. But what bit of it were you thinking about?'

'I was thinking that I need a god on my side, too.'

Anyone with half a brain treated all the gods with the respect that was their due. But still, for most men and women, there was one god or goddess in particular that they worshipped with special reverence.

For Piay, his chosen deity was Khonsu, god of the moon, and son of the gods Amun and his consort Mut. Khonsu meant 'the Traveller', but he was also known as the Embracer, the Pathfinder, the Defender and the Healer. When he was in a lighter mood, Piay would joke that he had never done much healing, but he more than made up for that with the number of beautiful women he had embraced, the places to which he had travelled, the new paths he had found, and the people (himself, first and foremost) that he and his sword had defended.

But this was not the time for joking, least of all about the gods. Piay needed Khonsu's protection as a matter of life and death.

The sun was at its zenith and the people on the streets of Thebes were as hot as loaves in an oven when Piay, Hannu and Myssa reached a crossroads in the centre of the city. Myssa looked around, trying to get her bearings. Then she pointed up a road and said, 'I think I have to go that way.'

'Have a good time with those dusty old scrolls,' Piay said, knowing that Myssa was getting down to work on the research that Taita had outlined for her.

'Give my regards to your god,' she replied.

Myssa had no more desire to offend the heavens than anyone else, but the only Egyptian deity she recognised was Bast, and then only because of her cat. Myssa's true divine lord was the ram-god of Kush.

Piay watched his lover until she was lost in the bustle of a city coming back to life after decades of defeat. Then he turned to Hannu, pointed in another direction and said, 'This way.'

The interior of the Temple of Khonsu was blissfully cool after the sweat and dust of the city. Hannu stood guard by the door, his sword drawn, facing the outside world, as Piay walked into the centre of the building and bowed before the statue of Khonsu that stood at the far end.

The spicy scent of incense hung in the air, and a lantern hanging from the roof cast a glow over the crystal orb of the moon that was placed atop the statue's human head. The god's face was painted green, as were the hands that emerged from the white-painted bandages in which his body was wrapped. He wore a necklace – blue beads dotted with contrasting beads of red and gold – and the *was*-sceptre, flail and crook that he held in his hands were also decorated in the same colours.

If Taita was the mortal man whom Piay considered his second father, then Khonsu was his immortal equivalent. Khonsu had been Piay's companion through his many adventures and kept him safe from harm each and every time. He had come to Piay in his dreams on so many occasions, always appearing with the head of a falcon, that Piay was certain the god had chosen him for some task. And then one night, came the experience that bound Piay to Khonsu forever.

During the long march up to Egypt from the south, they stopped by a vast lake, from which the waters of the Nile itself were said to flow. The elephants stepped into the lake waters to wash themselves and slake their thirst. The Tumisi tribesmen speared fish to be wrapped in leaves and baked in the embers of an open fire. Piay and Myssa ate their fill and then, as they lay together on the grass beside the lake, Myssa said, 'There is magic in the air. Can you feel it?'

Piay sensed something, and so, too, did the elephants. They all stood still, silently looking out across the waters. Piay offered up a silent prayer to Khonsu, asking for his protection in the dangerous days to come.

Then, in a vision which he alone experienced, Piay saw Khonsu coming towards him, with his falcon head, seeming to glide over the surface of the lake without ever touching the water. Khonsu held out his hand and conferred his blessing on Piay, and in the presence of his god, the young Egyptian had felt overwhelmed, terrified but also filled with awe and wonder at the gift he had just received.

Who could know the minds of the gods? Not even the priests who claimed to divine the purposes of those higher powers. But in his heart, Piay had come to believe the struggles of those beings were played out on earth, and that Seth, that dark god of the desert, and Khonsu, the god of the cool night, were in opposition and that they had chosen their mortal champions to do battle.

Now, Piay fell to his knees and asked for Khonsu's blessing once again.

'Protect me upon my travels,' he said softly, bowing his head, 'and guide my hand in the struggles that lie ahead.'

The interior of the temple was dark, lit only by a few openings high up in the walls, but now it seemed to Piay that a shaft of moonlight lanced across his eyes. He blinked and, when he opened his eyes again and looked up at the statue, he thought he saw a faint white glow.

'You are here with me, my lord,' Piay said. 'And as far as I journey, I will always be with you.'

A breeze had picked up as Myssa passed through the gateway of the precinct that surrounded the Temple of Amun, causing the dust to whirl and eddy around her ankles. Bast was walking beside her. Her pet's reappearance at a temple made perfect sense to Myssa. It was only natural for a cat with the soul of a goddess to wish to be among her own kind.

The people of Thebes worshipped Amun above all other gods, and his temple complex was therefore much bigger than his son Khonsu's. The sound of chanting priests, somewhere in the depths of the sacred space, was just audible as Myssa strode across the courtyard and skipped up the limestone steps that rose to the temple itself, but she paid it little heed, for as the woven straw bag she carried indicated – containing as it did a roll of papyrus, a bottle of ink and three pens made of reed stems – she was a woman on a mission.

'I need you to do two things for me,' Taita had told her, when they had spoken together in his tent. 'First, I need you to learn everything you can about Imhotep, his architecture and all that is known about the riddle. Most of the information you need will be in Memphis, but you need not be idle while you are waiting here in Thebes. When the Hyksos barbarians first approached Thebes, so long ago that I was still a young man, the ancient records of the Upper Kingdom, dating back hundreds, even thousands of years were deposited for safekeeping in the Temple of Amun. So start your work there, but be sure to tell some other story to cover your true actions.'

'I imagine that great works will be planned to celebrate the victory of the people of Egypt over the Hyksos,' Myssa said. 'Doubtless you would wish your servants to consult the records of previous projects, the better to avoid any mistakes that might have been made.'

'Indeed I would,' Taita smiled, 'so you have the great advantage of being able to tell a false story that in fact has a kernel of truth. Now, there is one more favour that I ask. Piay has the heart of a lion but he can be . . .' Taita paused for a moment, as if unwilling to criticise a man in front of the woman he loved.

Myssa had no such scruples. 'Rash, headstrong, too convinced of his own abilities, prone to act first and think second?' she suggested.

Taita smiled. 'An excellent summary, which I only tolerate as it comes from someone who cares for that young man as much as I do.'

'She does, yes,' Myssa said.

'Then you must strengthen him where he is weak. Use your knowledge, your intelligence and your intuition to provide the clear-eyed guidance that will steer this vital mission to its rightful conclusion. Above all . . .' Taita placed his hands on Myssa's shoulders and looked deep into her eyes. 'Look after Piay for me. He is heading into terrible danger, and there may . . . No, there will be moments when he risks himself to help others, where men with cooler, more calculating heads would put their own safety first. Be that cool head, that word of caution in his ear. He will not be grateful to you for it, as a proud Egyptian man, but be assured, I most certainly will.'

'I will do as you ask, but if I am to go into your people's greatest sacred places and examine their most precious archives . . .'

Myssa paused just long enough to allow Taita to see where her words were leading.

'Ah, yes,' he said. 'Of course. I quite understand. Come with me.'

Myssa revelled in the tasks with which Taita had entrusted her. He was not the first wise man to have spotted her gifts. Even when she was a girl, barely past her first moon, she had served as an advisor to the chieftain of her tribe. But then her people had either been slaughtered, or, like her, sold into slavery. Piay had given her back her freedom. Taita had renewed her sense of purpose. She was not going to let either of them down.

A priest wandered out of the depths of the temple – a shrivelled, desiccated old man. He was fresh from his daily ablutions, smelling of the fragrant unguent he had applied after washing, his head freshly shaved, his linen robe perfectly clean and white, the leopard skin of his class slung across his scrawny shoulder.

Bast looked at the priest and hissed in his direction.

'What brings you to these far lands?' he asked Myssa officiously.

'I have been sent by the Pharaoh's advisor, Taita, to study the records for the reconstruction that is to come. I seek admission to the House of Books and for the Keeper to guide me in my understanding.'

Myssa had spoken with an air of calm, confident authority, but the priest was not impressed. The way he looked her up and down, his nose twitching, made Myssa feel as though she were back in the slave market once again. The priest barely saw her as a human being. She was just another object to be traded. The shame and fury of the memory cut her to the very core.

'From Taita, you say?' the priest said. 'No, I think not. You are a woman and, what is more, as black as a Nubian. Why would a man as wise as the great Taita choose an underling who is inferior on two counts for a task that should surely be conducted by a true-born child of Thebes?'

Myssa swallowed her anger and showed a sweet face.

'Truly you are wise and perceptive, holy one. I am, indeed, both female and a Kushite. But I assure you that Lord Taita has nonetheless seen fit to enlist me to do his bidding.'

'No,' the priest snapped before she could continue. 'I cannot believe a word you say. Away with you.' He waved a hand and turned. 'If you return here I will have you taken away and beaten.'

The priest stalked off into the depths of the shadowy temple.

Bast aimed another angry hiss at the cleric.

'Good girl,' Myssa murmured.

She felt humiliated, infuriated and sorely tempted to scream in sheer rage, right there in the middle of the temple. But Taita had shown his faith in her capacity to keep her mind calm and her wits sharp. And they had both anticipated the possibility that – given the undeniable facts of her race and sex – problems such as this might arise.

Myssa thought of the confidence with which Bast had walked among the elephants. Now it was time for her to draw on her own inner goddess. She drew herself up to her full height and raised her head high, then she hurried after the priest.

He sped up, hearing her behind him, coming as close to a run as his feeble frame could manage.

With her long legs and cheetah's stride, Myssa swiftly caught up with him.

'Stop! Please! I need to show you something!' she called, but the priest paid no attention.

Myssa was close enough now to touch him. She reached out, intending only to tap him on the shoulder, to make him turn and look at her, but as she did so she felt her fingers close around a handful of his spotless robe.

The unexpected contact was enough to cause the priest to lose his balance. His sandals slipped on the shiny stone floor and he fell backwards, his arms waving, before landing hard on his bony backside.

The priest gave a yelp of pain.

'I'm so sorry,' Myssa said, bending over him and holding out her hand to help him get up.

The priest stared at the tall, strong woman with blazing eyes looming over him, and pushed himself away, wailing.

'Help! Sacrilege! A barbarian has assaulted me!'

'It was an accident,' Myssa said.

'Help!' the priest repeated. 'A woman has violated our sacred space!'

For a moment nothing happened, but then Myssa heard the slapping of sandals on stone floors. When she looked up she saw half a dozen men in clerical garb all rushing from various corners of the temple.

The scrawny priest allowed his colleagues to help him to his feet. Then he glared at Myssa, jabbed his forefinger at her and began a lengthy account of what had happened, in which his civilised, perfectly reasonable behaviour was contrasted with the primitive savagery of the woman who stood before them.

Myssa said nothing. She just looked from one man to the other, wondering which of them would be the first to forget that he was a servant of the gods and become just another violent man attacking a lone woman.

Then she heard more footsteps. They were heavy, steady, confident.

Good, Myssa thought, *the headman is approaching*.

As he got nearer, and she could see him properly, Myssa could tell from the sheer size and glittering gems of the man's ceremonial collar that he must indeed be the high priest.

'What in the name of Amun is going on here?' the newcomer asked.

The scrawny priest told the story of the brutal assault he had suffered.

'She attacked me here, in the god's house. Amun has been insulted and defamed. She must be made to pay . . .' He looked at Myssa with barely hidden glee. 'And the penalty for such blasphemy is death!'

Other priests chimed in with their own observations, all to the effect that the priest and Amun alike had been abused, and that death was the only fitting verdict. The chill grip of fear began to clutch at Myssa's guts as the men began shouting and waving their fists. It would take very little to tip them over the edge into attacking and killing her.

The high priest watched for a moment, then held up his right hand.

'Silence!' he called.

The noise abated. The fist-waving stopped. But the hunger for violence in the eyes of the priests who surrounded Myssa was as fierce as ever.

The high priest looked at her. 'Did you lay a hand on a man of god, within this holy place?' he asked.

'Yes, but—'

'There is no "but". You have admitted your own guilt. Proof has been provided. The case is closed.'

Now injustice was being piled upon insult. But Myssa refused to give in.

'Proof of what?' she asked. 'Proof that you do not allow an innocent woman to defend herself? Or proof of your own deafness and stupidity?'

'By Amun, I will not be insulted in this way!' the high priest bellowed.

By now, the commotion had attracted people from all over the temple. Worshippers, other clerics, even temple guards had gathered, forming an audience to the drama in which Myssa and the high priest were now taking the leading roles.

'Then, for your own sake, you had better listen to what I have to say. Your position, and even your life, may depend on it.'

Myssa looked the high priest right in the eye. He stared back at her. Neither spoke.

The high priest cracked first. Affecting a lordly, untroubled air, as if he were merely humouring her, he waved a hand and sighed.

'Oh, very well, then. Speak, if you think it will do you any good. But be brief.'

Myssa reached inside her bag and pulled out a papyrus, tied with a black linen bow. But it was not the one that she had set aside for her notes.

'I told the man who now accuses me that I was working for Lord Taita, the victor of yesterday's battle, whose standing is second only to the Pharaoh—'

'And I paid no need to such babbling, because it is plainly nonsense!' the old priest interrupted.

'It is so, and it explains why I hurried after you – for your sake, and for the sake of your master, the high priest.'

The first traces of concern crossed the high priest's face. 'What do you mean?'

Myssa handed him the papyrus. 'Perhaps you should read this,' she said. 'And it might please you to read it aloud, so that all can hear that justice has been done.'

The high priest untied the bow and unrolled the document. His eyes widened in horror as he read it. His mouth opened, but he could manage no more than a long, 'Aaaahhh . . . Yes . . . I see . . .'

'I can easily recite the message from memory, since I was with Lord Taita when he wrote it,' Myssa said. 'It reads, "Myssa the Kushite is my trusted servant and messenger, and the work that she is conducting on my behalf is of the utmost importance. She is to be given every possible assistance by all who read this parchment."'

A gasp went up from the still-growing crowd of onlookers, and the priests began exchanging nervous, cowardly looks.

'Do you agree that I have recited the message accurately?' Myssa asked the high priest.

He nodded.

'And is Lord Taita's seal imprinted upon the bottom of the message?'

'Yes,' he said.

'Then perhaps your holiness might consent to do as the words suggest . . . if it pleases you.'

A short while later, Myssa was in the temple library, being conducted along row upon row of scrolls, some dating back a millennium to the time of Imhotep himself. But though the high priest had been forced to relent, and the librarians were fawning over her as if she were a queen – even fetching milk and scraps of meat for Bast to feast upon – she had been given a hard lesson by the priests of Amun.

Piay will do anything for me because he loves me, she reflected. *Hannu will fight for me, because he is loyal to Piay. Taita will support me because he loves Piay, too, and also because he is a good and wise man, who values and respects me. But they are only three men among a multitude, and I am still an imposter in this land, and an outsider to those who inhabit it. And all the messages and seals in the world are never going to change that.*

Days passed as arrangements were made. Piay waited for a messenger from Taita, but none came, though news drifted back among the Nile boatmen that the siege of Memphis was underway. King Khamudi had abandoned the city's ancient port of Peru-nefer and burned all the vessels moored on the banks of the Nile. So, for this reason, the flow of trade to and from the great capital of the Lower Kingdom had ceased, and the waters of the great river were being left to the fish and the crocodiles.

Every morning Piay would hurry down to the riverside to catch any scraps of news that had floated back from the Lower Kingdom. One day it was said that Taita had set his men burrowing under Memphis' walls. Then came reports of hundreds of refugees who had fled the doomed city, laden with their valuables, only to have their prize possessions relieved from their grasp by Hurotas' men.

Everyone knew the spoils of war belonged to the victor. Once it had been the Hyksos pillaging the settlements that fell under their rule. Now those barbarians were learning the hard lesson they had inflicted on everyone else.

Myssa had thrown herself into the task given to her by Taita, spending long days with the scribes and the priests in the temples and libraries of Thebes and nearby Karnak as she learned all she could that might help in their quest for the Riddle of the Stars. Piay felt proud of her dedication and sense of duty, but he was embarrassed to admit to himself that he was jealous of the time she spent away from him.

Every night, at Hannu's insistence, they slept in the barracks of the Theban guards, surrounded by soldiers keeping their watch. Hannu himself rested with his sword under his bed.

'They'll come for us when we least expect it, mark my words,' he said. 'Try to take us by surprise.'

Shamshi was confined to a cell deep beneath the garrison, his guards carefully chosen by Gatas. No risks were to be taken.

Then, one night, Piay was jolted awake from a troubling dream of jackals howling at the moon in the desert waste. Hannu's face loomed over him, the shadows shifting across his features cast by the lamp swinging from his hand.

'Our time has run out!' he hissed.

Piay lurched to his feet, shaking the last clots of sleep from his head. When he began to ask questions, Hannu pressed a finger to his lips and shook his head.

Within moments they were hurrying through the night and out of the River Gate to the banks of the Nile. Limping on his ruined leg, Hannu headed south as fast as he could and soon Piay caught sight of a light burning. As they closed upon it, he saw it was a lamp held aloft by a man in a drab cloak, with the hood pulled low over his brow. He was standing beside a papyrus bed. The wind rustled through the rushes as if a beast moved there.

Hannu took the lamp from him and said, 'Remember, say nothing of this to anyone. You will be well rewarded.'

The cloaked man nodded and strode off into the night.

'One of my spies,' Hannu said. 'A boatman. He's been keeping watch for me along the riverbank at night.'

'You have spies? I didn't know.'

'You didn't ask.'

'Hope they're not spying on me.'

'Maybe they are,' Hannu said, with a wicked grin. Then he stepped into the sucking mud of the reed bed and squelched towards the water, turning from one side to the other, so that the flames cast their light across the rushes all around.

Piay watched him for a moment, puzzled, and then eased in after him.

A moment later he heard Hannu mutter, 'Ah, there you are . . .' He raised his voice just a little louder. 'Over here!'

Piay splashed over and recoiled when he saw what lay within the circle of light. The body of a man was sprawled across a flattened bed of reeds – or rather, half a body, for the legs were missing, the torn flesh and bone suggesting the remains had been feasted on by a river crocodile. Quite why the whole body had not been consumed, Piay did not know.

Leaning in for a closer look, he saw jewels gleaming through the mud and bloodstains on the ragged white robe. A man of status, then. But when Hannu lowered the lamp over the face, Piay winced. At first he couldn't discern the identity, for the features were contorted into a hideous mask. The lips were pulled back from the teeth and the milky eyes bulged. It was as if the skin of the head had shrunk to half its size.

'Wait,' Piay said, bowing even closer, 'Is that . . .?'

'Lord Azref,' Hannu said. 'The man Taita said would knock Memphis into shape while we got on with our mission. The man who was supposed to protect us.'

Piay took the lamp and held it just above Azref's face. Sapphire crystals crusted the dead man's grey lips.

'Aye,' Hannu said, taking the lamp back and swinging it to one side. 'Now look here.'

The shadows rushed away to reveal a dead river crocodile lying on its back, the belly bloated.

'Poison, then,' Piay said. 'That beast had a meal it could not digest.'

'I reckon it was those tattooed bastards,' Hannu said.

Piay nodded and looked back at the body of Azref, his mind shuffling through what had been discovered here.

'Taita told me about potions that can loosen a man's tongue before they finally kill him.'

'Well, that would come in handy if you wanted to find out why we were going to Memphis, or even who had the Eye.'

'Azref didn't know anything about the riddle,' Piay said. 'So far as he was concerned, we were going to survey all of the libraries and monuments in Memphis, once the Hyksos had been kicked out.'

'But if it was the tattooed men, or . . . what do you call them . . .?'

'Ghost-warriors.'

'Right, well, either way, chances are they now know that we're going to Memphis. And even if Taita had their precious Eye the last time they saw it, they're going to reckon we might have it by now, and they'll want to find out for sure.'

Piay looked from the mutilated body to the crocodile and then to Hannu.

'Then we leave tomorrow, whether we have news of Memphis falling or not,' he said. 'There's no time to waste.'

The expedition to Memphis was not expected to encounter any hostile ships on their way, and in any case all the available war galleys, and the oarsmen to crew them, had already been sent ahead to support Taita's campaign against the Hyksos. Instead, Piay and the others would be travelling on a large sailing vessel.

Now Piay stood on the quayside in the bright morning sunlight, just a few paces from where he had last talked to Taita, watching a thirty-strong detachment of the Blue Crocodile Guards boarding the ship. They were the best fighting force in Egypt, perhaps in the world, and Piay realised what a sacrifice Taita had made to release even a few of them from the army besieging Memphis.

Azref's body had been reclaimed. The official conclusion was that he had been taking a moonlight stroll when the crocodile had attacked him. Those who dragged his remains out of the rushes were not concerned enough to notice the signs of murder, but Piay's thoughts kept turning to those blue crystals crusting the dead man's lips, and the strange dust he had breathed in during the attack at the palace. Whether the guardians of Imhotep's secret knew sorcery, he could not tell, but it seemed to him that they were in command of what Taita liked to call 'the old knowledge' – skills passed down the years and known only to a few.

Myssa drifted down to the riverside soon after, with Bast curled in her arms. She was wrapped in an ivory sheath dress that made her seem even more dazzlingly elegant, but Piay had seen her slit a man's throat without a second thought. He knew the hardness that lay beneath Myssa's beautiful surface.

'You're taking the cat with you?' he asked with a note of incredulity.

'Of course,' she replied. 'We're going on a dangerous journey. Don't you want the goddess's blessing?'

As Myssa spoke, Piay caught Bast's green eyes. They were staring at him with an intensity that seemed to be daring him to deny that the cat goddess was present.

'Very well, then,' he said, as if he had some say in the matter. 'You'd better both come aboard.'

Myssa stepped onto the ship, took Piay's arm and said, 'Let's take in the view from the bows,' as if she were just another woman wanting to be close to her lover. But once they had reached the vessel's prow and she had nestled closer to Piay, she whispered, 'I've spent hours examining the Eye of Horus. I can't quite tell how it functions as a key, but there's a secret to it, I'm sure.'

'Keep it well hidden,' Piay said. 'I wouldn't want anyone to know that you're carrying it.'

Hannu was already prowling around the deck as if he was on the brink of battle, pausing every now and then to lean against the rail and peer out across the river to where the necropolis brooded.

Piay strode aft, where Captain Gatas scowled at his barbarian captive Shamshi, looking as if he was trying with every fibre of his being to resist hacking the Hyksos priest to death.

When he saw Piay, Shamshi stood and threw his arms wide.

'My brother,' he declared.

'I'm no brother of yours,' Piay replied.

'Come now. We embark on a great adventure, shoulder to shoulder.' Shamshi grinned. 'Once we were enemies, that is true, but now we share the same aim. Partners.'

'Keeping your head on your shoulders,' Hannu rumbled. 'That's the only aim you need to think about.'

Shamshi shrugged, but his grin remained. How he could keep his spirits so high in captivity, Piay didn't know.

'An enemy on board my ship! What is this travesty?'

The voice boomed across the deck and Piay turned. At first the figure was lost to the glare of the sun, but as the new arrival neared, Piay saw a nobleman in a shimmering white robe studded with more jewels than he had ever seen before. He had to be the one that Pharaoh's advisors had chosen as a replacement for the kindly Lord Azref, but he looked as if he had barely seen forty floods of the Nile, and lacked any air of wisdom or authority.

Taita would never have allowed someone like that to come with us, if he'd still been here, Piay thought.

The new arrival pushed up his chin and peered down the length of his nose at those who stood before him. He was slim, his muscles unformed, his hands as smooth as a child's. The skin of his face looked as if it was continually massaged with creams, and the lack of any visible lines gave it an odd mask-like quality.

'And who are you?' Shamshi chuckled.

'Throw him overboard. He will make a fine feast for the river crocodiles,' the lord commanded with an airy waft of his hand.

Piay stepped forward and bowed. 'My lord, we need this barbarian. He has information that will be useful when we sail into the lands the Hyksos once occupied.'

The nobleman looked Piay up and down, making no attempt to hide his disdain.

'And who are you?'

'Piay, my lord. Taita has placed me in command of this expedition—'

'Don't be absurd. You are not in command. I am here now. I am Lord Harrar. Pharaoh has chosen me personally for this vital work. Only a man of my intellect and wisdom could see it through to fruition. You would be wise to remember that.'

And with that, Harrar floated away along the deck, calling out to the galley's captain to attend to him.

Shamshi threw his head back in a hearty laugh.

'Obey your new master, Piay of Thebes. Obey this wise and experienced leader!'

'Still your tongue, dog,' Hannu snapped. 'Or we'll take Lord Harrar's advice and throw you to the river crocodiles.'

Shamshi only laughed harder. He understood their need for him as much as he, too, recognised the hollowness of the nobleman's authority.

Piay watched Harrar gesticulating to the galley captain and felt his unease mount.

Hannu snorted. 'This just got a hundred times harder.'

The crewmen at the bow and stern of the ship cast off the lines that had bound it to the shore. The helmsmen pulled on the great steering oar and they drifted out into the river, letting the current provide momentum until the single linen sail caught the breeze, snapped tight and set them on their way on the long journey to Memphis.

No crowds gathered on the banks to cheer them on their way as they had done for Taita's flotilla, and the only noises to be heard were the calls of the captain to his crew, the creaking of the hull, the snapping of the sail as the wind died down and then picked up again, and the running of the water as the bow pushed it aside.

Piay's eyes were fixed on the river and the scattering of small ships dotted about on the water. But he hardly even registered what he was seeing, for his thoughts were concentrated on the journey ahead and the dangers that lay on every side. They were being hunted now. But what else could they expect, given the nature of their quest? They would not be able to rest for a moment.

A skiff sped past them, heading downriver with heaps of silver fish glistening aft. They passed a great barge laden with creamy stone from the quarries upriver, its sails billowing. Trade with Memphis may have been halted for now, but there were other ports and customers to serve. And the waters of the eternal Mother Nile flowed on, blithely indifferent to the troubles of mortal men.

As they neared what had once been Hyksos-occupied territory, the river traffic thinned – even fewer smaller boats plied their trade, and they barely saw any larger vessels from one hour to the next. Harrar kept apart from the men as much as he could, settling under a canopy of white linen to protect himself from the heat of the sun and adopting a disdainful expression. Occasionally, he would call for olives or flatbread to be brought up from his own personal store in the hold.

As the setting sun painted the water blood red, the ship moored for the night. Piay joined the captain of the vessel and the commander of the Blue Crocodile Guards detachment to determine the best arrangements for the night. Under normal circumstances, the crew would sleep on the deck, to make the most of the night's cool air. But for their own safety, and much to their displeasure, they would have to go below, into the cargo hold.

Meanwhile, half the Blue Crocodile troops would join the crewmen in the hold, while the rest remained on deck to form watches, guarding the vessel till dawn. The following night, they would be the ones to sleep below.

'We've had it easy all day,' Hannu said, when Piay told him what had been agreed. 'This is when it gets serious.'

'Yes,' Piay agreed. 'If there's one fact we know about our tattooed friends, it's that they like to work at night.'

'So does Bast,' Myssa said, smiling. 'She's down below, hunting mice.'

The three of them walked across the deck to where Shamshi was being held under the hawklike vigilance of Captain Gatas.

The barbarian nodded when he saw Piay approaching.

'Ah. Serious talk.'

'We are carrying you towards Memphis,' Piay said. 'Now it's time for you to keep your side of the bargain Taita struck with you.'

'But we are not there yet.'

Gatas whisked out his sword and jabbed it towards the captive.

'Don't test my patience. I can easily whittle off a limb or two and still keep you alive until we reach our destination.'

Shamshi weighed this, then said, 'I will tell you a little now. More when we reach Memphis.'

'Very well . . . but remember, you are speaking for your life.'

Piay sat on the deck, leaning against the side. Hannu and Myssa made their way over to join the conclave.

'Speak,' Piay said, holding out the flat of his hand.

Shamshi rubbed his chin with his thumb, thinking.

'The ones who guard the secret are called the Sons of Apis,' he began.

Hannu grunted. 'That explains the bull inscribed upon their flesh.'

'I had already drawn the link with Apis,' Myssa said dismissively. 'It was obvious. The sacred bull Apis has long been worshipped in Memphis, the city of Imhotep. He is an intermediary between men and gods. If one were trying to forge a link with the gods, he would be a natural ally.'

Shamshi looked at her, and once again Piay noticed the divergence between the fierceness of his eyes and his ironic, almost playful style of speech.

'You know a lot,' Shamshi said to Myssa, 'for one who, like me, is considered a barbarian.'

'I learn quickly,' she replied. 'So now tell us something that I don't already know.'

Shamshi smiled. 'If only I were not a priest, the lessons I would give you . . .'

'Watch your tongue,' Piay snapped. 'Or I'll finish you now, and damn what secrets you know.'

Shamshi shrugged and held up both hands. 'What can I say? I have been away from my temple too long. I apologise if I forgot my vows.'

'Enough of this!' Myssa snapped. She looked at Shamshi and said, 'I don't need any lessons from you on that subject, and if I did, I would choose a different teacher. And as for you . . .' She turned her attention to Piay. 'I know you mean well, and I thank you for defending me, but if a man insults me, I will respond to him myself. For now, though, I just want to know about these Sons of Apis. So, I make the same request, priest. Tell me something I do not know.'

'That may be difficult, since you know so very much . . .'

Again, Piay saw the mouth that smiled and the eyes that had no spark of humour in them.

'But I will try.' Shamshi shrugged. 'So . . . the old stories say Imhotep himself first created the Sons of Apis to guard his secret from the unworthy. Their sect is thus as old as the great monuments themselves, always hidden, always watching. But there is more to the Sons than that. Yes, they guard Imhotep's secret, but their main task is to find the one about whom Imhotep prophesied, a worthy man who can overcome all obstacles and who will then prove himself wise enough to be granted access to the source of all power. And the Sons of Apis will find that person by challenging everyone who sets foot upon the path to the ultimate prize.'

'By "challenging", you mean trying to kill them,' Piay said.

Shamshi nodded. 'If you escape death, you will be granted access to power over all life.'

Shamshi had not told Piay much that he did not already know, or that Taita would not have told Myssa, too, but it was useful to know that Shamshi was, in this respect at least, telling the truth – or what the truth was believed to be.

Piay glanced at Myssa and, sensing that she was about to tell Shamshi once again that he had not surprised her, gave a tiny shake of the head that only she would notice. She gave him the merest hint of a nod in return. It would not be good for Shamshi to be aware of exactly how much the Egyptians already knew. Better now to flatter him.

'I must admit, you have kept your side of the bargain, priest,' Piay said. 'This is remarkable information. But tell me, do you Hyksos know where the secret is buried?'

'Ha!' Shamshi laughed. 'If we did, we would now be in Thebes, and you would be our slaves.'

'Then you know nothing of value.' Hannu exhaled with disdain.

Shamshi tightened his grin.

'Go on,' Piay said.

'Some of your people now consider Imhotep a god. I can see how they would think that. His wisdom and his knowledge of all things have never been equalled. He watched and he learned and his mind made calculations. It is said that when he closed his eyes, those calculations opened up to him the great sweep of days yet to come. His prophecies caused some to call him a sorcerer. Perhaps . . .' Shamshi shrugged. 'But there is no doubt he predicted a dark time for Egypt—'

'Caused by you bastards,' Gatas hissed.

'. . . and he was determined to prepare for that age, even though it would come around many lifetimes beyond his allotted span. So, let me tell you now, not what I know, but what I think. You are aware that Imhotep was known as the Great Architect?'

'Of course,' Piay said.

Shamshi glanced at Piay, and as their eyes met it struck Piay that they might both be playing the same game: bluffing, dissembling, trying to find out exactly what the other knew, where they stood and what their intentions might be.

Then that brief moment was over and Shamshi was saying, 'We believe, as maybe you do, too, that Imhotep had a hand in all those monuments that brood across the wilderness at Giza, not far from Memphis. One he designed himself. For the others, he left . . . who can say? Plans, perhaps. Guidance. So consider now the nature of these monuments. See how they have survived for a thousand years, untouched by fires, floods, storms and wars. Imhotep knew that time could not touch them. What better place could there be for him to hide his clues?'

As the last of the sun's rays were swallowed by the dark, Hannu lit the lamp that stood next to the steersman's platform. Faces glowed in the circle of light.

'What if the clues open a path?' Shamshi said as he stared at the flame. 'A path that is also a ritual. Each step taken along it opens another door, and another threat, for death lurks on every side. Only the wisest will find a way to the ultimate reward. This was Imhotep's plan, for only then could he be certain that the treasure he had left behind would be used in the manner he intended. The greedy and the weak and the unworthy would be doomed.'

'Aye, and you and your barbarian brothers are trying to prove him wrong,' Hannu rumbled.

Shamshi smiled. 'Perhaps we are not barbarians. We may have among us the man who will be fit to answer Imhotep's call.'

'No!' Piay said. 'Imhotep could not possibly have wanted someone who was not of his people – our people – to solve his riddle!'

'Do you think you can be sure of what a man of such wisdom would want? A man born of a god who himself became a god . . . Who are we to claim to know his ultimate intentions? You, Egyptian, believe that you have the right to solve this riddle. But ask yourself this – are you sure that you are wise enough and worthy enough to solve Imhotep's puzzle? Or is it only death that awaits you?'

Silence fell on the group for a moment, so that the only sound was that of the waves lapping against the hull.

Is the barbarian right? Piay wondered. *Am I up to that challenge?*

He glanced around the faces and was warmed to see neither Hannu nor Myssa were looking at him with that doubt.

'Ho!' A watchman's cry echoed across the deck, jolting everyone from their own thoughts.

'Who's making that infernal noise?' Harrar snapped from the shadows beneath his shelter. He sounded as if he had been dozing.

Piay jumped to his feet and leaped from bench to bench until he reached to where the soldier leaned against the rail, peering towards the bank.

'Thought I saw movement. Out there.'

The watchmen pointed, but the dark across the fields and the papyrus were impenetrable. Piay searched back and forth along the bank, but no movement caught his eye. He felt pleased that he had taken the decision to drop the ship's stone anchor just beyond the shallows, so that there was an expanse of water between them and dry land. They would, he had hoped, hear anyone splashing in the river if they tried to reach them.

'Be on your guard,' he called to the other watchmen along the rail. 'At the first sign—'

An arrow flashed out of the night and punched into the throat of the watchman standing next to him. The man keeled back, choking, his hands clutching at the shaft. He staggered, bumped into the guardrail and toppled backwards.

The Sons of Apis were on the attack.

'Bowmen!' Piay bellowed so that his voice would carry to the other galley. 'Keep your heads down!' He turned towards Captain Gatas, 'Get the priest and Myssa down below!'

Barely had the words left his lips than arrows whirred through the air across the length of the galley. Most whisked across the deck and splashed into the river on the other side; one or two crunched into the wood of the guardrail.

A high-pitched wail rose up and Piay wrenched round. At first, he thought Harrar had been wounded. The nobleman was lying on his belly, his hands over his head, screaming. An arrow had ripped through the canopy of his shelter; that was all.

Damned coward! Piay thought.

More shouts came – dripping apparitions were hauling themselves over the starboard rail, their skull-like faces ghastly in the torchlight. Each of them carried a curved knife as they heaved themselves up. On the rail, bronze hooks dug into the wood, hide ropes trailing behind them. Whether the Sons had swum around the ship or used vessels unseen in the dark, Piay couldn't be sure.

Piay heard the commander of the Blue Crocodile Guards firing orders to the guardsmen who'd been on duty. Roaring battle cries, they threw themselves at the attackers. A sword swung down like a butcher's cleaver, hacking into the shoulder of one of the Sons. As the tattooed man fell away, his knife nicked the arm of the guardsman who had wounded him. It was barely more than a scratch, but a moment later the man was staggering backwards, foam bubbling from between his lips, clutching at his throat as if he couldn't breathe.

'Their weapons are dipped in poison!' Piay yelled.

The soldiers caught up his cry and passed it along. Hannu was already at the rail, fighting off one of the tattooed attackers, bobbing and weaving out of the reach of his poisoned blade.

He fended off the initial attack, drew his opponent on, then saw the opportunity he had been waiting for. The attacker only left himself vulnerable for a blink of an eye, but that was enough for Hannu to lunge forward, stab his sword into the chest of his enemy and then rip his blade out in a sideways, cutting motion that dropped the Son of Apis to the deck, desperately clutching at his stomach, trying to hold in the guts that spilled out onto the blood-drenched wood.

'Draw up the anchor!' Piay yelled. 'Get us out into the flow.'

In the faster currents, their attackers would find it much harder to board and continue the slaughter.

As Piay ran to Hannu's side, so that each could watch the other's back, he heard the rumble of the stone against the hull as the anchor was drawn up. It would take several moments before the ship was carried far enough away from the bank.

He rammed his sword tip into the face of a Son of Apis who was pulling himself over the rail. The wounded attacker fell back and splashed into the river below. The blood would attract the river crocodiles. If the cultists were swimming, they would soon face a more frenzied foe.

The battle raged up and down the deck. Men were falling on either side, but then the Blue Crocodile Guards, who had been scattered around the ship, formed themselves into a battle formation. Standing side by side, holding their shields together in a solid wall and jabbing their short stabbing spears in unison, they marched in a solid mass, from the stern of the vessel towards the bow, sweeping the Sons of Apis before them like a broom clearing litter from a floor.

Finally, no new attackers pulled themselves up to replace the ones who had fallen. Piay hesitated at peering over the edge for fear it was a trap, but the only sound that reached his ears was the churning of the water where the river beasts fed.

'How many are there?' Hannu gasped.

'Fewer now.' Piay stepped back.

'We showed those bandits what sharp bronze in the hands of brave Egyptians can do,' Harrar declared, puffing out his chest as though he had personally led the fight to defend the ship.

'That's one way of looking at it, my lord,' Piay replied. 'Another was that this was just a skirmish to test our strength.'

Now that the battle was done, the only sounds came from flowing water and creaking wood, but the Sons of Apis were still out there, somewhere in the darkness, waiting to make their next move. Piay turned his attention to the arrogant, lily-livered man by his side and finished his sentence.

'. . . and the next time, they'll know precisely how to conduct their attack.'

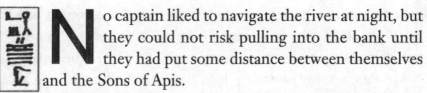

No captain liked to navigate the river at night, but they could not risk pulling into the bank until they had put some distance between themselves and the Sons of Apis.

Only two of the Blue Crocodile Guards had been lost, and the boat's crew, who were all now deeply grateful for being banished to the hold, were entirely untouched. Piay was sad to see any man die, but to have such light casualties was surely a blessing from Khonsu. With those knives dipped in lethal poison flashing back and forth, it had been a wonder they had not lost more.

Harrar had decided to retire to the comfort of his shelter, rather than to offer his praise to the men who had defended him. Instead Piay moved among the soldiers, commending them on their courage. Many he already knew by name, and if he did not, he took a moment to find out about them and their families, so that they knew they were seen and appreciated. Piay knew that the greater the concern he showed for the men, the greater their willingness would be to risk their lives defending him.

Sometimes it helps, coming from nothing, he thought. *A man like Harrar, who has been waited on hand and foot all his life, has no idea that slaves, servants and soldiers are even really people at all.*

Piay fetched Myssa from below decks.

'It's safe now. They won't come back tonight,' he said.

They walked together up to the prow and laid their bedding on the deck so that they might lie down together and gaze, side by side, at the sea of stars in the sky. Soon enough, they were both fast asleep, and it barely seemed like a moment later that Piay was awoken by a rough, calloused hand shaking his shoulder.

Hannu's face was looking down at him.

'Time to get up,' the old soldier said. He was holding two pottery cups, filled with wine and water. 'For you two lovebirds.'

Piay got to his feet and looked around, raising his hand to shield his eyes from the glare of the sun rising over the eastern bank of the Nile. The ship was sailing peacefully down the river, and the only obvious reminder of the night's events was the sight of crewmen on their hands and knees, scrubbing blood from the deck.

In the growing light, the land looked less foreboding. It was far easier to see any enemies moving among the irrigation ditches and the gently clacking shadoofs that dipped leather buckets down into the river, then popped up with those buckets brimming with fresh water. Piay looked at Myssa, standing in the prow, her eyes closed and a faint, beatific smile on the face that she raised to the rising sun. For her, this was a daily ritual, as it had been all her life.

'The same sun shines on me here as shone on me in my village,' she had once told him. 'So, every day I am reminded that my homeland is still there. That thought comforts me. And one day, if the gods will it, I may be able to go back.'

'And every day, when I see you looking at the rising sun,' Piay had replied, 'I am reminded of how beautiful you are and how much I love you. And if you ever go home, I will go beside you.'

When he finally saw Myssa's eyelids flutter open, Piay strolled up behind her and put his arms around her waist. Myssa leaned back against him and said, 'Do you trust that man who calls himself a priest?'

'The one who also calls himself Shamshi? The only thing we know for sure is that he's a Hyksos, and that everything he has said so far about Imphotep's riddle matches what we ourselves know. But do I trust him? No, not one little bit – in part because he's a Hyksos. But also, there's just something about his eyes . . .'

'How they never laugh, even when he does? It is because he is always calculating. Maybe the Hyksos have sent him to test us. He gives us information and watches our reactions to see how much we know and how much of a threat we might be.'

'Like the Sons of Apis last night, testing our defences,' Piay said.

'Well, I would not know,' Myssa replied, in a tone that gave Piay the sense that he had just poked a hornets' nest. 'I was sent down into the belly of the ship, away from all the fighting. Do you really see me as such a helpless little woman?'

'No, of course not,' Piay fought back. 'I see you as someone who is so vital to the success of the task that Taita has given us that her safety cannot be risked.' He stepped right up to her and lowered his voice. 'Particularly when she is carrying the Eye of Horus that may be the key to the entire mystery.'

'Huh!' Myssa was not ready to forgive him just yet. But she was at least willing to change the subject, just a little. 'About Shamshi . . . There was one thing he did not mention last night, and I cannot decide whether that was because he did not know it or was simply choosing to withhold it from us.'

'What is that?'

'Imhotep's tomb . . . It would make sense that if Imhotep wanted to take his secrets with him, he would have them by his side on the journey to the afterlife.'

'So where is it?' Before Myssa could answer, Piay gave a half-whispered little 'Ha!' and said, 'Stupid question. No one knows, or else the riddle would already have been solved.'

'No one knows . . . for certain. But from what Taita knows, and I have been able to find in all the old documents I've been reading, the tomb is believed to be somewhere within the Saqqara necropolis, close to Djoser's pyramid. But somehow, no matter how hard people search the necropolis, the tomb remains undiscovered.'

'Well, the necropolis is not far from Memphis—'

Piay's words were interrupted by a cry from the ship's lookout. 'Fire!'

A second or two later, he could smell the first acrid hint of smoke on the air. The lookout was pointing towards the left bank of the river and shouting, 'Over there!'

As he squinted in the direction the lookout had indicated, Piay spotted a crouching woman tearing at her hair and beating her fists upon the ground as she wailed. A second later he saw the cause of her distress.

A man had been strapped to the frame of a shadoof. His head lolled onto his chest and there was a dark stain down his front: blood from where his throat had been cut. As the boat drew closer, Piay could see smouldering ruins of peasant homes and farm buildings a short way inland.

He did not think it was the work of the Sons of Apis. What interest would they have in attacking a small farming village? But still, there was something about that body . . . Someone had gone to considerable trouble to display it in that fashion, where it could be seen from the river. What message were they trying to send?

A small rickety jetty stuck out into the water, not far from the shadoof.

'Pull in over there,' Piay called to the captain. 'I want to take a closer look.'

The moment Harrar realised what was happening, he started complaining.

'What's the meaning of this? Why are we slowing down? I do not want to spend a single moment longer on this smelly, flea-bitten barge than is absolutely necessary!'

'My lord, we need to find out what has happened here,' Piay replied.

'It is perfectly obvious what has happened. Some sort of disreputable bandit gang has attacked and killed a few farmers. The affairs of criminals and peasants are no concern of mine . . . or of yours.'

'Surely the killing of innocent farming folk is always of concern to those who govern this kingdom. And if there are groups of bandits at large, laying waste to the land, should Pharaoh not know about it? I am certain that Lord Taita would wish to know. And I for one would not want to find myself before him, explaining why I had ignored such a tragic event.'

If there was one thing that was likely to worry Harrar, it was the possibility of his life becoming even fractionally less comfortable. He would not want to fall out of favour at the royal court. He sighed and gave one of his airy, dismissive waves of the hand.

'Very well, then, if you must. But be quick about it.'

A few minutes later Piay, Myssa and Hannu were walking along the jetty, heading for the shadoof. Half a dozen guardsmen had come with them, just in case.

'Don't like the look of that,' Hannu said as they drew closer to the hanging body. 'Two farmers get into a fight, it turns nasty and one of them ends up dead. The last thing the killer wants to do is stick the body up on a bloody shadoof. He's going to hide it away or bury it somewhere.'

'How about bandits?'

'No. They want to get in, take what they want and get out again, fast as possible.'

'I agree – so someone did this to let the world know they were here. Like a warning of what they can do.'

'Aye. And who would that be?'

Piay followed Hannu's searching gaze as it swept across the fields.

'Some straggling Hyksos troops, trying to loot whatever they can before they flee back home?' he mused.

'Perhaps. But they wouldn't slit that farmer's throat. They'd stick a sword in his guts or chop off his head with an axe. Then rape all the women, steal all the food and flee. Oh, and before you say anything, no, I don't think it's those bastards with tattoos. They're evil and they're dangerous, but they've got no more interest in common people than that gutless son of a concubine over there on the boat.'

Piay glanced back at the galley, where Harrar was standing by the rail, letting them know that he wanted to be off. He sighed.

'You're right, Hannu. There's nothing here to keep us.'

Myssa flashed him a look. 'If you two want answers to your questions, why don't you ask that poor woman? And we can find out if she needs any help, while we're at it.'

Piay nodded, chastened. 'Yes, my dear.'

He let Myssa take the lead as they approached the weeping woman, since she would seem infinitely less threatening than two armed men and a group of soldiers.

Drawing closer, Piay could see that the woman's black hair was threaded with grey. Tears cut paths through the dirt that streaked her deeply lined face. Her frayed dress, cracked, dirty fingernails and calloused hands spoke of a lifetime of hard manual work for very little reward.

Piay stood in silence as Myssa rested a hand on the woman's head. Instantly her crying ceased, as if a spell had been uttered. Myssa dropped beside her and whispered some soothing words. The woman blinked her tears away and looked up at Piay with hopeful eyes.

'Tell me what happened,' Piay asked in what he trusted was a comforting tone.

'It was the Shrikes.'

So this was the work of criminals, after all. But criminals from another age.

Piay summoned up a memory of Taita telling him about the bands of vicious thieves and cut-throats that used to roam the fertile Nile valley in the days before Piay had been born.

The Shrikes had grown more and more daring as the authorities failed to get a grip on them. They became a threat to the very stability of the Upper Kingdom, even roaming into the cities, robbing and killing and wreaking havoc among the people. It had taken the renowned General Tanus to crush them once and for all.

So it had been believed. But now they had returned.

'They came at dawn,' the woman cried. 'Raided our home, and when they'd taken what they wanted they set fire to it. We tried to fight back, but . . . but . . .'

She glanced up at the dead man hanging from the shadoof and was racked with another bout of sobs. When she was done, she said, 'They took our daughter too, and . . .' There were more sobs before the woman managed to gather herself enough to say, 'They left my husband there as a message to all who live around here. They will be back and they will not be resisted.'

Piay looked towards the soldiers and said, 'Get that body off there, so that he can have a proper burial.' He turned back and gently told the woman, 'Don't worry. Your husband will be able to make his journey to the afterlife. He will be at peace.'

'Thank you, master,' the woman said, and her mood lifted a little, for the loss of a safe passage to the world to come was feared more than death itself.

'How long have these Shrikes been a problem?' Piay asked, wondering whether there was any connection, other than the name, between these raiders and the Shrikes of years gone by.

'They came after the barbarians fled. No thieves would ever have risked an attack like this before. The Hyksos would have hunted them down like rats and cut them dead. Oh, if only the barbarians had stayed behind! We were safe then—'

'And you will be safe once more,' Piay interjected. We have come to help. Does the leader of this band have a name?'

'Akh-Seth. That is what he calls himself. His true name, no one knows. No one has even seen his face.'

Akh-Seth meant the brother of Seth. Piay felt his mood harden at the sound of that name. Once again the god haunted him.

Piay swept out an arm. 'Do you see these soldiers? They are men of the Blue Crocodile Guards of the Upper Kingdom, the fiercest warriors in all the world. This Shrike – this Akh-Seth – will stand no chance before them. He will flee in terror the moment he sees their faces.'

The woman nodded. 'But . . . but . . . my daughter. He has my daughter, my little girl. If these soldiers are so good, can they not bring her back to me?'

Piay winced. He looked around the gathered soldiers and then back at Harrar's furious face as he stood at the rail. It was one thing stopping to gather information. He would have a far harder time justifying to himself, as much as to anyone else, the time and potential risk of chasing after the Shrikes.

The woman must have noticed his hesitancy, for she grabbed at Piay's arm.

'And not just my daughter! Others . . . They take others! A captive was with them, a man – a demon! Covered in strange marks from head to toe!'

Piay flinched. 'Tattoos? Black tattoos, circles and stars and—'

'Yes, yes, all of that!' the woman enthused, now that she could see Piay was interested.

'Tell me,' Piay said, 'this man with the tattoos, this demon . . . Was he with you when the Shrikes arrived? Or was he with them? Had they already taken him prisoner?'

'He was with them.' The woman shivered in revulsion. 'We would never have let such a creature remain in our village. We may be poor, but we are good people, respectable people. We worship gods, not demons.'

'I quite understand. Please excuse me one moment, while I speak to my friends.'

Myssa shared a few reassuring words with the woman, then got up to join Piay and Hannu.

'What in Ra's name does a bunch of criminals want with one of the Sons of Apis?' Piay asked the other two.

'Maybe they don't know what they've got?' Hannu suggested.

'Then why are they keeping him alive? Why not just kill him?'

'The real question is, why did this Son of Apis allow himself to be captured?' Myssa said. 'First the Hyksos catch the man with the Eye of Horus. Now this . . . not to mention all the attacks. For centuries, these men are invisible, no more than rumours or passing mentions in ancient scrolls. Now they have come out into the open.'

'Surely this means that it is the time for Imhotep's prophecies to come true and his clues to be solved,' Piay said. But then he sighed, shook his head and said, 'But we can't just go chasing after this tattooed man.'

'Then chase after that poor girl,' Myssa said. 'We can't just stand by and let her be sold into slavery. I know what that's like. Please, I'm begging you, we must go after her.'

Piay closed his eyes and screwed up his face as he tried to find a way out of an impossible situation: his duty on one side, the woman he loved on the other.

He took a deep breath, sighed and said, 'I'm really sorry, my love. I know . . . I really know how much this means to you. But we have to get to Memphis. That's where our real work is. I hate to say it, but Lord Harrar's right about that.'

'Helping those in need is important work,' Myssa said. 'Whatever lies ahead has waited a thousand years. It can afford to wait a few more days. If it is within your power to save this mother's daughter, then you have to do it.'

Piay looked at Myssa, knowing how furious and, even worse, how desperately disappointed in him she would be if he sided with a man they both despised.

'A confrontation with the Shrikes would be dangerous,' Hannu said, seeing the conflict tearing Piay in two. 'And do either of you really think Lord Harrar's going to wait here, where the Shrikes have been? That man's afraid of his own shadow. Oh, and one more thing . . . What if the Sons of Apis come looking for their brother?'

Piay glanced once again at Myssa and knew his mind was made up.

'I say we do what we can to bring the daughter back. We can tell Harrar that if we rescue the Shrikes' captive, then we can learn the Sons of Apis' plans, and that way we'll be better able to protect him.'

Hannu shrugged. 'Maybe he'll fall for it, if you lay it on thick enough. But he's not going to send one single, solitary Blue Crocodile guardsman marching off into the wilderness. He'll want them looking after him. So then what are you going to do?'

'Go alone,' Piay said. 'There's no other way Harrar will agree to it. He won't give a damn risking my neck, so long as his is safe.'

'He won't care about my neck, either,' Hannu said, and Piay knew just by the way the words were said that it would be a waste of time to argue with him. 'I'm just going to take a look around this place,' Hannu added. 'See what we're up against.'

He wandered off, his face pointing down at the ground like an old hound following a scent, while Piay returned to the farmer's widow. She raised a trembling hand and caught at Piay's wrist when she heard he was heading after the Shrikes.

'Ten thousand thanks,' she all but sobbed. 'May the gods watch over you for all your days.'

As Piay turned away, Myssa leaned in and whispered, 'You are a good man.'

Piay gave her a wry smile. 'You'd better ask Captain Gatas to tell our esteemed passenger what I'm doing. That kind of man would be affronted by a woman telling him what's going on.'

'And my kind of woman doesn't want to waste a second of her life arguing with him, so Gatas is welcome to do it.' Myssa rested a hand on Piay's forearm. 'Good luck.'

Piay gave a quick smile of acknowledgement, then said, 'Thanks . . . and don't worry, I'm not planning on a long exped-ition. If I'm not back by nightfall, set sail without me.'

'Then come back quickly, because that would break my heart.'

'Wait,' Piay said.

The pouch containing the Eye of Horus was tied to the belt of his kilt. Now he undid it and gave it to Myssa.

'Just in case I don't come back,' he said. 'Use it well.'

'But you will come back,' she said softly, laying a hand on his arm.

'I will . . . but just in case . . .'

Piay kissed Myssa and she returned to the ship with the guardsmen.

Hannu made his way back to Piay.

'I've been checking footprints. This farm was attacked by a large band. I'd say forty men, at least. And that Akh-Seth character knows what he's doing. They came in from two directions, using the trees and bushes for cover before creeping along the ditches. This isn't going to be easy. You know, just the two of us.'

'It would be harder with others,' Piay said.

'What? Are you serious?'

'Absolutely. Look, if we set off with the soldiers, they'll see us coming a mile off. But if there's only two of us, we can sneak up on them.'

Piay grinned. 'Hey, who knows? If the gods smile on us we could be in, out and back to the boat . . . and the Shrikes won't even know that we've been there at all.'

 Soon the fields of barley fell behind them. As they followed the trail out of the lush, irrigated land and into the scrub that bordered the wilderness, Piay said, 'I remember Taita telling me that the Shrikes stole girls to sell into the brothels, so this one should still be alive. That's something.'

'And do you have even the faintest inkling of a plan when we do catch up with them?'

'I'll know when the time comes.'

'I thought we'd agreed not to use those kinds of plans anymore.'

'How can I think with all your wittering?'

Before Hannu could reply, Piay strode off, picking up his pace, waiting until he had found the point at which his companion, with his wounded leg, could not match him. Then he slowed down and let Hannu catch up.

The spiky bushes and tufts of yellowing grass eventually gave way to the ochre rock and drifting dust of the wasteland. The trail was easier to follow there – a mass of footprints trudging across the rolling desert.

As they crested a ridge, Hannu pointed towards the azure sky ahead. Black shapes circled: vultures, their wings catching the hot currents.

'They spy carrion,' Hannu said.

'At least we're not it,' Piay replied.

'Yet.'

Sweating in the heat, the two men picked up their pace again. Piay could see that Hannu was working hard to keep up, but they still marched side by side before skidding down a slope, then clawing their way up the next dune. At the top, Piay shielded his eyes against the glare and peered ahead. Underneath those slowly descending vultures, he spotted a figure spread-eagled across a rock.

'Now who could that be?' Piay mused. 'Another farmer? But why bring him all the way out here?'

Piay and Hannu hurried across the shifting dust to try to reach the remains before the vultures began tearing the flesh from the bones. As they rounded a boulder, Piay slowed his step when the body fell into relief.

'Do you see what I see?' he said.

'Aye,' Hannu replied. 'This changes things.'

Flapping his arms to frighten the vultures away, Piay raced across the remaining distance until he stood by the remains. His eyes had not lied. The dead man was one of the Sons of Apis, the tattoos stark on the pale skin. It must have been the man the Shrikes had held captive. He was naked, and he had been tortured by the looks of it. Open wounds scarred his flesh and his member had been lopped off and stuffed in his mouth.

Hannu limped up to his side, gasping for air, and studied the corpse.

'So even a Son of Apis can't beat a gang of Shrikes,' he said. 'Could be a lesson for us there.'

Piay did not respond. He was studying the pattern of the wounds.

'Tortured to get the information they needed,' he said. 'And look, there are scars and fading bruises under the new wounds. They've been working him over for quite a while.'

'So did they kill him because he wouldn't speak, and they got bored waiting?' Hannu asked. 'Or did they kill him because he'd already told them everything and they'd got no more use for him?'

'The only way to find out is to go and ask the Shrikes.'

'And I would imagine that's not something you plan to do, seeing that it would be mad.'

Piay peered across the waste to a ridge of bronze-coloured rocks.

'Tell me that's not your plan,' Hannu said.

'We still need to find the camp so we can tell the mother where the girl is being kept,' Piay replied. 'If there is some way to free her ourselves, that is good. If there is a chance to capture one of the Shrikes so we can find out what the cultist told them, that is also good.'

Piay sensed Hannu wearily sagging his shoulders. He didn't look round. Instead, he pressed on towards the ridge.

'There's more of them than I thought.' Hannu lay on his belly, peering around the edge of the boulder. Ahead, the Shrike camp lay in a hollow so it could not be seen by anyone approaching from any direction. Tents were jumbled around a central campfire, their cloth stained in earthy colours so that they merged with the desert landscape. 'Too many for us, I'd say.'

Piay had to agree. This Akh-Seth had amassed a body of men that was more like a military unit than a gang of thieves and cut-throats. True, the men wandering around the camp or squatting in conversation near the fire were dressed in ragged robes stained with filth, and had scarves tied around their heads like the desert wanderers, but they were all well-armed.

Piay spied bronze swords hanging from waists, axes and bronze-tipped spears, all of them no doubt looted.

'There's a lot of lads with crescent swords down there,' Hannu said. 'Must've taken them off what's left of the Hyksos army.'

'Unless they're Hyksos, too,' Piay said. 'Deserters, maybe . . . or deliberately left behind to cause trouble. Either way, I've only counted three guards on the perimeter of the camp. They're not expecting trouble.'

'Who's going to give them any? There are two armies in Egypt and they're both busy in Memphis. This lot can do what they like.'

The wind whined among the rocks, whipping up whorls of dust. Then it died down for a moment, and in the calm that followed, Hannu tilted his head and frowned.

'Can you hear that? Coming from the camp.'

Piay cocked his head, too, and made out women's voices. They seemed to be coming from a larger tent close to the camp's edge.

'Well, now we know where the girl is,' he said.

Piay imagined the farmer's daughter who had been stolen by these cut-throats, and her terror at being snatched from the heart of her family. His own feelings of being abandoned by his parents stabbed into his mind. But here there was no Taita to make things right for a lost child. So now it was all down to him.

Without looking at Hannu, keeping his eyes on the camp, Piay said, 'Go back to the ship.'

Hannu stared at him, his face crumpling into a scowl as the truth behind Piay's words revealed itself to him.

'Don't be a fool,' he growled.

'Go back to the ship . . . and tell Harrar I have uncovered a plot by the Shrikes to capture him and hold him to ransom.'

'He won't send anyone to help you, if that's what you're thinking. He can feel the Sons of Apis breathing down his neck, and all he wants to do is get to Memphis and hide behind those big high walls.'

'If it's the Sons he's worried about, the walls won't help,' Piay said.

'Aye, but Harrar doesn't know that. Wouldn't surprise me if he'd already ordered the captain to sail on.'

Piay studied those lazing guards and the space that lay between where each one had been positioned.

'They won't be breaking up the camp now,' he said. 'Under cover of the night I can sneak into the camp there . . . and there.' He traced a path in the air with his finger. 'With the blessing of Khonsu, I can crawl into the tent where the women are kept.'

'And then what? Will Khonsu give you magic wings, so you can pick up that lass and fly back to the boat? Eh? A quick prayer and – oh look! – a miracle!'

'Don't insult my faith.'

'Then don't you insult my intelligence.'

'All right then, I'll tell you straight . . . I am going in there by myself. I am going to see it through, for better or worse. And the reason I'm going alone is that I fancy my chances of getting in and out more if it's just me. I need you to get back to the boat and do whatever you can to stop Harrar sailing off without me. And I'm going to have to get out, fast, and you can't keep up with me.'

'Then go faster and leave me behind,' Hannu said.

'You know I'd never do that.'

'I'd leave you, if I had to . . . wouldn't think twice.'

'Like hell you would. Truth is, we'd both stick together and then we'd both die. This way, one of us survives for sure, and the other has a chance of surviving, too.'

'A tiny chance.'

'A fighting chance, and that's good enough for me.'

Hannu seethed, torn between walking away from his friend and knowing Piay was right.

'You'd never make a soldier,' he hissed. 'You're too foolhardy. I just pray to the gods it doesn't cost you your head.'

With that, Hannu scrabbled around and crawled away until the lip of the hollow hid him from the eyes of anyone in the camp. Then he stood up and began to limp back along the trail of footprints that led towards the Nile.

Hannu was getting very drunk, very publicly. He had made his way back to the ship, arrived a couple of hours before sunset, and passed on Piay's message that he was going to rescue the missing girl by himself, and that they should wait for him to return. The only effect had been to persuade Harrrar that Piay was suicidal, that he was already as good as dead and they might as well leave immediately. Hannu had then lost his temper and started flinging every foul-mouthed insult he had learned in twenty years of military service at the haughty nobleman.

As negotiating tactics went, that had not proved a success. The captain of the Blue Crocodile Guards had stepped in.

'Leave it to me, your lordship. Hannu's an ex-guardsman, so he'll respect my rank. Believe me, sir, I'll give him a talking-to he won't forget.' He'd looked around, then added, 'We'll be using barracks language. Probably best to do it on dry land, out of your earshot.'

The guardsman had ordered one of his men to fetch him a wineskin.

'And make it a full one.'

Then he frog-marched Hannu down the gangplank, along the jetty and into the shade of some date palms, a short way from the still-burning village. For some time, the two men could be seen arguing and gesticulating, then the captain returned to the ship.

'You'll get no more trouble from him, my lord,' the captain had said, and, while Harrar appeared to be as close as he ever got to a good mood, he added, 'One other thing, your lordship . . . Some of my lads really did themselves proud in that fight last night. They're not on duty tonight, so, if it pleases you, I was thinking that maybe they could have some shore leave this evening – if we're still here, obviously. Just a drink or two, a decent meal and a few songs. It's good for their spirits, my lord. Makes them fight even harder next time.'

'Very well, then – but they must be ready to return at a moment's notice, when I give the order to set sail.'

A dozen or so of the guards had gone ashore. They'd found a goat wandering around the burned-out farm buildings, slaughtered it, and were now roasting it on a spit above a roaring fire. Hannu had woken from a wine-induced slumber and joined the guards' party. He could not shake the shame he felt for leaving Piay to fend for himself, and the fact that he had been obeying Piay's orders didn't make him feel any better. So, now he was resorting to the comforts that sustained all fighting men at all times, everywhere: hard drink, filthy jokes and loud songs.

And maybe – just maybe – that might do the trick.

Myssa was still aboard, standing in the bows, consumed by worry. She could not stop thinking of Piay out there in the dark, facing an overwhelming enemy. All too soon, the ship would resume its journey to Memphis, and Harrar would leave Piay behind to fend for himself.

All day, Myssa, Gatas and the commander of the guards' detachment had argued, pleaded and even begged Harrar to wait for Piay's return. Even the captain of the ship had joined them. Piay had treated the captain and his crew with the same respect as he had the soldiers, and won their loyalty as a result.

All their arguments had bought a little time, though Hannu's understandable but entirely counterproductive fury had brought Harrar within a whisker of leaving there and then. As he had pointed out, and it was hard to argue with him, 'These Sons of Apis have already attacked this vessel at night, when it was moored, and therefore much easier for them to board. And we know that there is a large band of murderous thieves in the area – these Shrikes, or whatever they call themselves. Plainly, the safest place for us is to be in the very centre of our beloved Nile, far from either bank and moving at the highest possible speed.'

Now the sun had set and only the faintest hints of light remained on the western horizon. In no time at all, darkness would fall, and then what case could be made for delaying departure?

Myssa stood at the rail and looked up at the stars appearing one by one in a sky turning from blue, to purple, to black. The time had come. Persuasion had failed. Now all she had were her prayers.

Someone moved behind her and she turned to see Captain Gatas. He was frowning, his mouth turned down. Behind him, in the glow from a lamp, Myssa could see Shamshi watching them both intently.

'What is it?' Myssa asked.

Gatas nodded to where Harrar was prowling back and forth along the deck like a leopard in a pen. His fear of the Sons of Apis hung around him like the stench around a rotting corpse.

'Bad news,' Gatas began. 'Harrar has told the captain to set sail.'

'But Piay . . .'

'It's too late. Harrar has decided that Piay is dead. We all know he doesn't give a damn. Saving his own neck is all he cares about.'

Myssa narrowed her eyes at the nobleman. 'I will not let this happen,' she breathed.

'What are you going to do?' Gatas asked.

'Come with me.'

'I can't.' He nodded towards Shamshi. 'I've got to watch him.'

'Find someone else to do it. I need you. Piay and Hannu need you.'

Gatas nodded, a little sheepishly. As he arranged a guard, Shamshi looked up at them, grinning.

'She has more fire in her belly than you, Captain Gatas.'

'Hold your tongue,' Gatas snapped.

'I like her,' Shamshi said. 'She is the only one on board this vessel with any wits.'

Myssa turned away from Shamshi and marched along the deck towards the stern, where Harrar's tent stood, just forward of the steering oar. But before she could get there, she was brought up short by the sight of the captain, a seasoned sailor with a face like old, worn leather. He was bent over the large hatch, which provided access to the cargo hold, shouting down at someone inside.

She quickly gathered that a crewman who was meant to be on duty was too drunk to work.

'I don't care how scared he is of the demon-men,' the captain shouted. 'Throw some water over him and get him up on deck.'

Myssa laughed to herself and was about to move on when a high, whining voice called out, 'For the gods' sake, stop making such a ghastly noise down there.'

The sound of Harrar's complaint gave Myssa an idea.

'Excuse me, Captain,' she said, 'but could I just have a word with you . . . in private?'

'Can't you see I'm busy?'

'Of course, I quite understand.' Myssa dipped her head and looked up at Gatas coyly. 'I promise I won't keep you long.'

The captain sighed. 'All right, but make it quick. His lord-ship is—'

'Why have we not set sail yet?' came a cry from Harrar's tent.

'He's getting impatient, I know,' Myssa said, 'but tell me . . . are there any members of the crew who are so important that the ship can't set sail without them – apart from you, of course?'

'One or two . . .' The captain jerked his thumb towards the hold. 'Not him, thank Ra.'

'But Harrar doesn't know that, and—'

The captain grinned. 'Oh, I get you. Leave it to me.'

Myssa watched him walk away towards Harrar's tent. She could see Harrar, with his shoulders hunched and his hands clasped together. Now he was the one who was pleading, 'How much longer must I wait?'

'Soon,' the captain assured him. 'Very soon.'

'But "soon" is just not good enough. For goodness' sake, man, can you not see the peril we are in? We were attacked last night. This village has been razed to the ground. There's danger everywhere – we have to get away!'

'Absolutely, your lordship, and we will cast off and set sail the moment we can. But I'm afraid that bad men and demons aren't the only things we have to worry about.'

'They aren't?' Harrar's voice sounded even more plaintive. 'You mean there's more?'

'Well, you see . . .' The captain looked around, sucked in his breath through his teeth and said, 'It's the currents – in the river. I mean, the Nile's like a woman. She may look calm on the surface, but there's all sorts going on underneath – particularly around here. This is a very tricky stretch, especially at night.'

'You must be able to do something. No one would ever get up and down the river otherwise.'

'Ah! My lordship, you are obviously a very wise man, and yes, I can do something. I can tell my sounding-man to go up to the prow and drop a line into the water, and tell me exactly how deep the water is in front of us.'

'Then what are you waiting for? Do that!'

'Ah, well . . . yes . . . that's the problem. The man's had a bit too much to drink . . . well, quite a lot too much, to be fair. It's his nerves. He's not like you, my lord, a tough leader of men who's cool and calm in the face of danger. Timid as a mouse, my sounding-man. But don't worry, we'll have him up and about in no time. Then he'll get down to work, and we'll be able to set sail.'

'Then get on with it,' Harrar said, very obviously making an effort to pitch his voice in a lower, tougher register. 'I'm not waiting a moment more than is absolutely necessary.'

Myssa mouthed a little kiss to Gatas as he passed her and he winked back in reply. By now, the captain had found two guardsmen to watch Shamshi and was standing beside her.

'The door's just a little bit open,' she whispered to him. 'Now we've got to get it wide open.' She thought for a moment and smiled to herself. 'I think I've got something . . . Just wait here, and I'll be right back.'

Myssa returned to the prow of the ship and darted a glance back to where Harrar stood. The ship's sail had been furled, and the moon had risen in the night sky, so her position in the bow would now be just about visible to him.

I'm the only woman on board this ship, she thought, *and even if he's only a pale shadow of a real man, he'll surely be looking in my direction.*

Myssa made a great play of peering out into the darkness directly ahead of the ship, and then across the full expanse of the Nile. She gave a little cry of alarm and then turned around. Holding her dress higher to make it easier for her to run – and to give more for Harrar to see – she dashed, apparently in panic, to his tent.

'My lord!' she cried. 'My lord!'

The nobleman saw her coming, and perhaps emboldened by the captain's description of his leadership ability, said, 'Calm yourself, my dear. How can I help you?'

'It's . . . It's . . . It's the Sons of Apis, my lord . . . They're out there, on the water, I know they are.'

Trying very hard not to reveal the bowel-loosening terror Myssa's words had instilled in him, Harrar asked, 'And how, exactly, do you know this?'

'Well, Lord Taita has been tutoring me in the ways of the Sons of Apis, and I've done further research of my own. And it is clear that they only attack at night – as we all know from last night's assault, which you so bravely defeated.'

'Yes, but that was last night. Are you saying that they are about to attack us again?'

'No, eminence, I believe they plan to trap us. I was up at the front of the ship just now—'

'Yes, I saw you.'

'Well, I glimpsed some small rowing boats, patrolling back and forth on the water up ahead. It was only for a moment . . . If it wasn't for the moonlight, I wouldn't have seen them at all.'

'You're certain?'

'The light was poor, but I think so. And there was something else . . . The men rowing them . . . they didn't look like ordinary men. They were just patches of shadow that were even darker than the water and the sky.'

'The Sons of Apis . . .' Harrar said, failing to keep the tremble out of his voice.

Myssa's eyes flickered to Gatas and he stepped forward. Without missing a step, he picked up the thread of her story.

'These members of the Sons of Apis are not fools. They know how many men we have, and how well you lead us. If they make another frontal attack, we will be ready for them. So their best hope is to lure us downriver, into the trap they have set for us.'

'We already know that the blades of their swords are poisoned,' Myssa cut in. 'But from all that I have learned, they may not need swords at all. If they can trap us, and surround us, they have spells and curses that can kill us without striking a blow.'

To someone who had never encountered the Sons of Apis, it would have seemed an absurdly far-fetched story, but Harrar had witnessed them at close quarters. And all day, the ship had been abuzz with soldiers and boatmen discussing these ghosts – these demons – and speculating about the terrible powers they must surely possess.

'At night we will not be able to see their trap until it is too late,' Gatas said. 'At least in daylight we can make preparation to avoid any dangers. We're safer here by the jetty, my lord. We can mount guards all around the ship, to make sure there's no surprise attack – and if all else fails, we can leave the ship and run to dry land. Can't do that in the middle of the river.'

The opportunity to run away was clearly the clinching factor to Harrar.

'I won't have that kind of defeatist talk around here,' he said. 'No, sir.'

'Bad for the men's morale. But I want the Blue Crocodile Guards to double the number of men in the watches.'

He stalked back to his shelter.

Gatas whispered to Myssa, 'Good work. Piay may owe you his life.'

'Now I just pray that he's back by morning,' she replied. 'There'll be no persuading Harrar to delay any longer if he isn't.'

The arguments had ceased for the night. The ship's passengers and crew had settled down to sleep, leaving only the watchmen awake. And on shore, where the guardsmen had finished every last scrap of goat and drop of wine and were making ready to return to their vessel, Hannu was getting to his feet.

For a man whose intoxication had been plain for all to see only a couple of hours earlier, and who was physically impeded at the best of times, Hannu looked remarkably steady and clear-eyed.

'Right, lads,' he said, gesturing to the men around him. 'Gather round.'

The milky river of stars swept across the sable sky and the moon cast stark shadows across the pale desert. In the centre of the camp, the fire roared. A rumble of voices rolled out across the night as the men gathered to drink beer and gnaw on whatever food they had stolen from the farms along the valley.

Piay rubbed the knots out of his muscles. He'd long ago given up hope of returning to the boat while the sun was still up. There was just no chance of getting in and out of the Shrikes' camp in daylight. He could only pray that Myssa and the others would find some way of preventing Harrar from giving in to his cowardice and sailing for Memphis at the earliest possible opportunity.

In the meantime, Piay had made the best of his long hours of waiting by planning his way in and out of the camp in the greatest possible detail. He had passed what remained of the day almost motionless, watching and memorising the layout of the camp and the movements of the men inside it. Soon it would be time for him to make his move.

In the wake of their successful raid, the Shrikes had thrown themselves a feast. Piay reckoned that they'd drunk more than enough to dull their wits, and their raucous revelry would drown out any sounds he might make as he crept into the camp.

As the cut-throats sang and laughed, two men heaved a throne of carved dark wood out of a tent and set it in front of the fire. A moment later a man strode out and sat in the chair like a king before his subjects. This must be Akh-Seth, someone who thought so highly of himself that he had styled himself brother to a god.

Though Piay couldn't discern the Shrike's features from that distance, he was tall and moved with an unusual grace for a mere criminal. He was wearing finer clothes than those who followed him: a ruby-coloured robe with wide sleeves and a similar-coloured scarf around his head.

Two other men walked out to stand on either side of the throne, folded their muscular arms and set their legs apart. It was almost as if they were daring the men in front of them to try their luck at killing Akh-Seth, Piay thought, but what caught his attention was not the men's attitude but their race.

They were Hyksos warriors, dressed in the familiar leather armour and caps, with their crescent swords hanging at their sides.

Are these men deserters? Piay wondered. *Or might they be a sign that these Shrikes have the blessing of King Khamudi?*

Slaves splashed whatever stew was bubbling on the fire into a bowl and knelt before the throne, raising the dish up. As

Akh-Seth lifted it to his lips and slurped a mouthful, a cheer rang out across the throng. A celebration of another successful day. More slaves hurried out with pitchers, slopping beer into cups waved in the air by the Shrikes. This Akh-Seth looked after his men well. That was how he earned their loyalty.

Piay rolled onto his back and watched the stars for a while, letting the Shrikes sink deep into their drunkenness. As he studied the constellations, he thought back to what Shamshi had said about Imhotep's secret being hidden in the stars. What could he have meant by that? If the Great Architect was as clever as legend said, could any of them ever hope to solve such a puzzle?

Pushing these pessimistic thoughts out of his mind, Piay turned his attention to the noise of revelry in the camp. When the laughter reached fever pitch, he decided the time was right. Easing out from behind the boulder where he had been hiding, he pulled himself along on his belly. The nearest guard had not moved since night had fallen – sleeping, no doubt, after the rigours of the day – but Piay was not about to take any chances. He chose a looping path, following the contours of the hollow, and using whatever rocks littered the slopes for cover.

Soon he reached the edge of the tents. A din of drunken voices rang back and forth. He could have danced into the camp singing and those cut-throats would not have heard him.

Easing along the line of tents, Piay found the large one he had identified earlier. He could hear the women's voices chattering within. Two were trying to calm one who sounded much younger, her cries cracking with sorrow.

'If you carry on this way they'll punish you,' one of the women was saying. 'And believe me, you can't even imagine what they'll do to you.' The voice was edged with the bitterness of experience.

The younger girl continued to sob. 'I want my mother.'

So there was the girl Piay was looking for. He glanced around, checked that he had not been spotted, summoned his courage and then wriggled under the edge of the tent.

One of the women shrieked in shock as Piay emerged from under the canvas. He hissed for her to be silent.

'I am here to save you,' he whispered, pressing a finger to his lips for good measure.

'Who are you?' asked a woman with a bruise on her cheek.

Piay recognised that voice. She was the one who had spoken so harshly to the girl, and now Piay could understand why. Sour lines were etched around her mouth, and the muscles of her face had hardened along with her heart, so that she looked like one of the desert rocks.

Piay had seen this before in those who had endured deprivation. The suffering of days past, and the fear of days of hardship ahead, formed a shell around their natural kindness and selflessness, sealing it away. Their own survival became all that mattered to them.

Piay counted ten women in the tent. All had been stripped of their clothing.

'My name is Piay of Thebes,' he began. 'The Pharaoh of the Upper Kingdom has sent an army to drive out the last of the Hyksos force. The two kingdoms will then become one and the misery you have suffered will be no more.'

The promise of good times to come did not impress the hard-faced woman any more than it had the weeping widow in the village.

'How does this help us?' she asked, contemptuously.

'Now that I've found the Shrike camp, I will send men here to free you – the finest soldiers in all Egypt. You have my word.'

The other women seemed to believe Piay. One or two pressed their hands together and rocked, tears of desperate joy streaming down their faces. He looked around until he saw a girl cowering.

'You,' he said. 'Are you the one the Shrikes took today?'

The girl nodded. She looked no more than ten, her eyes wide above her dirty cheeks.

'I have promised your mother I will take you back to her tonight.'

The girl's face lit up with joy.

'The rest of you need not worry,' Piay said, looking around at the other women. 'I swear I'll come back tomorrow, with the soldiers and—'

'Don't give us promises,' the hardened woman spat. 'Even if we believed them, words are no good to us. You don't get it. Every night here is an eternity. You cannot begin to imagine . . .' She choked off the words. 'We're not waiting another day.'

The other women were nodding. Piay felt his heart go out to them. But what could he do?

'I hear your plea,' he said. 'You are right, I cannot imagine the miseries you have experienced at the hands of the Shrikes, but I can only beg of you to endure one more night—'

'No,' the hard-faced woman snapped.

'If I try to take you all this night, we will be caught. I will be killed and your fate will be sealed.'

The woman's eyes flashed and Piay thought he could see a hint of madness in them. Whatever she had experienced had shredded her wits. There was no point even trying to reason with her, but he had to try one more time.

'I beg of you, let me take the girl,' he said, softening his voice. 'She is young. She has not yet had to bear the burden that has crushed you all down. Let her escape with her innocence intact.'

The other women stared at the girl as if remembering themselves at that age. One of them blinked away a tear. Another raised trembling fingers to her lips.

'You must take all of us or none of us.' The hard-faced woman with the bruise on her cheek narrowed her eyes.

'The stranger is right,' one of the other women said. 'This girl is untouched. She still has a chance to live the life that the gods have blessed her with.'

'Yes, take her,' another said. 'Take her.'

'This will be our sacrifice. One more night of misery to ensure this girl escapes suffering.'

'No!' The hard-faced woman balled her fist and hammered it into the ground. 'This is not fair. All of us or none of us.'

Piay felt despair. He understood the woman's anger, but he could not agree to her wishes. There was no possible way of getting so many of them past the guards and out of the camp.

One of the women had a split lip and a patch on her scalp where her hair had been torn out. She must have seen the plight in his face, for she leaned forward and said, 'Take the girl. We will see to this one.'

'If you take her and leave me,' the hard-faced woman said, 'I will scream until the Shrikes come running.'

'If you dare open your mouth, we will gouge out your eyes,' said the one with the split lip. 'You aren't the only one who's suffered.'

In defiance, the hard-faced woman threw back her head, preparing to scream, but the other women fell on her, stuffing their fingers into her mouth and beating her with their fists.

Piay grabbed the girl's hand and dragged her to the edge of the tent.

'Follow me,' he whispered. 'Do not make a sound. Can you do that?'

The girl nodded, her eyes still wide, and Piay smiled before wriggling out under the side of the tent. He crouched outside while he waited for the girl to join him. From within the tent, the sounds of struggle echoed. They had only a little time before the alarm was raised, he was certain of it.

'Move as fast as you can, but keep close to the ground,' he breathed to the girl.

Piay dropped to all fours and crawled back along the trail he had made in the dust on his way down the slope, with the girl following close behind. The raucous festivities in the camp rolled out across the night. That was good. There was still hope that the women's struggles would not be heard.

Around a low ridge of boulders they crept. Piay peered at the guard, silhouetted against the night sky. Still he had not moved.

Behind him, the girl showed no fear.

'Only a little farther,' he whispered. 'Beyond the edge of the hollow we will not be seen. Then we can run.'

As Piay clawed his way up the slope, he heard a commotion behind him and he felt his heart sink. Glancing back, he saw the hard-faced woman wriggle out from the edge of the tent, her naked body spectral in the moonlight. Blood streaked her face from a wound on her forehead.

'A stranger!' she screamed. 'Stealing a girl! Stop him!'

At the cry, the guard jolted to life. He whirled around and saw Piay and the girl framed in the moonlit sweep of the incline. His cry of alarm rang out, mixing with the high-pitched shrieks of the woman, and that frenzied sound cut through the din in the camp. A moment of silence followed and then Piay saw rapid movement around the campfire, like an ants' nest that had been disturbed.

He grabbed the girl by the shoulders and peered deep into her eyes.

'Run,' he said. 'Run as fast as your feet will carry you. Follow the trail of footprints and it will take you back to the valley and the fields and your mother. Go!'

The girl let out a cry and raced up the slope and over the rim. Piay prayed she would survive. If he had attempted to go with her, the Shrikes would have hunted them both down without mercy. At least now she would stand a chance. His days were done, though. Hannu had been right, as he usually was.

Turning, Piay whipped out his sword and braced himself. His hope was that he could at least delay the advancing horde long enough for the girl to put some distance between herself and the camp.

When the Shrikes streamed out of the camp, he felt pleased to see his calculation had been correct. The girl was already forgotten. All eyes were on the man with the sword who had dared challenge their authority.

The cut-throats raced up the slope with their stolen swords and axes and spears.

How many of them can I get before they get me? he wondered. Piay gripped the hilt of his sword with both hands.

'Who will be the first to die?' he yelled, putting on a show.

The Shrikes must have thought him mad to stand his ground and not flee in terror from such a number. And perhaps he was. But he could go to his death knowing that he had done some good in the world and that he had not let Myssa down.

The murderous thieves swept up the slope and surged around him, keeping a good distance. His cry had clearly done its work. No one was going to risk his life first.

Piay whirled around, watching for an attack coming from any direction. The cut-throats bounded forward, then leaped back as he slashed with his blade. Now they had started laughing at this sport. He was like a rat cornered in a mill and they could afford to take their time to wear him down.

Then their ranks parted and one of the Hyksos guards stepped forward. Piay glimpsed something in the warrior's hands. As the warrior spun it around his head, Piay realised it was a sling made of hide. That revelation came a moment too late. The warrior snapped the sling and a chunk of rock flew out, crashing off the side of Piay's head.

His wits flew away for a moment and he felt himself sag to his knees, his sword slipping from his grasp. The Shrikes roared as one, and an instant later they fell upon him.

The Shrikes jeered as Piay stumbled around the campfire at the end of a spear tip, with his hands tied behind his back. He felt the heat from the blaze sear his face and he choked on the smoke billowing off it.

His skull throbbed where the stone had cracked it, and blood from the wound caked his ear. But he was alive, for now.

The spear tip prodded into his back and he stumbled forward. On the far side of the fire, Akh-Seth still lounged on his throne. He was smirking, his chin resting on one hand with an index finger reaching up to the edge of his eye.

Even through the fug of pain, Piay felt surprise. Now that he was close, he could see that the robber baron was Hyksos, too. His eyes were dark and glittering in the firelight, and his nose was like a hawk's beak above an oiled moustache and beard. Under his ruby robe, he looked strong, and he exuded the pride and self-confidence of a battle-hardened warrior.

Akh-Seth raised his hand and slowly lowered it. At his signal the jubilant roars of the thieves ebbed away. The baron looked Piay up and down, a quizzical smile on his lips.

'My men say you must be mad,' he began, his voice rich. 'To come into this camp, alone? Did you seriously think you would survive?'

'I'm still alive,' Piay said.

Akh-Seth laughed at that.

'So, now I've got a question for you,' Piay said. 'Why haven't you and your Hyksos friends fled north like whipped dogs, with your tails between your legs, just like the rest of your kind?'

If Piay had expected the words to sting, Akh-Seth did not show it.

'Good question,' he said, thoughtfully. 'When there's so much plunder to be had, why indeed would I stay here robbing from farmers who've barely got more than the dirt under their nails?' He raised a finger in the air and waved it. 'Perhaps because I'm after a bigger prize. Riches greater than any man could imagine, buried a thousand years ago. Clues hidden in the stars.'

Piay felt a chill deep in his gut. He thought back to the body of the Son of Apis. How much information had the torture prised out of him?

Akh-Seth leaned forward, looking more closely at Piay's face, reading it for clues.

'Well, now, this is interesting . . . You know what I'm talking about, don't you? So, I'll be straight with you, and listen carefully because your life depends on it. I'm after Imhotep's secret, and you could be just the man to help me.'

Akh-Seth smiled, shrugged, then added, 'Or you could be just another dead body.'

Most of the camp was rank with the stink made by such a large number of men and the waste they produced, crowded into a small space. But when Piay was shoved into Akh-Seth's tent, the warm air was heavy with the scents of sandalwood and lavender. The two Hyksos guards prodded him forward until he stood in the centre of the space, caught in the glow of a single lamp. While Akh-Seth flopped onto a pile of sumptuous cushions, one of the guards pulled the flap of the tent down so they would not be overhead.

'Aren't you afraid your men will be inflamed by all that talk of riches beyond imagining and try to find the secret without you?' Piay said.

Akh-Seth shrugged. 'They're thieves. That's what they do.'

'What use is a band of men you cannot trust?'

'I don't need to trust them. I only need them to do my bidding, for now.'

'And when they have served their purpose?'

'They will get a reward, of one kind or another.' Akh-Seth looked at the two bodyguards and said, 'Untie his hands.'

As Piay was rubbing his wrists and feeling the tingle of blood pouring back into his hands, Akh-Seth gave another command and one of his men poured wine from a pitcher into four cups: one of them gold and encrusted with jewels, the other three plain fired clay. The guards gave the gold one to their master. They each took a clay one and handed the final cup to Piay.

Piay stared into the blood-red depths of the wine, caught off guard by this show of generosity.

'Drink,' Akh-Seth said. 'It is from the finest Syrian grapes. There's no reason why we can't talk like civilised men.'

Piay raised the cup to his lips and felt the sweetness of the contents flood his mouth.

'Akh-Seth,' he said. 'That's a grand name you've chosen for yourself.'

'I was not the one who chose it.' The barbarian sipped his wine. 'My true name is Khin.'

'I am Piay.'

'Well, Piay, let me start our conversation by stating something that should be perfectly obvious. But a man can never be too careful.' Khin smiled as an afterthought occurred to him and added, 'A point you should have considered before walking into a camp filled with armed men on your own.'

Then, in an instant, Khin's face hardened, and his eyes were hard and cruel as he leaned forward and said, 'You will only live for as long as I think you can give me information that can help me in my quest. If you possess information but you refuse to share it with me, my men will torture you until you either talk, or die. And if you truly know nothing, then you will die at once, for why would I waste food and water on a man who serves me no purpose?'

It struck Piay that Khin's terms were little different to the ones Taita and Gatas had placed before Shamshi. He sighed and gave a rueful shake of the head. He hadn't expected to be in the exact same situation as the Hyksos priest.

'Do I bore you?' Khin asked, misreading Piay's reaction.

'Not at all. Please, continue. Who knows, you may mention something that I do know about, and then, perhaps, we can reach an agreement . . . like civilised men.'

'Very well, then . . .' Khin paused for a second to order his thoughts and said, 'Those men out there, those thieves and vagabonds, are merely a means to an end. I serve His Majesty King Khamudi, may the blessing of Re be upon him.'

'As well as serving yourself—'

'Of course! Every loyal general lusts for the glory and plunder that victory will bring him. Every fawning courtier dreams of favour and advancement. Why should I be any different? I faithfully reported that I had found a man who was unlike any I had ever before seen, and I passed on the one thing he had said.'

'Which was?'

'Let's just say it related to the quest. Now, I admit, I also told my superiors that those were his dying words. But . . .' Khin shrugged. 'The man was going to die anyway, it was just a matter of where and when – as with us all. And, happily, it turned out that he was not as unique as I had first thought. Perhaps you saw what's left of one of his friends on your way here.'

'Perhaps.' Piay shrugged. 'What of it?'

'Come now – you saw him, and you knew exactly what he was . . . And I'll wager you saw the state of him and wondered, "Did they get him to talk?"'

'How could he say anything? His mouth was full.'

'Ha! Very good! Perhaps I should keep you as my jester.'

'Maybe you should tell me the rest of your story. It may be such a joke that I can't possibly compete.'

'Or maybe you should learn to curb your tongue, before it gets you killed.'

'All right then,' Piay said, 'tell me more and I will listen seriously. As I recall, you were just describing how you told your superiors about the man you'd found.'

'That's right . . . I delivered my information. Then the priests and scribes went away to investigate, and the next thing I knew

I was being told that I was now a part of a quest for something of the greatest possible value to my king and my people. So, of course, that seemed like a noble task, and yes, it could also be of value to me, too. But then matters became more complicated . . .'

A look of profound irritation, verging on fury, crossed Khin's face, but this time Piay was not its cause.

'You see, my superiors wished to double their chance of success, so they gave another man the exact same task as me . . .' Khin had to pause to calm himself before he added, 'And that man was my brother – Akkan.'

The way Khin had emphasised the name, along with the seriousness of his face, suggested that he was expecting a reaction, but Piay could only reply, 'I'm sorry, I don't understand. Am I supposed to know who you're talking about?'

This time the question was asked without a hint of mockery and Khin knew it.

'You have truly not heard the name of Akkan – the one they call the Child-Killer?'

'No.'

Khin frowned. 'So . . . you are obviously lying when you say that you do not know what my quest is about, for if you were truly ignorant you would have asked me to explain. On the other hand, you are plainly telling the truth when you say that you do not know about Akkan. Yet I find it hard to believe that both of those things can be so.'

'Now I really am confused. How does any of this connect to your brother?'

Khin made a sour face. 'He and his men were ambushed by your troops in the desert outside Thebes. I had thought that he was captured, but there are no reports of Akkan being taken prisoner. No one can say where he has gone.'

'Maybe he just ran away, like the rest of your army.'

'Ha! Akkan is not like the rest. He has never run away from anyone or anything.' Khin paused, as if to consider his next move. 'What do you know about the Eye of Horus?'

'Every peasant in Egypt wears an Eye of Horus,' Piay said.

'Not like this one, or they would not be a peasant for very long. This one is the key to the entire quest.'

'Did your brother take this Eye of Horus with him, then . . . when he went missing?'

'No. If Akkan had that amulet, the earth would be shaking, the cities would be in flames and the dead would already be stalking our mortal world . . . And yet, I believe that someone must have found it, for I have had news from Thebes of bloodshed in the palace . . . murders in dark alleys . . . strange men like ghosts or demons racing through the streets in pursuit of fleeing Egyptians . . . tombs cracking open. There are many stories, but I believe they all point to the same thing. There is something very powerful at work, and the tattooed men are trying to recover it.'

Khin paused and looked hard at Piay.

'And in all these stories the same four people appear.' Khin gave the dry smile of a game-player about to make the winning move and said, 'The great Lord Taita . . . a young Egyptian man . . . an older Egyptian with a limp . . . and a beautiful woman with skin as dark as the night. So, now I look at you, such a fine young example of Egyptian manhood. And think of the old man my scouts saw painfully making his way back to the river today. And the woman on board a ship, moored at the riverbank, who is probably, even now, begging the Egyptian lord to wait just a little bit longer before he orders the ship they are on to set sail . . .'

Like the losing opponent who stares silently at the board, seeking an escape where none exists, Piay said nothing.

'A ship whose passengers could not resist the sight of a man hung from a shadoof, and would feel bound to investigate, just in case this might be a sign of something relevant to their mission. You see, I knew you had boarded a ship in Thebes and I wanted to lure you, in the hope of just such a moment as this, when one of my principal rivals for the prize we all seek would be at my mercy . . . and here you are.'

'Why do you call me your rival?' Piay said. 'I came here with the sole intention of rescuing that poor girl, which is what I was doing when a woman driven half-mad by the suffering your men inflicted gave us away. That's it – I've got nothing more to say.'

Khin sighed. 'Have I entirely wasted my time with you? Are you really so stupid that you don't understand what is happening here? I am your best option. However bad you may think I am, I am as weak and innocent as that little girl, compared to my brother. Did you not hear me when I said he was called the Child-Killer?'

'Men choose all sorts of names when they want to sound important, or dangerous. Names do not frighten me.'

'You stupid, arrogant, self-satisfied little piece of Egyptian camel dung,' Khin said, slowly, calmly, relishing every detail of the insult. 'You should be afraid. In fact, you should be more terrified than you have ever been in your entire life. Because if Akkan ever finds you, believe me, you will get no cups of wine from him . . . and all you will want is to be allowed to die, rather than be forced to endure what he is willing to do to another man.'

It was obvious Khin was not making threats for effect. He meant every word.

'All right then,' Piay said. 'I will ask you humbly, please tell me about Akkan.'

'Ah, so you do have a shred of good sense, after all. Then I will tell you this . . . Akkan is my older brother. We are the sons of Abisha, a spice merchant from the city of Uru-Salim in the land of Canaan. But even though I was not the firstborn, I was always my parents' favourite. I was born to be a warrior – Akkan was born to be a clerk. He could never make a woman look twice at him. I had my pick of whichever young beauty I wanted.

'When he became a man, Akkan worked as a record-keeper in the king's treasury, noting all the gold that flowed in and out. He found a wife and she bore him a son, whom they called Qar. So Akkan had a life, but it was dull and drab, while I was entertaining my parents with tales of battles, conquests, journeys to distant, exotic lands.

'Akkan burned with envy and frustration . . . and then, one day, he met a man called Tallus, who liked to be known as "the Cobra".'

Khin paused for a moment to finish his cup of wine, then went on. 'Tallus had been a priest at the Temple of Seth in Avaris, but he had a falling-out with the high priest, Mut-Bisir, so he became a wandering preacher, a mystic and, he claimed, a healer. He told Akkan that he had the answer to all his problems. Of course, it would come at a price, but that was no problem to Akkan. He had the whole treasury at his disposal.'

Despite himself, Piay found himself being drawn into the story. Somewhere he had heard that name before – Akkan, son of Abisha – but where?

'Tallus began by introducing Akkan to the potions and powders that can be made from the flowers of the blue lotus,' Khin said. 'I am sure you have heard of the lotus – it can bring deep slumber to those who cannot sleep, it can numb the pain of a warrior's wounds, and, if taken in greater quantities, it can provide far headier intoxication than the strongest, sweetest wine. But Tallus and Akkan weren't interested in the lotus for these reasons. Tallus and Akkan wanted the power to contact the gods. And the lotus can, if you are willing to take enough of it, if you are willing to enter a state of living death, lead you to the door of the afterlife. The god whom Tallus and then Akkan communed with was Seth.'

For the first time, Piay began to feel a faint, distant tremor of the fear that Khin was trying to instil in him.

'But Akkan wanted more. He wanted Seth to grant him the strength of mind and body that I had always taken for granted. Tallus went away into the wilderness. He took his lotus potions, he communed with the gods, and when he came back he told Akkan that Seth was ready to instruct him. He should go into the wilderness, just as Tallus had done, and he should take his son Qar, so that the boy, who was seven years old, could also see his god and become his devoted follower.'

Both men had forgotten that they were a captor and his prisoner. They had become a storyteller and his audience, both equally lost in the drama as it unfolded.

'So, my brother, too, went into the wilderness, leading Qar by the hand,' Khin said. 'He heard the word of Seth and obeyed the deity's command and when he came back to the city, he was a changed man. He stood tall and strong, fully a head taller than me. His voice was deep and commanding. His eyes burned with a fire that terrified men and drove women mad with desire. The king rained gold upon Akkan, for fear of what he might do if he were not paid his tribute.'

'But what about Qar? What happened to the little boy?' Piay asked, though he already suspected, and dreaded the answer.

'When Akkan came out of the wilderness, he was carrying Qar's body in his arms. Akkan said that they had been attacked by a lion. He even had the beast's freshly severed paw to show the world, just as a soldier cuts off a dead enemy's right hand. But the whole of Avaris knew what had really happened. For how could a man get such a gift from his god, without sacrificing something of equal value in return? And a god who had murdered his own brother might easily ask a man to murder his own son.

'My brother did that so that he might become Seth's right hand in this world. That is why he is called the Child-Killer. And as for me, I did not name myself Akh-Seth out of arrogance, as you imagine. I was given the name, whether I liked it or not, because I am the brother of Seth . . . My brother is the embodiment of violence, the distillation of evil, and the one man who must never, ever be allowed to complete the quest on which we are all embarked.'

Khin looked Piay in the eye and said, 'Think about that, why don't you, before you decide your next move.'

Then he made a gesture of dismissal. His two Hyksos henchmen pulled Piay to his feet and marched him towards the opening of the tent. Just as one of them was pulling the flap open, Khin called out, 'Wait! Turn him to face me!'

The bodyguards did as they were told.

'I have just thought of something that may help to concentrate your mind. You may not have the Eye, but every instinct I have tells me that one of your boat party does. And that beautiful woman . . . What is she – Nubian? Kushite?'

'She's none of your damn business!'

Khin smiled. 'As I thought, you are lovers. Her pleading to your lord indicated as much, and you have just proved it. So, she is doubtless wondering what is happening to you. Let us reassure her that you are in safe hands by sending you back to her . . .'

Khin waited just long enough for Piay to get his hopes up, and then he added, '. . . one piece at a time. Think of that, Egyptian, as you ponder what you should do. Imagine losing an ear . . . a hand . . . your tongue. And with them the same message – all they have to do to stop your mutilation is to hand over the Eye of Horus.

'Ponder all that, and then remember this . . . I'm the nice brother.'

weat trickled down Piay's brow as the sun moved up the sky and the dawn chill gave way to stifling heat. His wrists ached where they had been bound to the side of a cart with hide strips. The muscles in his arms and back cried out for relief, and his head still ached from where the stone had clattered against him.

Still, his captors had not beaten him further. That was some small comfort. Now he only had to wait until they began chopping him into pieces.

The two Hyksos guards had dragged him from Khin's tent and strung him up here while the festivities in the camp were dying down. Now the camp was waking.

Piay watched the Shrikes claw their way out of their tattered tents. Many of them still looked drunk. Some cast murderous looks in his direction before their attention skittered away to filling their bellies or emptying their bowels.

The two guards stepped out of Khin's tent and began barking orders. They moved steadily across the camp, their voices ringing out. Piay strained to hear what they were saying, but only snatches of words reached his ears above the chatter and braying laughter of the Shrikes.

'They're breaking the camp and moving on.'

Piay jerked his head around at the sound of the voice. It was the woman with the split lip and missing patch of hair who had heeded his pleas for help the previous night. Still naked, she was crouching at the end of the cart, glancing around to ensure no one could see her there.

'We're leaving for Memphis,' she added. When she looked back at him, her eyes were filled with pity. 'I fear for you,' she breathed.

'Khin has plans to reduce me in stature, that is true.' Piay forced a grin to show his lack of fear. 'But as long as I'm still breathing there's still hope of escape.'

The woman did not look convinced.

'What is your name?' he asked.

'Maye.' Her face creased in surprise, as if the name sounded strange on her lips. 'The Shrikes took me from Lahun.'

Piay had heard of that city. It had been largely abandoned when the Hyksos first invaded, but some Egyptians had crept back to shelter behind the city walls.

'I am Piay,' he said. 'I am grateful for the aid you gave last night. That could not have been easy.'

'The girl escaped?' Maye asked.

He nodded.

'Good.'

'She is young and strong. She should be home with her mother by now.'

Maye smiled – a little sadly, Piay thought, and he realised it was because her own hopes of escape had been dashed.

'If I free myself, I will not forget you or the other women—'

'There's no need,' she said. 'I've made my peace with my lot in life. I will endure this suffering as best I can before my time in this world is over.' She glanced around and saw one of the guards walking close by. 'I must go.' She slipped away among the tents.

As the Shrikes pulled down their tents and stored them with their plunder in mule carts like the one to which Piay was bound, Khin strode over.

'Your ship sailed without you this morning,' he said.

Piay couldn't help but let his disappointment show. It was only an instant before he regained his self-control, but that was enough for Khin's sharp eyes.

'Aaaahhhh . . .' he mocked. 'Your friends don't care about you after all. Still, this is good for you in one respect. There is no purpose in cutting pieces off you just yet.'

'Is this where you tell me that your brother would have chopped me up anyway, just for sport?'

'No, he would have tortured and then killed you last night. But I like to play a longer game. You see, that ship is sailing downriver, towards Memphis, the city of Imhotep. We both know the significance of that, even if you pretend not to. And I have just received word that Memphis has fallen to Lord Taita and his Greek allies.'

'That's bad news for you. Hyksos warriors aren't going to be welcome there.'

'Really?' Khin's voice was heavy with irony. 'You mean I might have to adopt some kind of disguise?'

Then, as was his way, he reverted to absolute seriousness.

'Everything is converging on Memphis, I can feel it. All the competitors are assembling. They feel the same pull that I do. So, that is where we will go. You will find it a long, hard, thirsty journey. You will receive just enough food and water to keep you alive. And when we reach the city, you will be dismantled, piece by piece, until Lord Taita or your other friends give me the Eye.'

'That won't happen. Lord Taita never gives in to threats or blackmail of any kind.'

'Then we will find another way. Tell me, how well do you know Memphis?'

'Not at all.'

'Well then, let me tell you. For years now, Memphis has not been the city that it was in the days of its glory. And it will be even worse now, after a long siege, after the deprivations of war, after starvation and disease. My Shrikes can move with ease through a city like that, a city of shadows, where there is a blade around every corner and always a hungry mouth to feed.

'Sooner or later your master, or your friends, will make an error. They will walk unguarded along a narrow street as dusk falls. Or they will look up and notice those soldiers that are paid to keep them safe are no longer at their posts, because they have been paid even more not to be there. Or they will swallow a mouthful of wine that has not been tested by the food-taster. And in that moment the Eye of Horus will be mine.

'So, I have work to do before we leave.' As Khin walked away, he called back, 'Prepare yourself. We have a long march ahead. Enjoy it, while you still have feet upon which to walk.'

The column of Shrikes trudged through the parched wasteland, a cloud of dust billowing in its wake. The men bowed their heads into the wind blasting from the north, scarves pulled tight across their mouths and noses. Khin was carried on a chair by six of the stronger Shrikes, the filthy canopy that covered it protecting him from the heat of the sun, but not the sand lashed by the air currents. Near the rear of the column, donkeys hauled the laden carts, and beyond them Piay tramped with the nine remaining women behind him, all of them with their wrists bound behind their backs and tied together so that it would be impossible to flee.

The Shrikes were following one of the age-old trails that the desert wanderers used, trekking from oasis to oasis while avoiding the major settlements spread along the Nile.

How far away was Memphis? Piay couldn't tell, but each step brought him closer to the moment when the first blade cut into his body. He had begun to pray that the Sons of Apis would fall upon them, but why would they? Those tattooed fiends wanted, above all else, to recover the Eye of Horus. Since the Shrikes did not possess it, they were – for now – an irrelevance.

That was absolutely not the case, however, for Myssa and Hannu. And so, as Piay trudged on, he offered silent prayers to Khonsu. He asked his god to ensure that his friends could survive whatever the Sons were prepared to do to get their hands on the sacred object.

'And get me a drink of water – even a drop . . . Anything to slake this terrible thirst.'

'Do you regret coming to rescue that girl now?' the hard-faced woman shouted from further down the line. 'How much of a hero are you now?'

Her face was a mass of cuts and bruises from when she had been subdued. The other women chimed in with cries and catcalls, shouting her down.

'Leave him be,' one of them said. 'He saved one of us. That's more than anyone else has done since we were dragged away from our homes.'

'See what good that does when we're sold into the brothels in Memphis,' the hard-faced woman shouted back.

The trail wound between jagged strips of rock that burst from the ground like the bones of giant beasts and then ran along the rolling dunes, so that the walk became a constant, energy-sapping series of climbs and descents. Finally, Piay heard the rustle of excited voices moving down the line from where Khin was being carried. Straining, he heard the Shrikes telling one another that the next oasis was close and the going would soon be easy.

Piay wondered whether he would be allowed to share any of the water from the oasis. His mind was so focused on his thirst that he barely noticed the trail disappearing between two high ridges. Then he felt the air cooling as they walked from the full force of the blazing sun into the shadows between sheer rock walls on either side. The little ravine also provided some respite from the harsh wind and the biting sand.

It reminded Piay of walking into Khonsu's temple, but there he was at liberty to pause and kneel before his god in the cool, incense-laden air. There would be no opportunity to rest his weary legs and moisten his cracked lips here.

Maybe at the oasis . . . They might let us all rest there, he thought.

He could hear laughter up ahead. The Shrikes were in high spirits. They, too, were thinking of that tantalising oasis up ahead. When Piay heard the blood-curdling shriek that echoed around the ravine, his first thought was that it was some kind of joke.

Then he saw the looks of alarm on the faces of the bandits nearest to him. He looked along the line and there, barely twenty paces ahead, lay a Shrike sprawled in a swelling pool of blood, an arrow deep in his neck.

For a moment, silence suffocated the valley and then someone yelled, 'We're under attack!'

As if that were a signal, a volley of arrows rained down into the ravine, some punching into the Shrikes as they ran for cover, others clattering harmlessly off the rocks. Another volley followed almost immediately, then a third with equal speed.

Piay's first thought was, *It's the Sons of Apis!*

Then he cursed himself for missing something obvious.

Forget the Eye of Horus, they just want revenge for their dead friend.

Barely a pace from where Piay stood, a Shrike fell as an arrow hit. Another spun away as two more punched into his chest. Piay saw another three men go down in a single one of the volleys loosed by the unseen bowmen, somewhere up above.

The Shrikes were well-practised at killing peasants, looting buildings or ambushing traders' caravans, but most were not trained soldiers, and though Khin was shouting out orders, trying to organise a proper response to the attack, few of his men were listening. Most were simply running as fast as they could towards the end of the ravine, up ahead.

None of the arrows had touched Piay or the women to whom he was tied, but he couldn't count on that remaining the case. He had to find shelter, and that meant they all had to find shelter together.

'Follow me!' he shouted. 'I'll keep you safe!'

One of the women tried to run along the line and became tangled up in the rope that strung them all together.

'We have to go in the same direction!' he roared. 'Otherwise we'll all die!'

Maye saw the wisdom in the words and joined in with Piay's commands, urging her sisters to follow his lead. He had seen the direction the arrows had come from – along the western edge of the ridge – so he herded the women to that side, where they crouched among the boulders. The arrows kept raining down into the chaotic mass of Shrikes. Then came a new threat: a volley of short spears.

Piay frowned. Those spears were the standard weapon of Egyptian soldiers, equally well adapted for throwing or stabbing. So, who was hurling them now? He craned his neck, squinting as he looked up towards the silver glare of the sky.

Now Piay could see figures silhouetted on the top of the ridge. Then he felt his heart leap. Those men were not the Sons of Apis. They belonged to the Blue Crocodile Guards, he was sure of it.

'Keep your heads down,' he called to the captured women. 'With any luck you will soon be freed.'

He glimpsed flickers of hope in those faces, but still they could not bring themselves to quite believe him. The remaining Shrikes might have had no thought on their minds apart from the desperate need to get out of the ravine, but from the women's point of view, the victors of this battle might just be another group of bandits or slave traders.

Piay saw one of the women flinch.

'Over there!' she shouted, pointing towards a male figure, scrabbling from the cover of one boulder to another as he made his way towards them.

'Hannu!' Piay shouted. Then he turned to the women and said, 'Don't worry, he's a friend.'

'I thought you'd gone for good,' Piay said, as Hannu used his sword to saw through the rope that bound him. 'They told me the boat had sailed.'

'Yeah, well, the others all left . . . But me and some of the lads wanted to tell you, in person, just how unbelievably stupid you were to go into that camp on your own. And this was the only way we could do it. Word of thanks wouldn't go amiss.'

'Thank you, thank you, my dear friend, my most trusted companion,' Piay exulted. 'I don't know what I'd do without you!'

'Huh!' Hannu grunted, as if he didn't believe a word of it.

But as he moved down the line of women, his mood improved, for with every one that he released from her bonds, he received hugs, kisses and expressions of gratitude, often followed by floods of tears as the women's emotions overwhelmed them. The Blue Crocodile guardsmen, too, were coming down from their perches atop the ravine wall to help cut ropes and hand out leather flasks of water.

Maye turned to Piay and threw her arms around his neck, burying her face in his chest.

'You, too, have our endless gratitude,' she whispered, 'for none of us would now be free if you had not risked your life to come into the camp for the girl. You are a good man, Piay of Thebes. The gods will see this and know.'

'Thank you,' he said. Then, as the excitement of his release gave way to more practical thoughts, he asked Hannu, 'If the boat's sailed, what are we supposed to do?'

'Walk along the river and around the next bend. It's waiting for us there.'

'It's so good of everyone to think of me . . .'

Hannu sniffed. 'Nah, they don't care. They just want to tell you what a total ass you are, too.'

The patchwork of green fields spread out to the edge of the shimmering Nile. Piay breathed in the scents of the vegetation, soothing after the dry desert air.

The Shrikes had left their baggage carts behind as they fled, so the freed women had been able to scavenge a selection of garments, fabrics and tent-cloth that would serve to cover them until they got home. They and the guardsmen then shared out the most valuable, portable items of booty, to compensate the women for their suffering and the soldiers for their service.

Now the women had all gone their separate ways and Piay was marching with Hannu at the head of the guards.

'I bet Harrar wasn't happy when he heard you were coming to get me,' he said.

'Pah! He didn't have a say in the matter. I'd got the whole thing sorted with their officer yesterday afternoon. We left before dawn, so his lordship was still asleep. We got close to the camp as the Shrikes were packing up, saw which direction you were all going. Just a matter of finding a good place for an ambush, after that.'

'So what was their captain going to say when Harrar found out what had happened?'

'Simple – the Blue Crocodile Guards are currently under the overall command of Lord Taita. Taita gave orders to guard you. That's what his men are doing, and if Harrar's got a problem with that, he could take it up with Taita.'

'How about Myssa?'

'Ah, yes, well . . . I reckon she might go after you like we went after the Shrikes.'

'That bad?'

'Well, look at it this way . . . That girl's been worried sick about you. She's begged Harrar not to sail. She's made up crazy stories about the Sons of Apis laying ambushes on the river, just to scare Harrar into staying put all night. So she'll be crying her eyes out with joy when she sees you.'

'And then she'll make me pay for making her suffer.'

'Got it in one.'

'Even though she's the one who said we had to go after the girl.'

Hannu grinned. 'You expect a woman to be reasonable? You're even dumber than I thought. So . . . did you learn anything useful, while you were there?'

'Yes, as a matter of fact I did.'

'So, what's the news?'

'We're in a three-way race between us and two Hyksos brothers who hate each other's guts. We all want to be the first to work out what Imhotep was up to, a thousand years ago.

And, as we have both seen with our own eyes, the Sons of Apis will go to any lengths to stop the lot of us.'

'So who are these brothers, then?' Hannu asked.

'One of them is called Khin, alias Akh-Seth,' Piay told him. 'He's the leader of the Shrikes. As a matter of fact, I had a nice chat with him last night, over a cup or two of superb Syrian wine.'

Hannu gave a disapproving grunt and said, 'If I'd known you were having it easy, I'd have stayed on the damned boat.'

'Well, not that easy. Khin was planning to cut me up and send me to you piece by piece until you handed over the Eye.'

'That's more like it! Hyksos bastard!'

'Yes, well, Khin says his brother, who goes by the name of Akkan, is way worse than him. He claimed that Akkan can speak to Seth. Seems Akkan asked to be given strength and power. Seth said, fine, but you've got to sacrifice your only child to me.'

The blood drained from Hannu's face. 'Tell me he didn't do it.'

'He did it – killed his seven-year-old boy.'

'I don't believe it . . .' Hannu shook his head in horror at what he had just heard. 'I mean, I have met some evil sons of whores in my time. But killing your own son . . . What kind of a man does that?'

'That's a fair question,' Piay replied. 'And here's another . . . Just how much power will Seth grant a man who is willing to do that in his name?'

The sun was already beginning its descent to the western horizon when Khin and his two Hyksos henchmen finally managed to gather all the fleeing Shrikes into a single group again. The operation had taken shouts, orders, kicks, and even the occasional whipping, and it had left Khin in a foul temper.

'I feel like a farmer rounding up a flock of runaway sheep,' he told the Hyksos, as he tried to calm his nerves with a brimful cup of wine. And though he knew it might make him look weaker in the eyes of his underlings, he could not stop himself from adding, 'I'd wager my life that my brother doesn't have to put up with nonsense like this.'

'So what are you planning to do, master?' one of the men asked.

Khin paused for a second to control his temper and then said, 'Well, for a start, we need to establish a new camp, somewhere nice and private, where we'll train these ill-disciplined vagabonds. Let's see if we can knock some basic military discipline into them. Meanwhile, I intend to keep my eyes peeled for any sight of that cocky little pup, Piay of Thebes.

'Believe me, if he should ever cross my path again, I'm not going to waste time talking to him. I'm certainly not going to give him any of my food or drink. I'm just going to kill him. And you two men are welcome to join me in making sure that his death is so painful and protracted that he will be begging us to let him die, just to stop the agony.'

Bast stared at Piay with her unnerving eyes and purred as Myssa stroked her.

'I was worried for you at first,' Myssa said with a smile. She was sitting cross-legged with her cat by the steersman's platform. 'But then I decided that you must be alive. Bast would have let me know if it were otherwise.'

So far, Hannu's assessment of Myssa's mood had not been accurate. She had greeted Piay with a loving hug and kind words, without a trace of irritation over what he'd put her through.

Maybe she's saving her anger up for later, thought Piay, who was learning that he could always trust Myssa but should never take her for granted.

'It was really just a long walk,' he said, feeling duty-bound to assume an air of manly indifference to his ordeal. 'I'd been on the boat too long, needed a chance to stretch my legs.'

Myssa laughed at his little joke, as she always did.

He tried his luck again. 'I met some charming people and decided to stay the night. Always nice to meet fresh faces, don't you think?'

Piay was just about to try another line including the phrase 'ten naked women', when he realised that the hairs on the back of his neck were prickling. He turned his head to see Harrar, sitting in front of his tent and glaring at him with a poisonous look on his face.

'You've got to build bridges with that man,' Myssa said, glancing in Harrar's direction.

'I'd rather fight every member of the Sons of Apis single-handed.'

'Well, you don't have a choice. Taita is expecting you and Harrar to work together in Memphis.'

'No – he was expecting me to work with Azref. Harrar's a very different proposition.'

'But you need him, just the same.'

Piay sighed. 'I'm going to try my luck with a Hyksos,' he said. 'That's a lot easier than Harrar.'

He made his way along the deck to join Captain Gatas, who was leaning against the rail with Shamshi squatting beside him like a pet dog. The barbarian didn't seem troubled by his captivity. In fact, he appeared to be enjoying himself, whistling through his teeth and nodding at everyone who passed.

Piay levelled a finger at him. 'We need to have words.'

The barbarian raised his eyebrows in a show of innocence. 'Surely I have already told you so much—'

'Well, I've got some new questions to ask you.'

'You may count on me.' Shamshi pressed his right hand against his breast. 'I am a man of honour.'

'Then tell me all about Khin and Akkan,' Piay said. 'I met Khin last night and he told me about his brother. It took me a while to remember where I had heard that name before – Akkan, son of Abisha – but it was from your lips. I'm assuming you know them both. When Gatas captured you, you were working for Akkan – even if he did run away the moment he saw an Egyptian.'

'Akkan is not a coward,' Shamshi said, with an intensity which suggested that he still, even now, had faith in his former leader.

'Well, then where is he?' Piay asked. 'He cannot simply vanish into thin air.'

Shamshi twisted his mouth into an ugly smile. 'I think you will be surprised, Egyptian, at what Akkan the Child-Killer can and cannot do.'

'So, tell me about those two brothers. We are entering a contest in which the losers will probably die. Why would one brother fight another to the death?'

Shamshi shrugged. 'Maybe because they are too alike, so there is only room in this world for one of them.'

'How do you mean?' Piay asked, thinking that Khin's assessment of himself and Akkan was very different from Shamshi's.

'If you met Khin, then you know that he is a sly dog, always plotting this and that.'

Piay laughed. 'Oh, he's sly all right. But mostly he was plotting how exactly to kill me.'

'That he did not choose a simple knife to your throat is all that you need to know about the kind of man Khin is. But other than that, he is no different from Akkan. Both are bloodthirsty, cruel, as likely to stab a man as slap him on the back and . . . Wait.' Shamshi held up a finger. 'I have deceived you, forgive me.'

'In what way?' Piay asked.

'Because there is another way in which the two sons of Abisha the Canaanite differ. Akkan is driven to solve the riddle of Imhotep for the glory of the Hyksos. And now that we have been defeated, for the first time in the long story of my people, I am sure that he wishes this more even than before. But Khin's only desire is to solve the riddle for himself.'

'That's not what Khin says,' Piay observed. 'He swears that he is still a loyal follower of King Khamudi.'

Shamshi's only response was to spit contemptuously onto the deck.

'So, you've taken sides in the quarrel,' Piay said. 'Very well, then, tell me what you know about about Akkan, and the lengths to which he will go to serve his gods.'

'Ah . . .' Shamshi said. 'So you have heard the story of the Child-Killer?'

'Is it only a story?'

Shamshi shrugged. 'Who can say for sure what happens when a man and his son are alone in the wilderness? Still, as one who is himself devoted to the service of Seth, the all-merciful, I can tell you that, yes, Akkan has the god's great favour. But he is not the first of our warriors of whom that is true. There was another before him, who claimed Seth spoke to him. Sakir was his name.'

Piay felt a deep chill to hear that name again, and he locked eyes with Hannu. Sakir was the murderous, seemingly indestructible warrior who had claimed to be Seth's agent upon this earth, and had tracked Piay halfway across the world to destroy him. Neither sword, nor axe, nor fire seemed to kill Sakir. Only when Piay had stabbed him with a spear and trapped him in the hold of a sinking galley did his end come.

Shamshi noticed the look. 'So, you have heard of him?'

Piay ignored the question. 'Was Sakir connected to Akkan?' he asked instead.

'Only because they were both led to Seth by the same man.'

'You mean Tallus, the renegade priest?'

'You might call him a renegade. I would say that the high priest and his followers were envious of Tallus. His spells and potions brought him closer to Seth than Mut-Bisir had ever managed to come. But I paid Tallus little attention. To be honest with you, Egyptian, he made my skin crawl. He stared too long, too hard. There is a reason people called him "the Cobra". He was poisonous.'

'Do you think Tallus and Akkan are still allies? If the Cobra is as much of a sorcerer as people say, a man who was searching for the answer to a magical riddle might consider him a useful ally.'

'He might, yes, that is true.'

'And where do you think this sorcerer might tell Akkan to go to find the answer?'

'How would I know?'

'Stop playing games,' said Hannu, his hand hovering over the hilt of his sword.

Shamshi looked back at him without fear, and once again Piay was struck by the thought that the priest was tougher and sharper than he liked to let on.

'In every marketplace there is always a man with a monkey,' Shamshi said. 'The monkey does tricks, the people laugh, and then, if the man is lucky, they throw him a few coins. And here, too, we have a man with a monkey. But the monkey has to hop because he only has one leg. His tricks are feeble and when people laugh, it is with pity and contempt.'

Hannu sprang to his feet, his sword now drawn. Piay had to put himself between the furious soldier and Shamshi, who had not moved a muscle, nor shown any sign of alarm.

'Sit down,' Piay ordered Hannu, who did as he was told, still muttering.

Piay turned his attention to the priest. 'Now, you do what he said. Stop playing games. Tell us what you honestly know about the riddle and the men who are chasing it.'

'I know that everyone is playing games, you included,' Shamshi said. 'The game we are playing, you and I, is to try and discover what the other one knows, without revealing our own secrets. But I am bored of the game, so I will be straight with you.

'Everyone involved in this quest, this contest – whatever you wish to call it – knows that the riddle we seek to answer was devised by Imhotep, the Great Architect. We all know that he lived and worked in Memphis. We know he built his first pyramid for the Pharaoh Djoser. And we surely all suspect that he was buried there, though we do not know exactly where. What do we conclude from this? Simple . . . Imhotep is likely to have left his clues in the places that mattered most to him – his tomb and his pyramid. You know this, Egyptian, with your pet monkey and your ebony concubine.'

Now it was Piay who wanted to leap up, brandishing his sword, and Hannu who had to lay a hand on his arm to restrain him.

'He's just playing with us,' Hannu said. 'Don't give him the satisfaction.'

'Oh, I am not playing,' Shamshi said. 'I am simply observing the group of people who have in their possession the one thing that might help solve the riddle – the Eye of Horus. And I am comparing them with Khin and Akkan, and thinking that they are just children beside those two brothers. And so I pity them, knowing the lengths to which my countrymen will go to take back the Eye.

'And there is one other thing that I consider as I watch you blundering towards Memphis. The riddle was set by a dead man. So, if you wish to discover Imhotep's secret, surely you must travel to the kingdom of the dead.'

The searing sun spun the river into a shimmering cascade of reflected light. The wind dropped in the verdant valley and the date palms stilled their rustling until the only sound was the gentle lap of the oars as the ship cruised on.

In the prow, they caught their breath and stared in awe.

Out of the wavering heat haze, the Great Pyramid of Giza rose up in the distance, a dazzling white beacon, topped in gold, its presence as mighty as the gods themselves and a testament to the glory that was Egypt.

Piay breathed in the dank river scents and the sweet aroma of the ship's cedarwood heated by the midday sun. He felt the sweat trickle down his brow, but he did not move – he was as bewitched as all those who travelled with him. This was a moment he had never dared to imagine – the Great Pyramid was once again in the hands of Egyptians.

In that moment Piay felt like a child again, caught in stories of the grandeur of days long gone, of mysteries and whispered secrets. Ahead of him, Harrar was silhouetted against the silver sky. He was rigid, his weak shoulders pulled back, his chin slightly raised as even he greeted this marvel with respect.

Piay stepped up to join Harrar as two more pyramids emerged from the haze.

'For all the tales that were told, all the elaborate descriptions of their majesty, no words did them justice,' Piay breathed.

'Here is the beating heart of Egypt.' Harrar's voice cracked with emotion, something Piay had never expected to hear. 'Once our work is done, the lifeblood will again course through this land of ours. Egypt will rise up once more, reborn in shining glory as Osiris himself was resurrected after Set, his brother, had murdered him.'

Piay glanced back and saw the seasoned soldiers of the Blue Crocodile Guards massed on deck, standing in silence, all gripped by the same sense of wonder. They, like him, were seeing this land and these monuments for the first time, and they all knew what this moment of reunification between Upper and Lower Egypt meant.

'We have much work to do if we are to meet Pharaoh's expectations,' Harrar said, still gripped by the pyramids.

'The people here will welcome their liberators,' Piay replied. 'They'll want to do all they can to help. Now that the siege is over and the Hyksos have fled, they must long to see some order brought to their lives.'

'Perhaps.' Harrar turned to look at him and behind those cold eyes, Piay sensed something squirming.

'You see problems ahead?'

'There are always problems ahead,' Harrar replied with a waft of his hand. 'They wait like jackals hiding behind the next dune. I received a messenger, sent upriver by Lord Taita, while you were busy trying to defeat a gang of criminals single-handed.'

'Did he have any word for me?' Piay asked, feeling annoyed but hardly surprised by the fact that Harrar had chosen not to inform him of the messenger's appearance.

'I have no idea,' Harrar replied. 'Why would he?'

'Because I—' Piay stopped himself. Harrar knew perfectly well that Taita was his master. This was just his way of letting Piay know that he did not care who he worked for, or how important his job might be.

'What news did the messenger bring?' Piay asked, wondering why Myssa, Hannu or Gatas hadn't mentioned anything, and then, in his mind, answering his own question: *Because Harrar regards them as even more lowly than me.*

Harrar looked at him. 'His information was confidential. Taita would surely not have wished anyone but me to hear it.' Harrar looked at Piay, letting his contempt sink in, but then shrugged and said, 'Still, I suppose I can give you a rough idea of the situation. When Memphis fell, our forces behaved in the manner appropriate to a victorious army. They sacked the city. Apparently the looting and pillaging went on for days.'

'But how could they do that to fellow Egyptians?'

'Because many of the looters were not Egyptians, but Spartans – I believe you had some hand in bringing them here. Evidently, neither you nor your master had the foresight to see what they might do.'

'Was King Khamudi in the city?'

'Yes, the king of the Hyksos, his wives and his children were found hiding in the dungeons beneath the former palace of the pharaohs. His children and wives were drowned in the river, then Khamudi was skinned alive in front of the city walls. Lord Taita is now heading back to Thebes to receive his orders from our new Pharaoh, and, no doubt, to make preparation for the reunification of the Upper and Lower Kingdoms.'

Piay felt a pang of sadness that he had not had the opportunity to see his master before Taita left Memphis, but his greater concern was the effect that the death of Khamudi would have on the quest for the Riddle of the Stars. Whatever oaths Khin and Akkan had sworn to their king, they would now be acting for no one but themselves – any constraints upon their behaviour had been ripped away.

Piay was jolted from his thoughts by Harrar sighing. His immediate assumption was that Harrar was reacting to the sight of the pyramids, which were even closer now, but when Piay followed Harrar's eyes, he saw that the nobleman was looking at a much more humble sight, right in front of them on the river-bank: a shattered shadoof; crops dried to a sea of brown by the sun; ragged bands of men and women in filthy tunics, who called out to the passing river vessels for aid, food, passage to Memphis.

'They look so poor,' Piay said.

'Mm . . .' Harrar agreed, his noise wrinkling in distaste. 'When the Hyksos invaded, they let the Egyptians rule themselves while they stood in the shadows and guided the hands of those who showed their faces to the people.'

Piay's nostrils flared. Now he could smell more burning and the odour of human waste on the breeze.

'I had hoped that the governors the Hyksos appointed would keep Lower Egypt functioning once their masters had departed, at least until we could tie the two parts of our land together. I now see that I was mistaken. Plainly there is no rule of law here. Bandits are attacking with impunity. Crops are failing and people starving. If the trade along the river is in a parlous state, too, then the entire Lower Kingdom may be close to collapse.'

Piay had thought for a moment that Harrar's concern might at last be that of a great nobleman for his people, but he was soon reminded that this particular nobleman only ever had one priority.

'In a place like this, where enemies lie around every corner, I will require protection,' Harrar said. 'The Blue Crocodile Guards will therefore accompany me at all times. Egypt cannot afford to lose a man of my value, not at this time of great potential.'

And what about us? Piay wondered. *Can our lives be thrown away without a second thought?*

His fears were proving well founded. Lord Azref would have protected them, as Taita intended. Now they were on their own.

'Then we have work to do,' Piay said, adopting a light tone. 'More than we thought, perhaps. But if anyone can bring the Lower Kingdom back to full health, it is you, my lord.' He hoped his sardonic tone did not ring clearly in Harrar's ears.

Harrar did not reply. His gaze skittered across the landscape, the great monuments in front of him forgotten in the face of his fear. And Piay knew full well that frightened men could not be trusted, particularly when they were as powerful as Harrar.

Piay stood on the deck of the ship, looking towards Memphis, the ancient capital of all Egypt, which sprawled across the landscape on the west bank of the Nile.

'It's even larger than Thebes,' he marvelled.

He could just make out the rooflines of the city's great buildings, including Hout-ka-Ptah, which was the greatest of all Egypt's temples to Ptah, the Master of Truth – and the father of Imhotep.

Myssa walked along the deck to join him, but stopped a few feet away and looked him up and down appraisingly.

'I like your new kilt,' she said.

'Taita gave it to me He said I should wear it when I get to Memphis.'

'Well, it's very smart, and it makes you look more important. People will take you more seriously.'

'I think that was Taita's intention. And there's something else.' He gave her a cheeky, flirtatious grin, held out his arms and said, 'Come here.'

Myssa went to him. She let him wrap his arms around her and pull her close. Then her eyes widened, she giggled and exclaimed, 'Oh my!'

'It's not what you think,' Piay said, laughing.

'Oh . . . that's a disappointment.' Myssa sighed. 'So what is it?'

'I'll show you later.' Then something caught Piay's eyes. He turned his head back towards the city and said, 'By all the gods . . . Look at that!'

Up ahead, they could see where the eastern ramparts of the great walls that encircled Memphis had collapsed during the siege, and the breaches through which Taita's army had poured. Black sooty stains scarred the creamy stone. For the first time, Piay fully understood the scale and savagery of the final blow that had sent the Hyksos reeling from the city.

The twin dominions of Upper and Lower Egypt had been reunited. But at what cost?

The captain bellowed the order to bring the ship in to the wharf. The crew furled the great sail to cut their speed as the steersman guided them out of the deeper water.

As their destination loomed ever closer, the air was sour with the oppressive reek of charred wood. Beyond the prow, Piay could see the blackened bones of the ships that Khamudi had ordered put to the torch while they had been moored along the stone jetties.

But this was the great port of Peru-nefer, and the siege was over. There should have been trading vessels crowding the river as far as the eye could see. Instead, only a few small boats bobbed up and down on the swell of the water.

Piay jolted as the hull thudded against the stone wall of the wharf. Four sailors jumped over the side to tie the galley up.

There was absolutely no one to greet Harrar and the ship's other passengers and crew as they stepped ashore.

'They knew we were coming.' Harrar sniffed, trying to hide his irritation. 'Messengers were sent ahead. The governor was pleased to hear of the Pharaoh's plans to bring the Upper and Lower Kingdoms together, or so he said. Since I am the Pharaoh's representative, he should have been here to welcome me.'

'Where is everyone?' Myssa asked as she and Piay followed Harrar down the gangplank. For it was not just that there was no welcome for their party: there was barely anyone at all.

The workshops and factories beyond the harbourside, that should have been thundering with the sounds of labour, stood idle and deserted. There were no dockers loading und unloading vessels. No crews, each from a different corner of the earth, speaking countless different tongues, coming ashore or setting off again on their travels. No merchants strolling the quay, enjoying their new-found freedom now that the Hyksos had been driven out.

There was just an eerie silence that set Piay on edge.

Hannu limped up. 'Can you feel it – the hostility?' he growled. Sweat matted the black hair across his chest and pooled in his navel. 'I don't care if this used to be our capital city. It's enemy territory now.'

Myssa allowed herself a sly smile. 'Who'd have thought these people wouldn't take kindly to their city being looted?'

'But at least they are free from Hyksos rule,' Piay said. 'That has to count for something, surely.'

'Yes, but now they have the rule of the new Pharaoh of the Upper Kingdom,' Myssa noted, 'and they don't yet know if that will be any better.'

Hannu grunted. 'Better sharpen my sword tonight, then. No doubt it'll soon be needed.'

Harrar plainly felt the same sense of danger as Hannu. His response, however, was not to reach for a sword of his own – Piay would have bet all his worldly possessions that Harrar had never in his life used one in combat – but to order the Blue Crocodile Guards to surround him on all sides as he walked towards the city.

Soon they were marching out of the sprawl of the port and into a cool open space of verdant grassland dotted with date palms that stretched all the way to the city walls. The fabled Gate of a Thousand Stars loomed in front of them. In days gone by, all who found their way to Memphis were expected to fall to their knees and kiss the ground in front of it. Piay wondered if Harrar would revive this ritual, but the nobleman strode on, his expression sour.

Piay craned his neck up as he passed through the towering gate, which was surely the height of at least six men. Two sullen guards stood there, leaning on their spears as they eyed the new arrivals. They looked thin, their cheeks gaunt, compared to the strong, well-fed soldiers of the Blue Crocodile Guards, and they made no move to stop or question the column.

Once the shadow of the gate fell behind them, Piay breathed in the scents of the city: the aroma of baking flatbread, the tang of fish oil and the reek of human waste. There was more life here, too. Children chased each other, laughing and rolling in the dust just as they did in Thebes. Groups of women chattered as they collected the provisions for the day's meal. Builders boomed at their apprentices and travelling merchants called to passers-by to stop and buy their wares.

Piay felt relief creep over him at the familiar sights and sounds. The tension in Harrar's face eased, too. Yet even now, wherever he looked Piay could see the scars of the Hyksos occupation. Monuments had been dismantled, the bones of their foundations still poking up from the earth, their stones perhaps transported north to add grandeur to Avaris. Statues had been damaged, struck with axes and defaced with paint, or simply removed, leaving empty plinths littering courtyards and thoroughfares.

Much of the city had fallen into disrepair, but the palace was resplendent. It was painted white so that it glowed like the sun itself in the afternoon light. And it was huge, with annexes stretching out on all sides, larger even than the pharaoh's residence in Thebes.

The perimeter wall was high, and both the appearance and alertness of the guards at the gate showed that they, at least, were not going hungry.

Behind the wall lay a parkland of lush gardens and still pools. The air was filled with the scent of jasmine. Pink flowers bloomed on the tamarisk and shade fell beneath gnarled grapevines strung between stone columns.

'This used to be the home of the pharaoh,' Myssa whispered as they were ushered along an avenue of sycamore that led to the palace. 'It looks like the governor has now claimed it for himself.'

The entrance hall was cool after the heat of the day and perfumed from the bowls of rose water set around the walls. Here and there stood pieces of fine wooden furniture, imported from the East. The whole place looked entirely untouched by the looting and destruction that had scarred the rest of the city.

'Honoured guests!'

The voice echoed off the white walls as a figure lumbered into the shadowed chamber. The man was fat, his belly stretching the jewelled robe he had chosen for this occasion, and his arms and legs were short. His jowls wobbled as he moved and his green malachite eyeshadow appeared to have been hastily applied, as if the new arrivals had taken him by surprise.

A gaggle of servants and scribes, and a musician plucking a lyre, swept into the entrance hall in his wake.

'Welcome, welcome to the glory of the great capital of Lower Egypt,' the man said, throwing his arms wide. 'I am Zahur, the governor. We have been eagerly awaiting your arrival to discuss what lies ahead for the Lower Kingdom.'

'I am Lord Harrar, envoy from the Upper Kingdom,' Harrar replied in a high-pitched tone that sounded even more haughty than usual. 'The power of the Pharaoh is vested in me, and I have been sent to commence the discussions that will bring the two halves of Egypt together.'

'Greetings! This moment has been eagerly anticipated. You bring with you hope for better days. As you have seen on your journey from the Upper Kingdom, we exist in misery. The Hyksos looted everything they could carry when they fled back to their homeland. I have, of course, done everything within my power to keep Memphis functioning, but after the siege, and the bloodshed, and the barbarians stealing everything of value they could lay their hands on . . . And trade has collapsed, and we are short of even the most common goods. We have prayed to the gods and they have sent you to save us.'

He was babbling. Piay looked the governor up and down. He liked to give every man a chance, but there was something here that left a bad taste in his mouth. He'd seen Zahur's kind before, during the long years of occupation: weak, greedy, corrupt men who were prepared to do anything to advance their own self-interest. They were governors who had no skill in governing, merely a knack for dragging more taxes out of the poorest citizens and then skimming a little off the top for their own comforts.

The Hyksos could not have survived so long as masters without this breed. For now, the new pharaoh would need Zahur, but surely, Piay thought, Harrar would have this leech replaced as soon as he had outlived his usefulness.

'There is much work to do,' Harrar began, clearly as irritated by the man's chatter as Piay.

'Yes, yes, of course,' Zahur interrupted, 'but first you must get to know this great city and its people. You will find much magic here, my good friends, seeping from the very stones that were first placed upon this land when the world was young.'

Zahur clapped his hands and the musician began to draw a lilting song from his instrument. As if from nowhere, three female dancers appeared and swayed around the room, throwing handfuls of petals across the floor.

Trying to curry favour, Piay thought, watching anxiously as the governor's gaze danced from face to face.

The governor was clearly unnerved by the thought that he might be removed.

How far would a man like Zahur go to keep power? Piay wondered.

'Your slave may dance, too,' Zahur said.

Piay flinched when he realised the governor meant Myssa.

'Myssa is a free woman,' Piay snapped, 'and a wise advisor. It would be in your interest to stay on her good side.'

'My apologies, my apologies.' Zahur bowed again, deeper this time, so that he came up wheezing. Seeking to distract attention from the awkward moment, he clapped his hands again to stop the music and the dancing. 'Let me show you the wonders of Memphis,' he boomed, his voice echoing off the walls as the slave girls hurried back to wherever they had sprung from.

'Have you seen the way they look at Zahur?' Hannu whispered, as alert as ever to even the slightest hint of danger.

Piay turned his attention to the men and women who had ventured out into the street to watch the passing cavalcade. Zahur was perched on an ornate golden chair that sat on a frame carried by eight muscular slaves, his delicate skin protected by a white linen sunshade. His lyre player had been joined by musicians with a flute, a shaker and a drum, and their strident music rang off the walls of the buildings along the street. Ahead of him, his female slaves continued to throw handfuls of flowers across his path. Twenty of his well-fed guardsmen marched on either side of the slaves who carried his chair.

It was a grand display that would usually have been reserved for a king, not a governor, but Zahur revelled in this show of pomp and majesty. With his chest puffed out, he waved his hand to those he passed, as if he was the most beloved of leaders.

Instead, Piay saw scowls. Some people waved fists or spat, but there were no smiles, no hint of joy. A few brave souls shouted out their contempt, but they remained at the back of the crowds where they would not be seen. Now Piay understood why Zahur had insisted on so many soldiers accompanying this procession through the streets of Memphis. Some of these citizens looked as if they would happily drag Zahur from his chair and slit his throat.

'This is what happens when whipped dogs see that their master has lost his whip,' Hannu murmured.

Myssa leaned in. 'Harrar will have to tread carefully. If the people see us as allies of Zahur, we will become their enemies, too. That will make our task even harder.'

Harrar was seated in a slightly less ostentatious version of Zahur's palanquin, also borne on the shoulders of slaves. A dozen men of the Blue Crocodile Guards walked on either side of him. As ever, the nobleman was leaving nothing to chance when it came to his own safety.

As they progressed, the crowd thickened, the raised voices becoming a constant rumble. Hannu's hand slipped to the hilt of his sword.

'If this carries on, we may have a fight on our hands.'

Zahur, too, must have sensed the mounting threat, for he barked an order and the slaves turned his chair towards twin stone pillars. At the base they were painted with the crossed symbol of the mallet and chisel, and halfway up their length the all-seeing eye stared back at visitors. Beyond them was a large courtyard and beyond that, the white stone of the city's great temple soared up against the azure sky. A doorway the height of three men led into the cool, dark interior.

'The Temple of Ptah,' Zahur called to his guests.

As if in response to his announcement, three priests emerged from the shadows of the entrance. They were shaven-headed and wore white robes with a single strap over one shoulder.

The slaves set Zahur's litter down and he heaved himself to his feet. Bowing his head, he intoned, 'Great Ptah, husband of Sekhmet and father of Nefertem. Ptah, who blesses craftsmen and architects, who has always held Memphis under his protection.' He turned back to his guests. 'Come! Make an offering with me! Let great Ptah bless your mission in the Lower Kingdom.'

Piay marched along with the others into the temple precinct. Then he glanced back. The crowd heaved just beyond the gateway. Though no one ventured into the sacred compound, dark eyes glared.

'This can't go on,' Myssa said. 'The people are hungry – it's obvious just looking at them. They'll never forgive Zahur if he doesn't look after them now.'

They followed Zahur, Harrar and the priests into the temple. The vast, windowless hall was lit by lamps placed at intervals along the walls. As the air currents shifted, shadows swooped.

At the far end, the statue of Ptah loomed. Here he was in mummy form, with a skullcap and a short, straight beard. Zahur grabbed two flowers from one of his slaves and handed one to Harrar. He shuffled forward and placed the offering on the floor in front of the god. Harrar did the same, bowing his head and muttering some words that no one could hear.

Once they were done, Zahur turned and called in a disrespectfully loud voice, 'Here! See here!'

He pointed to a much smaller statue of a man in robes, pressing a large scroll to his chest.

'If you are ever to understand Memphis, you must understand this,' he said, raising a trembling hand to the wise alabaster features. 'This is the great sage Imhotep, the son of Ptah and the One Who Comes in Peace. Even in the Upper Kingdom you must have heard that name.'

Piay stared in silence at the face of the statue. It was serene, but with a mysterious expression that he could not quite read.

Zahur took Piay's lack of response for ignorance and said, 'Ah, then this day your life will be enriched. Imhotep was the wisest of the wise. Indeed, a man so wise, he could see far into days yet to come. Magic, perhaps. Some say it was. Or perhaps the gods merely blessed him with far sight.'

'I have heard much of you, too, great Lord Harrar,' Zahur added fawningly, turning to the Pharaoh's representative, 'and to my mind you have all the wisdom of Imhotep. Perhaps the gods have even blessed you with his spirit. Your name will ring out across the years, as Imhotep's has. I have no doubt of it.'

Harrar was a man easily moved by flattery. He nodded and smiled.

Piay jolted as an elbow jabbed him in the ribs. Hannu was wagging a finger towards an alcove that they had not noticed when they entered. One lamp now lit a portion of the chamber that lay beyond. Piay squinted in the gloom. A great beast seemed to be hunched there.

'The bull,' Hannu breathed.

Piay strode across the temple to the entrance to the alcove. Hannu was right. A statue of a bull was the only object in the space. The creature's head was lowered and its front hooves splayed as if it was about to attack, just like the tattoos they had seen on the chests of the Sons of Apis.

'The Bull of Apis,' Zahur said at his shoulder. 'I can understand how this caught your eye. Such power. You could almost think it alive.'

'The Bull of Apis,' Piay repeated, thoughtfully.

'The Keeper of Mystery,' Zahur said. 'The living manifestation of Ptah. You should make an offering at the Temple of Apis, not far from here, where the great bull himself resides. He is an oracle, reincarnated many times, who can guide your path in uncertain times.'

Hannu folded his arms and looked at the bull.

'I don't like secrets,' he muttered to no one in particular. 'I don't like surprises and I don't like mysteries. They've all got a habit of biting you in the arse.'

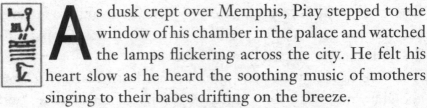As dusk crept over Memphis, Piay stepped to the window of his chamber in the palace and watched the lamps flickering across the city. He felt his heart slow as he heard the soothing music of mothers singing to their babes drifting on the breeze.

Looking down into the gardens, he could see Zahur's personal guard patrolling between the sycamore trees. The Blue Crocodile Guards were on watch inside the palace, but would they be enough to keep danger at bay if the people of Memphis finally rose up against Zahur, or the Sons of Apis came looking for the Eye?

And then there was Akkan the Child-Killer. If he was anything like as dangerous as Sakir then he would be a fearsome enemy indeed. He might have vanished, but it would only be so that he could reappear all the stronger.

Piay was not afraid of Akkan or the Sons of Apis, but the state of Memphis and its people bothered him. His task was hard enough without having to worry about a city in crisis.

I need to be out there, he told himself, as he looked over the city. *And I need someone to watch my back.*

Soon afterwards, Piay and Hannu slipped out of the palace gates and into the darkening night. They made their way along the streets of the age-old city, past the clusters of old men moving their pawns across the narrow boards on which they played torchlit games of senet, which mimicked the path of their souls to the afterlife.

Here and there, merchants were still bartering over their wares, and the women whose trade was immune to changes of kings and dynasties leaned against the doors of their brothels, beckoning any passing man to come inside.

In one of the taverns, Piay and Hannu sipped cups of beer and cast discreet glances at the men around them. Eventually they identified the ones drunk enough to engage in conversation without too many questions being asked.

The first three men they approached were just about willing to whisper their dislike of Zahur, having first looked around to make sure they couldn't be overheard, but they didn't give any sense of an uprising in the offing. And they certainly hadn't heard anything about men with tattoos or a Hyksos warrior who'd sold his soul to Seth.

The fourth man was a lot more useful. He was a mason, working hard to repair the damage inflicted on the city during the siege. Already deep in his cups, he babbled easily, waving a hand still white with stone dust. After a rambling discussion about the shortage of limestone from the quarries, Piay said, 'We've heard tell that there are still Hyksos men roaming near the city, preying on travellers.'

'True, true,' the mason slurred. He leaned in to a conspiratorial clutch and said with a blast of fruity breath, 'And they're led by a demon.'

'Why do you say that?' Piay asked, wondering which of the possible demon-men the man had in mind.

'The travellers he robs are skinned alive and left to die in the heat of the desert sun. Men. Women. Children. This is no lie. I heard it from one who found the bodies. Life means nothing to him, only death, and he kills in honour of Seth, so they say. If you see his face, you will never survive.'

'Do you know this demon's name?' Hannu asked.

The mason shook his head. 'No one has lived to tell it.'

This description could fit either of the sons of Abisha of Uru-Salim.

'Does he ever venture into the city?'

'No, this demon lives in the desert waste where he can be close to his god.'

'A fine story,' Hannu said with a nod. 'I will make sure never to go wandering in the desert around Memphis.'

'A good decision,' the mason said, raising his cup to his lips.

'I've heard about another band,' Piay said. 'Men covered in black tattoos with faces like skulls.'

The mason said nothing, but his face darkened.

'Have you heard of them?' Piay asked.

Their new friend shook his head. When Piay pressed once more, the mason drained his cup, mumbled an excuse and walked away.

'The Sons of Apis have made their presence known here,' Hannu grunted.

'So, there's no safe place in Memphis, then.' Piay chewed on his lip. 'Which means that there's no time to waste. Sooner or later they'll come for us, however many guards we have.'

'We have a lot of work to do and we need to begin immediately.' Piay stared into the face of the governor, who seemed baffled by his display of eagerness. 'I have strict instructions from my master, Taita, about what needs to be done here.'

Nearby, Harrar perched like a bird on a cushion, popping plump olives into his mouth. Hannu leaned against a wall, his arms folded, while Myssa waited at Piay's elbow in case he needed to draw on her store of knowledge.

'Yes, yes, much work to be done,' Zahur burbled.

Piay drew in a steadying breath. 'The great monuments are the symbols of the Egypt that was once and will be again. They must be returned to their former glory, to inspire the people and to show visitors to our land that Egypt is once more a power to be reckoned with in the world.'

Zahur wrung his hands together and bowed his head, pretending to let tears flow. There seemed little honesty in any of his emotions, Piay thought.

'Truly, the condition of the ancient remains is parlous indeed,' Zahur said. 'The Sphinx, that great, wise lion, lies all but buried in the shifting sand. Even the pyramids themselves have every one been looted and left to crumble.'

'They must be repaired,' Piay stressed. 'That is one of our main tasks here.'

Zahur shook his head. 'The cost—'

'You must have something in your vault.'

'All looted. The barbarians and the Spartans—' Zahur caught his tongue and bowed. 'Our happiness overflowed at the chance to offer any small gift we could in thanks for our liberation. But now, what little tax revenue we raise goes to keep the city alive – though barely.'

Zahur's eyes flickered furtively around the works of art that adorned the walls of the chamber.

'We cannot tax any more than we do,' he said, forcing what he no doubt thought was a disarming smile. 'The people will not bear it.'

'The monuments are not the real issue.' Harrar's voice cut through the sunlit chamber. 'The first priority is to get this city back on its feet. We must restore the rule of law and clamp down on criminality. Without those things, Memphis is doomed. With them, trade can be restored, wealth will flow, and the people will enjoy a life here that has not been dreamed of in an age.'

'My lord . . . Governor . . .' Piay persisted. 'I remain under orders to inspect the monuments to see what work must be carried out on them. My intention is first to examine the pyramid of the Pharaoh Djoser, which remains a testament to the greatness of Imhotep.'

Zahur had been greatly cheered by Harrar's image of a rich, peaceful Memphis, particularly since he had not heard anything to suggest that he would not still be ruling it.

'The Djoser pyramid, you say . . .? Yes, very good. In the Saqqara necropolis. North-west of the city. I will make the arrangements.'

Zahur waddled away and Piay followed with Hannu and Myssa before Harrar could find some way to interfere in their plans.

'We'll need to take the Blue Crocodile Guards along to keep watch on us,' Piay said.

'I'll have a word with their officer,' Hannu replied.

'And Shamshi?' Myssa asked. 'Is this his moment of reckoning?'

Piay thought he heard a note of sadness in her voice. For all that he was a barbarian, she liked Shamshi's good humour and his wit, he was sure of it.

'His last chance to reveal what he knows, or he dies,' Piay said.

Leaving the others to return to their chambers, Piay had just stepped out into the gardens when he heard a cry rising up from the direction of the gate. He raced towards it to find four men of the Blue Crocodile Guards dragging Shamshi back into the palace compound. His face was bruised and blood caked the corner of his mouth, but he was grinning.

Gatas hurried up and bowed his head.

'I have let you down. You may take my sword if you wish.'

'What happened?' Piay asked.

'I took my eyes off the barbarian, but only for a moment, and when I looked back he was gone.'

'Tomorrow is your judgement day,' Piay said to Shamshi. 'You must fear what the ruling will be.'

The Hyksos priest laughed silently. 'I merely wanted to stretch my legs in this city my people once called home.'

'He was too slow,' Gatas said. 'We found him in conversation with a merchant, trying to buy passage out of the city.'

'You'll be out of here soon enough,' Piay said to Shamshi. 'Perhaps for the last time. Take him away.'

As the soldiers dragged the barbarian back to the palace, Piay said to Gatas, 'No harm was done, so you're forgiven . . . this time. But when we head out to the Pyramid of Djoser, keep your blade close to his back in case he tries to flee again.'

Gatas nodded and marched away, chastened. As Piay turned to follow him, a voice rang out. 'It is you! It is!'

Piay glanced back to see an old man beckoning to him from the gate. One of the palace guards was attempting to restrain him. The creases in the man's face mapped out a life of hardship; white bristles edged his chin and his head was wrapped in a stained cloth, but Piay could see that he had once been a tall, powerful man.

'This old dog claims to know you,' the guard growled as Piay approached. 'He is a thief, the kind who'd steal the bread from a blind old mother. I told him that he could not know you as you've only just got here. Just say the word and I'll have him thrown back among the rabble.'

'I can see it now, in your face,' the old man gushed, reaching trembling fingers towards Piay's features. 'You are that boy.'

'Go back to your home, old man,' Piay said. 'Whatever you think, you're mistaken.'

'No, no,' the old man insisted. 'You are Piay. You are my son.'

iay felt as though the very ground beneath him had shifted. As he had led the old man to a chamber in the palace, where they could talk in private, he had felt unsteady on his feet, as if he might stumble at any moment. Now, as he stared at the old man sitting opposite him on a richly embroidered cushion, he tried to tell himself that it was a lie. It had to be a lie. There could be no other explanation.

'You will not remember my face. Of course you won't. You were just a boy when I said goodbye to you in Thebes.' The old man peered at him from eyes rimmed with tears.

'What is your name?'

'Asil.'

That was the name Piay recalled – Taita had mentioned it several times.

'I understand you cannot believe,' the old man began, 'but—'

'Why would you be here in Memphis? Why now? This makes no sense to me.' Piay heard the harshness in his voice, but he was helpless in the face of his emotions.

'The story is long and this is not the time for it,' Asil said. 'For now, all you need to know is that my heart was broken when I was no longer able to see my beloved son—'

'That is not all I need to know,' Piay snapped. He got to his feet and prowled around the old man, watching every movement, every tic, trying to spot some hint of a lie. 'If you are my father, why did you abandon me? And how could my mother . . .?'

Piay could not go on. He bent his head, his face twisted by the force of his feelings. Then he gathered himself, took a deep breath and stood straight again.

'All my childhood . . . Night after night I dreamed of you returning to see me. Whenever my master had visitors, I always hoped that maybe it was you. But you never came . . . not once.'

Asil bowed his head. 'If only we could have.' His voice was a croak. 'When we left Thebes that first day, the caravan in which we were travelling was attacked by a Hyksos war band. Your mother . . .' He swallowed. 'Your mother was killed. I was driven all but mad with grief. I was carried away to work as a slave and . . .' He sighed. 'There's so much to tell you, far more than we have time for now. All that matters is that for a few years now I have been free, and living here in Memphis.'

'As a common criminal, apparently,' snapped Piay, bitterly.

'It is very easy for those who have so much to condemn those who have nothing,' Asil said. 'I'm not proud of some of the things I've done – but I'm poor, and I do what I must to survive. Perhaps you are now too mighty to understand this.'

'I know exactly what it means to have to fight to survive,' Piay retorted. 'I've done it all my life – alone, with no family to turn to. You abandoned me, deserted me and forced me to be strong!' He grunted and then added, angrily, 'Maybe I should thank you for that, eh? Maybe you did it all for my own good.'

'We just wanted—'

'Enough!' Piay interrupted Asil. 'I don't want to hear your excuses, just tell me why you're here. What do you want? Are you so lacking in shame that you have come here to ask me favours?'

'No, please . . . my darling boy . . . believe me . . .' Asil pleaded. 'I just heard rumours of new arrivals from the Upper Kingdom, and a man who was said to be an assistant to the great Taita. Someone gave me a name – Piay of Thebes. I could scarcely believe it. I had to see, with my own eyes, whether it was really you. And so the gods have blessed me. Just to see your face, after all these years . . . what more could I desire?'

There were tears in the old man's eyes. Piay crouched in front of him.

'You swear this is the truth?'

'I do. I do. My son . . .' Asil reached out a hand once more and this time Piay allowed his father to stroke his face.

The old man bowed his head. 'I am not proud of what I have become.'

Something that Piay had always imagined, but long since ceased to believe in, had actually happened, and now he felt battered by a slew of contradictory emotions: joy and fury, love and hate, compassion and bitter resentment.

He told himself to gather his thoughts and make a rational assessment of the situation. Assuming that this man who called himself Asil really was his father – which was itself a highly debatable proposition – he had not denied that he was a petty thief. That dishonesty and lack of care for others made Asil inherently untrustworthy.

Far more significantly, if Asil really was his father, Piay already knew what it felt like to be deserted by him. How terrible it had been to be that sad little boy abandoned in the chamber of the great Taita, watching his mother and father slip away into the shadows. How could he possibly risk letting Asil into his heart? How could he risk being abandoned a second time?

Piay pushed himself up. He could not face dealing with whatever this encounter was revealing – not now, when there was so much at stake.

'I need to think about this,' he said with a coldness that he couldn't prevent. 'Go back to your home. Perhaps we'll talk some more another time.'

'But Piay . . .' Asil pleaded. 'My son . . .'

'I will fetch a guard to show you out,' Piay said. 'Try not to steal anything before he gets here.'

Then he walked out without a backward glance.

A new morning had come and a cool wind washed over Piay and Myssa as they stood in the shade of the sycamore avenue and waited for the Blue Crocodile Guards to assemble. Soon they would be marching into the necropolis towards the Pyramid of

Djoser and the brutal heat of the day. There would be no respite out in the desert and they both knew it.

'But this must be wonderful news,' Myssa said, her eyes sparkling, after Piay had told her of his meeting with his father.

'I suppose so,' Piay replied. 'I mean, of course, yes, seeing my father, after all this time . . . That's what I've always wanted.'

'So what's wrong?'

Piay shook his head. 'I don't know. I just feel . . . odd. I feel . . . I cannot tell what I feel.' He sighed. 'The man's a thief. He as good as admitted it. How can I trust a man like that, when I know what he did to me? But if he really is my father, I—'

'Come here,' Myssa took Piay in her arms and then, like a mother comforting a crying child, gently stroked his head. 'I understand . . . This is so hard for you.'

'Crazy, isn't it? I can charge a whole army of Hyksos without thinking twice. But then one old man appears at the gate, and I'm as helpless as a little child.'

'Yes . . . but that's only natural. Because it is the child in you who met your father last night. The child who is still hurt by what he did to you.'

Piay nodded. 'Maybe . . .' Then he cocked his head at the sound of marching feet and a moment later spotted the Blue Crocodile Guards with Hannu at their side.

'Now this I understand,' Piay said, with a grin of sheer relief.

Myssa returned his smile, gave him a quick kiss on the cheek, then dropped her arms so that they could both turn to face the soldiers.

Just ahead of the column, Captain Gatas was prodding Shamshi forward with his sword.

'Our barbarian friend has promised to reveal what he knows once we reach the pyramid,' Hannu said, glowering at Shamshi.

'Good,' Piay replied. 'The sooner we get there, the sooner we can be back safe within these walls.'

Before he could add another word, a loud, aristocratic voice could be heard.

'What is the meaning of this?' Harrar shouted, storming out of the door of the palace, waving his arms in the air.

Piay bowed as the other man rushed up.

'My lord,' he said, 'we are conducting the work that Taita charged me with – in this instance, an inspection of the Pyramid of Djoser.'

'With the Blue Crocodile Guards?' Harrar fumed.

'We will need protection once we leave the city.'

'I forbid it!'

'My lord—'

'The Blue Crocodile Guards must stay here,' Harrar said. 'How am I expected to be kept safe if my own guard is not here to watch over me?'

'We will only be gone a little while.'

'And it will only take a little while for a poisoned blade to nick my flesh. No, no, no.' Harrar turned to the Blue Crocodile Guards and bellowed, 'Back to your posts! You will not leave the palace under any circumstances. Do not forget you have one task – to watch over me.'

Without waiting for a response, Harrar swept back into the palace. The soldiers of the Blue Crocodile Guards all knew that they had ignored his wishes once, by coming to Piay's rescue. If they disobeyed him again, here in Memphis, it would undermine his position, and, even more importantly, his precious dignity. And if Harrar took his grudge back to Pharaoh, they would all pay a price.

Piay nodded and waved a hand to dismiss the warriors.

'What do we do now?' Myssa asked.

Piay glanced at the position of the sun. 'It will be dangerous out there, but we have to go to the necropolis. All our answers are there.' He looked at Myssa. 'Do you agree?'

'Yes – the closer we get to Imhotep, the closer we are to his secrets.'

'As always, the lady is as wise as she is beautiful,' Shamshi said.

'I wasn't asking you,' Piay snapped, though his anger had in truth been provoked by Harrar.

'Forgive me, Egyptian—'

'So let's get going, then,' Hannu said.

Piay paused for a second. 'No. If we go in the middle of the day, too many people will see us. That wouldn't matter if we had an escort, but it's too big a risk now. We're better off going at night.'

'When the Sons of Apis come out to play,' Hannu said.

'Could you just, for once in your life, try obeying an order without questioning it or making snide comments?' Piay said, hearing the tension in his voice. Evidently this day was starting as stressfully as the last one had ended.

'I was just trying to point out that—'

'Yes, I know, it's dangerous going to the necropolis at night. It's dangerous at any time. But my judgement is that right now it's just slightly less dangerous at night. All right?'

'Yes, sir,' Hannu said.

'Good, so that's when we go.'

'Just the five of us?' Gatas asked.

Piay nodded. 'Just the five of us.'

'If our departure has been delayed,' Myssa said, 'I might as well use the time until then. I'm going back to the Temple of Ptah, to see if they have any useful documents about Imhotep, or even scrolls that he himself wrote.'

'I'll walk with you to the gate,' Piay said.

As they were making their way across the palace grounds, Myssa gave a little laugh.

'What's so funny?' Piay asked.

'I was just thinking that there might actually be six of us tonight, not five.'

'Really? How?'

'Well,' she said, 'won't you be bringing your little friend?'

Now it was Piay's turn to laugh.

'You're quite right. On a night like this, I'd be a fool to leave him behind.'

The blasting wind whipped stinging clouds of ochre sand around the hunched figures trekking across the vast necropolis. Their mouths and noses were covered with scarves and they bowed their heads, leaning into the gusts as they staggered on.

Every now and then Piay raised his head and squinted, but he could not see more than a spear's throw ahead.

'Are you sure this is the right way?' he bellowed above the howl of the wind.

Myssa had spent much of the day ensconced in the library of the Temple of Ptah, learning all she could about the huge complex of tombs and temples that comprised the necropolis, and, above all, the Pyramid of Djoser that lay at its very heart. Now she grabbed Piay's arm and stabbed a finger towards a track of stones almost hidden beneath the shifting sand.

'Keep your feet upon this!' she shouted. 'It should lead to the pyramid.'

When they had first crept out of the city, the sky was clear and the moon lit their way. Then the sandstorm had blown in, wiping out the stars, blocking the moonlight and whipping up vortexes of sand around them. As they struggled on, the wind dropped and the storm abated. Now Piay could just make out white walls appearing through the ochre curtain.

'When Imhotep designed the temple complex it was as big as one of their cities,' Myssa said. 'Even now it's a great undertaking.'

Piay ground to a halt and stared at the structures slowly revealing themselves.

'One thousand years ago,' he marvelled. 'Who could imagine anything would still stand after such an age?'

'Stones piled on stones,' Hannu grunted. 'Made by men just like us.'

'Not like you,' Piay said. 'Or me, for that matter.'

They pushed on until they neared the necropolis wall. Piay gasped at its scale – it was as high as the Gate of a Thousand Stars. In front of the wall was a deep trench that disappeared into the sandstorm in both directions. Myssa grabbed Piay's arm and tugged him along it until they found a bridge made of two knotted strips of hide: the lower strip to step on, the upper one to hold. Piay edged along it. The others followed behind.

Once across the trench, Piay ran to the first opening in the wall, but just inside it, a wall of stone blocks, previously hidden in shadow, barred the way.

Frustrated, Piay glanced around and saw Myssa coming towards him. In the shelter of the opening, it was possible to talk without shouting.

'Imhotep cut thirteen false doors into the wall to deter unwanted visitors,' Myssa said. 'There is a reason he chose that number. It has meaning.'

Piay stared at her blankly.

'In your tale of Isis and Osiris,' Myssa went on, 'it is said that when Osiris was slain, his enemy Seth cut him into fourteen pieces and scattered them across Egypt.'

'Everyone knows that,' Piay sniffed.

'But when Isis tried to resurrect her consort she could only find thirteen pieces. The missing one was—'

'Osiris' prick.'

Myssa nodded. 'Isis created a pillar of gold to replace the missing part. And so when Osiris was reborn, the most potent part of his masculinity was made by a woman.' She smiled. 'Imhotep was a man of great humour, so the records said, and here he is being playful. What lies ahead will unman you.'

'There might be more to it than that,' Piay said.

'What do you mean?' Myssa asked.

'If Imhotep could truly see across the years, then this night may have been preordained. So maybe, whoever wants to solve the riddle needs a woman to complete them, just like Osiris. And here you are.'

'I like that idea.' Myssa smiled.

Piay smiled back. 'Then you'd better get on and do what Imhotep wanted. We're in uncharted territory now.'

Myssa reasoned that if the entrance was not where it obviously should be, then perhaps it might be found where it was least expected. But it took a long walk around the perimeter wall and several false starts before they finally found an entrance in the south-east corner of the complex that did not lead to a dead end.

At last, they stepped into the necropolis, and as they did, the wind fell to a gentle, barely perceptible breeze. The sands were calm again, the clouds in the sky parted and finally there was clear, shimmering moonlight.

Piay gasped, and he was not alone, when he saw the full extent of what Imhotep had created in his city of the dead. There were temples, whose soaring columns were delicately carved to represent bundles of reeds and papyrus; magnificent tombs guarded by statues of the gods; cloistered courtyards; shrines; living quarters for the army of priests who had once served here, stretching out as far as the eye could see.

At the centre of it all stood the vast pyramid, rising in six giant steps to the skies. Its grandeur made Piay's breath catch in his throat.

'Now I can see why Taita wants all the old monuments restored,' he said. 'Who could lay eyes on a place like this and not feel the glory of Egypt?'

He looked at Shamshi. 'Isn't that right, Hyksos?'

The priest shrugged. 'Lord Taita has not seen the royal palace in Avaris.'

'Yet the king who once lived there sought the wisdom that lies hidden here, because Avaris could not provide it,' Myssa pointed out.

Piay smiled. 'Well said, my love.' Then he turned back to Shamshi again. 'So, are you ready to tell us what you know?'

'Soon. When the time is ripe.'

'Playing for time won't get you anywhere. Before we leave this place, you will either be dead or free, depending on what comes out of your mouth.'

'I am aware of what is at stake,' Shamshi said. 'Soon you will see the true value of bringing me along on your quest.'

'I'd better – for your sake.'

Piay led Myssa to one side, and spoke quietly, so that Shamshi could not hear him.

'This place is huge. We can't possibly search it all. So where do we even begin?'

'We try to think as Imhotep would have done. To understand him as a man, to know his mind. I've been thinking hard about that ever since Taita first spoke to me about, well . . .' She looked around. 'All this.'

'And?'

'It seems to me that Imhotep was very much like Taita. His thoughts were like quicksilver, his knowledge immense. But he had a sense of humour and he understood the way people think. One of his teachings was that we see but do not really see. We miss what is right before our eyes. So . . . the secret Imhotep has hidden was reserved for Egypt's darkest hour. Not hidden for all time. He made it very difficult to uncover, because it had to be found by the right person. But still, he wanted that person, whoever they might be, to find it.'

'So, you're saying that the clues can be seen, if someone knows how to see them?'

'Yes, exactly.'

'And do you know how?'

'I only know that we're looking for a sign that others might pass by and not give a second thought.'

Piay sighed. 'A sign that no one knows is a sign . . . Now I get why they call this a riddle.'

'Except that I'm sure Imhotep made the sign something obvious, once one sees what it means.'

Piay craned his neck up. 'Like the pyramid? That's obvious, all right.'

Myssa shook her head. 'Too obvious. No – the first sign is elsewhere. But I'll know it when I see it. I'm sure of that.'

They returned to the others and walked on, their footsteps ringing off the walls. All conversation ebbed away. Piay felt dwarfed by the weight of ages among the stones, too insignificant even to utter a word. The only voice was that of Myssa as she noted the buildings they passed from the descriptions the scribes had given her.

'The House of the South . . . The South Tomb . . . The Heb Seb Court . . . The Serdab . . . The House of the North . . . The Mortuary Temple . . .'

And then, when Piay was starting to fear that they would never see the damned sign and their entire expedition had been a waste of time, Myssa suddenly gasped. Her face lit up and she spun on her heel, hurrying back the way they had come. The others raced after her.

Finally she came to a halt.

'There,' she said, pointing.

Piay looked in the direction she was indicating and saw a temple, just one among many other buildings laid out to Imhotep's sophisticated plan. He shook his head, frustrated.

'I don't get it.'

Like a teacher patiently explaining to a slow pupil, Myssa said, 'Every building here has some ornamentation, some carving to beautify, to dazzle the eye and take the breath away. Except that one. It stands alone.'

Piay felt as if the sun was rising and he could see everything as clearly as Myssa.

'She's right,' Hannu said. 'I've not seen anything like that temple. It's plain, simple – you wouldn't look twice.'

'Then let's investigate it,' Piay said.

He glanced back at Shamshi. The barbarian's grin had gone; his eyes were narrow.

At the entrance to the temple, Gatas struck a flint to light the torch they had brought with them for just such an occasion. Once the flames licked up the brush, Piay grasped the brand and stepped inside. The dark rushed away from the circle of light and Piay gasped at what was revealed.

The inside of the temple was the exact opposite of that plain exterior. It was filled with opulent design and intricate carvings. The light licked up a series of gently curving pillars decorated with bands of different colours separated by narrow hoops of gold, as beautiful as the day they were first constructed. The style of the pillars was called *djed*, the gods' word for stability, and also for the spine of the god Osiris.

Piay could feel elements of the puzzle starting to come together at last. This place of divine inspiration hidden away behind an unimposing surface: a secret hidden in plain sight.

Myssa pushed past him towards something she had glimpsed half-hidden in the shadows and he followed, holding the sizzling torch high. On the facing wall was a carving of a half-opened door, so realistic it looked like an actual doorway.

'The door to the afterlife?' Myssa mused. 'Why would Imhotep have had this sign carved here if it had no meaning?'

Piay turned back to Shamshi. 'If you have something to say, now is the time.'

The barbarian stared at that half-opened door and a smile crept across his face.

'Let the Eye show you the way,' he said. 'Let the Eye light the way.'

Piay shook his head, unsure if Shamshi was merely saying something – anything – to save his own neck, or if this was some crumb of information he had picked up from one of his masters. Myssa pulled the linen package from the pouch on her hip and unwrapped it, holding the Eye of Horus up. The torchlight danced across the polished quartz and Myssa frowned as she saw it. With a slow movement, she turned the Eye back and forth, letting the glimmering of the illumination play across its surface.

She took a step forward and held the Eye in front of the carving of the door.

'Bring the torch closer,' she said, beckoning.

She positioned the Eye of Horus the span of a hand from the stone of the carving, then took Piay's wrist with her other hand and moved the torch so the light shifted. As if from nowhere, a blast of light surged from the Eye, brighter than any beacon, as bright as the sun itself, and everyone there gasped.

Something in the nature of that translucent quartz had magnified the flickering amber glow beyond all reason. The intense light sprayed across the surface of the stone, picking out the tiniest flaw.

How can this be? Piay wondered. *Is it magic? Imhotep's skill was far, far beyond even the greatest craftsman of contemporary Egypt.*

Myssa was gripped by the sight, too, and as she peered closer, her eyes widened.

'What is it?' Piay breathed.

'See here. And here.' Myssa traced a finger across the surface of the limestone.

Piay leaned in. Tracings of what looked like fire burned across the surface of the door: engravings that would have been invisible to the naked eye, so delicate as to have been put there by a master craftsman who knew how to keep the edges sharp for an age. They were coated with some substance that made them blaze to life when the brilliance of the Eye of Horus shone upon them.

Piay felt a shiver along his spine. Here was the signature of Imhotep, the Great Architect, a man who had lived one thousand years ago and now walked with the gods.

'We've been blessed,' Myssa said. 'If we had come here in the daylight we'd never have discovered this.'

'Then I have another prayer of thanks to make to Khonsu, for the night is his domain,' Piay replied.

'Let me see what it reveals,' Myssa whispered, seemingly as awed by the discovery as Piay was.

As she moved closer, Piay placed a hand on her shoulder to stop her and looked round.

'Take him away,' he said to Gatas. 'This is not for his eyes.'

Gatas prodded Shamshi with his sword and the two men disappeared into the dark, the echoes of their footsteps dying away as they passed through the entrance and into the night.

When they were alone, Myssa continued her search of the engraving on the stone.

'I see the Eye of Horus here,' she said, tracing her finger around the outline of the hieroglyph. 'So we have not found it by chance. This is the First Door – the clue that leads to the second, and then on, and on to the very end of the puzzle. And then here, beneath it . . . Oh!'

Piay sensed the excitement in her voice. She had found something – the location of the next clue, the Second Door, perhaps.

'Look,' she continued, pointing at the engraving. 'Just here, it's—'

But her words were interrupted by a sudden thud and the sound of something rolling across the flagstones towards him. Piay glanced down as an object came to a halt by his feet.

It was a human head.

Piay looked down at it and saw Gatas staring back. The soldier's mouth was open in a gasp of surprise. And the flames from the torch were dancing in his dead eyes.

Hannu whipped out his sword as he spun around to face the direction from which the head had come. Holding the torch high, Piay drew his own blade, too, as he turned.

Across the temple hall, figures were emerging from the dark. At first around ten men were visible, then fifteen, then yet more. They came quietly, steadily, unafraid. Piay looked along the line as they emerged into the light. They were all Hyksos, black-bearded and coal-eyed, and most of them were dressed in the leather breastplates and caps of warriors. Swords hung loosely in their hands.

A few wore robes of grey and brown and their frames were slighter, their muscles not hardened by battle. All of them were streaked with the dirt of the road, looking as if they had spent an age in the wilderness. They had hacked off Gatas' head, and no doubt done the same to the fellow barbarian who had betrayed them, but Shamshi was no great loss. All they wanted was here: the Eye of Horus and the revelation of the path that would lead to Imhotep's secret.

Just beyond the light, they came to a halt, staring at their prey. Two at the centre of the line stepped aside. More footsteps echoed from the dark. Piay realised he had stopped breathing.

A figure stepped forward, taller than the others. At first Piay couldn't make sense of the shape that was presenting itself to him – more than a man somehow – and then he realised that the new arrival was walking with a staff that was as tall as he was. The staff was slim, smooth, as black as night, but the top of it flashed in the torchlight. Piay squinted and realised he was seeing a crescent moon made of what appeared to be silver.

And then the tall man passed through the line of barbarians and came to a halt. His weathered face was framed by a mass of black hair and a wild beard, all streaked with grey. Beside his commanding height, his threatening air was charged by those fierce eyes glowering under low brows. The robe he was wearing was of the deepest black, so that for most of his journey towards the light, it seemed as if his head was floating, an eerie echo of poor Captain Gatas' current state.

The tall man glanced at the warriors nearest to him and said, 'Take their swords.'

Faced by such overwhelming odds, Piay and Hannu had no option but to hand over the weapons. But all was not yet lost.

Just don't search me, Piay thought, as if the words in his head could somehow command the enemies all around him.

He was in luck. The newcomer waved the warriors back, so that he could take their place directly in front of Piay, Myssa and Hannu.

'I am Tallus, though some call me the Cobra.' His voice had the sound of pebbles falling on stone, thick with the accent of the wild lands to the east.

Piay flinched, remembering the stories that Khin and Shamshi had told. Tallus was the sorcerer that had made the bargain with Seth: the power of the god in return for the sacrifice of a beloved son. Without Tallus, Akkan the Child-Killer would never have existed: neither the man as he now was, nor the myth that surrounded him.

And if Tallus is here, can Akkan be far behind? Piay asked himself.

'You stand now on the threshold of ancient times,' the Cobra said. 'A door has been opened. A path has been lit, one that leads to a prize that will change the fate of this land.'

Piay forced himself to look away from that piercing stare. His eyes ranged across the line of Hyksos, trying to work out some way of getting past them. But none came to mind. He and his companions were trapped, at the moment of their greatest triumph. There was nothing that could save them. One word from Tallus and they would be cut down in an instant.

Piay flashed a glance towards Hannu and could see from the dour expression that his friend would far rather have gone out in a frenzy of bloody slashing and stabbing, right now, than surrender and then wait to be executed.

Then Piay's gaze was drawn to Myssa. She had her head held proudly and her chin was tilted up in an expression of pride and defiance. Even to the last, she would not be beaten down.

The Cobra, too, turned his attention to her. He took a couple of steps and stood directly in front of Myssa. Then he reached out a hand, palm upwards.

'The Eye of Horus. Give it to me now.'

Myssa backed away a step, her eyes flaring once more. She slipped the Eye behind her back.

Piay stiffened. Tallus would not be patient for long. And what good could he, Myssa or Hannu do if the Eye was in the hands of their enemy and they were all dead?

'Give it to them,' he murmured.

Myssa flashed him a look, her face hard.

'It's for the best,' Piay said, praying that Myssa could understand his reasons for conceding defeat, for now.

Myssa looked at him again. He gave her a little nod, and then, very reluctantly, she brought the Eye of Horus back and laid it on Tallus' hand. The sorcerer folded his fingers around it, his lips creeping into a victorious smile. When he saw that expression, Piay felt his anger surge and wished he still had a sword to ram through the Cobra's chest.

'Soon the treasure of the ages will be in our hands,' Tallus hissed, the faint sibilance in his voice echoing the sound of his namesake. He rapped the heel of his staff on the flagstones three times. 'You have opened the way for us. Now your time in this world is done.'

Piay heard more footsteps approaching from the entrance and he knew that the rapping of the staff had been a signal. Only one person could be approaching.

Piay could just perceive the outline of a shadowy figure, darker than the surrounding gloom, and felt a queasy twist in the pit of his stomach. The silhouette was unfamiliar, but the gait was not. He knew that walk. Then the leader stepped into the light and Piay reeled; what his senses had been telling him was true.

He cursed himself for his stupidity. *There were so many clues, why didn't I see it sooner?*

The man Piay had known as Shamshi stood beside the Cobra, as the renegade priest intoned, 'Here is the one who will usher you over the threshold into the afterlife. Akkan, the true brother of Seth.'

Gone were the grins, the cheery charm, the endless love of bargaining that had amused them all. This seemed like a different man entirely. He appeared to have somehow grown in stature, and with his shoulders pulled back and his broad chest, he conveyed an overpowering sense of sheer physical menace.

I should have known from the eyes, Piay told himself.

But now that Akkan had revealed himself, those same eyes were even more disturbing, for they told of a man who had done terrible things, witnessed untold suffering and communed with the most terrifying of all gods . . . and not once felt a flicker of pity or compassion.

Piay ground his teeth together. The demon had been in their grasp, right from the start. They had sheltered him and guided him to the thing he desired most, and in doing so, had brought about their own destruction. But there might still be one thing they could do.

Piay caught Hannu's eye. He then moved his eyes in two different directions, first up and then to one side. Hannu responded by lowering his head, as if in despair, but giving an extra little nod on the way down.

They understood each other. Now it was just a matter of timing.

'The woman is the only one that matters.' Akkan's voice rolled out through the dark of the temple. He no more sounded like Shamshi than he looked like him. His voice was low and resonant, like the echoes of a stone thrown into a deep pit. So little remained of the man who had been beside them as they sailed out of Thebes that Piay wondered if it were possible for two souls to reside in one body.

The flaming light of the torch twisted the shadows on the faces of the intruders. The Hyksos commander's men closed around Piay, Myssa and Hannu, with swords levelled, and the Cobra stepped forward, the end of his staff rattling on the flagstones.

Flames flickered in his dark eyes. He came to a halt in front of Myssa. Her eyes flashed with defiance. Unmoved, Tallus looked her up and down.

'You are certain?'

'She has the wits here,' Akkan replied. 'The knowledge that can unlock the riddle. These other two are of no use whatever.' He glanced to his right, at the men standing there. 'Kill them both.'

'No!' Myssa flung herself between Piay and Hannu and the approaching warriors and spread out her arms to bar the way. 'If you kill them, I will not help you.'

Akkan raised a hand. 'Hold.'

His men came to a halt. Their leader's brow twitched as he scrutinised Myssa. He seemed to be peering through the skin and bone and deep into her head.

'We could make you help us,' he said.

'I have no fear of pain, nor death,' Myssa replied.

'You have no power here. You have already opened the way. We can travel on ourselves from this point, if needs be.'

'You think Imhotep would have made this riddle so easy? Every step of the path will require wisdom, humility, knowledge. Things you do not have.'

Holding her burning gaze, Akkan weighed her words. 'Very well,' he said. 'You may have some use after all.'

Then he looked towards Piay and Hannu and told them, 'The woman will light our path through the darkness to our ultimate destiny. And we will keep you alive, as our slaves, for as long as she does everything we command and guides us truly. But should she falter, should she deny us at any stage, we will kill first one of you, then the other.'

'Why don't you threaten to chop me up, one piece at a time, if she doesn't tell you what you need to hear? That was your brother's bright idea. And yet . . . here I am, all in one piece.'

'Khin is nothing. He is a dead man who does not yet know he has walked away from the land of the living.'

Piay forced himself to grin. 'Ah, brotherly love. There's nothing like it.'

The Hyksos commander slid his sword out of its sheath and pressed the tip against Piay's throat. His flesh burned as the bronze edge bit.

'If you have any wisdom at all in your head, you would not anger me, Pharaoh's man.'

Piay lowered his head in a slight bow, feeling the blade dig deeper. 'If you say so.'

The gusting wind whined around the shadowed reaches of the chamber, sending gritty particles of sand skittering across the limestone floor. Akkan stared into Piay's face. Piay could see the other man was wondering if he should simply press hard on his sword and be done with it.

Akkan restrained that impulse. He stepped back.

'Tie them up,' he ordered his men. 'It's time we were on our way.'

Before the Hyksos warriors could move, Myssa cried out, 'My love!'

She lunged towards Piay, throwing her arms around him and burying her face in his neck so that it seemed she had fainted. But as she moved in close, Piay felt her hot breath on his ear and heard the whispered words that could not have been caught by anyone else there.

Two of Akkan's men pulled her away. Others moved to grab Piay and Hannu.

'Now!' he shouted; then, 'Run, Myssa, run!'

Piay rammed the torch towards the chest of the nearest Hyksos warrior, held it just away from him for an instant, then shoved it hard against his tunic. The light was snuffed out with a muffled hiss, plunging the temple into an all-consuming darkness.

An instant later, sparks glowed where the burning end of the brand had ignited the robe, and then a flame licked into life. In an instant, the fire rushed up the cloth, swallowing the man's head. Screeching, he whirled in a crazed dance, the desperate flapping of his hands only serving to further whip up the blaze.

An animal howl echoed through the dark reaches of the temple. Flames consumed flesh, and though his comrades rushed to extinguish the blaze, it was already too late.

The column of fire seared a circle of light in the dark, shifting in an erratic spiral with the man's slowing movements.

Piay snatched Hannu's arm and silently dragged him away into the darkness of the temple. One glance back was all he allowed himself. In the dying glare, Hyksos faces twisted with fury. But though Myssa was fighting like a wildcat, she had not escaped the hands that held her captive.

Piay had already memorised the direction of the entrance, and as the reek of cooking flesh fell behind them, they raced out of the temple into the cool night. The wind had picked up again and it moaned among the buildings of the temple complex, desolate and relentless.

Behind them, angry shouts rang out. Only now that their comrade was dead had Akkan's men realised Piay and Hannu had used their confusion to escape.

'You have a plan, I suppose?' Hannu asked.

'I have half a plan,' Piay replied. He was still holding the extinguished brand.

'That's better than usual.'

Piay led Hannu between the towering buildings, following a twisting path that he hoped would buy them some time before their pursuers caught up with them. He felt sick. He had been forced to abandon Myssa to murderous barbarians; he could only pray that her value to Akkan would keep her alive. But she had anticipated this outcome, he knew. Her whispered words still rang in his head. There was still just a shred of hope.

The wind had picked up again and howled around the pyramid complex.

'If we leave this place, they'll catch us in no time,' said Hannu. 'Unless you leave me behind.'

'I'm not leaving you behind.'

'Then they'll keep searching this place until they find us—'

'Perhaps.'

'. . . and trap us.'

Behind them, the call and response of the hunting pack rang out as the warriors fanned out in pursuit.

'It is only a matter of time,' Hannu insisted.

'Stop moaning – and start running!'

Their footsteps cracked off the walls. Piay pushed north, then swung along one avenue before doubling back along another that ran parallel to it. The sounds of pursuit echoed closer. Hannu was right – they could not outrun the Hyksos.

Piay cocked his head. Not far away he could hear the beat of leather soles drawing closer to their position. One man, by the sounds of it. He prayed it was just one.

Glancing around, he identified a hiding place – a deep alcove in a tomb where a massive statue had once stood. If they ducked into its shadow they could ambush the lone man as he went by. Piay tapped Hannu's shoulder and pointed in the direction of the alcove. Hannu followed him in, but no sooner had they disappeared from the sight of any passer-by than a voice rang out above the rooftops, deep and clear. It was Akkan.

'I have your woman. My blade is against her throat. Give yourselves up, or she dies.'

The words were blown away on the wind. Piay could not tell if his enemy was bluffing. Why would he kill the person best able to lead him to his goal?

As if reading Piay's mind, Akkan called out, 'I do not need her as badly as you imagine. I have another guide. Seth will show me the way.'

'If that's the case, why hasn't he already done it?' Hannu hissed in Piay's ear. 'Akkan needs Myssa and he fears us. We know too much.'

'I can't leave her. Just can't . . . And it's my fault. I should never have left her behind.'

Piay took a step forward, but Hannu grabbed his upper arm and held him fast.

'Look, you tried. It didn't work, but we're still alive and so is she. And that Hyksos bastard isn't going to kill her. Not yet. Not till he's got what he wants.'

'I'm not my father. I don't abandon the people I love.'

Hannu pulled harder on Piay's arm, drawing him back into the shadows.

'Listen, I understand,' he whispered. 'I felt the same about my wife before those Hyksos savages slaughtered her. But you must trust Myssa.' Hannu gripped even tighter. 'Trust her.'

Piay swallowed, then nodded.

'Good. Now put it out of your thoughts, and you just tell me what two unarmed men are going to do against a boatload of Hyksos.'

'We're not unarmed,' Piay said, plunging his hand into his kilt and rummaging around his crotch.

'Brother, this is hardly the time or place . . .'

Then Piay withdrew his hand, which was holding a short but viciously pointed dagger.

'Taita gave it to me, after the battle, along with this kilt, which has a hidden pocket. Myssa calls it my little friend, because . . . well . . . Anyway, do you want to hear my plan?'

It didn't take long to describe. Within seconds, Hannu had slipped out of the alcove and into the shadows of a narrow path that ran between two high walls. Piay eased around the corner of another wall and pressed his back against the limestone. He breathed in the musky scents of great age seeping from every part of that place, of dank stone and dust.

Footsteps came closer, pausing every now and then when their pursuer stopped to look around. One man – Piay was certain of that now.

He pictured the Hyksos warrior, prowling along the avenue just around that corner, hunched over his sword, dark eyes darting. The footsteps were getting closer and closer.

Holding his breath, Piay waited until the very last possible moment, then stepped out onto the avenue, in clear view of the man who'd been searching for him.

The warrior jolted in surprise, then grinned. Piay didn't even have his blade in his hand.

Piay stepped back, once, twice, feigning hesitant movements, as if he was gripped by fear. The warrior's full attention lay upon him.

Hannu burst from the shadows, bent low. The Hyksos did not even sense the blur of activity until the cruelly sharp blade of Piay's dagger sliced across the back of his right leg just above the knee, severing the muscles and tendons. As he crashed to the flagstones, his agonised scream tore across the pyramid complex.

Hannu limped to Piay's side, holding the curved Hyksos sword he had just taken from Akkan's follower.

'That should bring them all running,' he said. 'And here's your dagger. Taita knows his weapons.'

Making sure the crippled warrior was aware of their movement through the mist of his pain, Piay led Hannu to the west. Once they were out of sight, Piay twisted back to the north and then east again. The roars of Akkan's men swept towards their wounded comrade, but Piay and Hannu had already passed them by and were moving towards their original route.

'I would say that was almost a plan,' Hannu grunted as they ran.

'The start of one,' Piay replied.

Ahead, the stepped pyramid blocked out the stars. As he stared at the towering stone mountain, a mountain created by mortal men, Piay felt himself shiver. The eyes of the dead would be upon him – perhaps those of the gods, too – in this place where the living walked among the departed. He could feel age-old fears suffocating him.

'We should not be here.'

On the north side of the pyramid, Piay crept to the edge of a deep pit disappearing into a black void. A hide rope dangled down one side.

'Grave robbers dug this when they looted Djoser's tomb in days long gone,' Piay murmured.

Hannu stared into the abyss. 'I'm not going down there.'

'Down there is the only chance we have of escaping this alive.'

Hannu chewed his lip. 'We're desecrating the grave.'

'Or dying up here.'

'How did you know about this place?'

'Myssa told me, when she got back from the temple.'

Piay dropped the extinguished torch into the pit. On the wind, he caught the sound of angry voices.

'They'll find us here soon enough,' Hannu said.

'That's the idea.'

'In a pit where there is nowhere to run.'

Piay grasped the hide rope and braced himself as he stepped backwards over the edge.

'See you in the land of the dead,' he said.

'Why did you say that?' Hannu snapped, but Piay was already walking down the wall of the pit into the void.

As the darkness closed around him, the raging voices above died away, suffocated by the deep silence of the tomb. Gradually Piay felt his eyes adjust to what thin moonlight made it down the shaft. When his feet touched the bottom, he felt around for the torch and waited as Hannu's grunts and grumbles drifted down to him. Finally, Hannu was standing beside him, holding the torch and striking his flint. The flames burst back into life and the darkness rushed away to reveal tunnels reaching out on all sides.

'A labyrinth,' Piay said, 'designed to confuse robbers and thereby protect the tomb.'

'Not likely,' Hannu growled. 'In my experience, the lust for gold overcomes all obstacles.'

'That kind of lust can easily prove fatal. By all accounts, these tunnels are endless. A man could get lost down here forever. So use your flint to mark our way on the wall. A little arrow to show the direction we came. But do it down low, where no one else will see it.'

Grabbing the torch, Piay pressed on along the nearest tunnel, stooping so he didn't crack his head on the roof. Hannu followed behind, dutifully scratching on the wall every twenty paces or so.

The space was tight, the air dry and stale. Piay tasted the bitterness of the dust of ages whisked up by the trudge of their feet. A little way along the tunnel, the dancing light of the torch illuminated a chamber to the left. Vessels of different shapes and sizes filled the room, constructed from limestone and alabaster, slate and siltstone. Names were inscribed on each one: Adjib, Sekhemib, Qa'a . . .

'Old kings,' Piay muttered, remembering fragments from Taita's lessons.

A little further on they came to a cross-tunnel. As Piay turned left he felt something hard under his foot, then a snapping as it broke under his weight, like a twig.

He looked down and started as he saw the skeleton, with the broken shin bone, on which he had just trodden.

'Not a god!' he joked, trying to make light of the gruesome sight.

'No,' Hannu said. 'A message, and we should listen to it. I'd rather take my chances with Akkan's mob than die in the dark down here.'

'Trust me,' Piay said, 'we'll get out of here, alive and well. Promise.'

As he walked, Piay burned the route he was taking into his mind, counting the paces between one tunnel junction and another, trying to imagine the pattern of the maze. After they'd circled a few times to be certain, following the marks Hannu had carved into the walls, Piay felt satisfied. He could walk this route without eyes, he was sure of it.

Slipping into one of the many chambers along the way, he eased aside some of the vessels until there was a space behind them in which to hide.

'What now?' Hannu asked.

'Put out the torch.'

'And stay here in the dark?'

Piay could hear all Hannu's fears crackling behind his words.

'Yes.'

'And then what?'

'And then we wait.'

P iay felt as if he was swimming in an endless black ocean. The darkness was so complete that he could find no barrier between the world without and the thoughts racing through his head. He breathed in, tasting the bitter tang of Hannu's sweat drifting from where his friend was crouching somewhere nearby. The silence crushed down. They were entombed, experiencing death before death.

As a cold wash of dread rose in his guts, Piay forced himself to focus on Myssa's face like a beacon in the night.

The beat of his heart thumped in his head and he was gripped by what appeared to be white sparks floating in the endless dark. Were they imagined – some hallucination – or truly there? He turned his head, but if Hannu had seen them he could not tell. His friend did not move, his breathing regular. Perhaps he was asleep.

The sparks swirled, then began to coalesce into a shape. A figure was forming.

Piay's heart beat harder.

Had Djoser returned to punish him for defiling his tomb? He swallowed, but his mouth was as dry as the dust that lined the tunnels.

As the sparks blurred into a shimmering pale glow in the shape of a man, Piay felt a calm descend on him. Now he sensed a familiar presence. It was the Traveller. Surely this could only be a dream. But dreams, as everyone knew, were the way that the gods communicated with men.

In the dark, Khonsu hovered before him in his mummy form, with the sidelock of hair of the innocent child hanging to his shoulder. The *menat* necklace gleamed on his chest and he gripped the crook and flail.

Piay mouthed a silent prayer.

'One day, and soon, I will be the Greatest God of the Great Gods.' The words echoed deep in Piay's head.

'I am your servant.' Piay heard his words, though he had no idea if he had actually spoken them.

Khonsu raised his left hand, palm outwards, and Piay felt his vision swim. An instant later he was standing on the cooling sands under a sky filled with stars. The patterns of the constellations were clear to him, and at the heart of this night sky glowed the crescent moon of Khonsu, the god of light in the night.

As he stared in wonder at the bright celestial bodies sweeping across the sable sky, Piay felt a familiar dread swell within him. Something tugged at his attention and he lowered his gaze to look out across the sands that rolled out to the horizon. The Great Pyramid loomed in front of him, and not far away, the Sphinx, still in its original, undamaged prime before the desert had started to claim it, proudly stared towards the east.

Piay shuddered as he finally saw the source of his dread. Seth towered above those monuments, almost obscuring the stars, the beast-head staring down at Piay. The god of deserts, of chaos, of violence, the god of the Hyksos. Seth opened his mouth, revealing rows of gleaming fangs, and then he began to swallow those vast stone structures, the desert, the night sky, even the crescent moon.

The vision vanished in the blink of an eye and once again Piay was staring at Khonsu. The god slowly lowered his hand and once again words echoed in Piay's head.

'They are coming.'

Piay jolted as if shocked from a deep sleep. Khonsu was gone; the dark was all that remained. But now Piay could hear the distant rumble of voices. Akkan's followers had found the shaft and were descending to explore further. Perhaps they had seen

Piay and Hannu's footprints in the dust. It mattered little. This had all been foreseen.

'It is time,' Piay said.

The flickering glow of an oncoming torch played across the tunnel wall. Piay crouched in the shadows of a side passage, watching the light grow stronger as the Hyksos warriors came closer. The sporadic bursts of conversation were low, occasionally whispered. They were as afraid of venturing into the tomb as Hannu had been.

Piay's fingers tightened around the handle of his bronze knife. The vision of Khonsu had somehow given him strength. His wavering faith in his own ability was fortified once again.

But as the first of the warriors crept into view, his sword swinging from side to side and his eyes darting, Piay stiffened. Perhaps it was a trick of the light and the shadows on the hewn rock, but the glow upon the tunnel wall seemed to shimmer into the form of Seth, the beast-head hovering just behind the approaching Hyksos as if the god was protecting them. Piay shuddered. The air itself seemed to grow heavier, like the feeling in the desert before a storm struck, and Piay felt certain he could sense that dread presence simmering through those claustrophobic tunnels.

He held back until the last of the Hyksos warriors passed the end of the cross-tunnel, counting each one. He felt a rush of relief. Only six of them. If his preparations had been good enough, there was a chance.

Darting forward, Piay ghosted around the corner into the other tunnel. He clamped his hand across the mouth of the last in the line of Hyksos warriors and slashed his short blade across the man's throat in one fluid movement. Blood showered, drumming into the dust on the tunnel floor.

His enemy flailed, bouncing from wall to wall as he clutched at his wound, but Piay was already gone, dancing back into the shadows from where he had come, with no sound to mark his passing.

As the dead warrior crashed onto the flagstones, Piay heard cries of alarm ring out from the other warriors. Following the map he had burned into his mind, he ducked down one tunnel and then another before slipping into one of the side chambers.

The voices that floated to him were laced with fear. Someone was blaming the death upon a curse – they had desecrated the tomb and now they would pay for their foolishness. Another poured scorn on the idea of a curse, pointing out that the wound had been made by a blade. That only seemed to whip them into greater anxiety. If the enemies they were stalking could strike with impunity, unseen, unheard, this meant they had badly misjudged their foe.

In the gloom, Piay grinned. So far, so good.

One of the Hyksos warriors was howling that he wanted to get out, right away. Another warned him that the fury of Akkan would be far worse than anything they encountered in those tunnels.

'The Cobra will feast on your soul,' another said, his voice strained.

Finally they reached an agreement to press on while taking the utmost care.

Piay waited until he heard the footsteps drawing in his direction and then he slipped out of the chamber and hurried along the tunnel to where Hannu was hiding.

'Are you ready?' Piay whispered.

He couldn't see his friend's face, but he imagined Hannu's eyes gleaming and the curved blade in his hand. An instant later, Piay sensed, Hannu had gone.

Piay turned back to the sound of muffled voices. They drew nearer and then he glimpsed the first hint of the torchlight. Swathed in shadows, he watched as the light washed closer and then, when it was almost up to the tips of his toes, he lunged into the light.

The Hyksos warriors cried out in shock, reeling back as their crescent swords swept up. Piay didn't wait to see any more. He threw himself back into the dark, counting his hurried steps until he reached the point where he knew the branching tunnel lay, and then he slipped into it. He could hear the pounding of feet at his back, just as he had anticipated. Then a scream of agony rang out.

Hannu had burst from one of the chambers and hooked his blade around the neck of the last of the warriors, before disappearing into the dark in the direction from which the warriors had come. The convulsions of the dying man would block the tunnel and buy Hannu some time to make his escape.

Piay muttered a prayer of thanks to Khonsu and then he raced back towards his enemies. As his eyes adjusted to the torchlight, he saw them churning in the confined space, consumed with fear. Confusion reigned. Two were kneeling, trying to staunch the flow of blood from the dying man. The other two had their backs to him.

Holding his dagger as he ran, Piay focused his attention on the warrior who had been guiding the way with the torch. Piay's feet made not even a whisper as he swept near. He hacked his blade into the man's wrist. His opponent shrieked and the torch spun to the ground. Letting his motion carry him forward, Piay stabbed the point of the dagger upwards, catching the warrior under his chin and driving the blade in up to its hilt, thrusting into his skull.

Piay caught the dying man's body as he dropped and heaved it towards the three surviving Hyksos. Then he stamped on the torch, crushing out the last of the flames.

That impenetrable dark swept in.

Piay had planned to retreat, to allow Hannu to strike from the rear again, but the blood was thundering in his head. Thoughts of Myssa and what she might be forced to endure consumed him. Suddenly, without even thinking, overtaken by the raging bloodlust of battle, he was picking up the dead man's sword and rushing at the men who had been hunting him.

Now Piay was the predator attacking his prey, slashing his sword from side to side in front of him and stabbing the dagger whenever the sword hit human flesh. All his senses felt heightened. Each jolt as the blade bit into bone or cut through skin and muscle fanned the flames of his frenzy.

The Hyksos warriors were screaming. Every now and then the tip of Piay's blade raked across the stone wall, raising a shower of sparks. In that fleeting light, Piay glimpsed bloodstained faces, mouths torn wide with agony, eyes staring in horror. They knew their end was upon them.

And then, soon enough, there was silence.

Once they'd relit their own torch, Piay and Hannu headed back towards the shaft. While Hannu remained in the tunnel so the torchlight would not be seen from above, Piay crept to the base of the pit. The murmur of voices drifted down.

'Where are they?' someone was saying. The light of a torch suddenly swayed into view against the square of stars overhead. 'Ciran should have returned by now with news.'

Piay stood in the dark, far beyond the reach of the torchlight, and felt his anger harden. Every fibre of him wanted to clamber up that hide rope and attack the remaining warriors to free Myssa. Not so long ago, the reckless Piay that he once had been might well have done that, but now he pushed aside those feelings until a steady calm settled on him. His only hope of rescuing Myssa alive came from biding his time.

The voices continued, murmuring back and forth until Piay heard the sound of running feet approaching.

'We leave now,' the new arrival barked.

'But Ciran—'

'He and the others can catch us up when they have ended the lives of those two dogs. Akkan does not want to waste any time. He and the Cobra want to get to work on that Kushite bitch.'

After a brief muttering, the voices trailed away until there was only the moan of the wind across the top of the shaft.

Today should have been the first day of their journey to uncovering the secrets of the ages. Instead, Piay had lost Myssa – the person he valued more than anyone else in the world. He'd lost the Eye of Horus. And his enemies now had the advantage.

But at least he had learned the path was real. They were not chasing some wavering illusion hovering over the hot desert sands, nor some story dreamed up to entertain children. They had passed through that half-opened door carved in the temple wall, as Imhotep had intended. What wonders and terrors lay ahead?

Piay grasped the hide rope and began to climb.

The wind howled across the waste like a lost soul screaming for deliverance. With a scarf bound around her mouth and nose, Myssa bowed her head into the blasting sand, feeling the exposed skin around her eyes burn as if from a thousand needle pricks.

Akkan's warriors were positioned all around her, with the Child-Killer himself marching at the head of the column. The Cobra strode at the rear, a little way behind, using his staff to lever himself over the dunes. Since they'd left Djoser's pyramid, they'd marched in silence. Myssa couldn't tell if the barbarians were angry that they hadn't seen Piay and Hannu's bodies, or that they'd left good men behind in the labyrinth beneath the monument. But they had the Eye of Horus now, and with it the belief that they were on the secret road that Imhotep had hidden so many centuries before. For Akkan, that seemed to be all that mattered.

As the dust storm raged once again across the desert, Myssa let her thoughts drift to the monotonous rhythm of her foot-steps. She was not afraid. She had long since learned she could endure any deprivation. After all, she had watched the people she had loved in her village slaughtered by ravening slavers. She had been captured and beaten and thrown into the stinking hold of the slavers' galley, clawing faces and gouging eyes to fight off every man who had tried to rape her. She had been stripped naked and humiliated, forced to stand on the selling block. All of that had washed over her like the cool surf of the incoming tide.

Now she was a captive once again, but she knew she would never be broken. She would do as she always did: watch and wait and turn over every new piece of information until she found an opportunity to escape. And if there was a chance to slit Akkan's throat in the process, she would take it.

Myssa's mouth was dry and she moistened her lips beneath the scarf.

Where are Piay and Hannu now? she wondered.

She did not for a minute think they were dead, as Akkan and his band seemed to believe. She knew them better than those Hyksos cut-throats. They were survivors, as she was. What lay ahead for them was now in the hands of the gods.

As Akkan, his followers and their captive trekked a little further into the wilderness, the wind dropped and the dust storm drifted away. A stillness fell across the desolate landscape of rock and sand as the moon painted it silver and shadow black. A scream rang out in the distance – a jackal hunting, yet another portent of misfortune.

Myssa pushed that thought aside.

On the crest of a dune, Akkan raised a hand and his war band dropped down, slaking their thirst from the water hides that hung at their sides. Myssa settled away from the group, peering out across the red sands as if she had never been so at peace.

After a while, Akkan wandered over and thrust his hide at her. Myssa took it and swilled back a mouthful of the sweet water. When she handed it back to him, she said, 'You played your part well on the galley. You deceived all of us.'

Akkan dropped to his haunches, and as Myssa traced her eyes across his features, she saw the muscles were taut, his mouth was a slash that turned down, deep lines that were carved into his forehead. And she winced when she looked into his eyes, for they seemed to offer her nothing but pain.

'Shamshi was the man I used to be,' he said.

Myssa narrowed her eyes. 'I liked him more.'

'I can still put him on, like a bearskin cloak in the chill of the mountains. But he is only a memory now. He saw the world a different way. I cannot be that man again.'

'And how is the world as you see it?'

'A hard place where only the strong can thrive. There is no space for weakness.'

Myssa weighed this stranger presenting himself to her, trying to understand how such a dark truth could have been hidden from her so easily. The more she could find out about this two-faced man, the more likely she was to see some crack that she could prise open to her advantage.

'What changed you?'

Akkan glanced to where the Cobra stood like a sentinel staring up at the moon.

'In the days of my youth, I was nothing, a weakling. Even when I grew into manhood, my own family despised me. Then I was introduced to the magic of the blue lotus. I walked with my god, and I became Akkan. He emerged from me, like the Dream Flower drawing up from the waters of the Nile to greet the sun at first light. I was ushered into a new life, a better one.'

'A life where you walk alone?'

Akkan made to speak, then caught himself, but in his intense gaze Myssa glimpsed a hint of his attraction to her that she had first felt on the galley from his other self, Shamshi.

'I will see where this road takes me,' he said.

Myssa smiled non-committally and said nothing.

Akkan was looking at her face, just as she had at his, searching for clues to the person who lay behind it.

'You have sharper wits than anyone I have ever met, man or woman,' he said.

'I'll never help you. I don't care what you do to me, it won't work.'

Akkan shrugged. 'We'll see. But I admire the fire in you. I have since we first met. I would like to see into your mind. What made you the woman you are?'

'A hard world.' Myssa showed a defiant face and considered leaving it there. But his question had untethered something inside her. 'My freedom was stolen from me. Men tried to force me to obey their will. I did not bow or break. I did not become another to survive. I am Myssa. I am who I always was.'

She held Akkan's searching gaze until he nodded as if he had learned some great secret, that slash of a mouth shaping into an inscrutable smile.

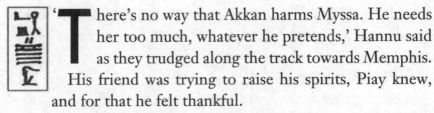'There's no way that Akkan harms Myssa. He needs her too much, whatever he pretends,' Hannu said as they trudged along the track towards Memphis. His friend was trying to raise his spirits, Piay knew, and for that he felt thankful.

The heat of the morning was already rising. Piay licked his dry lips, wishing they had a water hide.

'If only we could work out where they are going next . . .'

'I know where Myssa is taking them.'

Hannu frowned. 'How?'

'You remember how she saw something in the inscription . . . just before . . .' Piay paused, wondering how to phrase what he wanted to say.

'Before we were rudely interrupted by a severed head, rolling across the floor like a great big hairy watermelon, you mean?'

Piay had to smile. 'Something like that.'

'Yeah, I remember,' Hannu said. 'She was really excited, it was obvious. I thought to myself, "She's gone and found another clue."'

'I thought the same thing . . .' Piay said, 'and she had. She told me so, just before they grabbed her.'

'So, where is it, then?'

'I don't know – not exactly. But I know where she's going.'

'All right then. What did she say – exactly – word for word? Every word could matter.'

'She said, "Half a day south of Khem . . ." and then, "Not the Door, but close". The clue at the necropolis was the First Door, so this would be the second one. And she's not telling Akkan where it is.'

'Well, that's good,' Hannu said. 'But she's taking him close to it, and they've got a head start. Khem's not that far from the necropolis . . . Those Blue Crocodile lads could do it in a day, if they went hard at it. Akkan's mob aren't as good. But nor are we . . .'

Piay looked at Hannu.

'Yeah, all right, nor am I. But even if you went by yourself, they could find this new clue and be off again before you got there.'

'I don't think so. Myssa's smart—'

'I'd noticed.'

'She can keep them going around in circles, never quite find-ing the right place, until we get close enough to rescue her. With any luck we should be able to cut across their trail. We killed six of Akkan's men, but there are still at least fifteen people out there, marching around the wilderness. Hard to do that without leaving signs that we can follow.'

'All right, that sounds reasonable. But you just said it – there's about fifteen of them, and only two of us. We need to even those odds.'

'Well, the Blue Crocodile boys would love a few days off from Harrar,' Piay said.

'We both know he won't let them out of his sight,' Hannu replied.

'But we've got to try.'

They had almost reached the cracked and crumbling walls of Memphis, and soon they were passing through the shadows of the gate and into the sullen city. The mood was, if any-thing, darker than when they had left the previous evening. Piay looked around at the drawn faces of the men and women passing by. A mother was sitting on the step outside her home, brushing away the fat flies that buzzed around her baby's face. Her cheeks were hollow, her eyes moving slowly, drained of all passion.

'These people need feeding,' he said. 'But there's no chance of that while Zahur runs this city. And Harrar . . .' He shook his head. 'This would all have been a different story if Azref had lived.'

They hurried along the dusty streets and up to the palace gates. As the guards let them in, one of them said, 'Oh, sir, that old gentleman who was here the other night . . . The one who said he was your father . . .'

Piay stopped in his tracks. 'What of him?'

'Well, he came by and left word of where he lived, said we should pass it on to you.'

Piay almost said, 'I don't want to know.' But then he thought better of it. Like it or not, he still had unfinished business with Asil: answers and explanations that he'd yet like to receive. He nodded. 'Go ahead.'

'He said that his house is in the lane behind the old fish market, beside the tavern run by Malachi of Ashkelon. That's a very rough area, sir, a proper den of thieves.'

'No wonder my father feels at home there.'

The guard waved Piay and Hannu through the gate and into the palace gardens, where they were soon walking in the cool shade of the sycamore trees. Within these walls there was no trace of the suffering that existed across the city. The guards ambled, bellies full, wanting for nothing. Slaves dutifully heaved baskets of figs and pitchers of wine. The air was rich with the scents of the lovingly tended flowers.

They found Harrar in an ornate chamber facing the garden. He was sprawled on a sumptuous cushion, chewing on a honey cake. Zahur's huge bulk spilled over the edges of his own cushion nearby. The two men were laughing heartily as they broke their fast.

'They're the best of friends, aren't they?' Hannu whispered.

'Well, they've got a lot in common,' Piay replied.

He strode forward before one of the slaves could announce him.

'Lord Harrar, I beg your indulgence.'

Harrar's laughter drained away and his face shifted to one of weary irritation.

'I'm trying to enjoy these honey cakes.'

'I can see that, my lord, but this is a matter of great urgency. Captain Gatas is dead, murdered by a band of Hyksos. They have captured Myssa.'

'Ah! Your woman!' Zahur exclaimed, waving a finger in the air before dipping his hand down for another honey cake. 'Such a pretty black thing.'

Piay nodded, gritting his teeth to stop himself from telling Zahur exactly what he thought of his description of the woman he loved.

She's got more brains in her little finger that you have in your fat head, he thought.

But if he was to have any hope of saving her, he could not afford to antagonise the two most powerful men in Memphis.

'How did this happen?' Harrar asked, though he seemed more intent on brushing the crumbs from his robe than hearing Piay's tale.

'A small group of us went to the Pyramid of Djoser last night to begin the work that Lord Taita instructed me to do.'

Harrar sighed. 'You went to examine the pyramid in the middle of the night – when you couldn't see a thing? That sounds like complete madness to me.' He tilted his head towards Zahur. 'Don't you agree?'

'Absolutely,' Zahur replied, though the word was muffled by the cake in his mouth. He swallowed, burped and then added, 'The act of a madman or a fool, if you ask me.'

'We went under cover of the night in the hope that we would not be spotted by our enemies.'

'Another foolhardy notion!' Zahur smacked his lips. 'Cut-throats skulk everywhere beyond the walls. Shrikes, too, now, I hear.'

'I've already met them,' Piay said.

'On another of your grossly irresponsible attempts to win personal glory, no matter what the cost to others.'

Piay had had enough. Trying to keep his counterblast polite and not overtly insubordinate, he replied, 'With great respect to your lordship, in my time with the Shrikes, I gained an enormous amount of valuable intelligence that I would be happy to share with you both at your convenience. And I can now give you detailed information about the Hyksos warlord Akkan, whose men attacked us last night.'

'So you let your woman be captured, but saved your own skins,' Harrar said, with venom. 'What splendid warriors you are!'

Zahur giggled. 'Very droll, Lord Harrar,' he said. 'Such wit!'

Piay ignored Zahur and kept looking at Harrar.

'My lord, we need the Blue Crocodile Guards. They're our only hope of getting Myssa back.'

'We cannot risk seasoned fighting men in battle for one woman.'

'My lord, I know you require protection against the Sons of Apis – you have made your views clear on that – but if the gods are with us, we will be back before nightfall, and during the hours of daylight the palace guards will be able to keep you safe.'

Harrar tossed aside his honey cake, his face taut with irritation.

'Any fight with Hyksos warriors will be fierce. We cannot afford to lose a single soldier, and certainly not for a woman.'

'A man was stabbed last night,' Zahur explained through another mouthful of cake. 'Stabbed for a loaf of bread – in Memphis! The people are restive. The war . . . the siege . . . It has all taken a terrible toll. The people want the comforts they enjoyed during the long years of peace under Hyksos rule, and we cannot rest easy until we fill the grain warehouses and get the river trade moving again. That requires order to be restored and maintained.'

Confounded, Piay looked from Zahur to Harrar, and then to the heap of honey cakes and the slaves bringing in yet more tasty morsels for their delectation.

'The Blue Crocodile Guards will stay garrisoned here in case they are needed,' Harrar said. 'That is my final word. And as for this scheme of Taita's, to map the monuments and to return them to the glory of ancient times . . . What on earth is the point? And how could we ever afford such vast expenditure?'

'Lord Taita said—'

'I know what Taita said. But he is just a man, do you hear me? He is not always right.'

He's right a lot more often than you, Piay thought.

Once again, he restrained himself and instead said, 'In any event, my lord, he specifically ordered the Blue Crocodile Guards to protect me and my colleagues while we were carrying out our work here in Memphis.'

'The necropolis is not actually in Memphis,' Harrar observed, provoking another snort of amusement from Zahur. 'And, in any case, he did not inform me of any such arrangement.'

'No, my lord, because Lord Taita had already left Thebes by the time Lord Azref was . . .'

Piay just managed to stop himself from saying 'was poisoned', but he had left himself open to Harrar, who leaned forward and said, 'Was what . . .?'

It was suddenly clear to Piay from the tone of Harrar's voice, and the way he was daring him to finish the sentence, that his lordship knew exactly what had happened to Azref – and might even have played a part in his death. And with that realisation came another. Harrar was not as physically intimidating as Akkan. He had no powers conferred on him by the gods. But he was no less malicious, no less hateful, no less evil. And that made him, in his own way, no less dangerous.

'Before he was eaten, my lord . . . by the crocodiles,' Piay said.

'Hmm . . .'

Harrar gave Piay a look that signified that, as far as he was concerned, the conversation was over. Myssa was lost. There was no way of getting her back. But the very act of thinking about her reminded Piay of something.

'Excuse me, my lord,' he said.

He dashed out of the room, along a corridor, up a flight of stone stairs and into Myssa's bedchamber. Piay just had time to notice that Bast was no longer curled up on her mistress's bed, as she had been for most of the time since their arrival. Then he found what he was looking for and ran back the way he had come, pausing for a second to catch his breath before he walked back up to the two self-indulgent masters of this sprawling, suffering city.

'Excuse me, my lords,' Piay said.

Harrar looked at him with bored, unwelcoming eyes. 'What now?'

'There's something you need to see, sir. It's proof of Lord Taita's intentions.'

Piay handed him the scroll on which Taita's order to give assistance to Myssa was written.

Harrar shrugged. 'I fail to see the relevance of this.'

'Surely it's clear, my lord. Myssa the Kushite is to be given every possible assistance.'

'But you are not Myssa the Kushite, are you?'

'No, sir, but I want to give her vital assistance. I insist, on her behalf, that the Blue Crocodile Guards unit that was ordered to protect her should now be allowed to do so.'

Harrar looked at Piay, and there it was: the same total absence of common humanity in his eyes as in Akkan's.

'I have never been formally informed of any such orders being given to our brave guardsmen. And in the absence, and by now, almost certainly the death of Myssa the Kushite, this document' – he tore the scroll in two, and let the pieces drop to the floor – 'is no longer of any relevance or authority. Lord Zahur and I are in charge here. And I have made my decision. I strongly advise you to abide by it, or you, too, may soon suffer the same fate as your woman.'

'Yes, my lord.' Piay choked the words out, then he spun on his heels and marched away with Hannu close behind him.

In the far corner of the garden, out of earshot of anyone in the palace, Piay let out a volley of foul-mouthed insults relating to the parentage of Harrar and his resemblance to various human body parts and excretions. It ended with the words, 'He's no better than Akkan!'

'Huh!' Hannu said. 'That's quite a statement.'

'Well, if Myssa's been killed, they're both dead men.'

'Hey, don't go talking about Myssa being killed. You said it yourself – she's smart, and she can make Akkan and that Cobra fellow feel like they've got to keep her alive.'

'Maybe, but the longer we wait, the harder it'll be for her. We've got to try to get to her today, even if it's only just the two of us.'

'It's been that plenty of times before,' Hannu said.

He craned his neck up at the sky, and Piay knew he was looking at the position of the sun to judge how much time the two of them might have left.

'Hang on,' Piay said. 'Maybe it's not just the two of us. Maybe there's a third . . .'

On the edge of the market, a cloud of dust billowed as two men fought like rabid dogs. Snarling and spitting, they threw each other across the ground, gouging, tearing and rending with dirty fingernails. A crowd swelled around them, roaring in support of one or the other.

Piay glanced at the scuffle as he drifted past. He didn't care to discover what had motivated either of the combatants. It was the third fight he had seen since he had walked out of the palace gates. The city was a bubbling cauldron of anger, a stew formed from want and despair. No one could understand why their plight was not being addressed or their suffering alleviated.

The market was filled with citizens shuffling around as if their shoulders were weighed down by invisible bales, but the blocks where the merchants hawked their wares were mostly deserted. The bread vanished almost as soon as it arrived, and there were no olives at all, no honey, no dates.

The temples were bustling, though. Desperate men and women queued at the gates to make offerings to the gods in the hope of divine intervention. Piay weighed up making a devotion to Khonsu, but there was no time. Right now, he needed mortal men.

The fish market looked as depleted as everywhere else in the city. Piay could not think of any reason why there should not be fish to be caught in the Nile, or salted and transported from the great sea that lay beyond the river delta. But here, too, most of the stalls were deserted, and those that were still operating had only a pitifully small selection to tempt the few customers with the energy, or the means, to come and buy.

Piay found the entrance to the lane that the guard had mentioned. It wasn't hard to find the tavern – halfway down the alley, two drunks were lying flat out on the dirt. Even in the worst of times, there would always be those who had coins to spare for beer and wine.

Just beyond the tavern, Piay saw what he supposed must be his father's house. He'd half-expected a hovel – his father's clothes had been worn, and his slumped shoulders and downcast eyes had suggested someone who had long suffered deprivation. Yet this was a modest but perfectly acceptable dwelling. Asil must be doing better than he pretended, which might also explain the broad-shouldered, unshaven, surly-looking young man who was leaning against the wall beside the door, constantly looking up and down the street for any sign of trouble.

When he saw Piay approaching, the doorman stood erect and glared. He was doing his best to look fierce. But he still had a very long way to go to match Akkan or Khin.

'I'm looking for Asil,' Piay said.

'What's your business?' the man demanded.

Piay cocked an eyebrow. 'He's my father.'

The man did not question the statement. He just nodded and stepped aside.

So, he's been expecting me, Piay thought.

Piay stooped under the lintel and stepped into the cool, dark interior. Embers smouldered in the hearth. There was a low table, but little else.

Asil stepped out of a room at the rear.

'My son,' he said. A smile sprang to his lips.

'Who's that?' Piay asked, glancing back to the door.

Asil shrugged as he gestured for Piay to sit on the floor.

'The son of a friend. These are dangerous times. Since the siege, life here in Memphis has gone from bad to worse. There's not enough to go round. People steal from their neighbours. I don't have much, as you can see' – he swept out an arm to indicate the bare room – 'but I'm an old man, easy prey, and my friends thought it best to keep me safe. We look out for one another. That's all we have now – friendship.'

Piay slumped to the floor and leaned against the clay-brick wall. After the physical and emotional strain of the night and early morning, it felt good to rest. He closed his eyes for a moment and then immediately forced them open again. He had not slept for a full day and night, but he could not afford to give in to his fatigue.

Asil slipped into the room at the rear of the house and returned with a cup of beer, which he offered to Piay. Piay sipped it and felt grateful for the kindness. He eyed the old man, weighing him up.

'You seem troubled,' Asil said, sitting.

'That's because I am.'

'Surely there is no problem that the great Piay of Thebes cannot solve.'

'Those are the words I've lived by all my life. But now . . .' Piay shrugged. 'These days I have something that I can't bear to lose. It means more to me than life itself. And for the first time, I just can't see a way to save it.'

'A woman?'

Piay nodded.

'If you have chosen her, my son, she must be great indeed. Tell me about her.'

Piay sank deep into his thoughts. He found himself talking about Myssa, hesitantly at first, but then the words flooded out of him and he was caught up in a torrent of feelings and memories. Once again, he was there in Sparta, seeing Myssa for the first time as she stood on the slaver's block. Had he sensed then how much she would come to mean to him? A part of him thought that perhaps he had.

'And now she's gone,' he said as he came to the end of his description. 'Captured by a band of Hyksos.'

'I had thought they'd all fled,' Asil said, frowning.

'This lot are searching for buried treasure. Their leader is Akkan, a demon in human form. He believes Myssa can guide him to its location.'

'And can she?'

'If she told the truth, maybe. But she'll be trying to deceive him. You know, to buy time for me to rescue her.'

'So you're here in Memphis searching for treasure.' Asil sipped on his beer.

Piay stiffened. Was his father thinking of how he might turn this information to his own advantage?

'Among other things. That doesn't matter now. All that I care about is Myssa. How do I get her back? There's a detachment of the Pharaoh's guards at the palace. They're supposed to be helping me, but Lord Harrar and Governor Zahur insist on keeping the soldiers for themselves.'

'That doesn't surprise me. I saw them both when they paraded through the streets the other day. I don't know how Zahur dares show himself before people who are starving when he's flabbier than a fattened pig. He's asking for an uprising.' Asil smiled. 'Sorry, got carried away. Let's go back to your problem.'

'It's very simple. How do Hannu and I – two men – defeat a Hyksos warlord and his entire band of warriors before Myssa's deception is discovered and she's killed?'

Swirling the beer in his cup, Asil stared into the depths.

'You know, son, we knew you were special when you were barely more than a babe, your mother and me. When we looked into your eyes we saw something there, some spark that the other children didn't have. When we heard of the great Taita, we thought perhaps he could shape you into a man who could achieve wondrous things. And then . . . And then, perhaps, you would return to us.'

The old man sighed. Piay looked into his father's face, still trying to decide whether his words were a display of sincere affection and regret, or just cold, hard, manipulative deceit.

'Your mother never lived to see it,' Asil continued. 'But she would have been proud, my son – so, so proud – as I am proud of you. I have faith in you. There's a solution to your problem and you will find it. I'm sure of that.' He thought for a moment more, sipped on his beer and then said, 'All right, why don't I tell you what I think about your situation?'

'Go ahead.'

'Right, then. You've got to attack this warlord to rescue your Myssa. But you can't do that because you don't have the numbers, owing to your so-called superiors being flabby-arsed cowards. So, you need to find someone else who will fight for you.'

'Yes, obviously . . . but where am I going to find them? And even if I can find them, how can I pay them? I mean, I can't see anyone risking their necks just out of the kindness of their heart. Why would they?'

'Out of kindness, no, they wouldn't. But they might just do it out of loathing.'

Piay frowned at the old man. 'What do you mean?'

Asil drained the last of his beer and set the cup aside. 'Hard times demand hard things of us. You can't always be honourable or do what other people call the right thing. Not if you want to survive. Let me tell you, I wasn't always a man you'd look up to, Piay. I did terrible things just to reach the next rising of the sun. I'm not proud of it. But I survived, and I'm here now to see my son once again, to praise him for reaching the heights I always knew he would.'

'Thank you,' Piay said, who for the first time since he'd met Asil felt that the old man was speaking from his heart. 'But what has this got to do with me finding Myssa?'

'It's very simple. You are an honourable young man. You don't do business with bad men. You fight them, because you believe in justice and helping those who can't help themselves.'

'You make that sound like a bad thing.'

'Well, what if, in order to defeat one bad man, you had to enlist another one to help you?'

'Why would I do that? And if I did, why would he agree?'

'Because he hates your enemy even more than you do.'

Piay suddenly realised where this was going.

'Tell me, exactly, what you mean by that.'

'I mean that there are two bands of Hyksos near this city, and they are led by two brothers. Both these brothers have taken Egyptian prisoners lately. One of them has taken your woman. The other captured a man, but then his band, who call themselves Shrikes, were ambushed and—'

'Where did you hear this? Who is your spy?'

Asil shrugged. 'I don't have spies. But I have friends who hear things in taverns, and others who pass on information for the price of a meal, or a flask of wine.' Now his eyes hardened. 'I told you, boy, I'm a survivor. And even now, with half the city in ruins and the people starving, I survive. Why? How? Because I make it my business to know more than my competitors. That way I stay ahead of them.

'That's how I know that Khin and Akkan, the two sons of Abisha of Uru-Salim, both have reason to hate you, as you hate them. But the greatest hate of all is between one brother and another. That is the hate that you must harness, like a horse to a chariot, to carry you across the sands to your woman.'

'Are you seriously saying that I should go to Khin and suggest that he join me in attacking Akkan?'

'That is the only suggestion you could make to him without being killed, yes.'

'But it will be hard enough to find Akkan. How can I possibly find Khin, too?'

'As I said to you, my boy, I know more than anyone else in this city – and what I don't know, I can soon find out.'

'And you would do that for me?'

'Of course. I am your father. Why would I not want to help my son? But . . .'

'There's a condition.' Piay sighed. 'There had to be a condition.'

'No, there is an understanding of the world as it truly is. You and I are father and son. But we are also two grown men, doing business. If I do this great favour for you, you must do a favour for me.'

'What is this favour?'

'I don't know . . . But there will come a time when I will call on you, and then you can be a good son to me, as I am now being a good father to you.'

It struck Piay that he was in many ways his father's son. He, too, was a survivor. He, too, prided himself on having the ability to outwit his enemy, perhaps not with knowledge – he left that to Myssa – but with cunning, charm and the capacity to think on his feet. That being the case, he wasn't just going to roll over and give in to his father without at least trying to negotiate with him.

'Surely you are in my debt because I have not taken my revenge on you for the harm you did me when I was a little boy.'

'Harm?' Asil exclaimed. 'What harm was that? If you had stayed with us, you too would have become a slave of the Hyksos. Instead, you've spent half your life in the pharaoh's court, bedding every pretty lass in Upper Egypt—'

'How . . .?' began Piay, and then stopped himself. 'I forgot . . . you have the best information. Though you clearly had no spies in my bedchamber, when I cried myself to sleep every night, or in the classroom, where Taita beat me for the slightest mistake.'

'Taita, the wisest man in all Egypt, beat you because he wanted you to know all that he knew. He is still your patron and protector. What would less fortunate men pay to be as close to him as you are? No, Piay, my dear son, I owe you nothing. So, tell me straight, do you want me to locate Khin and his Shrikes? Are you prepared to accept my terms? And, boy, just remember this . . . the life of the woman you love is resting on your answer.'

'You utter bastard,' Piay said.

Asil smiled. 'Yes . . . and be thankful that you inherited my ruthlessness and determination to win at all costs. I heard they pulled six dead Hyksos from the tomb of Djoser, early this morning. Tell me . . . how many of those did you kill?'

Piay looked him right in the eye. 'Five.'

'Ah . . . That's my boy! Now, do we have a deal?'

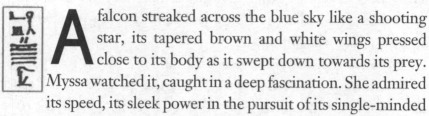 falcon streaked across the blue sky like a shooting star, its tapered brown and white wings pressed close to its body as it swept down towards its prey. Myssa watched it, caught in a deep fascination. She admired its speed, its sleek power in the pursuit of its single-minded vision, and for a while she imagined flying with it.

She lay on a slab of bronze-coloured rock on the edge of the wilderness, looking out across the patchwork of fields and clusters of swaying palms that stretched to the winding river in the hazy distance. The air there was rich with the loamy scents of that fertile zone, and it seemed to her that she felt more at peace than she ever had done in her life.

The Hyksos sprawled around, resting after the long march. Had they been walking for days and days and days, Myssa wondered? It seemed as though they had, but that surely could not be true. Time had lost all meaning.

Stretching like a cat in the heat, Myssa heard someone approaching. When she turned, a towering figure was silhouetted against the sun.

'Here,' Akkan said, offering her a water hide.

Myssa grasped it and swallowed a deep draught, marvelling once again at the sweetness of the water as she had the very first time Akkan had offered her the hide on the trek from the Pyramid of Djoser. She did not know what source he had used to fill the sack, but it tasted better than any water she had ever drunk before.

As she handed the hide back, Myssa frowned at an unusual sight.

'You have two water hides,' she said. 'Why is that?'

Akkan showed a sly smile. 'One for you, and one for me.'

Myssa shrugged. It was an odd thing to say, but she felt no need to question it further. Her thoughts drifted in the cooling breeze blowing along the valley from the north. It seemed to her that she was caught in one of the wavering heat hazes that hung over the desert, her memories indistinct. Who she was and where she had come from mattered little. It was where she was now that was important.

Somewhere nearby, she heard Akkan say, 'She is ready.'

The thump of the Cobra's staff on the ground drew nearer and then his wild mane of hair loomed over her, his black robe seeming to draw in all light so that he appeared little more than a shadow.

'Come with me,' he said in a gentle voice.

'Where are we going?' Myssa asked.

'To meet Seth.'

Myssa couldn't understand why she didn't resist, but she took his hand and allowed herself to be pulled to her feet. Tallus guided her away from the other men, away from those views of the green valley and into the baking wilderness.

A little while later, Myssa looked around and found herself in a bowl-like depression with ochre dust sweeping like a low mist across the base. The only view was of the sky above. In that restricted space, she felt choked by the trapped heat.

'Here is the home of Seth, the god of the desert, the god of war, the god of chaos,' the Cobra intoned.

He lowered his flattened hand and Myssa dropped to the sand and sat cross-legged, looking up at him.

'You are a sorcerer,' she said.

'Of a kind.'

'Are there many like you among the Hyksos?'

Tallus sat cross-legged opposite her. 'I perform a sacred role. It is passed from father to firstborn son, a duty to the god we worship and to our ancestors. We are keepers of the ancient knowledge, of the rites and prayers and spells that can call Seth to aid us. We understand the sacred plants, and the potions that can be made from them.'

'A priest, then.'

'Of a kind.'

'But now you're an advisor to Akkan.' Myssa cocked her head, trying to understand how this work fitted with what Tallus had said.

The Cobra smiled as one would smile at a child. 'The pattern of Seth's plan for his people is hard to see. We Hyksos are a proud race, but filled with yearning. We dream of our ancient home, far away, the vast grasslands that lie beneath the snow-capped mountains. But we travel beyond the furthest horizons. We take Seth with us wherever we go, and his power increases with every new land we conquer.'

Myssa found herself drifting with Tallus' words as if she was in a dream. Deep in her head, she heard a small voice warning her that she wasn't herself – that perhaps she had been poisoned by the water Akkan had given her – but she pushed it away.

The Cobra pulled out a smaller hide pouch and offered it to her.

'Drink some of this,' he said.

'What is it?'

'A potion that our people have carried with us from the earliest days. It is only given to those who have been chosen. It will nourish you, warm you and put strength in your limbs, so you have the power to deal with what is to come.'

Myssa felt uneasy, but she took the pouch and sipped from it tentatively. The first draught tasted bitter, but as it made its way into her stomach a gentle heat flowed with it, just as Tallus had promised.

'What is to come?' she asked.

'You are about to meet Seth, and you will be reborn in his service.'

Myssa felt no fear, felt nothing beyond the soothing warmth spreading throughout her body. Her eyes fluttered shut and when she opened them again, it seemed as if an age had passed.

'Seth is coming,' she heard Tallus saying, though he was no longer in front of her. 'Can you see him?'

'N-no.'

'Seth is coming. Can you see him!' The Cobra's voice boomed all around her.

Myssa jolted and looked up above the ridge of rocks around the bowl. The sky had turned crimson, and against it a vast shadow was rising up and filling her with dread. She heard jackals screaming all around, but she could not tear her eyes away from the shadow. It wavered, took on form and substance, and then she was peering up at the beast-head of the god, and she thought she must faint away from terror.

'The woman you were is gone,' the Cobra was saying. 'All that transpired before this moment means nothing to you. You have no feelings for anyone you once knew. They are nothing. Forgotten. Do you hear me?'

'I . . . I hear you.'

Despite her words, Tallus repeated what he had said, and again, and again, until it became a chant that burrowed deep into her mind.

All Myssa knew was that the terrible face of the god would haunt her for the rest of her days.

There were bright white sails on the river, and the sound of sailors singing to the beat of the sounding poles echoed across the landscape. The wind had dropped on the high ground and the merciless sun beat down on the roasting sand. As she walked back to Akkan and his men, with the Cobra beside her, Myssa looked out at the familiar view. Though nothing had changed, everything seemed transformed, for she was seeing it with new eyes.

'You lied about the location of Imhotep's next sign,' Tallus stated. There was no accusation in his voice, only friendly understanding.

'Yes.'

'We had no doubt that that was the case. We are not fools. You are sharp-witted and cunning. Of course, you would attempt to delay us to buy the others more time.'

'Others?' Myssa felt something prickle in the depths of her mind, as if she was striving and failing to remember a half-forgotten dream.

'You will now tell us the true location,' the Cobra said, ignoring her question.

'I will.'

As she neared the Hyksos warriors, they stood in a semicircle and watched her like vultures waiting for the last gasps of life to depart from their coming meal. Akkan stood in the centre, his arms folded.

'Welcome our new sister, Myssa,' the Cobra called out to the men.

Grins cracked the faces of every man there, except the Child-Killer, whose lips only twitched with amusement. Bast prowled around the edge of the group, but as Myssa leaned down to beckon to her, the feline reared back and hissed before dashing away.

Myssa shrugged and turned back to Akkan. He reached out both of his large hands and Myssa took them, puzzled but not deterred.

'Welcome, sister.' The Child-Killer raised Myssa's hands and kissed the back of each one. 'We have much to talk of, you and I. When camp is made, come to my tent and we will discuss what may be and what should be in the days ahead. But first, a gift.'

Akkan let go of her hands – a little reluctantly, Myssa thought – and dipped into the pouch at his side, removing a bundle of cloth. He shook it out and Myssa saw that it was a dress the colour of the sun, or a golden wheat field, just before the harvest, made of linen so fine that it flowed like water over his skin.

'For you,' the Child-Killer said, 'to befit your status. Let us see you in your splendour.'

Myssa looked around the faces of the men gathered there, seeing cheeks flushed with lust and hungry eyes. She cared little. She had more power than all of them combined. They could not touch her, and their impotent desire only made them weaker. She stripped off her dress, tossing it aside, raising her chin in defiance and letting their eyes range over her hard muscles and soft curves.

As if in a dream, hardly feeling the ground beneath her feet, Myssa stretched out a languid arm, took the dress from Akkan and slipped it on. She looked down at herself and nodded at splash of blazing brilliance against her ebony skin. Those lustful stares had changed now. The gathered men were dazzled, their lips parting with an exhalation of wonder.

Myssa fixed her eyes on the Child-Killer.

'Why are you dawdling?' she said. 'There is work to be done.'

The sky shaded from black to magenta to pink in the east. The stars still glimmered, but the pools of shadow were ebbing away in the hollows among the dunes. Piay and Hannu trudged across the sand with Memphis at their backs.

Piay had been woken in the middle of the night, after a few hours of desperately needed sleep, to be told that a messenger was waiting for him at the palace gates. It was a small boy, his face and legs as grimy as his kilt. He gave Piay the information, which was formed of stars to guide them and landmarks to indicate where they should change course. Then he added, 'Your father said to tell you that you owe him.'

'Send him my thanks, and tell him that I always pay my debts, in equal measure to what I owe.' He looked at the boy. 'Don't forget that part. I pay what I owe, and no more. Got that?'

The boy nodded and ran off through the city. Piay woke Hannu and the two of them filled their water hides, strapped on their sword belts and set off.

'So, you bringing your little friend along?' Hannu had asked.

'Always,' Piay replied.

They left the city through the western gate, telling no one where they ventured – not that Harrar or Zahur would care.

As was his way, Hannu had grumbled that, 'Khem is a full day's march to the north, maybe a bit more. So half a day's march south from there is basically half a day north from here, right?'

Piay had to agree that half of one was, indeed, half.

'Right . . . so what are we doing, marching all night to the west?'

'Because that's where Khin and the Shrikes are.'

'Yeah, but, one, it's mad to walk in the wrong direction, and two, it's even crazier to go and talk to a man who tried to kill you, before we killed a dozen of his men, minimum, and took everything worth having from his mob's baggage.'

'Yes, I agree,' Piay said. 'Both those things are mad, but they're still not quite as mad as trying to beat Akkan by ourselves. That really would be crazy.'

'Yeah . . . I know. But still, just saying . . .'

That issue settled, they walked on in companionable silence. Luckily, Asil's directions were easy to follow. Now they could see the final landmark, the outline of a rocky outcrop that seemed to resemble a jackal at rest. There was said to be a well at the foot of the outcrop, which explained why the Shrikes were camped there.

Hannu turned his head to take in the air.

'I can smell them.'

'Right, then,' Piay replied. 'I'm only going to say this once. This is all just as mad as you said, so you don't have to go any further. I can carry on alone.'

'I'm not walking all this way on one good leg just to stop now,' Hannu replied. 'We're doing this for Myssa. Both of us.'

Piay nodded. 'For Myssa.'

The first rays of the sun were rising in the east as Piay and Hannu walked up the jackal ridge. They crouched as they drew closer before dropping to their bellies and peering over the crest. A guard was perched, cross-legged, on a boulder just below them. He seemed to have been dozing, but when Piay and Hannu appeared as if from nowhere he jolted and jumped to his feet. Jabbing his fingers into the corners of his mouth, he blasted a whistle which rang off the rocks surrounding the depression.

The guard was carrying a spear which he levelled at the new arrivals.

'Stand your ground,' he barked.

'We are here to speak to your leader,' Piay said.

He looked past the guard to where the jumble of tents that made up the Shrike camp nestled at the foot of the hollow. It was just a matter of days since the Blue Crocodile Guards had ambushed the Shrikes. Both Khin and his men would still be smarting from the injuries to their bodies and their pride.

In the camp, figures were dashing out of their tents in answer to the guard's whistle, and soon a steady stream raced up the slope towards where the three men stood.

Piay watched them, noting how different they were from the seasoned warriors of Akkan's band. The Shrikes were dressed in rags, not armour, and they were carrying stolen swords and axes and spears. He had seen for himself that they lacked discipline in battle. Their fearsome reputation came from their savagery – they attacked like a pack of jackals.

Piay and Hannu stood their ground as the Shrikes swept in a circle around them, jabbing at them with their weapons and jeering.

'I know that one,' someone barked. 'He was the captive who summoned those soldiers to attack us.'

'Cut him down now!' someone else bellowed. 'Let's not waste time on him.'

'Harm us and Akh-Seth will take your heads,' Piay boomed. 'We are here to offer him a prize beyond measure.'

The cut-throats wavered, looking to one another for guidance. Without their leader there, none of them was brave enough to make any decision.

'Tell him now that we can bring him the thing he values most in the world,' Piay continued. 'Tell him we can give him the Eye of Horus.'

The Shrikes looked at one another, jabbering, arguing, not knowing what to do. They plainly had no idea what he was talking about. Then one of them took matters into his own hands and smashed his fist into Piay's face. Another clouted Hannu. Then the group fell on their captives, punching and kicking.

'Don't draw your sword!' Piay shouted to Hannu.

The last thing he needed now was any more dead Shrikes. Then he was hit again and as he crashed down, his head spinning, he thought, *I got it all wrong. We're the ones who'll die.*

Then, as suddenly as they had started their assault, someone shouted, 'That's enough, lads!'

The Shrikes stopped punching and kicking and stepped back from Piay and Hannu, who were both lying on the ground, curled up with their arms up to protect their heads.

'Get up!' the voice barked.

Piay did as he was told. He took a look at the man who had saved them, thought, *I know that face,* and immediately realised it belonged to one of Khin's two Hyksos bodyguards.

'What in the name of Seth are you doing here?' the guard asked.

'We've come to make a deal with Khin. He gets everything he wants. I get the most precious thing in my life back.'

'What's that supposed to mean?'

'You must've heard him talk often enough. You know what he's looking for. And you know he wouldn't want me talking about it in front of this lot.'

The guard eyed the Shrikes. Clearly his opinion of them was no higher than Piay's. He nodded.

'Right then, you two come with me. But I'll tell you one thing for sure. The boss isn't going to waste time on Syrian wine and a nice little chat. You give him what he wants or you're dead.'

'Understood.'

They walked down the ridge and into the camp, past several mule carts like the one Piay had been tied to. The Shrikes must have doubled back to collect them on the day of the ambush, once the Blue Crocodile Guards had left the area. They would have found that most of their most precious booty had been taken from them.

One more reason to want us dead, Piay thought.

The smell in the camp was the same as ever, and, when he and Hannu approached Khin's tent, so was the scent of the perfumed smoke drifting from its interior. Piay was shoved hard in the back and fell to his knees. Hannu crashed down beside him with a grunt.

An instant later, the flaps of the tent flew aside and the other Hyksos guard strode out, followed by their leader in his ruby robe. Khin looked down his hawklike nose at the two men sprawled in front of him, his eyes widening when he saw who they were.

Piay stared up at him, watching his expression change from shock to anger. Khin hooked his thumb in the hide belt from which his crescent sword hung as he tried to compose himself.

'I never took you for a fool,' he said eventually.

Piay pushed himself up onto his knees and showed a confident face.

'I'm no fool. I'm here to make you an offer.'

Khin laughed silently. 'You think I'd listen to a word you say? You cost me several men, most of my treasure and all the women we had captured. My men follow me because I bring them warm bodies and cold, hard coins. Now we will have to start all over again. They're not happy about that . . . and neither am I.'

'I have something better to trade.'

Piay glimpsed a look of intrigue on the Hyksos commander's face, but Khin instantly stepped away, as if he were too infuriated to stand still, and began to prowl around his two captives.

'I can't even begin to imagine what goes on in the ringing, empty cavern of your head. Why would you even think you'd be able to deliver your message?' Khin shook his head. 'How can I take a word you say seriously when you'd have to be a total idiot to come here?'

'Or a man so confident of what he has to offer, and how good it is for you, that he's sure you'll want to listen to it.'

Khin stopped his circling and scrutinised Piay.

'What we discussed before?'

Piay nodded.

Khin flexed his fingers and turned back to his tent.

'Bring them,' he barked.

One of the Hyksos warriors hooked his hand under Piay's arm and dragged him into the tent. Hannu followed.

Once they were thrown to the ground, Akh-Seth nodded to his two guards and the flaps were pulled shut. Piay's hands were bound tightly behind his back, his sword was taken from its scabbard and thrown to the floor and, finally, one of the guards stood behind him, holding a knife across his throat. The other guard gave Hannu precisely the same treatment.

'Do not waste my time,' Khin said. 'If I think you're trying trick me, your friend dies. If that doesn't make you talk sense, you follow. And this time, it'll be quick. You'll be dead before you've even got time to plead for mercy. So . . . the Eye of Horus. Give me that or die.'

'That is exactly what I am offering. And this time I'll tell you where it is and who has it.'

'Why now and not before?'

'Because I want something . . . well, someone, too. And that person is in the same place as the Eye.'

Khin came up and stood very close to Piay, so that he could spot the slightest facial clue to his truthfulness.

'Too vague,' he said. 'I need more.'

'Your brother Akkan has the Eye of Horus. He also has Myssa the Kushite, who was carrying it before. When I told you that I did not have it, I was telling the truth – and I am telling the truth now, too.'

Khin's face hardened. 'No . . . I don't believe you.'

He looked in Hannu's direction, pondering whether to give the order to kill him.

'It's the truth!' Hannu exclaimed. 'Believe him!'

Khin looked back at Piay. 'Tell me everything. And remember, you are pleading for your friend's life.'

'You know a lot of the story. Your brother captured one of the Sons of Apis – the tattooed men. They're the guardians of Imhotep's secret. The one that Akkan captured must have been important because he had the Eye of Horus. But Akkan didn't know that. Don't ask me how, but the captive managed to hide it. Then, as you said, Akkan disappeared—'

'Yes, yes,' Khin said impatiently. 'Just tell me something new.'

'Akkan did not disappear. He was with us all the time. Except we knew him as a priest called Shamshi . . . and all I can say is that though they were one and the same man, they also were not. Shamshi was no threat to anyone, while Akkan is, I would say, one of the most frightening men I have ever seen.'

'So it's true . . . Akkan can become his old self. I'd heard that, but you've actually witnessed it.'

'Yes. And I can tell you this. I left the Eye with Myssa, whom I love as much as you hate your brother.'

'Then you love her as much as any man can love a woman.'

'Yes . . . and I saw Tallus, the Cobra, take the Eye from her. Then Akkan and his men took her captive. And I know where she is leading them.'

Khin frowned. 'You say you love this woman, but you let another man take her from you. Either this is not much of a love, or you're not much of a man.'

Piay looked at Khin for a moment, shook his head sadly and said, 'I failed her. In that moment, when I let her be captured, I abandoned her as I had once myself been abandoned. If you think I should be ashamed of that, you're right. And if you imagine that a man who had known such shame would not do anything, no matter how desperate, to make up for what he has done, then you know why I just walked into your camp.'

'Very well,' Khin nodded. 'You've told me about the past. But what next?'

'It's very simple. There's a race going on to answer Imhotep's riddle and grasp the power and treasure it brings. Akkan is winning that race. He has the Eye and he also has the person who best understands how to solve Imhotep's clues. Myssa can make herself think as Imhotep would have done. I've seen her do it. She's already found one clue. Now she'll be trying not to give the next one away. But you know your brother. If anyone can force someone to obey them, it is Akkan.'

'Not just Akkan . . . The Cobra and the blue lotus, too.'

'Well, then, believe me when I say that if nothing is done to stop Akkan, he will win the race, and then we will all be doomed.'

'That may be true. But why would you let me win in his place? You have already led me into one trap. I have no intention of entering another.'

'Because . . .' Piay paused.

What he was about to say would be a betrayal of Taita, of Hannu, and of his entire people. But his life and Hannu's depended on his speaking the truth. So that was what he did.

'It's very simple. I don't care who solves the damned riddle. The only thing that matters to me is Myssa. If I'm with her, then you or your brother can turn all of Egypt into a burning wasteland and I won't care, because I'll be in Paradise. And if I'm not with her, then Egypt can become a paradise, and I won't care about that, either, because I'll be in eternal torment. So, I'll make any deal with anyone, if it means I get her back.'

Khin glanced across at Hannu and, seeing the horrified look on his face, said, 'Your friend believes you . . . and maybe he is now not your friend. So, what is your plan?'

'Simple. I know where Myssa is leading Akkan. Not exactly, but close enough that if you send out scouts, one of them will find Akkan, the Cobra and the rest. Then we attack them. Even allowing for your losses when our guards attacked, you should still have enough men to overpower your brother's forces.'

'Suppose I do that. If my brother and the Cobra are dead and the Eye of Horus is in my hand, why should your woman help me solve the puzzle?'

For a moment, Piay was dumbfounded. He suddenly realised that he had been thinking so hard about his needs that it had not occurred to him to consider what Myssa might think.

'Because . . . uh . . . Well, because she will be doing that to save me, just as I have saved her.'

Khin smiled. 'Ah, now that is the biggest of all the risks you are taking – relying on the will of a woman. How do you know that she loves you as much as you love her? You may be willing to abandon all your principles, but what if she is not so easily swayed?'

'She loves me, I know she does,' Piay said, realising as he did so that he was trying to convince himself as much as Khin.

'Hmm . . .' Khin murmured, a sceptical expression on his face. 'I fear I may have to persuade her, but no matter. My brother is not the only man who knows how to make people do what he wants. So, one last question – what about the Blue Crocodile Guards? Are they getting ready to ambush me again?'

'If they were, I would have brought them with me today. Instead, they're stuck in Memphis, playing nursemaid to Lord Harrar and Governor Zahur.'

The words were spoken with a genuine anger that seemed to give Khin the final reassurance he needed.

'Very well, then,' he said. 'I will move against my brother. As for you two, I will have your hands unbound, but I will keep your swords. And remember this – you are both still only one lie, one false move, away from your deaths.'

Myssa was awoken by her own shivering. She could see that the sun was rising. She knew that the heat of the day had not yet come and that the air was still cool. But the cold she felt now was something else. It came from deep inside her. Her head ached, too, and when she placed a hand to her forehead it was sweaty and burning hot. When she swallowed, her mouth was parched and her throat felt as though it was being scraped by thorns.

She could not understand what was happening to her. How could she be burning up and yet feel so cold? Was this some kind of fever?

It was only when she lifted the heavy woollen blanket that had covered her during the cold desert night that she became aware of Akkan's naked body, lying next to where she had been sleeping.

Myssa closed her eyes and tried to recall what had happened. She could not remember what – if anything – they had done together. And she didn't care. She was still entirely naked, but she didn't care about that, either.

Her entire focus was on the two water hides, which were placed on the ground, just beyond Akkan, on the far side of the bedding. But when she tried to stand up, Myssa felt dizzy and unsteady. Her head was as heavy as a boulder, so that her neck could barely hold it up. And when she tried to walk, her feet and legs were numb, so numb that she could barely lift them.

All she knew was that she had to have some water, so she fell to her knees and crawled around the bed. A man was standing, watching her, but she barely registered his presence.

Finally, Myssa reached the water hides. Still on her hands and knees, she looked at them, unable to remember which held the sweet, sweet water she craved so deeply. She reached out for one of the hides, but as she did so the man who was watching her spoke in his deep, gravelly voice.

'You want the other one.'

Obeying his command, Myssa took the other hide, pulled out the stopper and lifted the spout to her lips. The moment the water touched the back of her throat, the rasping she had felt there just melted away. A few seconds later the warmth that the water brought her was bringing her body back to life. And then came the blissful sense of seeing the world in all its beauty, more clearly than ever before, and at the same time being free of all its cares and troubles.

Myssa felt at peace. She looked back at Akkan. His body looked magnificent, like a sleeping lion: peaceful now, but terrifyingly powerful once awoken. She took another long drink, and was about to have a third when the hide was taken from her hand.

'That's enough,' Tallus said. 'The lotus is a fickle mistress. Take too much from her and she will kill you for your greed.'

The sound of the Cobra's voice had awoken Akkan. He propped himself up on one elbow and gave Myssa a lazy, half-awake smile. Just for an instant she saw another man in him – one who could be kind and gentle.

Akkan looked up at Tallus. 'You never told me how the lotus affects women,' he said.

'I confess, I did not know. I have never before guided a woman along its path.'

Akkan looked at Myssa, seeming to penetrate deep into her, and said, 'It softens them. It warms them. It opens them up so that they're . . .' He paused, searching for the right words, and Myssa felt sensations deep inside her, echoes of last night's pleasure that told her all she needed to know, as Akkan said, 'Helpless . . . and insatiable.'

Myssa didn't care. The sweet water had made her immune to anyone's opinions but her own. Her dress was lying where she had discarded it the night before. She walked to it and slipped it on. And now she felt the final gift that her water brought her: a sense of her own freedom and power.

He thinks he possesses me now, Myssa thought. *No one possesses me.*

Once again she sensed that faint memory, deep in her mind, of someone whom she had allowed to take her, body and soul, and whom she had taken in return. But it was as fleeting as a scent, caught on the wind and then blown away.

Akkan had risen to his feet and put on his kilt. He was buck-ling his sword belt as Myssa walked up to him and said, 'We must march towards Khem. Imhotep's clue is within marching distance of the city. I will know it when I see it. But it may be hard to find.'

Akkan eyed Myssa suspiciously. The lion had awoken. He was all danger and menace now.

'What do you mean?'

Myssa approached him and laid a hand on his arm, feeling the size and power of its muscles.

'Simply that the Great Architect did not leave this clue in a temple, or pyramid, or any kind of building. We will find it in a hole in the ground.'

'Is this a trick? Are you hiding something from me?'

Myssa stroked her fingers down Akkan's arm. She looked up at his face and said, 'Consider what you just told Tallus. Am I hiding anything – anything at all – from you?'

Khin and his men trekked north-eastwards across the sweltering wastes in the direction of the Nile, some way north of Memphis, but still well south of Khem. In their threadbare, filthy robes with scarves tied around their heads, the Shrikes trudged on. They had clearly learned from their last encounter with Piay, for they did their best to confine their advance to wide open spaces, going out of their way to avoid broken ground where enemies could be hiding, ready to ambush them again.

As the day drew to a close, Piay shielded his eyes and could just make out the dark smudge of vegetation on the horizon that marked the fertile valley that edged the Nile. It would soon be time to turn due north, and march directly towards Khem.

Up ahead of Piay and Hannu, at the head of the column, Khin held up his hand and one of his warrior-guards blasted a whistle. The column came to a halt.

'What now?' Hannu grumbled. 'The sooner we get to that dog Akkan, the sooner this can be over.'

Piay watched Khin whisper into the ear of his second-in-command and then the man moved down the column, barking out orders. The Shrikes nodded with eagerness, giving gap-toothed grins and clapping their hands together.

'Why have we stopped?' Piay asked, striding up to Khin.

'My men can't be expected to fight on an empty stomach,' Akh-Seth replied. 'This march has made them hungry and tired. They must eat well, and rest, to be ready for what this night brings.'

Piay followed Khin's gaze across undulating fields of wheat to a small farm. It was well-tended, despite the war that had raged across this land in recent times. His heart sank.

Khin must have seen Piay's feelings on his face, for he gave a contemptuous chuckle.

'Come. You are a fighting man. Don't tell me you've never killed anyone who was helpless, or innocent, or just happened to get in your way at the wrong moment.'

'Every man I killed deserved it,' Piay said. 'We met in battle as equals.'

'Ah, but you know what Shrikes are like. They kill for sport, like a cat kills mice. Do you expect them to change their nature? My men will take from that farm what they need and then we will move on, so that you and I can take what we need. That's how the world works.'

Piay knew then that he had damned himself by finding an ally in a man he knew to be a killer.

I'm no better than my father, he thought. *Maybe that's why he gave me Khin's location. He wanted to drag me down to his level.*

'Join my men in their raid,' Khin said, enjoying Piay's discomfort.

'I'll wait here. Let them do what they want and then we can move on.'

'If you don't join them, you can't eat.'

Piay felt his belly growl. It had been a very long time since his last decent meal, but he'd made enough moral compromises for one day. He wasn't backing down on this.

Khin tugged at his oiled beard, pleased with himself.

'Suit yourself. We'll see how long it takes for hunger to change your mind.'

He clapped his hands to gain the attention of the Shrikes and then, with a whistle, he flicked his fingers towards the farm.

Like ravenous beasts, the cut-throats dropped low as they prowled forward, with knives and axes in their hands. Piay felt sickened by the cruel glee on their filthy faces.

As the last man moved away, Khin called to him, whispering something in his ear before sending him on his way.

'This will be over in no time,' he said to Piay. 'These farmers have no idea how to defend themselves.'

The Shrikes disappeared into the wheat field and crept unseen towards their prey along irrigation ditches and through the waist-high crops. For a while the farmland looked as peaceful as when Piay had first seen it, but then he glimpsed a distant figure crawl up to the neat white walls of the farm. The lone Shrike waited there, sniffing the air and listening. Then, when he was sure, he raised one arm and waved.

With a great roar, the Shrikes burst from the field, racing across a dusty track and flooding through the gates. From within the walls, screams rang out, drowned out in an instant by the howls of delight of the attacking men.

'Don't punish yourself.' Hannu stood at Piay's elbow, his voice low.

'Is this who we are? Standing by watching while innocent farmers are attacked . . . just to get what we want? Have I betrayed Taita?'

Hannu had no answer. Piay watched, refusing to tear his eyes away from the unfolding scene. Bearing witness was the least he could do. The memory would remain with him for life: his punishment, and, perhaps, his lesson.

Soon a plume of smoke curled up into the clear blue sky, and then flames licked up through the roof of the farm. The crackle turned into a roar as everything the farm-folk had worked for was consumed by fire.

Then the Shrikes surged back out of the gates, jeering and whooping, their arms filled with bread, cheese and whatever other supplies they had raided from the kitchens. Behind them, a few of their number were herding three huddled figures away from the burning building. Piay saw a man in a grey kilt, a woman wearing a drab brown dress and a girl. At least that family had not been slaughtered in their home, but why were the Shrikes bringing them to their master?

Piay sensed that Khin was watching him intently, but he refused to meet the Hyksos commander's eyes.

The Shrikes carved paths through the field, not caring who saw them now. When they reached their master, they offered up their booty. Khin had his guards take some bread, olives and wine, and then flicked his hand to the rest of his men to divide their spoils among themselves.

As the Shrikes fell upon the stolen food, Khin beckoned for the farmer, his wife and daughter to approach him. The two women juddered with sobs, tears streaming down their cheeks, but the farmer kept his eyes down, sullen. He knew, as did Piay, that they had been brought here for a reason.

Khin tore off a chunk of flatbread and swallowed it, then stood and looked across at his feasting men.

'You have done well, brothers,' he called. 'Another great victory.'

He turned his gaze to Piay and his lips widened into a smile of contempt.

'But you!' Khin boomed, so the Shrikes could hear. 'You think you are a better man than us, just doing all we can to survive in this harsh world. Do you think you are better?' Khin pressed. 'Better than me, perhaps, the great and power-ful Akh-Seth?'

'That's not for me to decide,' Piay said. 'I only have my own code – that men should not prey on the weak, the defenceless.

Those who do that aren't strong, they're weak and cowardly and the gods will surely judge them.'

Piay half-expected Hannu to be nudging him to hold his tongue, but when he glanced at his assistant, Hannu's face was hard with defiance, too.

Khin nodded. 'Your code, eh? All right, then, let's see you live by it.' He wagged his finger at the three captives. 'One of these three must die, so that all who live in these parts will fear the Shrikes and cower when we visit them.'

After an instant of shock, the women's wails erupted like the sound of keening birds. They pressed their hands together and shook them in desperate pleas for mercy. The father stared at the ground, the blood draining from his face.

'Choose this one,' Khin said, pointing at the father. 'The one who works the land from dawn to dusk to ensure his wife and daughter do not starve. The one who provides. Or choose this one . . .'

Khin shifted his finger to indicate the mother.

'The one who offers comfort and care, so the father is free to labour and so her daughter is guided into a good life where she can survive and thrive. Or this one . . .'

Khin wagged his finger at the daughter.

'The hope for the future. Choose her, and her father and mother will be condemned to a life of bleak days and a joyless tramp towards the grave. Choose now. Their fate is on your head.'

Piay looked past the captives towards the burning farm, refusing to engage.

'And if you do not choose one, all three will die,' Khin added with a smirk.

The father stepped forward.

'Take me.'

'No!' The wife wrenched the man back. 'My husband can care for my daughter. I have no value here!'

'Mother! Father! Stop!' the daughter wailed. She thrust herself forward so that her desperate face filled Piay's vision. 'Save them, I beg of you,' she pleaded. 'I could not live knowing that I had cost one of them their life.'

Piay looked at the three faces and then turned to Khin.

'All three of these good people are better than you. Better by far.' He looked across the group of feasting Shrikes and boomed, 'Better than all of you!'

'Which one?' Khin laughed.

Suddenly his feelings of guilt overwhelmed Piay and he said, 'Forget them. Kill me in their place.'

Khin just laughed. 'What – and lose my best chance of becoming a god among men? Oh no, I need you. And you need to choose. One dies, or all die.'

So here he was, the son following in his father's footsteps, obliged to do something unforgivable because the alternative was even worse.

Piay looked at the family, his voice breaking.

'I'm sorry,' he said. 'I'm so, so sorry.'

The mother, who was calmer now, as people often are when their own death is very near, said, 'It is not your fault. We understand.'

Her forgiveness only made it harder for Piay to forgive himself. He closed his eyes, unable to look at the poor, defenceless people in front of him as he said, 'Take the father.'

Piay opened his eyes and made himself watch as the father was marched a few paces away from his family and forced to his knees. He listened as the condemned man offered up his last prayers to the gods. Then he saw the curved blade of the Hyksos swords cut so deeply into the front of his throat that his head flopped backwards, his eyes staring blindly at the darkening sky.

And as the woman and her daughter rushed to the dead body, Piay realised that there was only one way in which he could begin to make amends for his part in this murder. He had allowed himself to be so carried away by his passion for Myssa that he had forgotten the mission with which Taita, his master, had entrusted him.

It was his sworn duty to follow the clues left by Imhotep and solve the Riddle of the Stars. He therefore had to rescue Myssa, not for the sake of his love for her, but because she was essential to the success of his quest.

For a moment, Piay almost felt grateful to Khin for leading him to this new-found commitment to his proper cause.

But not so grateful, he thought, *that I won't happily kill you, or anyone like you, in order to get what I want.*

There was barely any light in the sky, but from the ridge where Piay and Hannu were standing, along with Khin and his two Hyksos bodyguards, it was still just possible to see the ancient city of Khem away in the distance.

'What do you think?' Piay asked Hannu. 'Does that look like half a day's march away?'

'Maybe a little more, but it's about right.'

'I think so, too.'

Piay did his best to sound casual, but the truth was that his guts were as tight as a clenched fist. This was the point of maximum risk. Once he gave Khin the location that Myssa had whispered in his ear, he was revealing the secret that had ensured his survival up to this point. There were reasons for keeping him alive a while longer, but Khin might not agree.

He's been wanting to do it from the moment we met, Piay thought. *He might not be inclined to put it off any longer. But if I don't tell him, it's a certainty that he kills me. So . . .*

He turned to Khin.

'Myssa told me that she would lead Akkan to a point half a day's march south of Khem. That point would be close to the location of the next clue, but not actually there. I guess she was thinking that she could delay Akkan a little longer.'

'That is not very precise,' Khin said. 'Everything we see before us is south of Khem.'

'Just what I said,' Hannu piped up.

'Yes,' Piay agreed, 'and I will repeat what I said to Hannu. Akkan and his men will be leaving a trail. If scouts are sent out from here, there is a good chance that at least one of them will find that trail and follow it to wherever Akkan is spending the night.'

'If they do not,' Khin said, 'I will take that as proof that you lied to me. And you know what will happen then.'

Five of Khin's best men were dispatched. The moon journeyed more than halfway across the starry sky as one by one they returned. None brought any news. Piay and Hannu tried to keep their spirits up by sharing funny memories of their adventures together, but the threat of imminent death loomed ever closer. At last Piay heard the faint whisper of approaching feet and saw a shadowy figure emerging from the darkness.

Piay took a deep breath. 'Here we go,' he whispered to Hannu.

The fifth scout looked around, spotted Khin, ran straight to him and spoke his news into his master's ear.

'Get ready to run,' Hannu said, and then, 'By the gods, I wish we had our swords.'

'Well, they never took my little friend,' Piay said. 'So that's a start.'

Piay watched Khin whisper an order to one of his guards, which was instantly passed down the line. The Shrikes melted away into the field on the other side of the track.

Khin gestured to Piay. 'You told me the truth, so you live . . . for now.'

'Can we have our swords back?'

'And what is there to stop you from sticking them in my back?'

'No more than stops you doing the same to me. We are about to take on Akkan and his men. Both of us will have better things to do than fight each other. And if we each get what we want, then we can go our separate ways – for good.'

Khin considered what Piay had said for a second, then told one of the two guards to fetch the swords. Emboldened by his success, Piay asked, 'Do you have a plan of attack?'

'Yes.'

'And . . .?'

'I will send all of my men against all of my brother's men, like a flood, wave after wave. His men are better, but there are more of mine. Meanwhile, you with your friend and me with my two friends' – Khin emphasised the 'two', by way of a reminder that a double-cross was inadvisable – 'can go looking for my brother, your woman and that venomous priest.'

'Won't Akkan be fighting with his men?'

Khin laughed. 'And risk the Eye of Horus? No, he will hold back, just as he did that night outside Thebes, ready to disappear again if things go badly.'

'Except that you will take him by surprise before he can do that.'

'Exactly . . . and you can go after your woman.'

Piay knew – as Khin surely did, too – that there was no chance of the two of them simply clasping hands and bidding each other a fond farewell if the battle went as planned. Each would want what the other had. But that fight could not happen unless the first fight, against Akkan, was won.

For now, at least, they would be allies.

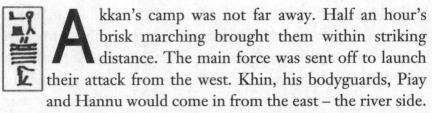**A**kkan's camp was not far away. Half an hour's brisk marching brought them within striking distance. The main force was sent off to launch their attack from the west. Khin, his bodyguards, Piay and Hannu would come in from the east – the river side.

The Nile was not far away now, and Piay could smell the water. After a little while, he heard the faint rumble of voices. Light spilled through a wall of acacia bushes.

Khin beckoned Piay to come forward to join him.

Piay dropped to his hands and knees and crawled to the edge of the acacias. He could smell the pitch from the torches and hear the gentle gurgle of the river as it eddied along the banks on its journey to the sea.

The voices, too, were clearer. Two of them were having a debate about diving into the depths. Piay could not make out what depths those might be, but he was sure he could hear an edge of frustration in those voices.

'I thought you said your woman wasn't bringing Akkan to the site of the clue,' Khin whispered.

'That's right.'

'Well, either she lied, or he forced her, because I reckon they're looking for it right here.'

Piay strained to hear Myssa's voice, but all those speaking were men. He told himself that was no cause for concern, but still a part of him began to worry.

Khin gave a short jab of his forefinger and they both pushed further into the shrubs to get a better look. Piay pressed down a branch just enough to get a clear view. The torches sizzled at the heart of a small camp. Some tents had been erected on the far side of what looked like a hole in the ground. More Hyksos were gathered in front of the tents, eating, drinking, talking, and occasionally casting glances towards their half-dozen comrades gathered around the hole.

Some of those men stood with hands on hips, peering into its depths. Others were squatting on the ground. Two of the men wore robes, rather than military tunics and breastplates. Piay remembered seeing robes like that at the necropolis. They must be priests of some kind, acolytes of the Cobra.

Piay recognised other faces he had seen that night, but he could not spot Akkan or Myssa, nor hear their voices. He prayed the Shrikes did not attack until he had discovered where his love might be, and taken her to safety.

There was still no sign of the Shrikes, either, though Piay knew that they must be lurking in the fields, ditches and under-growth, no more than fifty paces – if that – from the camp. As chaotic as they might be in some aspects of soldiering, their capacity for stealth was remarkable.

'Do we drag him out?' one of the Hyksos warriors was saying.

He leaned forward and looked into the hole, though it must surely have been too dark to see anything.

Another warrior shrugged. 'Might as well. What's the point of waiting?'

The first warrior grunted and said, 'Give me a hand, then.'

As they stooped, Piay noticed a hide rope running into the hole, anchored by a bronze peg hammered into the earth. The two warriors grasped the rope, braced themselves and heaved.

The other men clustered closer, peering into the depths. Their bodies formed a wall, so Piay could not see the activities of the two men hauling on the rope, but from their grunting he could tell that whatever it was on the other end was heavy, and from the time it took them to complete their task, that the hole was deep.

Piay was gripped by the activity. Surely a hole that deep so close to the river would be full of water. How, then, could they drag *him* out?

Finally the other warriors moved away as whoever was emer-ging neared the top. Heaving on the rope, the two labourers stepped back until they were almost inside one of the tents.

Then, with a sudden jolt and a slapping of wet skin on the muddy earth, a body emerged out of the hole. The two warriors hauled on the rope until the remains were fully out, face down in the soil. Dead. Without a doubt.

Squinting, Piay scrutinised the poor soul, trying to draw out details in the fading light. He was not one of the Hyksos, Piay was sure of it. The shaven head and the filthy, sodden kilt told him it was one of the farmers from the nearby fields. Why had they killed him in such a bizarre way? Was it some kind of punishment, or torture?

'Look – something's attacked him,' one of the men said, pointing.

The dead man's left foot was missing, the ankle gnawed.

'Crocodile,' another said, emphatically.

Piay glanced at Khin, who was frowning at the scene. He shook his head, baffled. When Piay looked towards Hannu, he looked equally bemused.

Folding his arms, one of the warriors stared down at the body and shrugged.

'Nothing for it but to throw him with the others.'

The others? Piay furrowed his brow. *Why are Akkan's men drowning farmers in a hole?*

Whatever he had expected when he found these treasure-hunters, it was not this.

Khin tapped Piay on the shoulder. He mouthed, as much as spoke, 'Akkan's not here. Going to find him.'

He and his guards disappeared, but as they left, one of the guards stepped on a twig that broke under his weight. The little crack was enough to get the attention of one of the Hyksos warriors.

'What's that?' he asked, looking almost exactly towards the bushes where Piay and Hannu were now lying flat on the ground with their heads down.

'Probably just a rat, or a fox,' one of his comrades said.

'Or the crocodile that ate this poor bastard,' said a third, making all his comrades laugh.

Piay waited a few moments, then very cautiously raised his head. The men around the hole had all turned their heads in another direction, and Piay soon saw why – they were looking towards the oncoming figure of Tallus, the Cobra.

In his black robe, and with his wild, silver-streaked black hair and beard, he looked like a pool of shadow in the torchlight. He came to a halt and stared down at the body, one hand gripping his long staff with the crescent atop it.

'You have failed again,' he said in his low voice.

Under his heavy brows, his eyes were lost to darkness, but when he looked from face to face each man shifted in discomfort.

'Once they're in the hole, they thrash like a fish on a line,' one of the men protested from the back. 'It's the fear – drives them mad.'

'Then perhaps one of you fearless men should do it,' Tallus said in a calm voice.

The man who had spoken bowed his head.

'Go and tell your master that he is needed here,' the Cobra said. 'It is time to make a decision.'

Piay felt his chest tighten. The only master here was Akkan. But there was still no sign of Myssa – and where were the Shrikes? Had Khin lost his nerve now that the prospect of confronting his terrifying brother was a reality? When he left, was he really just running away?

The man who had been sent to fetch Akkan ran back to the group. Soon after, Piay sensed movement on the far side of the camp. But as he stared he realised there was not one figure but two.

His heart began to thump so hard he thought his enemies might hear it.

The Cobra stepped to one side and Akkan walked towards the circle of warriors and wise men. But all Piay's attention was focused on the shadow just beyond Akkan's shoulder. His blood pounded harder, matching the beat of the silent prayer he was uttering. Then the torchlight glistened on soft, dark skin, and he felt a rush of relief so powerful he thought it would wash his wits away.

It was Myssa. She was still alive, seemingly unharmed. Akkan had not broken her. On the contrary, she held her head up as proudly as ever. Piay felt overwhelmed by his love for Myssa. He had never doubted her strength, not for an instant, and her mind was sharp enough to find ways out of any trap set for her. But he knew what the Child-Killer was capable of and that had filled him with a fear so deep that he could only now bring himself to admit it.

Yet when she stepped fully into the torchlight, Piay felt surprised. Myssa was now wearing a dress of brilliant yellow, quite unlike the one she had been wearing when Akkan captured her.

Now, in his tumbling emotions, Piay felt his anger simmer. Had Akkan offered Myssa this fine dress as a bribe to convince her to do his work for him? Or had the warlord dressed Myssa to show her off as his prize?

Piay gritted his teeth. He wanted so badly to separate Akkan's head from his body. He glanced at Hannu and saw that he thought the same. They were ready.

Then a throat-rending cry tore through the night. An instant later, frantic activity erupted on all sides as the Shrikes thundered into the camp, all of them howling war cries that merged into one great roar. As they raced forward, the Shrikes shook their plundered weapons, those dented swords and stained spears, the filthy rags that clothed them reeking of sweat and blood and mud.

The Hyksos warriors had been caught off guard, but they reacted with the speed of seasoned veterans. They snatched out their crescent swords and whirled into a circle with Akkan, Myssa and the Cobra at the centre.

As the first of the Shrikes dashed forward, whirling his sword above his head, one of the Hyksos warriors swept his blade, backhanded, across his attacker's exposed abdomen, tearing open his belly. The Shrike's battle cry became a howl of pain and he fell to the ground, his hands clasped to his body, desperately trying to contain the guts spilling out through the open wound.

Other Hyksos were dispatching their enemies with similar efficiency, but some were being overpowered, and for every Shrike that fell, two more appeared in the clearing to take his place. Piay waited, biding his time for the moment when – he hoped, he prayed – he could take advantage of the confusion, slip through the Hyksos defences and snatch Myssa from the heart of the circle.

She was still completely calm, Piay saw. His pride in her grew even greater. Akkan, too, looked self-assured, still confident in his men. Or was it his faith in Seth and the power the god had given him that gave the Child-Killer such certainty in his capacity to survive?

Piay could not spot Khin anywhere. He, too, must be biding his time, waiting for that one moment when Akkan could be caught unawares.

The fight raged on and Piay watched a Hyksos warrior being assailed by four attackers, their axes hacking as if they were cutting fresh wood in a shipyard. Unable to defend himself from every strike, the warrior collapsed under the assault.

Piay braced himself. Soon . . . soon. He looked at Akkan even more closely, wondering where, precisely, to stab his hidden dagger when the moment came.

The Shrikes were still flooding into the camp, fresh meat replacing the slaughtered. There couldn't be many of them still waiting in the night. But as the latest wave crashed into the camp, Piay glimpsed something that chilled his blood.

White foam frothed from the mouth of one of the Shrikes at the rear, stark against skin almost black with filth. His eyes spun and he reeled into the torchlight before collapsing to the ground, racked with convulsions.

Piay gasped, but he already understood what he was seeing.

Caught up in the brutal battle for life, no one seemed to notice the fallen Shrike. But then others clutched at their throats, gagging and choking, falling to their knees, crashing face down, dying without a single hand laid upon them.

'Oh no, that's all we need,' Hannu muttered. 'The Sons of Apis have arrived.'

As one, the attacking Shrikes realised their comrades were falling around them, untouched by any weapon. Terror was etched into their faces and they lurched away from the battle with the Hyksos, for they were mere mortals and now some supernatural force surely assailed them.

Akkan's men would not be distracted by such a sight, Piay knew, and he was right. The warriors seized their moment, hacking down those Shrikes now caught between death on both sides. The thieves and murderers fell in their ones and twos, their blood soaking into the rich, fertile soil, desperate to flee but afraid of whatever waited for them in the night.

Victory was within Akkan's grasp.

Piay crept to the edge of the shrubs, ready to make his move. The perfect moment had not arrived. Now he would just have to count on the element of surprise, and the good luck with which he had been blessed in so many battles.

But before he could move, a howl rose up somewhere deep in the night like a beast caught in the convulsions of death. It swept closer and closer, and then Khin crashed out of the undergrowth, his hands waving in the air, his face twisted with such terror it seemed he had no wits left. His ruby-red robe swirled around him as he ran, and his hands and face were the same colour, though whether it was his blood or someone else's, Piay could not be certain.

So terrified was the great and powerful Akh-Seth that he thundered past the poisoned Shrikes and into the very orbit of his hated brother. Piay glimpsed Akkan give a contemptuous grin.

He hooked one foot under Khin's legs and as the Shrike leader crashed down, the Child-Killer stepped over him and pressed the tip of his blade against the back of his brother's neck.

'Stay down,' he barked. 'Move and you die.'

From the direction Khin had fled, another figure staggered to the fringes of the torchlight. It was one of the Hyksos guards. His skin had turned as black as ebony from whatever poison coursed through his veins, and blood sprayed from his mouth as he hacked painfully. In his left hand he held the head of the other Hyksos guard.

The few remaining Shrikes backed away as if he had the plague, straight into the flashing blades of the Hyksos war band.

The blackened guard crashed to his knees, hovered there and then tipped forward, dead.

The grim scene was not yet over. Piay sensed movement in the darkness beyond the acacia. Figures floated like ghosts, wrapped in the interplay of shadow and moonlight. The Sons of Apis hovered there on the fringes of perception, pale faces turned into death's heads by those black tattoos. Silent. Summoning dread by their very presence.

Their leader stepped forward, surveying the camp with the same cold attention that Piay had witnessed that night when the hood had been ripped from his head in the palace in Thebes. With a gradual movement, he raised his right hand. His fingers curled around whatever he was holding.

'Protect yourselves!' the Cobra roared.

The warriors and the wise men tore at the scarves hanging around their necks and wrapped them across their noses and mouths.

Would that debilitating dust the Sons had released in the palace of Thebes still cloud men's minds out there in the open, where the slightest breeze would whisk it away? Piay wasn't sure, but the leader of the Sons seemed confident enough. His gaze didn't waver, and as he stood there his men pushed forward through the vegetation.

'How many of you are prepared to die?' Akkan roared.

He pulled his sword away from his brother's neck and stepped in front of his men, levelling his blade at the cult's leader.

The two men looked at each other, neither feeling the need to speak. One of the Hyksos warriors, panicked by all that had just happened, hurled a throwing-spear at the tattooed figure.

The spear was well-aimed. It was heading straight for its target's chest.

The Son of Apis did not appear to move a muscle. His gaze never left Akkan's. Yet the spear flew harmlessly past him.

Piay had been waiting for the tattooed man to fill the air with his poison dust. But then he realised that he felt no need to do that. He was sending a message to Akkan: we can kill you and all your men just as easily as we killed these Shrikes.

Then two more thoughts tumbled into Piay's mind.

He's not even trying to get the Eye back. He wants it to be out there, being fought over. That weakens all those who are trying to solve the riddle.

And then, cutting through his speculations, another, more urgent realisation.

This is the time!

The Hyksos' defensive circle had fallen apart. Now Akkan, his warriors and the Cobra were gathered in a line, their entire attention fixed on the tattooed man and the Sons of Apis lurking, unseen, behind him. Myssa stood behind Akkan and the Cobra, watching the two men at the centre of the drama. This was the perfect moment to rescue her.

Hannu knew it, too. When Piay nodded to him, they eased back through the shrubs and crept along the track that led towards the river. As they rounded the edge of the copse of acacia, Piay caught a clear view through the camp, with the backs of the Hyksos war band turned towards him.

He pressed his finger to his lips and then crept forward between two tents. The torches were dying down now, the circle of amber light closing in on Akkan's men and Myssa. The dark seemed to grow deeper and more impenetrable beyond it.

Here was his chance.

Piay waved his left hand to signal to Hannu to hold back, and then he crawled away from the tents without making the slightest sound, keeping low so any movement would not catch the edges of any of his enemies' vision. No one flinched. The Sons of Apis had not moved, nor had they retreated. Khin continued to lie face down, his hands over his head as if he could deny the existence of whatever had terrified him in the night by keeping his eyes averted.

Myssa watched the stand-off, as rigid as all the others. She, too, knew the threat the Sons of Apis posed. Piay weighed how he could gain her attention without extracting any cry of surprise.

His heart pounding, he crept on until he was level with the hole in the ground, his senses filled with the reek of the dead body. Reaching out a steady hand, he touched the hem of Myssa's dress – the merest brush, not enough to startle her but enough, he hoped, to get her to look round.

She did not respond. Piay tried again. This time she shivered with awareness and glanced back.

When she saw him, her eyes widened, but she did not start. Piay felt a flood of relief. Instead she wrinkled her nose – in puzzlement, it seemed, almost as if she was trying to comprehend how he had got there.

Piay pressed a finger to his lips again and beckoned as he backed towards the tents.

His intention could not have been clearer. Yet Myssa remained rigid, staring at him. Piay beckoned again, more furiously this time.

Why is she not following? Is she afraid of being caught? That is not like Myssa.

Then her eyes glittered and her face hardened. She whirled around, crying out, 'An enemy! Here, among us!'

Piay gasped, disbelieving. Ahead, Akkan and some of the wise men glanced back and saw Piay crouched there.

The leader of the Sons of Apis silently turned on his heels and walked away, his message delivered, taking his men with him. Now Akkan had just one more, far less imposing threat to deal with.

Piay's thoughts tumbled over themselves as he struggled to understand what he was witnessing. He lunged to grasp Myssa's wrist and pulled her back towards the tents. Yet Myssa only dug in her heels and wrenched her arm back.

'You will not take me!' she spat.

'Myssa, I beg you!' Piay pleaded. 'This is our last chance!'

'I will not go with you!' Myssa's eyes blazed with what looked like loathing.

Piay felt as if he had turned to stone, and in the time it took him to recover his wits, he realised he had lost his chance to escape.

'You should have kept running.' A smile ghosted Akkan's lips, as cold and cruel as the man himself. 'That would have been the action of a wise man.'

Piay peered deep into Myssa's eyes, desperate to see something that could explain her rejection of him. Nothing else mattered at that point, not Akkan, not the Sons of Apis nor the quest for Imhotep's secret: just Myssa.

But there was no respite. Those eyes told a deep and painful truth. In the short time they had been apart, Myssa had turned away from him.

'She has made her own choice. You have lost her to a stronger man, someone who can give her what she desires.' Akkan paused, letting the words that were to come gather weight. 'She is to become my bride.'

Piay reeled. That could not be. Myssa had professed her love for him so many times in so many different ways. Had it all been some grand deception?

He looked at Myssa, his eyes pleading with her to acknowledge him. But her stare remained cold and unknowing.

Akkan looked around, to make sure that the Sons of Apis were still hanging back, then he sprang forward and slammed the hilt of his sword against the side of Piay's head.

Piay fell to the ground, quite unconscious. When he came back to his senses, he was lying on the ground looking up at the Child-Killer.

'You are a fool to come here,' Akkan said. 'It has cost you your life.'

Piay's eyes fluttered open. The bright light of a new day flooded his vision, and with the gradual sensation of swimming up out of the depths of a deep lake, his memories of the night before returned. He recalled Myssa standing there glaring at him, but no Myssa he could comprehend. This was a stranger in every way he could imagine. Desperation swelled within him, and the grief of all-consuming loss. He felt as if he had been cut off from dry land, from everything he knew, and he was drifting out into the ocean.

Craning his neck, he looked around. Myssa was nowhere to be seen. Nor was Hannu – and that at least gave him some hope that his friend had escaped the mayhem unscathed.

Near that gaping hole in the ground, the Cobra and his acolytes bowed their heads together in deep conversation. The body that had been dragged out the previous evening was nowhere to be seen.

Around the perimeter of the camp, Akkan's warriors peered out across the fields, hands close to their swords, alert to the slightest hint of danger. The Sons of Apis had drifted away into the night, but who knew when they might be back.

Piay pushed himself up to his feet. His hands were bound behind his back.

This is getting to be a bad habit, he thought, with bitter humour. He had no idea why Akkan had decided to keep him alive, but it was not out of kindness; he knew that.

Not far away, Khin lay, also bound, his ruby-red scarf gagging his mouth. His Shrikes were all dead, his Hyksos guards, too. He had lost everything, and now he had nothing left but to throw himself on his hated brother's mercy.

Beyond Khin, Piay could see the perfectly worked limestone edging the lip of the hole and facing the walls leading down into the dark. Nearby a stone lid lay shattered. From the remnants he could just make out the broken design of the Eye of Horus.

'Imhotep,' he whispered to himself.

A gentle purring rumbled and Piay looked around to see Bast prowling up to him.

'Hello, little goddess,' he said. 'Does Myssa still love you, at least?'

The cat hunched down not far from his head and stared at him. Piay squirmed as he looked into those intense eyes. They never failed to unnerve him.

'Hear my plea,' Piay whispered to Bast. 'Help Myssa. Help her find her way back to me. Help—'

'And now you speak with cats. What possessed your master Taita to invest so much in you?'

Piay jerked around to see Akkan staring down at him, legs apart with his hands upon his hips. But it was Myssa who drew Piay's gaze. She stood beside the Hyksos leader, their shoulders almost touching, and it was that closeness which made Piay shudder. Her face was as stony as he remembered from the previous night. It was almost as if he looked upon a different person.

Piay winced from a pain so acute he could have been stabbed. Yet deep inside him, he knew that if he gave in to these feelings he would be lost. He swallowed his despair and showed a defiant face.

'Undo my hands,' he said. 'Face me, man to man, sword against sword. I'll show you why Taita placed his trust in me.'

Akkan laughed. 'Bravado is all you have left. Enjoy it.'

Myssa looked at Bast, and then pushed the tip of her foot towards the creature. The cat reared up, hissing as if she had been attacked, then darted away among the tents. Piay had never seen Bast behave like that. She and Myssa had been together from the day they first encountered each other.

Akkan nodded to two of his men and they hauled Piay to his feet so that he and the Child-Killer could at least speak eye to eye.

'So that hole . . . it's the next clue?' Piay asked.

Akkan shrugged. 'It's no ordinary well, that's for sure.'

'What have you done to Myssa? She would never have brought you here of her own free will.'

'On the contrary, she led us right here, quite willingly.' Akkan smiled. 'She was positively enthusiastic.'

'What have you done to her?' Piay repeated.

'I can speak for myself,' Myssa said.

At least Piay could hear some of the woman he knew in the fire that seared those words.

'I don't believe it,' he said, looking at her. 'No one changes this much, this fast.'

'Who are you to say that? I don't even know you.'

'What do you mean? We've been together, night and day, for so long. You love me! I love you!'

Myssa turned to Akkan, the hint of a frown on her face.

'What is this man talking about? I have never met him before in my life.'

'This isn't Myssa – this is sorcery!' Piay shouted, unable to hide his desperation.

'Believe what you will,' the Child-Killer replied, his voice perfectly calm. 'But this woman will be my bride. Meanwhile, you will be dead and she will never even think of you again.'

Piay looked deep into Myssa's eyes. He vowed that he would never doubt her, never give in to despair. He had known her love, and had told her his deepest secrets, just as she had shared hers. That Myssa – the one who knew and loved him – still existed somewhere, hidden inside the cold, hard shell that Akkan and the Cobra had somehow created. He would find some way to bring her back, or die trying.

Akkan glanced over at Khin.

'And you, brother. What am I to do with such a treacherous dog? You betrayed me. Tried to steal from me. Naturally, you failed, as you would. So, what will I do with you now, brother? What will I do?'

Khin looked away. Akkan continued to stare at the prone form, a look so filled with loathing that it was a punishment in itself.

The Cobra strode up, leaning on his staff.

'We cannot afford to waste time here. Now that the Sons of Apis know where we are and what we're doing, they'll keep coming back until they have destroyed us.'

'I am not the one wasting time,' Akkan said. 'This is our second day here – and how many dead? Five?'

'Six.'

'And you're still no closer to finding the answer.' The Child-Killer's voice was full of frustration.

'On the contrary,' Tallus said, and Piay, hearing those words, turned to pay closer attention to their conversation. He was curious to discover how the Child-Killer would take to being contradicted in front of his own men.

Akkan was taken aback for an instant, but then he composed himself and, in a voice that was all the more menacing for the politeness of his words, said, 'Really? Perhaps you would care to explain why I am mistaken.'

'We have not solved the riddle that Imhotep has set us,' Tallus said, 'but we do at least understand its workings.'

'Go on . . .' Now Akkan's curiosity was entirely genuine.

'This is a puzzle of the body, and solid, physical things, as well as of the mind. Imhotep used his skills as an architect and builder to turn what appears to be a simple shaft into a maze. About halfway down, there's a slab which seems to block the way. From what the men who've gone down there have told us, it seems to be counterweighted so that when you step upon the correct area, it tips, allowing access to the next slab below. And so on. Each slab must slot back into place before the one beneath it opens. When a slab closes, it does so completely, yet somehow the rope we use to lower our explorer is not cut. How that is done, we do not know, either.'

Tallus paused, his eyes glassy. He was no doubt imagining that journey down into the dark, sealed as if in a tomb.

'Imhotep's skill is beyond any that I have known,' the Cobra continued. 'His maze is also a trap. If the one descending does not find the prize in good time, the pit floods with water, drowning him before he can make his way back out.'

Piay found his thoughts drawn down into those dark depths, imagining the terror as water rushed in while the slab above was sealed shut. Each one of those captured farmers thrown in there to unlock its secrets had ended their lives trapped in absolute darkness, flailing as water was sucked into their noses and mouths and filled their lungs. A terrible death.

Akkan was not remotely interested in the suffering of others, unless it was for his own entertainment.

'How long will you need, and how many men?'

Tallus shook his head, still staring into those depths. 'Who knows?'

'You will know,' Akkan said, 'and soon. I will hear no other excuses.'

'Then we must do more than just throw farmers into this pit in the hope that they will solve this mystery for you. Imhotep did not construct his great puzzle for the benefit of ignorant peasants. Only a man of education and quick wits can even hope to comprehend the workings of a mind born of the gods themselves.'

'Ah, Tallus, thank you.' Akkan sighed, contentedly.

'For what?'

'Why, for answering my question. I was wondering what to do with my brother, who attacked me so treacherously. And now I know . . .'

Akkan walked back to Khin and said, 'You've always fancied yourself as a thinker. Sharp, cunning, smarter than any man you barter with. Well, here's your chance to prove it.'

Khin's eyes widened. He could not believe what he was hearing, but when he looked into his brother's face, he saw Akkan was absolutely serious. The Child-Killer was going to send Akh-Seth down the well.

As if reading Khin's mind, Akkan said, 'Now let's see who's really the brother of Seth.'

Khin thrashed back and forth, but his bonds held him tight. A high-pitched keening made its way through the scarf gagging him.

'Come, brother, come,' Akkan continued. 'If anyone can find a solution to this puzzle it's you. And I would think that saving your own neck will motivate you to bring me the answer I need.'

As Khin continued to thrash, Akkan nodded to his warriors. Two of them kicked and beat their leader's brother until he stopped his writhing. When he was still, they hauled Khin to his feet and wrenched the scarf from his mouth.

'If I were you, I would not struggle,' Akkan said. 'If you struggle I'll have to keep your hands bound – and then what will you do, down there?'

'Don't do it . . . please,' Khin begged. 'Yes, yes, I wronged you. I was a fool. Greedy. Proud. Tricked by that damned Egyptian. But I'll make it up to you, I swear.'

'Yes, you will,' Akkan said. 'On the end of that rope.'

'Think of our time as children!' Khin's voice cracked.

'When you beat me and kicked me and told the other children I was weak?'

Khin mouthed some response, like a gulping fish on the riverbank, but he knew that whatever he said was futile, as they all did.

'Very well,' he said finally. 'Maybe you're right. If any man can solve this maze, why shouldn't it be me?'

Akkan grinned. 'Very good. That's the attitude we need.'

The warriors slit Khin's bonds and guided him to the edge of the hole, where they tied a long rope around his waist. Two of the strongest-looking Hyksos, massive slabs of meat and bone, took the other end of the rope.

Khin stared down into the dark.

Everyone in the camp gathered around the hole. Akkan gestured to Piay to stand beside him. Myssa was on Akkan's other side.

Now that he was close, Piay could see the quality of the craftsmanship in the stone facing of the shaft. The edges were so expertly cut he could not have slid a sliver of papyrus between the joins. But he could not see the bottom. What lay down there was a mystery that would only be solved by accepting the challenge that the Second Door offered to all who would enter it.

Akkan leaned in to Piay and whispered, 'Pray that Khin finds a way. Because you're next.'

Khin shook his trembling hands and cracked his knuckles.

'I am ready.'

'May the gods go with you, brother.' Akkan sounded as sincere as if he was waving Khin off on a voyage along the river.

The two warriors braced themselves as Khin lowered himself over the edge. His leather soles scraped on the smooth stone, slipping as he fought to find purchase. He slammed into the wall and cursed.

The rope eased through the warriors' hands. Khin disappeared from view.

Piay stepped to the edge once more and peered in, hoping against hope that he would glimpse something that would help him. Khin dangled, bounced off the stone, his ruby-red robe disappearing into the darkness like blood dripping into ink.

For what seemed an age, everyone stood around the hole and waited. No sounds emerged from within that shaft. Every now and then, Piay flashed glances at Myssa, not sure what he was hoping for, but she didn't seem even to know that he was there. Her face had an odd blankness to it, as if she were drifting into sleep.

Eventually, Akkan said, 'Drag him out.'

The two warriors heaved on the rope. Piay imagined those counterbalanced slabs shifting as the dead weight of Khin slammed against them. After a while, he heard the slap and slither of wet fabric on stone, and then the body of Akh-Seth emerged from the dark. The men pulled the corpse onto the earth and let the rope slip from their fingers.

Akkan eyed the remains of his brother and shrugged.

'He was not as cunning as I thought. Dispose of him with the others. Give the crocodiles another feast.'

Piay was not surprised by the callousness the Child-Killer displayed, but there was no hint of compassion on Myssa's face either.

As Khin's body was hauled away, Piay crouched by the hole, trying to work out whether there was, even now, some way out for him. But none came to mind. From the moment he entered the Second Door, he would either fail to solve the clues that lay within it, and be drowned or eaten by what lay below. Or, he solved the puzzle, returned with the secret and Akkan killed him anyway.

First things first, he told himself. *Just get to the bottom alive.*

The second his mind had focused on that sole priority, inspiration came to him like a blast of light from the Eye of Horus: Myssa had compared Imhotep to Taita.

Well, I don't know how Imhotep thought. But I certainly know Taita.

Closing his eyes, Piay imagined himself as a child in Taita's classroom. He heard his master's mellifluous voice talking through this problem. It echoed as if from the depths of that pit. 'Where does the water come from?'

Looking up, Piay glanced past the tents to the river, close enough for him to hear it splashing over rocks in the shallows. This was no ordinary well that took its water from the earth down below. This was a tunnel to the river.

So, it's a way to get somewhere, Piay thought. *Like that carved door in the temple represented a way to enter the land of the dead. And this goes underground, like the underworld.*

The rope had been untied from Khin's lifeless waist. Piay hardly felt the hands that were now knotting it around him. His mind was on the lessons that he, like all educated Egyptians, had received about the path of the soul to the afterlife.

First test, Piay thought. *Ma'at, the goddess of truth, balance, harmony and justice weighs the heart against a single feather. If the heart is lighter or equal to the weight of the feather, the soul moves on to the next stage of judgement. If it's heavier, the unworthy soul is devoured by Ammit, who is part lion, part hippopotamus, with the head of a crocodile . . . Like the farmers have been eaten, because they aren't able to solve the puzzle!*

'What's so amusing,' Akkan said, spotting the broad grin on Piay's face.

'Oh, just remembering my schooldays.'

Akkan shook his head and let out a sigh of contempt at such idiocy. Then Piay added, 'By the way, if you want me to solve this puzzle, I need the Eye of Horus and a torch.'

Now it was Akkan who laughed. 'Are you mad? Do you really think I would hand over the single most precious object in the entire two kingdoms of Egypt?'

'What choice do you have? You saw it yourself – we needed the Eye to illuminate the hidden message on the stone door in the necropolis. The clues can't be solved without it. And the Eye doesn't work its magic without the light of a torch. So either you give me the Eye . . . or you keep it and go down there yourself. See if you have any more luck than your brother.'

Piay could hear Akkan's men talking to one another. They seemed to reckon he'd made a fair point, for a grinning Egyptian idiot.

Good, he thought. *Now Akkan has to consider how he looks to his men.*

Piay pressed home whatever small advantage he might have.

'Here's my suggestion . . . Put the Eye in a pouch. Tie the pouch to my wrist. If I fail, you drag my body back out and you still have the Eye. If I succeed, you also drag me out, because where else can I go? Then, who knows, maybe you'll thank me for doing you a big, big favour.'

Again, this proposition seemed to find favour with the barrack-room lawyers behind him. Piay just prayed that none of the

Hyksos had worked out that the well was linked directly to the river.

The Cobra's features remained impassive, but the scribes and advisors shuffled and looked at their feet. Piay felt proud of himself that he had reasoned his way through this puzzle, and was sure Myssa would be proud of him, too, once she was herself again.

'Get him a torch,' Akkan barked to one of his warriors. He turned to Tallus. 'Give it to him.'

Tallus had a small pouch hanging from a belt around his waist. He undid it, reached in, and Piay waited for the Eye to appear. But then Tallus frowned as a thought struck him, raised a hand and said, 'One moment.'

As the Cobra walked away, Akkan shouted after him, 'Where in Seth's name are you going?'

'One moment!' Tallus repeated, lifting his arm as if to silence Akkan.

The Child-Killer's brows lowered over his blazing eyes and Piay hoped for the priest's sake that he had a good reason for his disappearance.

Or he'll be going down instead of me.

Tallus returned holding a much bigger pouch.

'That's far too big for the Eye,' Akkan said.

'Indeed it is. But what if the Great Architect has left another, equally important treasure down there?'

Akkan shrugged, grudgingly accepting the point.

Tallus tied the pouch to the belt that held up Piay's kilt and whispered into his ear, 'The Eye is in there. No need for the men to see it.'

Piay nodded. He stepped to the edge of the hole. Blood thundered in his head as he stared into what was little more than an open grave. All the evidence, all his reasoning, told him he was going to his death.

With a deep breath, Piay eased himself into the dark.

The shadows danced away from the torchlight. Piay breathed in the dank air rising from below, braced his feet against the stone wall and lowered himself a few paces. Above him, curious faces were framed against the blue sky, but Piay's attention was all on the depths where the dark still swelled. He could see no sign of the bottom.

Swaying against the taut rope, Piay held the torch with his left hand, while his right rummaged around in the oversized pouch until he finally found the Eye of Horus. Then he positioned the Eye close to the stone facing, with the torch shining on it.

The light blazed through the polished quartz onto the limestone blocks. Piay strained, searching for the lines of fire, previously invisible to the naked eye, that they had found in the necropolis.

The stone facing was smooth and as unmarked as it must have been when Imhotep or his agents dug the pit and constructed the casing. Piay gritted his teeth in frustration, beginning a steady sweep around all four walls.

'What do you see?' the Cobra called down.

'Nothing, yet.'

Piay jolted the rope and the men holding it juddered him down a few more paces. Once again he moved the torch and the Eye of Horus across the stone slabs facing the shaft. Waves of light washed back and forth.

'What do you see?' Tallus called again.

'Nothing,' Piay barked back. His voice crackled with irritation. 'Leave me be to search.'

Another jolt, and he flexed his aching thighs as he walked down the wall again. He sucked in a deep draught of the chill air to try to ease the tension turning his neck and back muscles into cords, but he still felt as if he was teetering on the edge of the precipice.

Gripping the brand tighter, he eased the brilliant glow across the slick stone. Piay strained to see the faintest detail. The white light moved, and then, with a jump of his heart, he glimpsed the fiery lines leap out of the stone.

Piay had to stop himself calling out in jubilation. He had been right. He could scarcely believe it.

'What do you see?' the Cobra demanded.

'Nothing,' Piay lied.

Decipher these symbols as fast as he could: that was his task now, so those above would not realise he had uncovered the key to solving this puzzle. At least, he hoped that's what it was. The key to his survival. That was Piay's prayer. And he did not want Akkan stealing this discovery from him, thinking he could easily replace him with one of his men. If he was hauled back to the surface there would only be a sharp blade waiting to greet him.

Sweat prickled his brow.

'Why are you taking your time?' Tallus' voice echoed down to him.

'I need to be careful . . . deliberate . . . so I don't miss anything.'

The fiery lines illuminated the shape of a man – a single one this time, not the two that had been etched on the stone in the necropolis at Thebes. This was the Opener of the Way. This, he thought with a shiver, was him. He was the one being judged.

Beside that figure were three horizontal rectangles, each one with a small *X* carved in a different position: to the right on the first, to the left on the second, in the centre on the third.

That was all.

Piay felt queasy. What could it mean? He jolted on the rope again so those above would not become suspicious at the time he was taking. But his increasingly desperate thoughts tumbled over each other. He wished Myssa – his true Myssa – was there to guide him.

Somehow, Piay calmed himself. Imhotep had left instructions for a successful journey into the underworld. He would have to trust, even if he did not understand.

Weight . . . balance . . . feather. Then: *Right . . . left . . . centre.*

Piay turned those words over again and again, searching for inspiration. Finally, a notion struck him. The barriers were counterbalanced. Were the Xs the points on the slab where he should stand to tip them – perhaps shift them quickly so that he could reach the bottom before the water surged up? Could Imhotep have foreseen his size, his weight, so these barriers were perfectly attuned to him? Nothing would surprise him anymore.

'Lower me down,' he called up. 'I'm going to set the trap in motion and hope I'm fast enough to get through.'

After a brief silence, Tallus' voice floated down. 'Do what you will.'

Piay steeled himself. Now was the moment of life or death. He tucked the Eye of Horus into the pouch and yanked on the rope.

As he descended, Piay stared down the shaft, watching the receding darkness. Eventually it ebbed away and the torchlight revealed the first slab of limestone blocking the way.

When his feet settled on it, he felt the slab begin to move, but very slowly. At the same time, a dim grinding echoed from somewhere far beneath him, followed by the sound of rushing water. So now the test had become a race. He had to solve the puzzle and get out before the water filled the chamber, or whatever else was at the bottom of the shaft.

Piay had to move fast.

Muttering a prayer to Khonsu, he stepped to the first position indicated on Imhotep's engraving, to the right of the slab. Instantly the stone beneath his feet swung faster and he dropped through the gap. He fumbled to keep hold of the torch in his surprise. The movement must have shocked the men holding the rope, for they eventually slowed his descent. Piay jolted the rope twice, hoping it would send a message that he needed to move faster. That worked.

When his feet touched the second slab, Piay instantly moved to the left and the barrier swung open. He could hear the gurgling of the water below and smell the dank scents of the river.

On the third slab, he stood in the centre and this one tipped a different way. He felt his legs fall out from under him and he plunged down towards the final chamber.

Piay splashed into chilling water, his feet hitting stone almost instantly. He felt a rush of relief when he realised the level was only just above his knees.

His heart thumped. Time was short. He turned around in a full circle, sweeping the torch across the glistening stone walls to illuminate this new space. Shards of gold glinted across the swirling black water. At least there was no sign of Ammit, the terrifying composite of lion, hippo and crocodile waiting to devour him. But something certainly ate those other men.

Piay's attention fell on a large dark opening on one wall. Water gushed through it so fast the chamber would be engulfed in no time.

The echoes of the cascade boomed all around him as Piay threw himself into the search for Imhotep's secret. The torchlight swept in a delirious whirl, but the walls showed no distinguishing features and the water was licking up them at an alarming rate. Desperation spiked in his stomach.

Yet as he ranged around the space, his toe bumped against a raised object. Feeling his hope disappearing as quickly as the water was rising, Piay dropped to his knees. He held up the torch in one hand, praying that the water would not extinguish it while he scrabbled around with his free hand. His fingers slipped across something hard and slick. It was circular in shape, and seemed to be set into a groove in the flagstone.

Piay clawed at it with his fingernails, trying to get a purchase strong enough to pull the object out of its housing. Finally, he succeeded and stood back up with it in his hand. Then he held his torch to examine what he had found.

'Ha!' he exclaimed to himself. 'Tallus was right.'

The object he had just found was a slim disc, a little wider than the span of his hand. To judge by its weight, and the blazing gleam of the light on its untarnished surface, it was made of gold.

The object seemed to be a representation of Ra's great orb, with flames leaping from the edge at four points. It was intricately constructed with symbols and shapes etched into it – a star, a moon . . . too many for him to take in at that instant.

There was no time to examine it further. Piay slipped the disc into Tallus' pouch and peered up at the sealed third slab. One great puzzle had been solved, but an even greater one lay ahead.

Piay knew that the only reward he would ever get from Akkan for finding Imhotep's secret was his own death. If he allowed the guards to drag him back up, no protestations or bartering would prevent the warriors from cutting him down in an instant. But if he stayed where he was, he would drown.

Death at both ends.

The rushing water licked up to his thigh.

Piay hardened. He would not give in. He needed to lead Myssa to freedom for a second time, help her to escape from Akkan and whatever depravity he had planned for her. And Taita had placed his trust in him. He could not let down the man who had shaped him and showered him with kindness. Against those things, his own life meant nothing.

As Piay searched for a way out, his gaze fell on that now almost obscured black square where the water was flooding in. The water must be coming from somewhere, along a tunnel. So there was another opening, just like this one, at the other end of that tunnel. Piay just didn't know how far away that hole might be.

He felt a chill along his spine. Could he? Should he? Did he have any choice at all?

When he'd stood on solid ground beside the hole, Piay had judged the distance to the river from where he was certain the water was coming. Thinking about it now, he felt sure he could cover that distance in open water. But in a tiny tunnel in the dark? And what if Imhotep had set more slabs to fall in place along the way? The tunnel was not wide enough to turn around.

Piay felt a shudder of dread run through him. He imagined being trapped in the dark, deep underground, choking on the water filling his lungs as he thrashed and died.

He shook himself. What point was there in dwelling on such a terrible vision? It would not help him escape this trap. And he had no other choice. He had to gamble everything if he had any hope of living to see the next dawn.

Piay slipped his hand into his kilt to the secret pocket where he kept his knife. Drawing out the blade, he sawed through the hide rope that bound him to the men up above.

Let the Hyksos wonder what had happened when they drew it up and found their captive gone.

The water now chilled his waist.

Piay waded across the chamber to the tunnel entrance. He felt around the edge of the hole, his fingertips exploring the grooves where another slab would descend to seal off the flooding water.

Yes, there will be no way back.

He could not waste any more time. Steeling himself, Piay tossed the torch across the chamber. With a splash, the flames sizzled out and the dark engulfed him.

Piay gripped the edges of the hole, sucked in three deep breaths and plunged beneath the surface. The water shocked him with its coldness. In contrast, he felt a fire roar through him, searing strength into his limbs.

Thrusting into the tunnel, Piay kicked out to propel himself while using his hands to drag him along the walls. The darkness was so all-consuming he could not tell if he was swimming up or down.

Piay clawed his way forward.

In that constrained space, with no perception of the distance ahead, he felt the first flicker of panic begin to ignite in his mind. He could not afford to give in to it. If he did, he was lost.

The air began to dwindle in his chest. How much further could he swim before his air burned out?

Ahead of him, he sensed a disturbance in the water as shifting currents swept down to batter his face. He prayed it was some eddy from the entrance into the river, but the shifting water became stronger until he was being buffeted.

He could see nothing.

Yet he had the sense that something was sweeping towards him in the dark. A vision of the poor farmer's gnawed foot flashed into his mind, and suddenly he knew what was coming. Dread rushed through him once more, a dread even more powerful than his thoughts of drowning.

Though he couldn't see anything, Piay somehow sensed when the threat was almost upon him. It would be a river crocodile, those savage beasts with their ridged armoured hide, bronze in colour and flecked with black, camouflage that allowed them to hide in the mud in the shallows. He had once seen a child, who had foolishly ventured into one of the reed beds, bitten in half by one of these silent predators, so powerful were their crushing jaws and flesh-rending fangs.

In the river he would have stood little chance. Here, there were straws he could try to clutch.

The tunnel was so restricted that the beast would have to be young, not one of the powerful older predators. He knew their eyes were sharp enough to see well by starlight, but here there was no light at all. He prayed the creature would be as blind as he was, though whether it could scent him, he did not know.

The water churned harder and then the crocodile slammed into him, spinning him against the wall. As he flailed, he lashed out with his free hand, feeling it rake across the ridges of that armoured skin.

The beast thrashed, coiling and lunging in wild movements, but it was as limited in that confined space as he was. That restriction seemed to whip it to even wilder extremes, and though Piay imagined that jaw snapping, it could not gain a purchase on him.

Throwing his arm around the scaly beast, he slid it back up the body until it reached where he thought the head must be. He could feel the jaws cranking wider and he snapped his arm tight around the snout.

Khonsu must have smiled on him, for he clamped the jaw shut. The beast twisted and turned, smashing him against the wall with the tremendous power of those muscles, but Piay clung on for dear life.

His chest burned. Sparks flashed behind his eyes and he knew his life was draining away.

But then all that struggle, all that confusion, seemed to slip away into the darkness and his thoughts became as calm as a desert night under a clear sky.

Gripping the knife, he stabbed again and again into the soft flesh of the river crocodile's underside. The blade sank deep every time.

The beast whirled into a storm of rage. Time and again Piay slammed against the stone. How he held on he did not know, but he did. Finally he managed to rip with his knife, opening up the creature's innards.

And then he was kicking away along the tunnel, past the writhing crocodile. It would not be able to turn and follow him. He had survived that ordeal. But there was a worse one to come.

Piay could feel the terrible ache inside him and the almost uncontrollable urge to open his mouth and gulp. His thoughts fizzed in that death-panic, but a deeper part of him knew that if he did that he would be journeying to the afterlife.

On, he forced himself, on and on. Unable to tell how far he had travelled or how far he had yet to go. All that he knew was that he loved life and did not want to let it go.

A hazy grey patch appeared ahead of him. At first he thought this was some illusion, or a vision. Soon, he told himself, he would see Osiris opening the door to the afterlife.

But then he glimpsed silver fish flash by in shafts of sunlight breaking through the water, and his heart leaped.

Piay pulled himself out of the tunnel and into the river. Death beckoned. Up he thrust. With one final, desperate effort, he broke the surface and heaved in huge lungfuls of air.

His thoughts thundered into a rush of such joy he felt he would be carried away with it. With the last of his strength, Piay dragged himself into the shallows and clawed his way up the muddy bank. There he lay, laughing and crying.

He had been judged and had not been found wanting. His journey to the great reward continued.

Piay sprawled face down in the sticky mud for what seemed like an age. The hot sun prickled his back and the soothing whisper of the reeds rustled around him. With each deep, juddering breath, calm slowly returned until his body trembled with a rush of overwhelming joy.

He was alive!

Yet as the gulls swooped and shrieked overhead, as if celebrating his survival, he felt the weight of his responsibilities creep into his mind. With them came exhaustion, settling deep into the very core of his being. All his fire had been drained away by that ordeal.

But he could not afford to rest. He had plucked a great advantage from the jaws of what had seemed like certain death, and now he must not let that go.

Piay pushed himself up so he could delve into the pouch. The golden disc he had recovered from the bottom of the shaft was still there, as was the Eye of Horus. Without those, Akkan and his band would not be able to advance any further along Imhotep's path. But if Piay devoted every scrap of his intelligence and courage to the Riddle of the Stars, he might be able to move forward to the great prize. And he had solved the puzzle of that shaft. Perhaps he truly could solve the whole thing.

Piay staggered to his feet but kept his head down. The voices of Akkan's men echoed through the date palms and the shrubs lining the river. Some were still questioning what might have happened to him. Others were angry at yet another failure, and the loss of the Eye of Horus, too.

Piay strained to find Myssa's voice. He wanted to hear a wail of grief, as if she were tearing her hair or beating her breast at the thought of his death. But there was nothing.

Just accept it, you've lost her, he told himself. *Maybe she'll come to her senses, maybe she won't. But in the meantime, you just solved the puzzle of the Second Door, and you did it without her help. This is what Taita sent you to Memphis to do. So just obey your orders and try not to think about that woman.*

Piay had lost Hannu, too, although he should, with luck, be easier to recover.

He won't leave the area until he knows for sure that I'm dead, Piay told himself.

True, the sight and sound of the Hyksos, cursing the loss of yet another man down Imhotep's well, would be enough to make most men write him off, but Hannu might just be stubborn enough to stick around, precisely because no one else would.

So where was he?

Somewhere close enough to observe the camp without risking his own neck, Piay concluded.

He crawled up onto the bank, some way downstream from the camp, and then circled back around it at what he considered a safe distance.

Piay was counting on the idea that after all the time they had spent working and fighting side by side, there would be little to choose between his idea of a safe distance and Hannu's. Sure enough, he soon spotted his comrade lying on his belly in a field, peering towards the well. Piay felt sure he had not made the slightest sound, but Hannu leaped to his feet in an instant, sword in hand.

He gaped when he saw who was standing before him.

'By Ra's fiery chariot, are you a ghost?'

Piay grinned. 'Flesh and bone, like you. Though younger and much better-looking.'

'Doesn't seem to have done you much good with Myssa,' Hannu said, with characteristic disregard for Piay's emotions.

Piay knew that teasing was just Hannu's way of hiding his true feelings. And he could hear the barely disguised fear in his friend's voice when he added, 'I thought you were dead.'

'So did I. But it seems the gods had other plans for me. You know, it's not until we're on the threshold of the after-life that we discover what truly lies within us. Anyway, let's be off. Akkan's caught me once. I'm not giving him a second chance.'

'Seriously, though, what about Myssa?'

Piay swallowed. 'She's lost to me for now – maybe to all of us. We can talk about it on the way back to Memphis.'

On the banks of the Nile, they searched among the vessels moored in the shallows until they found a trader taking a break from his long journey from Busiris, in the far north of the country, to Memphis. He was returning for the first time since the siege, with bales of papyrus to sell in the market. He seemed pleased to have two polite but tough men on board his skiff in case they encountered trouble.

When he resumed his voyage, unfurling the sail to catch the hot wind blowing from the delta and the Great Green Sea beyond, Piay and Hannu settled astern under the shade of a canopy. The trader was too occupied with navigation to pay them any attention.

Once Piay had described what he had found in Akkan's camp, Hannu grunted and crossed his arms.

'Myssa would never have turned against you in that manner.'

'Perhaps she was fooling me from the day we first met. Just biding her time—'

Hannu snorted. 'Get a grip on yourself. Anyone could see she really loved you. Maybe she was pretending, to keep herself safe from the Child-Killer.'

Piay shook his head. 'No. I looked in her eyes. She truly believed what she was saying.'

'Then I blame the Cobra. He must have given her something – a potion. Maybe it was that blue lotus stuff that the Hyksos take. Never tried it myself, but they think it's got magic powers.'

'I've been hearing a lot about that lately,' Piay said. 'I know that Akkan has used it to contact Seth. He transformed himself.

Maybe he's planning to do that to Myssa. He, uh . . . He said that she was going to be his bride.'

'Ha! Can't see Myssa standing for that!'

'Not our Myssa, no . . . But Myssa as she is now . . . She was standing right by him, and the way she looked at him, and touched him. You know – a hand on his arm, letting him hold her close. It was like . . . Oh, Khonsu, help me . . . It was like they were already lovers.'

Hannu gave Piay a consoling pat on the back. For a while, they sat with their thoughts. Then Piay shook himself. With a glance along the skiff to check their host was still distracted, he pulled open his pouch and eased out the golden disc.

'This is what Imhotep had left at the bottom of the shaft,' Piay said.

The disc seemed to catch fire in the light of the midday sun.

Hannu marvelled. 'Well, that's treasure all right. It's got to be worth a fortune.'

Piay nodded, truly seeing the artefact for the first time. Lifting it, he turned the disc to examine it from all angles.

'I've never seen such craftsmanship.'

Now that he was looking at it in daylight, Piay could see that there were actually two discs on top of each other, revolving around a central pin. On the surface disc, an outer ring and inner ring slid separately. They could be moved by holding the flames of the sun that protruded from their edges. As they shifted, symbols on the bottom disc appeared in windows cut into the top one. But there were also triangular flaps that could be lifted and closed, revealing still more windows and symbols.

'What does it mean?' Hannu asked.

Piay shook his head. 'I have no idea. But considering where I found it, I've got to think it takes us to the Third Door. But how?'

'That Imhotep must have been a sorcerer, there's no doubt about it,' Hannu breathed. 'To create something like this, that would last a thousand years, until it was needed. No wonder people call him a god.'

Piay slipped the disc back in the pouch.

'I know – and this is so special, maybe it takes us all the way to the end of the quest.'

'I wonder where that'll be?' Hannu mused.

'I've been thinking about that,' Piay replied. 'First there was the opening of a door to the afterlife. Then a descent into the underworld, into the dark, filled with danger, where I had to face my own death.'

'Imhotep's telling the story of the soul's journey to the afterlife.' Hannu grasped the idea instantly. 'So the next stop on the way would be the judgement before you can enter the Field of Reeds.'

'Perhaps,' Piay said. 'Though I don't believe that this is a journey to Paradise and the eternal rest of those who have been judged and not found wanting. This is a journey to meet the gods.'

'The gods?'

'With his spells, Imhotep has found the path to move between the world of men and the world of gods. Anyone who goes on this quest is being prepared to do the same.'

Once again, Piay was struck by the similarities between Imhotep and Taita. Both were setting him seemingly impossible tasks in order to raise him up to become something better. And to raise all Egypt, too.

Hannu gave a sceptical grunt. 'This sounds like the crap the scribes spout when they've had too much beer. Give me a sword and an enemy to kill. That's the kind of problem I like – simple to understand and easily solved.'

Piay chuckled silently. 'If only. Our lives would be so much easier. But now our problem's getting very, very complicated, and all we can do is follow it through to the end and hope we get out the other side.'

'If only Myssa were here,' Hannu said.

'Yes . . . if only.'

The air itself seemed to ripple and melt in the blistering heat of the brassy sun. The natural bowl in the wilderness had become a simmering cauldron, the dusty air searing the back of the throat and plucking all moisture from the skin. At the sand-swept foot of this cruel, inhospitable place, Akkan's men stood with heads bowed in devotional silence. This was Seth's temple.

Myssa grimaced at the smell of the concoction the Cobra had brewed. It smelled like roses boiled in pitch, yet it had brought sweetness to the water in which it had been diluted, when she had first unwittingly sampled it. Now that she had been fully initiated into the cult of the blue lotus, no dilution was required. All she ever craved was more of the lotus, and stronger.

Every morning now began the same way, with the sweats, the aches, the pains and, above all, the desperate craving for the potion that would cure them. Tallus would bring a bowl to her lips and she would swallow the brown liquor, gagging at its strength. Soon after, that blissful feeling of warmth and peace would spread through her, and all her troubles would vanish like the early morning mist in the heat of the rising sun.

Then Tallus would whisper to her, a rolling jumble of words that became almost a chant, soothing her mind. What he said to her, Myssa could never remember. All she knew was that she was changed by it. And changed, she was sure, for the better.

This very morning, Akkan had come to her with a new gown, more beautiful than any she had ever seen, cut in a style that she had only seen the most wealthy, high-born women wear.

Straps the width of her middle three fingers, consisting of an open, criss-cross pattern of white cylindrical beads through which her skin was clearly visible, passed from the middle of her back, over her breasts, to just below her bust. The straps supported a close-fitting sheath of white linen so fine and so weightless that, though it fell almost to her ankles, it could hardly be said to cover her at all.

When she had first shown herself to Akkan, in the privacy of their tent, he had been so aroused by the sight of her that he had insisted on taking her, there and then. Suffused with the bliss of the lotus, she had felt somehow liquid, melting into the ecstasy of his hard, merciless strength. Now, scented and painted, she was standing beside Akkan as he grasped her hand and intertwined his calloused fingers with hers. He was eager for the ceremony to begin.

This was supposed to be a joyous ceremony. But as Myssa looked around the faces of the warriors and the acolytes, she saw only downturned mouths and sullen eyes.

When the rope that had lowered Piay of Thebes into the pit had been pulled back up with no body on the end of it, they had all felt the same terrible apprehension that he had somehow outmanoeuvred them. Outraged by the thought that a man he held in such contempt had somehow solved Imhotep's second clue and discovered some miraculous way to escape from the trap, Akkan had sent another helpless farmer down after him.

The farmer was told, 'Pull three times on the rope if you can see a body down there, twice if the pit is empty. As soon as you've done that, we'll bring you straight back up again.'

Two pulls, and the farmer was left down there to rot.

Myssa twitched her nose. These strong men had failed. Their weakness had been exposed. Now they brooded and plotted a way to recapture their advantage. No answers had been forthcoming.

The Cobra raised the bowl above his head and closed his eyes as he turned his face to the silver sky.

'Beneath the eyes of Seth, we will join this man and woman together,' he intoned. 'A union sanctified by the power of our god, as has been the way of our people since the first time.'

Myssa felt Akkan squeeze her hand. If he was expecting her to squeeze back, he would be disappointed. This ceremony, conducted so quickly, was his way of lashing out against the man who had got the better of him, a childlike gesture of impotent rage.

More weakness, she thought.

The Cobra lowered the bowl and strode over to put it to Myssa's lips.

'Drink now,' he said, 'and let the blue lotus transport you to a new life.'

Once Myssa had swallowed, and gagged, Tallus presented the bowl to Akkan, who took a deep draught.

'Now let us begin,' the Cobra said.

Myssa watched the heat haze rise over the desert. Over the days since her capture she had come to realise one thing. The sorcerer's rituals had not turned her into another person, as Akkan had insisted had happened to him. Instead, the lotus seemed to work in two ways. The first, immediate effect was to bring her pleasure. But the second, deeper gift, which only became apparent as the bliss began to fade, was to summon the essence of her being to the surface.

When she drank the potion, Myssa felt like her first, truest self – the young, free woman, proud and strong and defiant, who had stood at the heart of her people as she sought to guide her king. Yes, she had forgotten many things, and some that had once seemed important no longer intruded into her thoughts, but through this dream state, she had become the most potent form of herself. And that new sense of self remained with her, even when she was wide awake.

Myssa eyed Akkan. He flashed her a smile that at last had some warmth in it. She smiled back, but inside she was thinking that the Hyksos had misunderstood the subtleties of their own magic. Akkan was lying to himself, for perhaps that was the only way he could deal with the thing he had become. He had not been transformed by the lotus – or by Seth – into the Child-Killer. The killer was the true core of this man, always there waiting to be released.

'He is coming!' the Cobra boomed.

Myssa shuddered despite herself. In the distance, the howling of the jackals rose up, sweeping across the wasteland towards them.

'Can you see him?' Tallus called. 'Can you see him?'

Akkan craned his neck towards the sky and Myssa followed his gaze. For what seemed like an age, nothing moved. The Cobra continued to chant and Myssa felt her heart begin to beat to the rhythm of the words.

Then, as relentless and steady as the night creeping in at dusk, a soaring shadow formed in the northern sky. Myssa felt the blood pound in her temples as she watched the beast-head rise up. Deep dread rushed through her, heralding the arrival of Seth.

'He is here!' the Cobra thundered. 'Under his eye, let the bond be formed.'

Myssa felt Akkan's grip on her hand tighten. She glanced at him, but he was lost to a trance, mouthing the words that Tallus spoke. When she looked up once more, those fierce beast-eyes seemed to grow larger until they filled the entire sky. Myssa felt herself drawn into them, into the core of the god himself.

Time must have passed, though Myssa was not aware of it. Her next conscious sensation was the diminishing sound as the Cobra's final incantations drifted away and there was only the seething silence of that suffocating space.

Myssa swam up from what felt like a deep sleep to see that the sky was clear. She could no longer sense Seth's presence.

At her side, Akkan trembled. His hand fell away from hers, and when he looked at her a light burned in the depths of his dark eyes. that

'Come to me, my wife,' he said.

Myssa thought it sounded more like a command than a request, but she saw no need to resist. She stepped forward and the Child-Killer threw his arms around her, pulling her into a crushing embrace. She could feel the heat of his lust and the hardness of his member pressing against her belly. Evidently the morning's activities had not sated his appetite.

Akkan's dry lips clamped on her mouth and he forced it open with his kisses, penetrating the warm depths with his tongue. When he pulled back from the clutch, his eyes sparkling, Myssa smiled.

'Let's go back to the tent.'

Akkan needed no other prompt. Grasping Myssa's hand, he hauled her away from his men, up the steep rocky side of the bowl and across the waste to where the camp sprawled. The Child-Killer's tent lay at the centre of the jumble of shelters. He threw back the flaps and Myssa slipped inside, easing down onto the coarse blanket they used to keep the chill of the desert night at bay. She sat cross-legged, looking up at her new husband, smiling.

The Child-Killer stood in front of her, legs apart, and raised the flat of his hand, signalling to her to remove that fine white gown.

Myssa shook her head, teasing.

'First,' she said, 'show me your sword.'

Akkan removed his kilt and looked down proudly at what it revealed.

Myssa gave another calculated giggle. 'No . . . I mean your real sword. I want to see the weapon with which you have killed so many people, and feel its weight. I want to imagine the blood of your enemies staining its blade. You are my man. I want to feel your power.'

Akkan frowned in puzzlement. This wasn't what he had been expecting.

'Isn't a bride allowed to ask a favour from her man on her wedding night?' Myssa purred. 'Before she grants him her favours?'

Now Akkan smiled. That was more like it. He leaned down, kissed Myssa's lips and then, as he straightened back up, said, 'How can I refuse?'

When they reached the port of Peru-nefer, Piay and Hannu helped the trader unload his bales onto the wharf and then gave their thanks. The blackened bones of the burned-out hulks still protruded from the grey water as they had done since the siege, and blue sky shone through the collapsed roofs of the charred warehouses. No work had been carried out since their arrival.

'Harrar seems in no rush to bring Memphis back to its former glory,' Piay noted.

'He's the kind of man who likes to puff out his chest and speak loudly, but he shirks the hard work of getting things done,' Hannu replied. 'He'd rather sit with Zahur, getting fat on the food from the palace kitchens, and plotting how they can both get even richer at the people's expense.'

'Taita wants what's best for Egypt. Harrar and Zahur just want what's best for them,' Piay agreed. 'That's the difference between a great man and two worthless leeches.'

As Piay and Hannu trudged along the road from Peru-nefer to Memphis' white walls, Piay felt his inner fire burning low. More than anything, he needed rest and hearty meals to build up his strength, but he could not afford that luxury. Somehow he would have to find a way to struggle on.

'At least we're one step ahead of the Sons of Apis,' Piay said. 'They surely can't know yet that I've got the Eye of Horus and this Disc of Ra. With any luck they'll still be concentrating on Akkan.'

'But how long till Akkan discovers what's happened to you? We know he has spies within Memphis.'

'I'd love to see the look on his face when he knows I'm back in the palace, all nice and cool, while he's still sweating out there in the wilderness.'

'Personally, I'd rather not see his face at all,' Hannu said. 'Ever.'

As they came closer to the walls of Memphis, they could hear a loud noise coming from within: shouting, screaming, and the rumble and crashing of a throng of people in motion.

'Is the city under attack?' Hannu asked as they both picked up their pace.

There were no soldiers guarding the gate, and the street just beyond it was deserted, but the more they pressed on into the city, the louder the noise became. With a mounting sense of dread, Piay and Hannu hurried towards it.

They turned a corner, near the main market, and suddenly found themselves on the edge of a crowd filling the street with a milling, churning mass of people. Faces twisted with rage and fists shook in the air, their fury spiralling into a single deafening roar.

From the day that Piay and Hannu had arrived in Memphis the people's hunger and their hatred of Zahur – and the self-serving privilege he embodied – had been obvious. Discontent had been simmering, and now it had turned into outright insurrection.

'Wonder what set them off?' Piay shouted.

'Wouldn't have taken much,' Hannu replied.

Soldiers herded the citizens like cattle, prodding them with spears and swords as they attempted to contain the mob. In other times the people would have meekly obeyed, but Piay could see something had consumed them. Some passion burned in their eyes that made them oblivious to sharp bronze blades.

A gaunt man, driven mad by hunger, frustration and fury, threw himself at the line of grim-faced soldiers. More by luck than anything, he slipped past the lethal blades and slammed into one of the fighting men, clawing at his face and punching and biting like some wild beast.

The soldier crashed backwards with the emaciated man on top of him.

Most of the other troops were too busy trying to hold back the heaving crowd to go to their comrade's aid. If one more man went down, the dam might break. But a younger soldier dashed forward from the rear. He looked barely older than a boy, his sword unfeasibly large in his hands, and he had the awkward, long-limbed movements of youth, without the hard-muscled precision of a seasoned fighting man.

Piay felt struck by what he saw in the lad's face: terror. He had the wide-eyed, slack-jawed expression of someone who had never faced the horrors of battle before. Piay remembered that feeling well. Nothing could ever prepare a man for the chaos and demented emotions of war. And Piay had no doubt that this was war: a kingdom fighting its own people.

As Piay gaped, the young soldier lunged for the man who was now astride his victim, hammering his fists down like mallets in the shipyard. He, too, was lost to the madness.

From behind, the young soldier hooked his left hand around the attacker's neck under his chin and wrenched him off the fallen soldier, so that he too, was on the ground. Without a second thought, the raw recruit wrapped both hands around the hilt of his sword and rammed the blade downwards into the man's scrawny chest. When he yanked back his weapon, the blade was covered in blood from tip to hilt.

Piay felt as if the world had closed around him in that instant. The roar of the crowd ebbed to a distant throb, and his vision centred on the dying man and the growing pool around him.

Someone shouted, 'They've killed one of us!'

In an instant the news spread through the crowd: 'The soldiers are killing innocent people!'

The sound of the mob spiralled up, the roar of a mighty beast that had been prodded one time too many. As one, the throng hurled itself forward.

The soldiers had no time to brace themselves.

'They won't be able to contain them!' Hannu shouted.

His words became true an instant later as the line of fighting men crumpled. Some crashed down to the ground. Others spun away. The rest regrouped into a knot of fighting men, spears and swords at the ready, facing outwards towards the people surging around them like a racing stream around a boulder.

Piay shouted at the soldiers, 'Withdraw! Withdraw!'

It was still not too late to make an orderly retreat. But his words went unheard amid the noise of battle. The soldiers were filled with a poisonous blend of fury, terror and the raw, burning desire to strike back and shed blood. Their fellow citizens were enemies now. And enemies were there to be killed.

With a roar of their own, the soldiers went back on the attack, spears piercing undefended flesh, sparks of light flashing off slashing swords. The people at the front of the crowd, unable to resist the pressure of the protesters at the rear, were pushed directly towards the soldiers. They begged for mercy. They turned and pleaded with the other protesters to stop. And then, one by one, row by row, their shouts turned to screams as the soldiers mowed them down. Still the crowd kept moving, trampling over the bodies of their own dead, offering up more sacrifices to the blades of the fighting men

'We've got to do something!' Piay shouted, but Hannu caught his arm again and yanked him back.

'There's no point,' the veteran told him. 'You'll just get yourself killed.'

Piay knew Hannu was right, but how could he stand by and do nothing in the face of such slaughter?

Hannu continued to pull at his arm and eventually Piay relented, allowing himself to be led away from the battle. But as they eased into a deserted side street, past rows of clerks' offices, Piay glanced back. All he could see was blood washing across the road as if the tide was coming in.

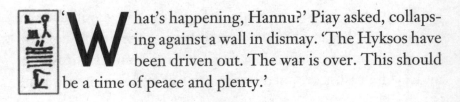'hat's happening, Hannu?' Piay asked, collapsing against a wall in dismay. 'The Hyksos have been driven out. The war is over. This should be a time of peace and plenty.'

'When the battle is over, the vultures descend, you know that.' Hannu kicked at the sand with his sandal. His head was bowed, his stare fixed. 'When one power leaves, there's always chaos until another takes over. That's just the way of the world.'

'This is the world Seth wants,' Piay said. 'His world is all chaos and disorder, and if that means mankind living in war and starvation, so much the better for him and his followers.'

'Aye,' Hannu said. 'If Akkan could see all this, he'd just love it.'

'It's everything Taita feared – and Imhotep must have known it was coming. This is what our quest is all about. To beat Akkan to the prize and make sure we live in a peaceful world, Khonsu's world, not the hell that Seth has in mind. The future of Egypt, its soul, depends on us . . . I just hope we're not found wanting.'

'Taita chose you for a reason, lad. Never forget that.'

Piay nodded. He said nothing for a moment, then he pushed away from the wall and strode off down the street.

'Where are we going?' Hannu called out after him.

Piay did not break stride or even turn his head as he replied, 'To someone who can tell us what's really going on in this city.'

The broad-shouldered man still leaned beside Asil's door, his eyes restless. When he saw Piay approaching, he nodded and this time allowed him entrance without question. Hannu glared up at the guard as he passed, as if studying a competing species; he barely came up to the other man's shoulders.

Beaming, Asil flung his arms wide as Piay stepped in.

'Young man!'

Piay found himself strangely happy to see his father again. He had been a thief, true, but his life had been hard. It was not Piay's place to judge. That was a matter for the gods.

'This is Hannu – he works for me.' Piay saw Hannu's face tighten and then, with a smile, added, 'With me.'

'I am happy to welcome you to my meagre home, Hannu,' Asil said.

'Hannu, this is . . .' Piay almost said 'My father,' but he was not yet ready to use that description, so settled for 'Asil.'

Hannu nodded, reserving judgement as he always did.

'I am pleased to make your acquaintance.'

'Sit, sit.'

Asil ushered them both to cushions next to the hearth. The old man fetched two cups of beer and handed them over.

'Tell me,' he said, 'about your woman. Did you bring her home?'

Piay shook his head. 'Your advice to join with my enemy's enemy was very wise. And it would have succeeded if, ah . . . How can I put this? If the situation had not changed unexpectedly, in ways I cannot explain.'

'Hmm . . . intriguing. Tell me all, my dear, and maybe we will find an explanation together.'

Piay took a sip of his beer and began the story of joining the Shrikes, his capture during the fight at Akkan's camp – though he omitted the presence of the Sons of Apis – and the revelation that Myssa had been transformed into someone he did not recognise.

Asil leaned his forehead against the tips of his fingers.

'I've heard of such things before, yes. You are right to think that this must be the result of some potion conjured up by the sorcerer. Of course, there are ways of undoing such changes—'

'What? Tell me?' Piay insisted.

'First, I need to speak with someone who understands this stuff.' He smiled knowingly at Piay. 'Let's just say, after all these years in Memphis, I can find people who know the kinds of things that rich folk who live in palaces will never understand.'

'Time is short,' Piay stressed.

'I won't let you down.'

'That man outside the door . . .' Hannu interjected.

'The son of a friend, protecting an old man.'

'He has three scars along his cheekbone.'

Asil nodded, still smiling.

'I've heard that's the mark of the Guild of Thieves,' Hannu continued. 'People say it's a brotherhood that's existed here in the Lower Kingdom for years, well before the Hyksos took over.'

Asil shrugged. 'My friend is a good man, but I don't know much about his son. Perhaps you should ask him yourself.'

Asil continued to smile. Hannu showed no reaction, but just like Asil, he knew many things that were beyond Piay's experience.

'I'm asking you,' Hannu said.

Asil smiled, but there was no humour in it. 'I'm just an old man. The Guild, if such a thing existed, would have no interest in me.'

'There was trouble of a kind I have never seen before,' Piay said, wanting to get back to the reason he had come here, before the growing tension between Asil and Hannu brought the visit to a close.

Asil listened to Piay's description of the riot, then said, 'Now you know why I stay at home with a guard at the door. Things have been getting worse here since the siege began. This morning, one of the kitchens producing bread burned down, and so did the grain store next to it. There's not been enough to go around in recent times, and now there's even less. And yet the governor's slaves went from bakery to bakery buying up much of what was available, for a feast perhaps, or simply to keep the larders full in the palace.'

'Taita would never have stood for that,' Piay said.

'But Taita's not here, is he?' Asil noted. 'And you can't rely on his guidance forever.'

Piay stared into the pot bubbling in the hearth. He had never considered a point when his master would not be around to help him.

'Your father is here now,' Asil said, as if he could read Piay's thoughts, 'and you have no more need to worry.'

He reached out and rested a wrinkled hand on the back of Piay's.

'Your father?' Hannu asked.

Piay and Hannu hurried through the small dusty streets lined with silent workshops and deserted warehouses. Piay had begun to explain how he had rediscovered the father he had not seen since he was five, but the conversation had quickly petered out as they encountered the aftermath of the riot. The streets were strewn with the dead and wounded. Here and there, women crouched in tears beside their dead or dying husbands. A little girl stood by her slaughtered parents crying, 'Mummy, Daddy, get up!' A thief rummaged through the pouches of the dead – he ran at the sight of Hannu drawing his sword.

As for the rest of the population, it was as if they had disappeared. The city was calm now, quieter than Piay had ever known it. But it was an oppressive calm, as if a great weight was pressing down on all Memphis.

Finally they reached the palace. The gates were closed, and the guards refused to allow them permission to enter until Piay persuaded them to send a messenger to the captain of the Blue Crocodile Guards to confirm their identity.

When they slipped through the gates, Piay felt as if they had been transported to another place entirely. The perfumed garden was still an oasis of tranquillity, and as he neared the palace he breathed in the scents of cinnamon, cumin and other expensive spices that were being used in the kitchens.

Inside, slaves bustled back and forth with arms filled with bolts of linen and flowers cut from the palace gardens. Piay followed them to the feasting hall, where gauzy curtains were being suspended from the ceiling. The fabric shimmered in the gentle breeze from the windows, obscuring then revealing the sinuous dancers who practised behind it.

Musicians plucked at their lyres and a flautist blew a sweet, gentle melody. Candles floated in bowls of water, the light flickering across the white walls. Slaves were strewing flowers across the floor around a low table where many places had been set. Herbs had been tossed on a brazier in one corner, filling the air with sweet aromas.

Piay looked around. How could anyone even consider such indulgence when the city was on the brink of total revolt? Surely Zahur and Harrar must understand what a provocation this feast would be if the masses ever heard of it. At a time like this, restraint was a necessity, as a matter of self-preservation.

Piay grabbed a slave.

'Where is your master?' he demanded.

Before the slave could answer, Piay heard the booming voices of Zuhar and Harrar approaching. The two men wandered into the chamber, laughing as if they had been friends since childhood.

When Harrar saw Piay, he held out his hands.

'Ah, Piay. How's your work going on those monuments? They still sinking in the sand?'

The two men laughed together.

Piay swept a hand towards the busy slaves and said in an incredulous tone, 'What's the meaning of this?'

'Why, we have reached an agreement,' Zahur said, his jowls shaking with mirth. 'One that will return Memphis to the glory of old.'

'The talks were arduous,' Harrar said, 'but it was important that no stone was left unturned. It has been decided how much gold Pharaoh must send to ensure the city can be rebuilt. I have agreed not to return to Thebes, but to stay here to oversee the work that will need to be done. And Zahur will remain as governor. We need someone who commands the respect of the people. It may take longer than the common folk think to make good the damage to the city.'

'Don't you know what's happening out there? The streets are running red with blood. Your own men are killing Egyptians – their own people – as if they were Hyksos.'

Zahur wafted a hand. 'The people are always complaining. No leader could ever satisfy their demands.'

'They're not complaining – they're starving.'

'There is more than enough food in Memphis, and more coming by the day.' Harrar's face darkened in annoyance. 'And in answer to your impertinent question, of course news of the disturbance has reached me. That is why I have increased the guard at the palace.'

'It's just troublemakers,' Zahur said. 'We know all about them, spreading lies and rumours to stir up trouble. Believe me, we're not letting them get away with it!'

Harrar scowled. 'We have identified a man who was making wild allegations by the site of the bakery that burned down. He's been arrested and will be executed at dawn, as an example to anyone else who so much as thinks of making trouble. His body will be hung from the wall until it has been pecked clean. People will see that we are in control of the situation, and that will be an end to it.'

Piay choked back what he wanted to say. He could not believe that these two men could be so deluded. How could they not see the terrible mistake they were making?

He tried a calmer approach, in the hope that he might be able to persuade them.

'My lord, may I suggest there may be another way to solve this undoubtedly worrying problem—'

'Who are you to suggest anything?' Harrar snapped. 'You are Taita's lackey, and that is all you will ever be. Waste your time completing the ludicrous task he has set for you, then return to Thebes where you can fawn over him.'

Piay eyed Hannu. Like all soldiers, he had long since learned to hold his tongue while his superiors made stupid decisions. His gaze was fixed on the far wall, and whatever opinions he had, he was keeping them firmly to himself, but Piay knew that Hannu could see the trouble that Harrar and Zahur were storing up.

Still, there was nothing further that could be achieved here.

'Very well,' Piay said. 'I will say no more on that matter.'

'Good,' Harrar said. 'Now hurry on your way. Soon the members of the court, the aristocracy of Memphis, will be arriving to hear our plans.'

Piay stepped forward, raising a finger. 'One more thing, my lord. The work I must carry out at the monuments will pass more quickly and easily if I can speak with the wisest, the most learned of your scribes. Someone who can guide me in my task. Someone who knows the work of the great Imhotep.'

'Zahur,' Harrar said, 'give this boy a name so that we can be left in peace. We've got a lot to do here before our guests arrive.'

'Yes, yes, of course,' Zahur said, clapping his hands. 'The man you need to speak to is as old as the desert and as wizened as a fig left out in the sun. If he does not have the knowledge you require, then no one else will. His name is Ankhu.'

There was a house that stood by itself in the corner of the palace compound. On the second floor, a large window gave a magnificent view of the moon, set against a glittering blanket of stars. Windows were set into the other walls, too, so there was a perfect view of the whole of the night sky for anyone who wished to study the constellations. Parchments were piled high everywhere except on a low table on which a fat candle guttered. As the shadows swirled, Piay felt an odd sensation of movement around him.

Here and there, strange symbols had been etched on the white walls in black ink. Piay had never seen the like before, but when he stared at them he felt his skin prickle. On one side there was a small alabaster statue of Osiris, some bowls containing dried leaves, a bronze mask with an ankh engraved on the forehead, and a scarab that gleamed in the flickering light as if it were made of gold, with eyes that appeared to be sapphires. Some riches, then, though why they would be in the hands of a mere scribe, Piay did not know.

Hannu flopped down on a sumptuous cushion and bounced twice, appreciating its stuffing.

'Better than I thought,' he grunted.

The faint aroma of incense floated in the air as if someone had been in the room only moments before.

'Ankhu will be with you soon,' they had been told.

Piay looked out of the window and felt the moon stare back at him. Khonsu was there with them that night, he was certain of it. He let his eyes drift down. Beyond the white walls, the night had settled like a sable cloak across the fertile valley and the desert to the west.

Music drifted up from the city – a woman's lilting song to her child, a man's yearning nostalgia for the days of his youth. The scent of the evening hearth-fires hung in the air.

Piay shivered. The night was peaceful, but the air in the room crackled with the tension that came before a storm.

From what Piay had been told by the guard who had directed him to Ankhu's residence, the man they had come to see had been a part of Memphis life for longer than anyone could remember. Zahur had inherited him from the previous governor, who had received the scribe from the one who came before. Everyone knew him, yet he seemed like a ghost drifting on the fringes of their memories, someone they were certain must have been at this or that event, although they could never quite remember for sure.

People told strange tales of how Ankhu roamed through the necropolis at Saqqara, sometimes staying out of the city all night, or how he had been found one dawn, sitting cross-legged in front of the Sphinx as if he and the ancient monument had been having a conversation.

However, his eccentricities were tolerated, because Ankhu knew everything. The names of long-forgotten kings. The names of the stars and the pattern of their movements across the sky. When the moon would rise and fall. When the Nile flood would come each spring. He could speak foreign tongues and read their writing. He knew the practices of the physicians, their potions and spells, and even had access to knowledge that was hidden from other men.

'Do you think he can help?' Hannu said, lounging back with his hands behind his head.

'Let's hope. We need to work out what this Disc of Ra is all about, and we don't have Taita or . . .'

Piay fell silent, so Hannu said it. 'Myssa. Then we'd better hope that this man can help us.'

'And that we can trust him.'

'There's no one in the city I trust, not completely. But what other choice do we have?'

The sound of soft shoes rustled on the steps up to their lofty perch. Piay turned in anticipation.

Despite his great age, Ankhu did not appear frail. His movements were strong, precise, potent. When he reached the top of the steps, he paused to study his guests. He was as wizened as Zahur had said. His small, round face was as coppery as the desert rocks and covered with so many wrinkles and grooves that it resembled a piece of papyrus that had been used and reused many times. Around his head was wrapped a scarf the blue-mauve colour of an iris, the colour of wisdom, and he wore a plain white robe that flowed around his gaunt frame.

Ankhu sighed when he saw them.

'Am I never to rest?'

Piay bowed. 'We will not keep you long, wise one, but we were told you may be able to help us with a matter of the greatest urgency.'

'As long as you were not sent by that fat slug Zahur.'

Hannu chuckled. 'Harsh words for the man who keeps you fed. Can't see him liking that!'

'I have reached the age where no man sees me as a threat. Besides, I am too valuable to Zahur to be dismissed. I could empty my bladder on his feet and he would still laugh and clap his hands.'

Ankhu strode over to the large cushion and flexed his fingers. Hannu grunted and moved to a smaller cushion so that the master of the chamber could sit where he pleased.

Once he was settled, the scribe looked Piay up and down.

'You are Taita's man, is that true?'

'Yes, my name is Piay. This is Hannu. You know Taita?'

'I know of him. A wise man. A knowledgeable man. And a long-lived one, I am told, for the stories of Taita have been circulating for a very long time.'

'So I am told. But he does not look . . .' Piay let his words die with a smile.

'Like me? The years have etched their story on my flesh, that is true. I wonder what Taita's secret is. Perhaps losing your balls to a knife traps a man's potency within him so that he can escape the ravages of time. But that is a higher price than I would wish to pay.'

Ankhu dipped his fingers into a bowl of dates and sucked on one for a while before chewing slowly.

'If Taita thinks you are worthy, then who am I to argue?' the scribe said eventually. 'These hours of quiet are normally reserved for my own investigations, but I will hear your plea.'

Piay felt relieved. Having seen how formidable Ankhu was, and how straight-talking, he felt more confident that he could get the guidance he needed.

'What I am about to show you is of great importance,' Piay said, moving to sit cross-legged in front of the scribe. 'To me, to Taita, to all of Egypt. Don't ask me why it carries such weight for I cannot . . . will not say. I hope you will trust me on this matter.'

Ankhu nodded. His eyes twinkled in the candlelight. He was intrigued now.

'And I know I cannot force you to do anything against your will,' Piay continued, 'but I must ask you not to discuss this matter with anyone else. Not with Zahur, nor with the other scribes. It must remain a secret between us. This is not something I say lightly. To speak of this thing that I am about to reveal could cost my life, your life . . . It could cost the very soul of Egypt.'

A playful smile flickered on the scribe's lips. 'The soul of Egypt.'

'Do I have your word on this?'

Ankhu sucked on the last sweetness of the date, weighing his response, and then said, 'You have my word. And my word is not given lightly. It is an unbreakable bond.'

Piay loosened his shoulders. 'Very well.'

He dipped into his pouch and pulled out the Disc of Ra. Balancing it on the palm of his hand, he offered it to the scribe. In the torchlight, the circle blazed like the sun itself.

Ankhu's eyes widened. 'Where did you find this?'

'I cannot say. But it has been hidden from the eyes of man for an age.'

'Yes, yes, I see. May I?' Ankhu reached out a hand, waiting for permission.

Piay nodded. The scribe took the disc as if he was afraid it would crumble to dust as soon as he touched it. He held it steady on his own palm, the reflected light of the artefact dancing in his dark eyes. Then he raised it, turning it so that same light could play across all the surfaces in the room, revealing details that would be hidden from a cursory glance.

'A magnificent work,' he breathed. 'I have never seen the like, and that alone tells me much about its origins. It is Egyptian, of course – the *medu netjer*, the gods' words, here and here and here.' Leaning back, he pronounced, 'Only one man could have created this. A man who is now a god, because the great powers breathed their spirit into him so he could construct wonders like this.'

Piay nodded again. 'Imhotep,' he murmured.

'Imhotep.' Ankhu returned his attention to the disc. 'You have not brought this to me to assess its value so you may sell it and make yourself wealthy?'

'No. We brought it to you to guide us in unlocking its secrets.'

'And secrets there are aplenty, I can see that with only the briefest examination. The disc is dedicated to Ra. You see the sun, the flames upon the edges? Imhotep was a high priest of Ra, in Heliopolis, the City of the Sun.'

'The parts of the disc move,' Piay prompted.

'I can see that . . . So this is not for decoration, not a work of art. Its beauty does not exist to dazzle the eyes, though it serves that purpose, as all great things do. The skill involved in the fabrication, the value of the gold used, make it something that would be constructed for kings. Or for the gods.'

'What is it, then?' Piay asked.

Ankhu tugged at the flames that rotated the discs with short, delicate strokes.

'It is designed to convey knowledge.'

'To a pharaoh?' Hannu muttered, turning up his nose. 'Knowledge is for those who advise them.'

'This is true, very true,' Ankhu said, 'and therein lies our mystery. Knowledge for the wise, but built from materials that only a king could access.'

'Unless . . .' Piay bit his tongue. What right did a man like him have to offer up his thoughts to a man of great learning like Ankhu.

And yet the scribe did not seem offended. He smiled and gently prompted, 'Go on, let me hear your opinion. You have lived with this object for longer than I and have had time to dwell on its meaning.'

Piay sucked in a deep breath. 'Papyri crumble and fade, but gold will survive the years, we all know that. If this knowledge was meant to reach across the ages, then what better a form than etched in gold?'

'Then why not carved in stone?' Ankhu pushed back. 'The monuments have lasted an age. Nothing can destroy them – not storm, flood or the baking heat of the sun.'

Piay had considered this. As an architect, Imhotep had understood the value of stone to stand the test of time. He had begun his quest with a carving and had etched his near-invisible messages in the surface of stones, to be revealed by the Eye of Horus, knowing they would last down the years.

'The great monuments have been all but forgotten, because men do not care enough to preserve them. But gold? That will never be ignored. It will always be desired and men will always keep it safe, and hunt for it, and fight over it. I can't say what a man as great as Imhotep thought or knew, but it seems to me that if he wanted his knowledge to last forever, he would make sure it was encased in gold.'

The scribe smiled and wagged a finger at Piay. 'You are wiser than you appear.'

Hannu snorted.

'So . . . let us see exactly what is so vital that Imhotep thought it worth preserving for so long.'

Ankhu leaned forward so his nose was barely a finger's width from the disc, and then he moved his attention slowly across every single part of the surface, examining every detail, searching for anything that might be half-hidden. He mumbled over the symbols that were etched there, talking to himself.

'. . . above . . .'

'. . . below . . .'

'. . . Osiris . . .'

The scribe rotated the discs back and forth, lifted the flaps, studying the different words and images that appeared in the windows. Nothing was left unexamined.

'I think it is true to say that without knowing Imhotep it would be impossible to decipher this puzzle,' Ankhu mused, looking up from under his bushy brows. 'The Great Architect walked a path between the world of men and the world of gods. He was an astronomer-priest. He looked from our world to the heavens above. And he saw the connection between the two.'

Ankhu bowed his head again, and once again lost himself to his task. The night deepened. The songs from the city ebbed away and then there was only the breathing of the wind as it rolled in from the desert.

Piay would not be distracted. He fixed his attention on the old man in front of him and it did not waver. He felt his shoulders tighten as his apprehension grew. What if Ankhu found nothing that could help? If a man so wise was confounded, what hope was there for him and Hannu? They would have reached the end of the road that Imhotep had shown them. He would have failed Taita.

And Myssa? Would I have failed her, too?

Piay cursed himself for the question. The only way to survive her loss was to drive all thought of her from his head. One day, he might let her back into his mind. But not now.

Then, after what seemed like an age, Ankhu looked up again, blinking, seemingly surprised that he had guests.

'What have you found?' Piay asked.

Ankhu's jaw sagged and amazement sparkled in his eyes.

'This disc is a construction of a mind beyond any I can imagine,' he said. 'Imhotep was truly a god.'

'So what have you seen?' Piay pressed, his frustration mounting.

'This is a map of the stars,' the scribe breathed, 'and of the earth, too. Both of them intertwined, as I surmised.'

Hannu jolted forward. 'The stars? A riddle of the stars?'

'In the days before days, when our civilisation was first forming along the valley of the Nile and the desert beyond, Egypt was shaped by the astronomer-priests,' Ankhu said. 'They looked to the stars, and to the gods, and saw how both cast their spell upon this land. Their wisdom flourished, a thousand blossoms – writing, architecture, numbers. What they discovered still guides us to this day. But the stars came first.'

Piay leaned forward, intrigued. 'The stars cast their spell upon the earth, all men know that. The rising of Sopdet signals the flooding of the Nile.[1] This has been known from the earliest times.'

The scribe nodded. 'But there is so much more. The stars hold our destiny.' Ankhu tapped the disc. 'This is what Imhotep learned, and he has left instructions on how to use this wonderful object he has created. See these words here – "The earth is a mirror. What happens in the heavens is reflected on the land."'

Piay winced. His thoughts felt like dull mud against the bright mercury of the scribe's thinking.

'And here,' Ankhu continued. '"The pathway to the gods lies at our feet."'

'It's a map, aye,' Hannu growled. 'A map to find a great treasure. The signs that point the way are over our heads. But the answers lie in the ground.'

Ankhu lowered the disc so they could all see. He lifted one window and behind it Piay glimpsed the mark for 'river'.

---

[1] The star we now know as Sirius.

'As the discs turn, this window reveals landmarks upon the earth,' the scribe said. 'And around the outer part of the disc are the stars as they appear overhead.'

He moved the disc one notch so that the window now showed a date palm. The stars etched on the outer ring had moved, too.

Ankhu tapped his finger on a notch in the outer ring which seemed to indicate a star beneath it.

'This is Sopdet.'

Piay grinned. 'When the window shows the Nile, the outer ring reveals the star with power over the river.'

The scribe nodded. 'Then we move this inner ring until Sopdet shows in this window. And in this window here, we now find . . .'

He lifted the flap to reveal the symbol for 'river' once more.

Hannu shook his head. 'What help is that? It's just the same.'

'Let me look,' Piay said.

Ankhu handed over the disc. Piay began to revolve the plates one step at a time, noting the symbols that appeared in the first window. He paused at one.

'What is that?' he asked.

The scribe examined it and shook his head.

Piay glanced at Hannu. 'This looks to me very much like a shaft in the ground. What do you say?'

Hannu shrugged. 'Your guess is as good as mine.'

The notch in the outer ring now pointed to a trail of three stars.

'And these are?' Piay asked.

'Sahu,'[2] Ankhu replied. 'The Hidden One.'

Piay nodded. 'The Hidden One,' he repeated. 'That speaks to me.'

He shifted the inner disc until he found the three stars of Sahu.

'Now,' he said. 'The moment of truth.'

---

[2] The constellation of Orion.

Piay lifted the third window.

'What is that?' he asked.

Ankhu leaned in once more to examine the symbol.

'That,' he said with confidence, 'is the Pyramid of Khufu, the greatest of all the monuments.'

'**M**en aren't supposed to set foot inside the tombs,' Hannu said. 'Once is enough . . . And now the Pyramid of Khufu? No living man should ever do that. There are curses, and spells. Khufu himself will likely rise up to drag us down into the underworld.'

'Imhotep has set us this challenge,' Piay replied. 'So we either run away or we face our fears.'

'I'd rather face the whole Hyksos army, single-handed.'

Piay turned and gripped Hannu's shoulders. 'This is where we are tested. If we're found wanting, then all is lost. It is time for us to risk everything. Even our souls.'

Hannu sucked in air, steadying himself. 'All right . . . I don't like it, but I will be there – as always.'

Piay clapped him on the shoulder. No further words needed to be said.

They walked on through the peaceful gardens, breathing in the cool scents of the night. The moon was reflected in the dark mirror of the pool. Everywhere was still.

Piay paused and looked up at the stars.

'Tonight has seen another door open for us. But the candle's burning low and we can't afford to hang about. Akkan must know by now that we've survived. He and Tallus will come looking for us.'

'As long as those bastard Sons of Apis don't realise we're moving closer to their precious secret. Swords I can deal with, but poison and magic dust in the air?' Hannu shook his head.

'Yes, but we're at the front of the race,' Piay said. 'And that's where we have to stay.'

The gods came to men in dreams – everyone knew that.

Piay felt the cool night wind caress his face as he looked along the majestic Nile. Across the expanse of water, the full moon hung over Thebes, its lambent rays turning the City of a Hundred Gates into a majestic citadel of white light.

On the far bank, Taita walked. Piay realised that for some reason he was standing alone on the other side of the river from his master, in the necropolis, surrounded by the great monuments to the dead. He called and waved, his voice growing increasingly louder, but Taita seemed not to hear him and eventually his master vanished into the night.

Piay was alone, and yet he sensed a presence all around him – invisible, intangible. It felt as if someone was about to tap him on the shoulder. He knew this sensation by now.

A band of light unfurled from that vast moon and rolled down to the land, forming a shimmering white path across the black water of the river. Piay half-remembered the last time he'd had this vision, on the vast lake in the highlands where the Nile began.

A figure strode along the white road over the river. As it drew closer Piay could see the mummy wrappings, the *menat* necklace and the crook and the flail. The Traveller was coming.

Khonsu came to a halt in the centre of the river, the glow from the moonlit band enveloping him.

Though the god's mouth did not move, Piay heard a voice in his head, as soothing as the sound of the wind through the rushes. 'I am three things – Embracer, Pathfinder, Defender. You are three things – Embracer, Pathfinder, Defender. Let love, wisdom and courage guide you.'

Despite the calm words, Piay felt a shiver of unease. Why was Khonsu telling him these things now?

As if in answer to his thought, the god pushed his flail forward. Piay turned, following the direction Khonsu was indicating.

Beyond the monuments of the necropolis, a red glow was rising along the dark horizon, as if a great conflagration raged there. The wavering crimson haze seethed upwards until it blocked out the sky and then, in the heart of it, Piay could see two fierce eyes burning. The beast-head of Seth emerged from the cloud, looming over the necropolis. The figure was vast, dwarfing Khonsu, seemingly enveloping the entire land.

This great war is coming to a conclusion, Piay thought. *This can be the only meaning of this vision. A final battle above the land of the dead.*

Piay felt a horrible apprehension at the disparity in size and strength of the two combatants. Khonsu had chosen him, but he stood alone against the power of Seth and all his malevolent followers.

How could he hope to win?

Piay jolted awake. He was slick with sweat and his mouth was as dry as the desert sands. The instant his eyes snapped open, he cried out.

A face hovered just above his own, instantly merging in his mind with the dream of Seth's beast-head.

He scrambled back across the bed until he realised a low chuckle was echoing all around him.

Ankhu juddered with mirth.

'A man so easily scared has something on his conscience.'

'What are you doing in my chamber?'

'I have consulted the gods since our last meeting,' Ankhu said, 'and they have spoken. It is my belief that what you are undertaking is of such importance that I should accompany you to the Pyramid of Khufu.'

Piay pushed himself up, stretching his limbs. He felt that one half of him was still trapped in his vision.

'Because you don't believe that something of such importance should be entrusted to a pair of thick-headed adventurers?'

Ankhu shrugged, 'Your words, not mine.'

'But you agree?'

'Yes . . . but a man who knows his limitations is better off than one who does not.'

'I should warn you, there will be danger.'

'I am not afraid of danger.'

'Very well . . . but why do you want to accompany us? What is there for you?'

'Knowledge. What you showed me last night unlocked the secrets of a long-gone age. It was as if I had sat with Imhotep himself and he had opened his mind to me. You cannot imagine, you who live by the sword, what that means to a man like me. I have devoted my life to learning. Now I have an opportunity to discover things I've never dreamed of. If I do not see them with my own eyes, that lost opportunity will haunt me until my dying day.'

Ankhu pressed his hands together as if in prayer. Piay could hear the sincerity in his voice, and yet to open up Imhotep's quest to another, a stranger, would create consequences that he could not control. He knew Hannu would caution against it.

'No,' he said firmly.

Ankhu narrowed his eyes. 'Tell me, my thick-headed adventurer . . . when you reach the Pyramid of Khufu, you will know the way to enter it?'

'We . . . we will find it.'

'You will not. And once you are inside, you will know where to go? What to do? What to say? I have studied the Pyramid of Khufu since I was a boy. I have read all the accounts I could find of the building and the tunnels. No man knows it better than me.'

Piay weighed the scribe's words. There could be no doubt that his knowledge would be helpful, but Hannu had often criticised him for being reckless. He did not want to face that accusation again.

'Answer me one question,' Piay said.

'Ah, a test.'

'Everyone tells me the Pyramid of Khufu was built after Imhotep's time. How then could it be part of Imhotep's quest?'

Ankhu smiled. 'A surprisingly wise question. And you are correct. Imhotep was not involved in the building. The architect of the Pyramid of Khufu was called Hemiunu.'

'Then how . . .?'

'The knowledge of how to build in stone is closely guarded. Architects and masons have kept their secrets from a time before even Imhotep. The knowledge is passed on only to those who have proven themselves worthy of becoming one of their number.'

Piay was intrigued by the words 'proven themselves worthy' – for was that not the very nature of the quest Imhotep had set for those who wanted to discover his secrets?

'They have a guild?'

'Of a kind,' Ankhu replied. 'From the earliest time they were known as the Followers of Osiris. Anyone who wished to become an architect or a mason would be tested. If they were found to be worthy they were accepted in a ritual – a ritual that even I have never heard described, and it has been my business to uncover secrets.'

Piay moistened his dry mouth. The more he heard from Ankhu, the more what he said fitted with all he had learned on this quest.

'If the Followers of Osiris, the architects and masons, pass their secrets down across the years . . .'

'Then, yes, any plan Imhotep had could also have been delivered in the same manner,' Ankhu said. 'When Hemiunu designed the Pyramid of Khufu, was he working to Imhotep's plan? We can never know. But it is not impossible.'

'And you know what lies within the tomb?'

'The texts reveal the details of the passages and chambers.' Ankhu paused, thinking, and when he looked back at Piay his eyes glittered. 'I will give you a word of advice. You will come to a point where one passage goes down deep into the ground and one rises up. Do not take the downward passage.'

Piay frowned. 'That doesn't sound right. If Imhotep has created a version of the journey into the underworld here on earth,
then surely the passage that travels down would be the right one.'

'Heed my words.'

Piay stroked his chin, reflecting. This advice troubled him.
Could Ankhu be trusted? Imhotep's secret had attracted greedy
men, hungry to snatch their prize. What if Ankhu, too, wanted
to keep it for himself?

Piay still worried that it was too dangerous to take this old
man along, with Akkan's men and the Sons of Apis stalking their
every step. But Ankhu's knowledge could be invaluable. And the
gods knew that without Myssa, he and Hannu would be wading
through a sea of mud to reach the isle of enlightenment.

'Make your arrangements,' Piay said. 'But do not make me
regret this.'

'This has slowed us down,' Hannu grumbled. He was squatting against a wall outside the garrison, sharpening his sword with long, singing strokes of a whetstone.

'Once we reach the Pyramid of Khufu and begin our search for the next sign Imhotep has hidden, Ankhu's knowledge may guide us to the prize faster than the two of us stumbling around on our own.'

Piay folded his arms, peering into the courtyard at the heart of the garrison, where the Blue Crocodile Guards were now forming into ranks under the curt commands of the captain.

His thoughts drifted back to when he had walked through the gardens with Myssa's hand in his. He forced the memory aside. He felt haunted, as if the ghost of Myssa was always with him, a few steps behind his left shoulder.

A call rang out across the courtyard as soldiers marched up the steps from the cells under the garrison block. The man deemed responsible for the bakery fire trudged between them. His hands had been bound behind his back and his head was bowed so Piay could not see his face. Two spear tips prodded his bare back should his step slow. He would meet his doom on time.

Hannu stood, setting the whetstone aside and sheathing his sword. He watched the knot of soldiers turn past the ranks of the Blue Crocodile Guards and make their way out of the garrison.

'I don't like this one bit,' he mumbled.

'You're not alone in that.'

'There's been no trial,' Hannu continued. 'There's no evidence that this was the man who led the revolt. For all we know, he's just a farmer who got caught up in all of this when he just wanted a fair price for his grain. There's no Ma'at here.[3] No justice.'

---

[3] The word for the Egyptian notion of balance, justice, morality and truth, as well as the name of the goddess who embodied those ideals.

'There's no law in Memphis,' Piay said. 'Least of all in the palace. Harrar thinks he's proving a point to the people – and so he is, but not in the way that he thinks. And as for Zahur, the people already hate him. What are they going to think if he's sent an innocent man to his death?'

'Folk were only complaining about empty bellies.' Hannu's voice cracked. 'Who can blame them?'

As the soldiers led the captive out of the garrison, he raised his head as if looking to the blue sky one final time. He still had the flush of youth upon his face, his eyes large, dark and filled with fear.

As Piay watched the poor soul pass, a slave ran up.

'Lord Harrar requires you to observe the execution,' the boy gasped. 'He wants all of Pharaoh's representatives there, so the people can take comfort in the security that is being brought to Memphis.'

'Wants us all damned together, more like,' Hannu muttered.

Piay nodded and the slave raced away to find the next person on the list of names he had been given.

The palace soldiers marched past, followed by the Blue Crocodile Guards.

'Bet Harrar thinks this is a show of strength,' Hannu grumbled as he and Piay slipped into step behind his old regiment.

'The sooner we're away from here, the better,' Piay said.

The soldiers marched along the street towards the Temple of Ptah. The execution was to take place in the hot, sun-baked square next to the temple enclosure – the very heart of the sprawling city. A good execution was normally an entertainment, a chance to break the drudgery of a hard day's labour, but this felt very different.

Piay had never seen so many soldiers in one place since his arrival in Memphis. They formed a wall across the square, staring at the sullen-faced crowd that had come to watch the execution.

Zahur, sweat beading his face, was sitting on a chair on a small wooden stage behind the line of soldiers, two slaves fanning him.

He was smiling like a child – a carefree, gleeful grin, as if he were about to be presented with a feast. The other dignitaries stood around him. Piay searched for Harrar, but he appeared to have chosen a position at the rear of the group.

The execution frame had been set up in the centre of the square, to the right of Zahur's dais – a triangle that consisted of two ladders set roughly fifteen feet apart and bound together at their apex. A wooden crossbar had been crudely nailed near the top of the structure to keep the whole thing solid. The wood was stained black with the blood of previous victims.

As the captive saw it looming up ahead of him, he began to wail in terror and tried to throw himself back. The vision of his impending death so consumed him that he ignored the spears jabbing at his back, and blood streamed down across his filthy kilt. As his struggles grew more frenzied, the guards were forced to grab his arms and drag him forward.

At the foot of the execution frame, they hit him several times, knocking him half unconscious, then they hauled him up the structure and bound his hands to the crossbar and his feet to the two ladders. He hung there, spread-eagled, his head slumped down on his chest.

The captive began to sob. He raised his head to proclaim his innocence, his wail rolling out across the strangely quiet city. None of the guards made any attempt to quieten him; the lamentations of those about to be executed were traditionally considered to be a part of the entertainment.

But as Piay peered at the crowd, he could see none of the usual excitement on the faces of the spectators. Their features were implacable, their gazes heavy, their attention fixed on the man bound to the frame.

The people all knew that the condemned man's punishment would not end with his death. A safe passage to the afterlife could only be guaranteed by observing ancient customs and sacred rituals. But the body of the accused would be denied a proper burial. Instead, it would hang on the city walls while the vultures feasted on its flesh. Then the remains would be dismembered and thrown into the waters of the Nile. No wonder the man was so terrified. He knew he would never find his way to eternal peace.

Piay felt Hannu nudge him.

'Over there,' he murmured.

Turning, Piay looked to the nearest corner of the square. His father stood among a large group of men, beckoning him.

Hurrying across the square, Piay pushed through the line of soldiers. Once he reached his father, the group of men closed around them so they could not be seen. These men were broad-shouldered, strong-armed, with eyes that held no compassion. Many of them bore the three scars that Hannu had identified the previous day.

'You have news for me about Myssa?' Piay asked, forgetting all his resolutions about driving her from his mind.

'I told you that I would find out what I could,' Asil said. 'I would not let you down, my son. We are blood, bound together by the life-force.'

Piay felt it odd to hear those words. He had been alone all his life, with Taita the only constant, and Taita had always had his own concerns.

'There are some in the city who know about poisons and potions and charms and spells,' Asil continued. 'They know how to make men sleep, how to fill women with desire, and how to kill and leave no trace.'

Piay glanced around the circle of hardened men, all of whom were now facing out into the crowd, their broad backs turned on Asil and his son. They were protecting this old man. Piay felt a twist of unease. He could no longer deny that his father had some connection to the Guild of Thieves. No wonder he knew poisoners and potion-mixers. Those who lived in the shadows clung together.

But Piay's desperation outweighed his moral scruples.

'So, can you help me?' he asked.

'Of course, of course – I would do anything for you, my son.'

The old man grasped Piay's hand and opened out the fingers, palm up. Into it he pressed a small hide pouch.

'In there you will find the flowers of the blue lotus and the leaves of some other plants which have the power to lull a person into a dreamlike state,' Asil whispered. 'You must roll the contents into pellets. When you find your woman, feed them to her, at dawn and dusk, for three days.

'During this time, you must profess your love to her. You must tell her clearly what her life was like before she was taken from you, and how the joy she knew then can be hers again. In the dream state the mind is open to suggestion. This is what her captors did to her when they took her. You will only be undoing their work, and she will thank you for it when she is once again the woman you knew.'

Piay felt a rush of relief, and then gratitude. He had fought hard to keep despair from overwhelming him, but there were times when he had wondered if the change that had come over Myssa was permanent. Finding her and rescuing her was work for another day. For now, there was hope.

'Thank you.' Piay grasped his father's hands and squeezed them.

The old man beamed again at this display of affection. In his hard world, perhaps he had not experienced such honest warmth for a long time.

'One more thing,' Asil said. 'You are now in my debt for a second time. And, once again, this debt must be honoured. Not now. Perhaps not for a season or more. But at some point you will be asked to repay it.'

Piay nodded. Whatever the price was, it did not matter as long as he had an opportunity to free Myssa from the spell she was under and bring her back to him.

'I must return to the others,' Piay said, 'but I won't forget what you have done for me.'

Asil glanced around, looking past his guards and into the crowd.

'You must take care,' he said. 'If you value your life, keep your distance from Zahur.'

'Have you heard anything that I should know?'

Asil shrugged. 'I hear many things. Keep your wits about you and your eyes clear, that is the best advice I can give.'

Piay closed his fingers around the pouch and nodded his goodbye, then he pushed back out into the square and strode over to where Hannu was waiting.

'Some news?' Hannu asked.

'I'll tell you later. For now, keep your eyes on the crowd.'

The captive's screams faltered, his throat clearly ragged from his exhortations, but his body continued to shudder with terror. Heaving himself from his chair, Zahur wobbled to the edge of the stage and looked out over the crowd.

'Ma'at is the way in this world and the next,' he called out, his voice wavering so that some words disappeared into the breeze. 'Truth, justice, order. There must be balance. There is no other way. This offender you see before you has betrayed the way of Ma'at. He sought to foment rebellion, to disrupt the peace of our city. That is a crime of such magnitude that only the highest punishment can be brought down upon him. Be witness now—'

A rock the size of a man's hand arced over the line of soldiers and clattered across the flagstones not far from where Zahur stood. He stared at it, bewildered.

'Uh-oh,' Hannu muttered. 'This is about to go very bad.'

Zahur was trying to summon up the words that he had bitten off when another missile spun his way. This one crashed against his chest and he cried out in pain. A third rock dropped out of the sky, cracking against the side of Zahur's head and leaving a spray of blood and torn skin in its wake. This time he howled in agony, clutching at the wound.

'Execute the offender! Execute him now!' Harrar's voice boomed out across the courtyard as he stepped out from behind the assembled dignitaries.

Dazed and uncomprehending, Zahur staggered around as more missiles rained down from all sides – stones, bits of wood, even clods of excrement. The dignitaries scattered. Zahur threw his hands over his head and stumbled after them, gesturing to his underlings to form a protective circle around him.

'Asil knew this was going to happen,' Piay said as the executioner strode towards the frame. In his hands he gripped the Tool of Opening, a long pole with a sickle blade at one end. He swung the pole up in a well-practised motion and raked the blade down the captive's belly.

The man screamed so loud and shrill that Piay felt his ears ring. As the glistening entrails tumbled out, the attack ceased. Piay sensed the weight of the crowd's attention on the act of execution and the dark thoughts that accompanied it.

They all knew that the so-called offender was trapped in that strange realm, dead yet not dead. He would live on for a while, watching his innards dry out in the sun before the final, fatal blow delivered him from his agony.

The lull only lasted a moment. Once the crowd had borne witness to what had happened, even more missiles rained down. The soldiers held their line across the square, while the Blue Crocodile Guards went to Zahur and the fleeing dignitaries and guided them back to the palace.

'We need to get out of here,' Hannu said. 'If people saw us arrive with Zahur, they're liable to think we're on his side.'

Harrar, Zahur and the others returned to the governor's compound and the gates were sealed. Piay watched as the bar was slammed into place before hurrying into the palace.

He found Harrar and Zahur sheltering in an opulent sitting room. Two female slaves were tending to the wound on the governor's head while another one stood by with a jug of Syrian wine, ready to refill the two men's cups.

'I have urgent business among the monuments,' Piay said. 'I must leave later today.'

'Out of the question,' Harrar said. 'No one may leave the palace until the mood in the city has calmed. You saw them at the execution. That rabble is out of control.'

'I do not know what has come over them,' Zahur wheezed, ignoring Piay's incredulous glance. 'I have never seen them this way. Yes, they have complained about the lack of bread. But to hurl deadly rocks? That is unthinkable!'

'I must leave today,' Piay pressed. 'Just seal the gates after I've gone.'

'Have you seen them?' Zahur exclaimed. 'You would never make it out of the city alive.'

'You will not disobey me,' Harrar said, wagging his finger. 'If you try to leave the palace, I will have you placed in the cells beneath the garrison. I do not care who your master is.'

Piay was simmering with rage as he strode out of the sitting room. He could ill afford to waste any more time, but Harrar's tone had made it plain that this was not the moment to challenge him.

When he found Hannu, they brooded over their options, but could see no easy way out.

'Look, the palace can't stay sealed forever,' Hannu said. 'We just have to hope that things calm down in the next day or two. Then we should be able to slip away.'

The desert wind dropped and the temperature began to rise as the sun climbed higher. Though the city remained quiet, Piay sensed an oppressive tension in the sweltering streets. When night fell, the heat barely seemed to diminish. He wandered through the gardens, listening, but this time he couldn't hear women soothing their babes or men in full-throated chorus, either yearning for days long gone or hoping for better times ahead. Those within the palace walls might as well have been all alone in the world.

The palace, too, seemed quiet, as if everyone within was holding their breath. Piay retired to his bed early, but it was too hot to sleep and his frustrations gnawed at his mind. From his window, Piay could see the candlelight flickering in Ankhu's house as he pored over parchments for any knowledge that would help them when they were allowed to begin the next stage of their quest. The only noise was Hannu snoring in the chamber next door.

Finally, Piay rolled out of bed and wandered back into the gardens. He half-thought he might visit the garrison and see if any of the Blue Crocodile Guards felt like gambling on a game of knucklebones over beer from the kitchens, but as he strolled along the walls once again, he passed a guard who grinned at him and nodded as if they both shared some secret. After a few steps, Piay turned to question him, but the guard had already continued on his round.

That nod of complicity preyed on Piay's mind as he walked. When he reached the gate, the two soldiers set to keep watch were leaning on their spears, engaged in bored conversation.

One of them looked up as Piay neared.

'She's come back, then.'

Piay shook his head, baffled. 'Who has come back?'

'Your woman.'

'My . . . woman?'

'Turned up at the gate—'

'When?' Piay snapped.

'Not long ago. Said she'd been captured by some Hyksos dogs, but that she'd managed to escape. They hunted her, but she hid in the fields till they'd gone, then made her way back here.'

Piay felt his heart leap. If anyone could escape from Akkan, it was Myssa. His mind raced as he imagined what might have transpired, from Myssa pretending to take the Cobra's potions and then slitting a throat and fleeing into the night, to turning those potions upon her own captors. Anything was possible if her mind was clear.

And yet he barely dared hope.

'Where is she?' Piay asked.

The soldier shrugged. 'Well, when we let her in, she said she was coming to see you.'

Piay raced along the avenue from the gate. Apart from the guards on their rounds, the gardens were deserted at that time of night. The palace, too, was still. The slaves had returned to their quarters; the kitchens were deserted.

He paused in the entrance hall and cocked his head. Nothing. No sound of echoing feet anywhere.

Piay bounded up the steps and raced towards his chamber. When he burst in, he was ready to throw his arms around Myssa and lift her off her feet, but his room was empty.

Piay felt his heart begin to thump. Where else could she be? Had the soldiers been playing some cruel joke on him?

He crept out of his chamber. He could still hear Hannu snoring, but he looked in on him, nonetheless. After that he moved on through the palace. His initial jubilation ebbed away – he could find no sign of Myssa anywhere.

As he paused by a window to reflect, he glimpsed a flash of pale yellow-grey in the gardens, sweeping along the white enclosure walls. It could have been the dress Myssa had been wearing at Akkan's camp, but he resisted calling her name for fear of waking the rest of the palace.

What a game of cat and mouse they were playing! Myssa had failed to find him in his chamber and now she was searching the gardens for him.

Piay raced back down the steps and into the garden. Ducking past the avenue of sycamores and around the pool, he dashed towards the wall, where he hoped he could intercept Myssa.

Through the trees and shrubs, he glimpsed flashes of pale grey in the moonlight. Then, when he looked along the wall, Piay finally caught sight of Myssa. She had come to a halt, her head bowed, looking down at the ground.

'Myssa,' he called, though his voice was so low it was barely more than a whisper.

He hurried towards her and tried again. This time she heard him. She raised her head and pushed her shoulders back, and though she still had her back to him, his heart jumped in recognition.

Slowly she turned and her lips curled into a smile of greeting. Piay felt overwhelmed at the sight of her.

'Thank the gods,' he gasped, then ran forward to sweep her into his arms.

But as Piay came closer to Myssa, the moonlight picked out more detail – something dark and glistening on her arms and hands. He slowed, trying to make sense of what he was seeing, and that was when he saw what she was clutching in the fingers of her right hand –a short-bladed knife.

Piay stumbled to a halt.

Two bodies were sprawled on the ground, one near her feet, still twitching as the lifeblood pumped out of him, the other a little further away. She must have circled around and taken the two soldiers guarding the gate by surprise.

'What have you done?' Piay croaked.

Piay had seen Myssa kill before. She had slit the throat of a pirate captain on the Great Green Sea, shortly after they had first met. But that was to save his life, and Hannu's. These were murders.

'What have you done?' he asked again.

'I remember you now, I think,' Myssa said, frowning, ignoring his questions.

'Remember? We were as one.'

Myssa shrugged. 'Ah, well, I have forgotten much recently,' she said dismissively. 'But I remember the woman I once was, long ago. I know what I deserve in this world and what is necessary for victory.'

Piay glanced past Myssa and saw the bar from the gate now lay across the ground. Before he could move, the gate creaked open and shadowy figures drifted in. When they stepped into the moonlight, Piay saw the Cobra, towering over the others, his wild hair limned in silver by the pale rays. Behind him strode half a dozen Hyksos warriors, their crescent swords drawn,

'We have come for you,' Myssa said. 'Or rather, for what you have.'

Piay's mind raced. The pouch the Cobra had given him still hung at his side, for he kept the Eye of Horus and the Disc of Ra with him at all times. He'd thought that he had been ensuring the safety of the two priceless objects, but now he had delivered them straight to a woman who considered herself his enemy.

'How you escaped the traps in that shaft, I will never know,' Myssa continued, 'but when my spies told me you had returned to Memphis, I knew you had discovered what we both wanted.'

'Your spies?'

Piay glanced around the gathered Hyksos and realised that their leader was nowhere to be seen.

Myssa nodded as if she could read his thoughts.

'I am in command now, Piay of Thebes. No man will make me a slave again. No man will tell me I must be his bride. I bow my head to no one.'

'Where is Akkan?'

Her smile grew darker. 'With his god. I killed him with his own sword. His men follow me now. If I give the word, they will end your life.'

As if to prove her point, two Hyksos warriors appeared behind Piay, their curved swords ready in their hands.

Myssa turned her head to Tallus and flicked her hand, beckoning him to join her. When the priest stood beside her, Myssa pointed at Piay.

'Do you recognise that pouch?' she asked, smiling at Tallus.

'Yes . . . I believe I do,' he replied, with an equal air of amusement, the two of them mocking Piay's folly.

'As I recall, you gave it to this man in case the Great Architect might have left something at the bottom of his pit – something that might be of great value.'

'Indeed.'

'Let's see if you were right.'

Myssa moved forward, and all at once she was so close to him that Piay could smell her scent . . . so, so close. Piay sensed the approach of the Hyksos warriors behind him, felt their calloused hands take his wrists, but he was helpless to resist with Myssa standing there in front of him. He could feel the warmth of her body through her dress, see her bare skin. As her fingers worked at the knot that held the pouch to his belt, his body betrayed him and he responded as he had always done when it was late at night and the woman he loved was at his side.

Myssa saw it, felt it, and as the knot came undone and she pulled the pouch into her hands, she gave a mocking smile and said, 'Men . . . all the same, all equally pathetic.'

She walked back to Tallus, opened the pouch and they both looked into it. Then she looked at the priest and said, 'Congratulations. You were absolutely right.'

Bast sat on the windowsill in the moonless dark that comes before the dawn. The cat's eyes burned with green fire and its tail flicked. Whether it had accompanied its mistress to the palace, Piay did not know, but the feline's stare gripped him as if the beast was trying to tell him something of great value.

'So, what I want to know is, why didn't Myssa kill you?' Hannu asked. 'Because it certainly wasn't because she still loves you, deep down inside.'

'No, it wasn't . . .' Piay paused. 'Just before she left, she told me that I posed no threat to her now. And then she said that she'd rather have me on my knees in front of Taita, begging for his forgiveness for my failure, than have Taita coming after her to avenge my death.'

'By the gods, she really doesn't think much of you.'

'No, and she wanted to make sure I knew it.' Piay sighed. 'I've been humiliated a few times in my life, but, by Khonsu, this really hurts.'

'So now what?'

'Now . . .' Piay said slowly, as if his thoughts were only just becoming clear enough for him to read them. 'Now, I'm going to prove her wrong, and make her pay for what she did to me. I don't know how, not yet, but I swear that whatever Imhotep left for us, I'm going to beat her to it.'

'Well, that's a relief,' Hannu said. 'I thought I'd lost you for a minute. Good to have you back. Now, what are you going to do to stop their lordships from kicking us out of the palace once they find out what happened tonight?'

'They're not going to find out. I had a long talk with the commanders of the palace guard and the Blue Crocodiles last night, while we were clearing up the mess. We agreed that there was no point in waking Harrar or Zahur. Harrar would have made a big show of being angry, Zahur would have cried like an overgrown baby, and then they'd both have lashed out at us.

'And then I said, "Do we have to tell them . . . at all?" I mean, those two don't see the men who guard them as human beings – they don't know their names, don't know their faces. So, we sent the bodies of the dead soldiers off to be prepared for a decent burial and the commanders adjusted their guard rotas so that there'll always be plenty of lads on show. Harrar and Zahur won't even notice anyone's missing . . . not for a few days, anyway. The way I see it, Myssa's going to want to use her new possessions as fast as she can. This will all be decided pretty quickly, one way or the other.'

'Makes sense.' Hannu nodded. 'But if Myssa's getting on with solving that riddle, how are you going to stop her?'

'By getting help from Harrar and Zahur.'

'*What?*' Hannu exclaimed, loud enough to startle Bast, who jumped off the window ledge onto a balcony below and disappeared into the garden. 'You'll never get help from those two. Never!'

Piay smiled. 'Just watch me.'

The Hyksos warriors huddled in the half-light of a single spluttering torch that sent shifting shadows across their faces. The air was thick with the scent of cumin – the walls and floor of the old spice warehouse had been richly stained by the merchandise it once contained. Its shelves were bare now, though – months had passed since fresh stock had been delivered.

Myssa leaned against a clay-brick wall, away from the others, her fingers dancing across the Disc of Ra, moving the rings back and forth as she unpicked its mysteries. Next to her was the empty bowl that had contained the serving of the blue lotus that Tallus had brewed for her.

It was the second she had consumed that day. Myssa was finding that a single draught was no longer enough to sustain her from one morning to the next. She felt as if she were floating, as she always did after consuming the lotus, but somehow the feeling was not quite as blissful as it had been when she had first fallen under its spell.

Myssa had begun to wonder what would happen if she ever decided to set it aside. Could she banish the aches and shivers? Would she still retain the power and clarity of thought that the potion had given her?

For a moment, her mind drifted away from the disc to the adventurer they had encountered at the palace, Piay of Thebes. His face floated in her memory like a half-forgotten dream. Feelings stirred deep within her, but they were half-formed, misremembered, and she couldn't tell if they were real or imagined.

Myssa pushed thoughts of Piay aside. Only one thing truly mattered – discovering Imhotep's secret. The Cobra, his acolytes and the warriors all thought she was aiding them. What would they say if they knew she was on this road for herself? The power and the gold the Great Architect had hidden would make sure that neither she nor her people, in her faraway home-land, would ever suffer at the hands of others again.

She nodded as she moved the rings of the disc. The Hyksos needed her sharp mind more than she needed anything they could offer.

The Cobra's staff tapped on the dusty floor as he drew towards her out of the dark.

'Dawn is not far off,' he said. 'We must be away before night fades if we wish to avoid unfriendly eyes.'

'I will have the answer soon,' Myssa said.

Tallus nodded. Myssa returned to the disc, but she could feel his gaze continue to lie heavy upon her, scrutinising every movement.

'Too many died tonight,' she murmured, distracted by one of the windows, which showed two stars.

'You are not a warrior. It is understandable that you do not have the stomach for this business.'

'It is not a matter of stomach. I just wonder if it is wise to provoke our enemies.'

'Let them be provoked. What can they do to us now that we have all the tools that Imhotep left behind? And if our enemies die, so much the better. They stand between us – between you – and what you most desire.'

Myssa felt the Cobra's words seep deep into her mind. Tallus had a way of speaking that always seemed to ease her thoughts: low, calming, sibilant.

She made one last movement of the disc and took note of the unmistakable triangular shape that was revealed in the open window.

'I am finished now,' she said. 'Tell the men to be ready to move out. I know exactly where we must go.'

 The first thing Piay heard, when he finally gained admittance to the garden room where his superiors liked to take their morning meal, was the high-pitched wail of Zahur.

'We are not safe anywhere!' he cried.

'We must conscript more men,' Harrar replied sternly. 'If the numbers defending the palace are great enough, no enemy would dare attack us.'

For a moment, Piay felt his stomach clench and the bile rise in the back of his throat. Had someone reported the previous night's attack after all? He gritted his teeth and prepared for the moment when the blame for everything that had occurred would be piled on him. But the two men ignored his presence, and it soon became clear that the current state of the city was quite enough to alarm them, without the news that a band of Hyksos warriors led by a homicidal Kushite had been wreaking havoc inside the palace gardens.

'You know what feelings seethe beyond these walls,' the governor whined. 'By conscripting men from the common mob, we would risk bringing enemies into our midst. Why, we would never sleep peacefully again.'

Harrar stared into the middle distance. He knew Zahur was right and he could see no other solution.

Piay folded his hands behind his back and let the two men stew for a while.

'What can we do?' Zahur stuttered.

Harrar chewed his lip.

Finally, Piay said in his calmest tone, 'I have a suggestion.'

Zahur and Harrar cast a look of suspicion Piay's way.

'More than a suggestion. I have knowledge to impart which may change the course of events.'

Piay bowed his head and wrung his hands together, an act he hoped would convey that he was wrestling with revealing a long-held secret.

'Speak,' Harrar said. 'But do not waste our time.'

'This will not be a waste of your time, my lord.' Piay raised his head and showed a confident face, as if he had reached a decision. 'I give you my strongest personal assurance of that.'

'Speak!' Harrar demanded.

'I have not been completely honest with you,' Piay said, feigning a look of contrition. 'Quite rightly, you questioned why Taita had sent me to assess the great monuments. Crumbling stones, as you say. What use are they to this age we find ourselves in? Now I feel obliged to reveal that this was not the full extent of the task my master set for me.'

Harrar narrowed his eyes. He could never believe that a man would act with honest intention; he was always looking for hidden motives, so Piay's words had hooked him immediately.

'What have you been keeping from us?' the nobleman demanded.

'My master, Taita, has studied at length the scrolls of the scribes and the tales the priests pass on to one another. Using these sources he has uncovered secrets lost for an age.'

The fear drained from the two leaders' faces and a flicker of greed glimmered in their eyes. To these two, the only secrets worth uncovering were ones that led to the feel of cold, hard gold in their sweaty palms. Piay was not about to disappoint them.

'You have heard me speak much about the Great Architect, Imhotep,' Piay continued, now adopting his gravest tone. 'His tomb has been lost for aeons, buried long ago beneath the shifting sands.' He paused for a moment and then added, 'Well, it is lost no more.'

Harrar's eyes widened. 'Taita has discovered where Imhotep is buried?'

Piay shrugged. 'He has determined the general area in which the tomb can be found, but not its precise location. One thing he does know for sure, however – Imhotep's tomb is filled with riches beyond imagining. More gold than even a pharaoh has ever seen.'

Harrar moistened his lips. Zahur closed his eyes as he no doubt envisaged Imhotep's hidden fortune. For a moment there was silence, then, 'Are you suggesting that Imhotep's grave should be robbed?' Zahur asked in an incredulous tone, obviously feeling obliged to put on a show of outrage.

'Surely no one would dare defile a grave,' Harrar said, sternly. 'Anyone who risked the wrath of Imhotep would be cursed for all eternity.'

'Quite so, my lord,' Piay said. 'That is why it is beholden upon us to find the tomb of the Great Architect and protect it from grave robbers, before the wicked and the damned can lay their hands on its contents.'

The governor nodded earnestly. 'To find the tomb . . . To protect it, yes . . . We would be doing a great good. This would be honouring the Great Architect.'

Piay bowed. 'My thoughts exactly. I knew you would want to do everything in your power to keep the contents of Imhotep's grave from falling into the wrong hands. This would be good work.' He reached out an imploring hand. 'Forgive me for not telling you sooner, my lords. I wanted to carry out a survey of my own, to confirm Lord Taita's hypotheses. I am now satisfied that he was correct, and so I come to you, in all humility, for fear that if this knowledge reaches the wrong people the tomb will have been desecrated before any work can be done to protect it.'

'So what do you suggest?' Harrar asked.

'Speed is of the essence here. Lord Taita had reason to believe that others, too, were searching for this treasure. Imagine what might happen if men sent from Avaris should ever seize it. The Hyksos could hire mercenaries from far and wide to replace the fighting men they have recently lost. They could march on Memphis once again. So, we must not let this opportunity slip through our fingers. My humble advice would be to bring together an army of diggers now, this very day, to set up camp on the north side of the Pyramid of Khufu where the tomb of Imhotep lies. They should begin work immediately.'

'An army of diggers?' Zahur said. 'Where could we find such a thing?'

'Beyond these walls there is a city full of able-bodied men,' Piay said.

Zahur crumpled his face at the thought of interacting with the people he led.

'But surely a man of your wisdom can turn this to his advantage,' Piay said, encouragingly. 'The people are angry because they are not being fed. But if you were to take the biggest, strongest men from the city – the very men who pose the greatest threat to its peace – and then give them work and food, you will be saving the greatest treasure in all Egypt from falling into the hands of our enemies . . . and you will be disarming the very men who are most dangerous to you. How could the gods not smile upon Memphis – and upon you both after that?'

Piay stifled a grin as he watched Harrar and Zahur bow their heads together in quiet conversation. He knew that they were united by their greed. They would not be able to resist the prospect of their coffers overflowing with gold. Perhaps they even believed they would be protecting it from the grave robbers, though Piay felt sure that this was the least of their concerns.

Finally, Harrar clapped his hands, beaming.

'We will make arrangements immediately. There will be a call in the market for all those capable of setting aside their daily work.'

'And a camp set up at the Pyramid of Khufu today?' Piay asked.

'Yes, you are right,' Harrar said. 'We cannot afford to waste time. There is too much at stake. Piay, I should be angry with you for keeping such a momentous matter secret from me, but when this tomb arises from the desert sands, you will be well rewarded.'

'Thank you, my lord.'

Piay bowed and left the room. But the moment he set foot in the garden he started wondering what he could possibly do to appease the two most powerful men in Memphis when the tomb was not found.

'What do you think of my plan?' Piay asked, after he had told Hannu about his audience with Harrar and Zahur.

'Not at all bad,' Hannu replied, which was, by his standards, high praise. 'An army of men digging in the shadow of the Pyramid of Khufu will certainly make it hard for Myssa to go hunting for clues inside.'

'Much harder.'

'And make it easier for us. And Harrar and Zahur will have to provide food to fill the bellies of the men labouring on their behalf.'

'Many men. I'll make sure of it.'

'You should think about their families, too. Make sure the women and children are looked after.'

'There's just one problem,' Piay said. 'What are we going to do once it's obvious that the diggers aren't going to find anything?'

'Hmm . . .' Hannu considered the question, and then said, 'That isn't your biggest problem.'

'It isn't?'

'No. The thing you really have to worry about is that you accidentally start digging in the right place. If you think Harrar and Zahur are bad now, just imagine what they'll be like if they're up to their ears in treasure.'

In the full heat of mid-morning, lines of women swayed through the streets, large jars balanced on their heads. Each vessel was filled with water collected from the canal. Once they reached their homes, the contents would be emptied into large ceramic pots that stood by doors or in courtyards, for drinking, washing and cooking.

Thoughts of Myssa still lay heavy on Piay's mind, for her new-found hatred of him brought him much pain. Still, he took comfort in watching the water-carriers perform their daily ritual. Life went on as it always had, despite the conflicts that raged around them all.

Minutes later Piay was weaving through the swaying women, with Hannu close behind him, making his way towards the steady heartbeat of a drum and the intermittent blast of a trumpet sounding out from the market. Bast pattered at his heels.

The air reeked of rotting refuse. Hannu flapped his arms to frighten off two vultures scavenging among the animal bones, rotting vegetables, soot, broken pottery and old rags that had been thrown out of houses. The flapping of their wings sounded like sails in a strong breeze as they swept into the air.

The waste crunching underfoot was a problem for the governors of all cities, but here, under Zahur's incompetent rule, it had piled up so high in the streets that it threatened to block the thoroughfares. Black rats scurried everywhere, feasting and breeding.

A crowd had gathered around the market. The throng of people bartering wooden chests for grain, or necklaces for pigs, had ebbed away. Now the citizens stood in silence, staring towards the block where the drummer thumped out his call.

The execution had not been forgotten, nor would it be soon, and the cold question of what new burdens would be heaped upon their shoulders with this day's announcement could be read on every sullen face.

Easing into the shade by a wall, Piay tucked his head into his chest. In that simmering atmosphere, he had no desire to be recognised as an associate of the hated Zahur. Hannu folded his arms and watched, as sullen as those around him.

When the crowd had swelled, the drummer stepped back and for a while there was only the whisper of the wind in the square. Then a gaunt man hurried forward, shifting from foot to foot as if he was ready to sprint away at any moment. He was wearing a pristine kilt marked with the symbol of a lion. Piay recalled seeing him at the palace. Khanay was his name.

Zahur had sent one of his officials, rather than face the crowd himself.

'Your pleas have not fallen on deaf ears,' Khanay began, a faint tremor just detectable in his voice as it rang out across the market. Piay noted that Khanay's eyes were fixed on a point somewhere on the distant western wall – he had obviously decided that the best way to deal with the crowd was to pretend that they simply didn't exist. 'Indeed, our governor, Zahur, has long been aware of the plight of the citizens of Memphis. He has been working tirelessly, night and day, to ensure that the warehouses are filled and no one goes without.'

A murmur raced around the crowd like the first tremor before an earthquake.

If Khanay heard it, he didn't show it. He continued to stare at the western wall.

'I come to you today with news that will swell your hearts,' he said. 'There is work to be done, important work, to prepare Memphis for the joining of the two kingdoms. This will ensure the days of want lie behind us.'

The official paused to moisten his lips. Piay watched as curiosity began to light up the faces around him.

'Able-bodied men are required for work beyond the city walls. Better rations will be provided for all who labour and for their families. The governor has found ways to . . .'

A joyful cheer erupted across the crowd, drowning out the rest of Khanay's words. That sound became one voice tinged with desperate relief. Fists punched the air.

'The work begins today!' the official bellowed. 'Make haste! Gather at the gate to the west . . .'

The crowd's voice surged into a roar. Khanay looked around, realising it was pointless to attempt to say any more, and with a sigh of relief he stepped back.

The roads to the west of the square were instantly full of pushing, shoving men, all fighting for the chance to sign up.

My plan has been a success, Piay thought. But when he glanced at Hannu he was surprised to see his assistant scowling.

'What's wrong?' Piay asked. 'That went perfectly.'

'For the diggers, maybe,' Hannu said. 'But they're not the ones who've got to go down to the kingdom of the dead.'

In the distance, the bronze hills wavered in the heat haze. The wind had dropped and the midday sun beat down on almost two hundred men crowding the dusty shade just beyond the western wall. Despite the conditions, the mood was bright. Grins flashed and hands clapped shoulders as friends greeted each other.

Scribes bent over their scrolls, making marks with their brushes as they questioned each new arrival. The youngest and strongest were welcomed. Those who were too weak or too old trudged away, complaining loudly.

The taskmaster, Adon, was watching the proceedings closely. He had a face that looked as though it had never known laughter. A whip was coiled at his side. Khanay circled him, clucking. Every now and then Adon would mutter something, and the official would scurry away to scold some poor unfortunate tasked with bringing in a cart with supplies or tents or tools.

'It seems like Zahur and Harrar can make arrangements fast enough when they want to,' Hannu said, scanning the mass of bodies.

'All it took was the promise of gold,' Piay replied.

'If they'd acted like this in the first place, they wouldn't have had a city filled with starving people who wanted to hang them from the walls.'

Piay looked out across the waste. It was half a day's march from Memphis to Giza. Could Myssa have already solved the puzzle of the Disc of Ra and reached the great monument before them? He prayed to Khonsu that this was not the case.

Bast rubbed against his legs. The trek would seem even longer if they had to take the cat with them, but Piay didn't dare leave it behind. Hannu had told him he had grown superstitious, but if Bast was a conduit to the protective goddess, as Myssa had once believed, he was not about to take any chances.

Hannu kicked up a whorl of dust. Piay had known him long enough to realise he was wrestling with saying something.

'What is it?' Piay asked.

'Just thinking about that woman.'

Piay did not need to be told who he meant.

'What about her?'

'Well, Akkan was a vicious dog, and a powerful enemy. But we could have taken him on, sword to sword. Myssa, though, she's different. That mind of hers is more dangerous by far than Akkan's blade.'

'She could defeat us – is that what you're saying?'

Hannu remained silent.

Piay nodded. 'Yes, that's possible. And if she's got Seth on her side, that'll only make it harder for us, but—'

'Piay!'

At the sound of his name, Piay looked up and immediately spotted his father hurrying through the gate with two of his burly guards beside him.

'My son,' Asil gasped. 'I came as soon as I heard the news.'

'What news?'

His father leaned in so he would not be overheard, his eyes darting towards the men preparing to march towards Giza.

'When I heard Zahur was conscripting men to work in the shadow of Khufu's pyramid, I knew I'd find you here. That fat fool would never have thought of doing that by himself.'

'It is true. I did offer the governor some advice.'

Asil grinned. 'I knew it. And such an army, arranged at such expense – that can only be for a work of great importance.'

My father is a shrewd man, there is no doubt of it, Piay thought.

'Then you have found what you were searching for?' Asil pressed.

'Not yet.'

'But you are close. I have seen the shovels and the picks in the carts. There will be digging, and in the place where the great monuments stand. With this help, I'd wager you'll find your treasure in no time.'

Piay smiled, humouring the old man. He was not about to reveal his plan, even to his own blood.

'I never doubted you'd be successful, my son,' Asil said. 'I'm proud of you.'

He reached out and squeezed Piay's arm, a simple act, but one that seemed infused with love.

Piay found himself moved by his father's words. It surprised him. He'd never felt such a thing before.

'And Zahur is going to feed all these men and feed them well, I hear,' Asil added.

'Carts will be sent from Memphis to the camp every day. These men will not go hungry. Nor will their families.' Piay paused, watching Asil's face, and suddenly he thought that perhaps the old man was yearning to be fed himself. 'Forgive me, Father. I never considered your needs. I will see what provisions can be sent your way.'

Asil shook his head. 'No, my son. I don't need favours. The gods will provide for me if that is part of their plan. There are others in greater need. Let them eat first.'

Piay felt a wave of warmth for the old man. 'Let us speak again when I return. You've had a hard life. I'll make sure that you are well cared for in the time to come.'

Asil blinked away a tear and hugged his son. When he pulled away, he said, 'When you return, my son.'

As Piay watched the old man walk back through the gate, he tried to make sense of the new emotions swirling around inside him. Was this what it felt like to have a family? And did everyone else find it equally confusing?

'Complicated man, your father,' Hannu said. 'He can be kind, all right, but then you remember he's best friends with the Guild of Thieves.'

Piay sighed. 'If there's one thing that we both should have learned by now, it's that nothing's simple.'

Behind them, the taskmaster barked a command and the labourers formed up into a disorderly line. As the carts trundled into place beside them, the column started out towards the necropolis. Someone began to chant a marching song that leaped from mouth to mouth, the words tinged with hope for better times. The wind whisked up the melody, carrying it back to where Piay and Hannu stood waiting.

'Where is he?' Hannu growled, looking round.

'Busy making last-minute arrangements, I expect,' Piay replied. 'When I visited Ankhu in his chamber, he was still keen to accompany us. More than keen. Excited.' He paused. 'The question is, can we trust him?'

'Hard to say. Gold has a way of messing with people's morals.'

They waited and they waited.

The army of labourers disappeared into a cloud of dust that drifted over the horizon. Midday became mid-afternoon. Hannu paced back and forth like a dog waiting for his master's return. Piay felt his own irritation begin to build.

'Night will fall before we get to the camp,' Hannu snapped.

'At least it will be cooler to travel now,' Piay said, trying to lift his own spirits, but it wasn't long before his frustration got the better of him. 'I can't wait any longer. I'm going back to the palace to find him.'

Barely had the words left his lips than Piay glimpsed Ankhu striding along the street towards the gate. He was hunched under the weight of a pack, and he leaned on a staff for support, his white robe pristine in the sun, a mauve scarf tied around his head.

Piay sighed. 'Can you believe that's our guide?'

'We should have left here hours ago,' Hannu snapped when the old man stood in front of them.

'The Pyramid of Khufu will be there whether we arrive early or late.' Ankhu shucked off his pack. 'I am an old man. I will tire quickly carrying this, and then we will be even later.'

Hannu spat and snatched up the pack.

'Old when it suits you,' he muttered.

'What kept you?' Piay asked.

'Preparations needed to be made. They took longer than I thought.' Ankhu smiled. 'You are venturing into a place where no man should walk. It is protected by spells and curses. Do you want to risk the wrath of Khufu if you disturb his tomb?'

Hannu shuddered, despite the heat.

'I have found a talisman that will protect you once you enter the monument, and a spell that should shield you from the eyes of those who watch from the afterlife. If the gods are with us, you will only need to trespass for a little while. Then, when you have found Imhotep's sign, the Disc of Ra should reveal—'

'We don't have the Disc of Ra,' Piay interjected.

Ankhu's eyes widened. 'How could you lose it?'

'It was taken from us.'

The scribe shook his head. 'How did a wise man like Taita choose such fools to aid him?'

'We will reclaim the Disc,' Piay said, 'when the time comes.'

He could feel Hannu's eyes on him, but he did not meet them.

'You imbeciles!' Ankhu exclaimed. 'An object beyond all value – and you let it slip through your fingers. If you were my students, I would knock your heads together. Let us just pray that the gods have a plan for you.'

Purple shadows pooled among the red dunes as night swept in across the desert. A cooling breeze whisked in from the north, and a hyena chattered away somewhere in the dark. Across the waste, the rising moon's lamp revealed a silvery road where the sand had been churned up by the feet of the labourers who had trekked there earlier that day.

As they walked, Piay looked up at the vast sweep of constellations twinkling in the ebony sky, a vision that never failed to fill him with awe. The home of the gods, the source of all magic. But now he saw them in a different light. Those ageless stars hid a message from a thousand years ago; they carried words to his ears from a man who had long since turned to dust. Or had the Great Architect truly ascended to sit beside the gods themselves?

Piay searched the sky until he found a familiar pattern.

'There,' he said to Hannu. 'The Four Sons of Horus.'

Hannu squinted up at the northern sky.

'Taita's old friend Admiral Hui took me aboard his ship once and pointed out those exact stars to me,' Piay continued, his voice low as he remembered. 'During times of trouble, he'd look to them and they'd be there, as they were when his own father showed them to him, unchanging, eternal . . . standing at the threshold between this world and the afterlife.'

'As you will when you set foot in the Pyramid of Khufu.'

Piay felt his neck prickle and he trudged on in silence for a while.

As they crested a dune and wound down into the hollow beyond it, Ankhu sank to the ground and crossed his legs.

'We will rest a while here.'

'We are never going to get there,' Hannu complained under his breath.

He slumped down beside the scribe, no doubt imagining a comforting campfire and some hot food to warm his belly.

As Piay sat, Ankhu pulled the pack off Hannu's shoulder and dipped inside, pulling out a flatbread. He broke off a piece and popped it in his mouth, chewing slowly before handing the rest to Piay and Hannu.

The laughter of a hyena once again echoed out over the desert from somewhere nearby.

'Smells carrion,' Hannu grunted.

'As long as it does not think we are easy meat,' Piay replied.

'I would ready your swords,' Ankhu said, through a mouthful of bread. 'If there is a pack, you may want to be prepared.'

Hannu sighed. 'Let me see.'

Piay watched his assistant crawl up the side of the dune to peer over the top, then turned to Ankhu.

'Will you join us when we go into the Pyramid of Khufu?'

The scribe's wrinkled face crinkled into a tight smile. 'Do you think me mad?'

Piay felt the weight of what they planned crush down on him. He prayed Khonsu would guide him through the terror that lay ahead.

A groan and then the sound of crashing echoed out across the sand as Hannu came tumbling down the side of the dune. He slammed to the ground, dazed.

Piay jumped up and whirled around to face the way Hannu had come, his blade already in his hand.

A tall, powerfully built figure loomed at the top of the dune, silhouetted against the star-sprayed sky. He was so dark against the night sky that Piay could not tell his identity, and yet there was something familiar about his brute physicality. He swayed slightly from side to side as if drunk.

'Death cannot touch me,' the figure said.

The voice was recognisable, but somehow changed – aged, desiccated. Piay frowned. It was not possible . . . Then the figure turned slightly and the light of the moon picked out the strong jawline and the sharp nose of Akkan.

Myssa had said she had killed him, yet here he was – a visitor from beyond the grave.

As Piay looked closer, he could see the Child-Killer's face was like chalk. A black stain covered the left side of his tunic, where a ragged, gaping wound was visible.

If Piay had not seen it with his own eyes, he would not believe a man could have survived such an injury.

Akkan was swaying on his feet, but he had managed to trek across the desert from wherever Myssa had left him for dead. Perhaps, like Sakir, he could survive by sheer force of will alone – that, and the power of Seth that burned inside him.

'The woman betrayed me,' Akkan said. 'She is a venomous snake, seemingly sleeping until she strikes.'

'She won't bend her will to anyone,' Piay said. 'You should never have taken her.'

Akkan stepped down the dune. In his hand a bronze sword gleamed in the moonlight – not the crescent blade of the Hyksos, but an Egyptian blade, stolen almost certainly from some unfortunate that had wandered across his path.

'That bitch couldn't kill me,' Akkan growled. 'Don't fool yourself that you can do any better.'

Akkan took another step, the sand flowing away from his feet.

'I hear the voice of Seth. He told me I would reach the edge of the afterlife, but I would not pass through the door. He would guide me back to the world of men and I would be his agent again.' He gave a croaking laugh. 'And here I am.'

Another step. Now Piay could smell the fruity odour of rot rolling off Akkan. That was what had attracted the hyena. It was almost as if he was dead, yet alive.

'Nothing will stop me from finding the treasure of Imhotep. And nothing will stand in the way of my revenge on the woman who betrayed me.'

When Akkan took another step, Piay levelled his sword.

Hannu shook off his daze and eased himself to his feet. Piay glanced towards Ankhu, but the scribe had crawled out of sight.

Akkan stepped down again. He was almost upon them now and his strength seemed to be growing, his shoulders pulling back, as if the thought of slaying his enemies filled him with power.

Piay watched Akkan's blade, settling into a defensive crouch, ready to duck and dodge and move. However strong Akkan might be, he could surely not match Piay's speed or agility when he was carrying such a wound. Akkan stepped down to the base of the dune. His features were taut from the pain he must have been enduring, but that did not slow him. Down here, where the air was still and close, the reek of rot was thick, like the stink of a battlefield the day after the war had ended, the day when the vultures feasted.

Piay shifted to his right, slowly circling the Child-Killer, while Hannu moved in the other direction. They had fought beside each other so many times that they needed no communication to signal their tactics; they acted as one.

Akkan's eyes flicked from Piay to Hannu and back again. He was alert – his suffering had not dulled his senses.

When Hannu lunged, the Hyksos captain flashed his sword. He parried the strike and instantly whisked his weapon towards Piay to block any move. When Piay delayed his thrust, Akkan dashed his sword towards him, the tip of the blade heading straight for his chest. Piay threw himself back at the last moment, stumbling in the soft sand and falling to one knee.

He had been too confident, but he had learned his lesson.

Piay and Hannu circled. Akkan eyed them, calm, unafraid.

'So much is at stake and yet you are the ones sent to stand in the way of the Kingdom of Seth.' A dark humour laced Akkan's voice. 'This quest demands warriors, not an arrogant young buck and a crippled dwarf.'

'If we're so weak, why waste your time killing us?' Piay asked, wanting to keep Akkan talking.

'You're like vermin. Unless you get rid of them all, they just keep coming back.'

For an instant, Akkan's attention was on Piay alone.

Hannu darted forward to strike, but Akkan's reflexes were quicker than Piay had anticipated. He evaded Hannu's blade and then spun around, slashing his sword in an arc. Piay's breath caught in his chest, but Hannu dropped to his knees beneath Akkan's stroke, then rolled back.

'Step back,' Piay said to Hannu, easing away himself so that he was at least three sword-lengths from his foe.

Akkan pushed his head back. His nostrils flared like some beast tasting the wind.

'I can smell the woman. She follows this path, too. She will not know what stalks her until the moment of her death.'

Piay stiffened. In the eye of his mind he could see Akkan bearing down on Myssa in the deep of the night. As much as he tried to force the vision from his head, he imagined her cut and bleeding and falling to her knees. And then he saw her die.

Gripping his blade tighter, Piay prepared to throw himself forward, but as he did so his senses told him that something was not right. The hollow was a pool of shadow nestled in a bowl of red sand. The darkness was deep and impenetrable in those areas where the moonlight did not touch. Something was not right.

The shadows were moving.

Akkan shifted in front of him. Piay could not afford to look away for even an instant. And yet, from the corner of his eye, he saw it again.

The shadows were moving.

One by one, figures began to rise up from the gloom, cloaked in darkness.

With his back turned to them, Akkan was oblivious. He grinned like a jackal, misreading the uncertainty he saw in Piay's eyes for fear. The Child-Killer lowered his blade so that he held it at hip level, ready to seize this opportunity to claim another life.

Hannu jerked round, sensing the movement on the edge of his vision. He scrambled away, gaping as he tried to make sense of what was unfolding before his eyes. He, Piay and Akkan had been alone, in that hollow, deep in the wasteland. They were all fighting men, attuned to the constant threat of life in a dangerous land. How could none of them have seen or heard the men approaching? Surely only sorcery could explain these figures appearing from nowhere.

Their movements were silent, so fluid that Akkan had still not noticed their presence. Piay marvelled at how skilled they were – they had crept in unobserved, slithering down the dunes, avoiding the rays of the moon and the starlight, not a whisper emanating from them. He felt awed by their abilities – and frightened, too.

Piay let his sword drop to his side. There was little use for it now. The Child-Killer's grin broadened.

As the figures moved closer to Akkan, there was just enough light to pick out their features – the pale skin, the swirl of black tattoos.

The Sons of Apis had come to claim the payment that was owed them.

Even at the last, Akkan had no sense of the fate that was awaiting him. Only when hands gripped his arms and his torso and grabbed him around his neck did the Hyksos captain finally come alive to what was happening.

His eyes widened as he glimpsed the tattooed skin of his assailants and realised what lay ahead. His mouth opened in a full-throated howl, a sound laced with a terror that Piay felt sure Akkan had not experienced in his life before.

The bronze sword slipped from his grasp and thudded into the sand.

And then the Child-Killer was being dragged back, hooked fingers clawing at the air. Into the shadows he went, the darkness swallowing him whole. Only his blood-chilling howl continued to echo through the night, until finally that, too, vanished.

When he felt a shiver of fur against his leg, Piay awoke from his reverie. He glanced down to see Bast sitting alert beside him as if waiting for something.

Piay looked back into the shadows and once again he glimpsed movement. A figure strode forward, the cloak of darkness falling from its shoulders as it emerged into the moonlight.

The leader of the Sons of Apis looked Piay in the eye. Piay's fingers twitched on the hilt of his sword, but this man stood alone, without his brothers to defend him, and he was not armed, at least not in any way Piay could see.

Piay's thoughts flew back to that night in the palace at Thebes, when the hood was yanked from the captive's head and Piay saw his tattooed face for the first time. He remembered the calm he saw there, the complete absence of fear, even though he was in the hands of his enemies. This man had known that whatever they did they could not harm him.

Now the tattooed head bowed and Piay realised that the obeisance was not meant for him. Instead, the Son of Apis was displaying deference to the cat that sat upright at Piay's feet. Bast stared back, her eyes as wide and unknowable as ever.

As he raised his head, the man flexed his upper body and the tattoos appeared to flow with a life of their own in the moonlight.

He looked back at Piay.

'We have not come for you.'

The voice was calm, almost gentle, the sound of a man who had no need to shout or bluster.

'You tried to end my life before.' Piay could sense Hannu willing him to keep his mouth shut in case he encouraged a change of mind. 'Why would you not try to end it again?'

'Judgement is pronounced on those who lay claim to what is rightfully ours.'

'The Eye of Horus?'

'The secret of the ages. We have guarded it for a thousand years. Now we are in an age of upheaval. Perhaps this is truly the time that the Great Architect imagined, perhaps not, but we will defend our master's secrets as we always have done. Any who dare to uncover the hidden knowledge will find the endless night draws in upon them.'

Piay felt the weight of that warning upon him.

'You have done well to venture this far. But you no longer have the Eye of Horus or the Disc of Ra, and so the way is closed to you.'

Piay narrowed his eyes. *How can this man know such a thing?*

'Your loss is your good fortune. You are once again a wanderer in ignorance, and so you are beneath our notice. But take heed – should we become aware of you again, we will come for you. And the next time will be the last.'

Piay had faced down the most dangerous men in all of Egypt, but those simple words brought a chill to his spine that he had never felt before.

'And Akkan?' Piay asked.

'We warned him that we would come for him, just as we are warning you, but he would not stop.' The leader's lips twitched into the faintest of smiles. 'We have plans for the Child-Killer. There are worse things than death.'

With that, he bowed to Bast one final time and walked back into the shadows until he vanished from sight so completely that it was as if he had disappeared from the very face of the earth.

'The Sons of Apis are unknown to me.' Ankhu shook his head in incredulity. 'How can this be? I have studied the scrolls and heard the histories whispered by the priests. I know the names of kings reaching back into antiquity. There are days when my arrogance tells me I have learned everything there is to learn. And yet I know nothing of a cult that has walked the black earth and the red sand for a thousand years?'

'They're like ghosts,' Hannu muttered.

He glanced over his shoulder, as he had been doing every few paces while they hurried along the trail away from the hollow where they had rested.

'The Sons of Apis are the Keepers of Mystery,' Piay said, 'so it makes sense that they're a mystery, too. Though the gods only know how they hid in plain sight for so long.'

'You can ask them yourself soon enough,' Hannu grunted. 'You heard what was said. Once we are back on Imhotep's trail, they'll be on to us again.'

Ankhu leaned on his staff as he heaved himself forward.

'And how do you hope to rejoin that path without the Eye of Horus and the Disc of Ra?'

'I have a plan.'

Piay ignored Hannu's snort.

Ankhu seemed not to hear. 'Then let us pray it unfolds as you hope. If we are nearing the end of the path, there is little room for failure.'

Piay winced. 'Yes, let us pray. For the Child-Killer just confirmed what we already feared. Myssa is way ahead of us.'

The Pyramid of Khufu was a beacon in the moonlight, drawing them on. The constellations hung over it, the great glistening snake of stars mirroring the life-giving Nile upon the earth.

If Imhotep had truly left such instructions, then he was deserving of the title the Great Architect. Such a sight spoke of wonder and mysteries and magnificence – of the glory of a king and the power of Imhotep's vision.

But what secrets did Khufu's great resting place hide? And what price would have to be paid to venture into the realm of the dead inside?

As they trudged on, their nostrils wrinkled at the smoke drifting from unseen campfires and the comforting aroma of dinners being cooked. The distant sound of laughter and song floated in the still night. Piay felt pleased to hear those warm sounds. The labourers were enjoying filling their bellies with the food Zahur and Harrar had provided on his instruction.

They pushed on faster towards the diggers' camp, keen to leave behind the lonely desert waste and whatever dangers it hid.

Soon Piay glimpsed the fires twinkling in the dark and the tents spread out across one side of the foot of the pyramid.

'That was a good idea,' Hannu said. He looked along the length of the camp, taking in the babble of voices rising from the large workforce. 'Myssa and her men will have a hard time sneaking past this lot without being spotted. And there are too many here for the Hyksos to fight their way through.'

'That won't deter Myssa,' Piay said. 'She'll find some other way to get what she wants, you know that. I'm counting on it.'

'What do you mean?' Ankhu asked.

'This Myssa – the new one – holds me in contempt. In fact, she feels that way about men in general. She'll never believe that I can possibly set a trap for her—'

'Not one that works,' Hannu said.

'Exactly. But that's her weakness, because she'll be just that little bit less careful than she would be if she did respect me. So now, we have to work out a way of taking advantage of that.'

'I wish you luck, friend,' Hannu said. 'Because I'm damned if I can think of anything.'

The three men edged into the camp, enjoying the warmth from the fires and the sounds of men whose spirits were good. Hannu paused by one fire and, after engaging the men around it in conversation, was offered three bowls of fish stew which the new arrivals placed to their lips and swilled down with joy.

Once they had all slaked their thirst from a water hide, Ankhu strode off ahead. Puzzled by his determination, Piay and Hannu followed the old sage as he made his way through the camp, between the tents, until he reached the foot of the great monument itself.

Piay watched, curious, as Ankhu rested one hand on the crumbling stones, bowing his head almost as if he were praying.

When he was done, he turned back to the two men and said in a low voice filled with awe, 'Here we stand on the brink of the afterlife. If you allow yourself, you can feel the presence of the gods themselves.'

Piay shivered. He craned his neck, letting his eyes find their way up the soaring wall of stone to the summit. A shooting star flashed across the vault of the heavens.

An omen, Piay thought, but for good or ill, he could not tell.

Ankhu was right – Khonsu is here.

The god's gaze weighed upon Piay, and he felt a sense of apprehension rise inside him – they were approaching the most dangerous time.

'The men told me you had arrived.'

Piay and Hannu turned to see Adon, the taskmaster, standing behind them. His right hand rested against the coil of the whip at his side, the telltale sign of a master who was ready to use it at the slightest provocation.

'Final arrangements had to be made,' Piay replied. 'The excavation will be long and arduous. It's vital to make sure the work is carried out in the right place.'

'I was not told what we were digging for, only that it was of the greatest importance.'

It was not a question, but Piay knew the taskmaster was probing for information.

'All will be revealed, in time, as the sand and the rocks give up their secrets,' Piay said.

Adon nodded. 'We begin work at first light. Show me where the ground must be broken.'

Piay, Hannu and Ankhu followed the taskmaster back through the camp, with Bast trotting at their side. On the edge of the tents, Piay looked out across the moonlit wasteland and searched for an area scattered with rocks where the digging would be hardest. The longer he could draw out this work, the longer these men and their families could benefit from the food released from Zahur's stores.

He made a great play of looking up at the stars and gauging the position of the Pyramid of Khufu and the two smaller monuments that stood nearby and then pointed.

'There,' Piay said, pointing towards a randomly selected patch of sand. 'Though I warn you now that the knowledge we have is not precise. We will continue to study the heavens, and if there is need to extend the work, we will tell you.'

Adon grunted. 'I will make the arrangements.'

'One more thing,' Piay said. 'Guards should be positioned around the camp every night.'

'Guards? What is there here to be guarded?'

'Shrikes roam the wastes. They will take anything they can find.'

Adon twitched his nose, unconvinced, but he nodded in agreement. Piay watched a cunning expression creep across his face. He was no doubt calculating that what the work band had been sent to find was of great value.

'But have your guards on the western approach pretend they are asleep,' Piay said.

Adon frowned. 'They should challenge no one who approaches?'

'No one.'

'Why protect the camp, but leave a path in for those Shrikes?'

'I have my reasons.'

The taskmaster shook his head in incomprehension and stalked away.

Ankhu pursed his lips. 'You are setting your trap.'

Piay looked back to the looming monument. 'Now we wait to see if it works.'

Piay and Hannu took it in turns to keep watch on the unguarded section for the rest of the night. Piay thought – hoped – he still knew a little about the way Myssa's mind worked. He anticipated she would make no attempt to enter the monument for a night or two. She was cautious. She would be watching, weighing up her options before she made her decision.

The next morning, the sun painted the dusty land crimson as it edged the horizon. The men crawled out of their shelters, stretching and hawking up phlegm. Adon moved among them, his voice like the crack of his whip as he barked orders.

With Bast beside him, Piay perched on the stones of the great monument, as the wilderness glowed rose pink in the first light. Soon the furnace blast of the sun would roast these labourers. The work would be hard, relentless, but at least they would be rewarded with food by day's end.

Adon paced back and forth as the men lined up to collect their tools. Some received shovels to shift the sand, others wooden mallets and chisels to split the rocks that lay just beneath the surface. Axes and copper bow drills were available for the more difficult terrain.

In no time the labourers were sweating as they broke the ground. Their tools thumped in a steady beat, and voices joined in song as they caught the rhythm of their labours.

Piay thought that the men seemed happy after the privations of Memphis. The knowledge that they would not be starving that night, and nor would their loved ones, had sparked a fire in their spirit. Though their task was a futile one, he felt pleased that some good would come of it.

Hannu limped up and waved a water hide at him to moisten his lips.

'I bet Myssa sent her men in the night to scout the camp,' he said. 'The Hyksos have sharp eyes. They wouldn't have needed to come close, not with the moon so bright.'

Ankhu wandered along the edge of the monument, trailing the fingertips of his left hand across the aged stones. Halting in front of Piay and Hannu, he shielded his eyes to look up at them and said, 'The Pyramid of Khufu calls to you. Can you hear it?'

'I hear nothing but the whine of the wind across the wastes,' Piay replied.

'These old stones speak if only you have the ears to listen.' He wagged the tip of his staff towards the top of the monument. 'Wise men built this. Wisdom is set deep in all parts of it. Why stone? Why so large?'

Piay shrugged. 'A king would want his name to be remembered.'

'The Pyramid of Khufu is different,' Ankhu said. 'In the age before this monument was raised, the pyramids of old sat above the burial chamber. They were the greatest of all tombstones, protecting the king and his possessions hidden beneath them. But not here. Khufu's burial chamber and a smaller one for his queen are suspended in that stone high above the ground. Why is that?'

Piay craned his neck around and looked up the soaring pyramid.

'How would I know?'

'You wouldn't. No one alive today does. But if the Pyramid of Khufu was indeed the vision of Imhotep, then he chose to go against the old traditions for a reason.'

Hannu shivered despite the heat. 'I don't like all this talk of tombs. Talk too much about death and you're just asking it to pay you a visit.'

Ankhu waved away his concerns. 'There is more here that puzzles the mind. The monument is empty.'

'Grave robbers,' Hannu said.

'That may well be. The royal treasures would certainly have been looted. But nothing remains. No canonic jars, No mummy. No shards of pot. The chambers within the monument were never completed. There are some who say that Khufu was never interred here.'

Piay thought back to the Pyramid of Djoser and how much remained within it, even though the grave robbers had broken into the very heart of it.

'Why go to all this trouble, then?' he asked, taking in the vastness of the pyramid. 'Why build all this and not even lay a pharaoh to rest here? That can't be true.'

'We are but ants before this magnificence and the men who made it,' Ankhu said. 'We can only wonder why.'

'Have you been inside?' Piay asked.

'I told you, I would not venture inside, not for all the riches this world can offer. But others have been inside and their accounts have been recorded.'

'So, how did they get in?' Piay asked.

'I have seen references to a hidden entrance, broken open by grave robbers, perhaps, or left there by the original builders. I do not know its exact location, but I'm hopeful that we could find it. But only when you are ready, and who knows now when that will be?'

Two more days passed. The labourers sweltered in the seething heat, their shovels biting into the sand, their chisels cracking stone. The music of the work filled the hot air from dawn to dusk.

Gradually the trenches deepened. From time to time Adon strode up to Piay, asking his opinion on the progress of the expanding trenches.

'You are certain this is the correct place?' the taskmaster asked.

'As much as I can be.'

'There is no more information you can bring to me?'

'None.'

'And if nothing is discovered in this place?'

'Then the work should be moved a step over, and so on. Something will arise out of the ground sooner or later.'

Adon nodded at this, looking across the dusty plain in the lee of the monument.

'Then your work here is done.'

'I will stay until you have found what is buried.'

Or at least until the secrets of the Pyramid of Khufu have been given up, Piay thought.

Once he'd solved the Riddle of the Stars, no one would care that the search for Imhotep's tomb had been in vain. And in the meantime, Piay hoped, men were being fed and the city was becoming calmer.

When darkness fell, he and Hannu took it in turns to keep watch on the unguarded approach. The night was still, the only sound the faint strains of the wind singing across the wastes. No noise of interlopers reached their ears, nor did Hannu catch any scent on the breeze. Would Myssa even try to reach the Pyramid of Khufu while so many people were there? Had his calculations been wrong?

That night Piay was jerked out of a deep sleep. Hannu had crawled under his shelter and was shaking him roughly.

'Get up!' Hannu said. 'That attack has come!'

'Attack?' Piay slurred.

'The Hyksos have struck from the east.'

'Not the west?'

'Hear me! They are attacking from the east – and there are more of them than Akkan had at his camp. A lot more. They're trying to drive all the diggers away, to take the monument for themselves.'

Piay levered himself up on his elbows and wiped the sleep from his eyes.

'On my way.'

'Bring your sword. We have too few fighting men.'

Hannu scrambled out of the shelter on his hands and knees. Piay followed him just seconds later.

A fire was raging on the eastern edge of the camp. Flames leaped up high from tents and painted the stones of the monument amber.

As Piay stared in incredulity at the blazing encampment, more streaks of fire blazed across the sable sky – burning arrows loosed from powerful Hyksos bows that could reach three times the distance of any Egyptian bow.

The shafts plunged down into the camp, setting fire to more tents. The terrified yells of the labourers rang out as they raced to stop the blaze spreading.

Piay dashed towards the fire, cursing himself for even thinking he could lure Myssa into a trap, or believing that a crowd of unarmed labourers would be any kind of deterrent. She hadn't bothered with trickery. She was making a direct assault.

Once the flames had panicked the occupants of the camp, the Hyksos would ride in on their warhorses, cutting down everyone before them. These labourers had no swords, few weapons that could be used to defend themselves beyond the tools they worked with every day. They could not be expected to fight.

Beyond the roar of the fire, Piay thought he could make out the thunder of approaching hooves to the east. He unsheathed his sword and was about to run towards the sound of the charge, when a thought struck him. What if Myssa's trick was precisely that she seemed to be attacking without one?

Skidding to a halt, Piay glanced back to the unguarded western approach. His sword and his ability to use it were essential for the defence of the camp. The Egyptian labourers had little hope under any circumstances, but without him and Hannu they would not stand a chance. He knew that.

And Myssa did, too. She had never believed in brute force to solve a problem. She'd always been cleverer than that. Why would she not be still? Why not use the attack from the east as a distraction to allow her to get to the pyramid from the west?

Unsure of what to do, Piay turned back and forth. There was no right answer here, just one that might cause less harm than the other. But which was it?

Finally, Piay made his choice, knowing full well he could come to regret it. Turning away from where the fighting was about to break out, he raced back the way he had come, passing the men scrambling to safety. When he came to the edge of the camp, he ducked down behind a tent and peered into the night.

The clamour at his back was as loud as thunder, and after a while he wondered if he had made the right decision.

Just at the point when he had all but decided to abandon his post and race back to the fray, he glimpsed movement in the dark.

Crouching lower, so he would not be seen, Piay watched a figure emerge from the gloom. It was a woman, slender, stooping to avoid drawing attention to herself, a cloak wrapped around her and a hood pulled low over her head so that her features were lost to shadow.

As she crept towards the monument and into the brighter light, Piay nodded. The dress she was wearing, visible when the cloak flapped open, was yellow. It was Myssa.

Piay slithered on his belly from his hiding place to a point where he could sprint to intercept her. Already he could feel his mind leaping ahead. She had separated herself from the Cobra and the Hyksos warriors. Alone. Undefended. That made it easier to capture her. And once she was in his grasp, he could begin the work of returning her to the woman he knew.

As Myssa neared the great monument, Piay launched himself out of his hiding place and raced forward. Using all the stealth he had learned as a spy, he arced around the rear of her, so that he would not catch her eye until it was too late. Myssa always carried her short-bladed knife for protection. He would have to be wary of that. She'd made short work of the palace guards, after all.

His feet barely whispered on the dust and the rocks. Yet as he closed on her, she jerked alert, sensing his presence. With barely a backward glance, she whirled away along the side of the pyramid into the gloom, her cloak billowing out behind her.

Myssa was leaving the camp, leaving the warriors who would be able to protect her, but she was strong and fit, and her long muscular legs made her fast. Piay had seen her run through the forests, far to the south, and he had marvelled at her speed.

But the fire in his chest gave him an advantage. He would not let her escape now that he was so close to bringing her back into his life. Piay hurled himself on, pushing himself to the limits of his strength, and the distance between them began to close.

At the far corner of the great monument, her steps slowed as her strength drained and she seemed to sense that she would not be able to outrun him. Piay braced himself for a struggle and that flashing knife.

'Run no more,' Piay called. 'Do not fight me. I am here to help.'

Myssa spun around in a swirl of her cloak.

Piay choked on his words.

The face that peered back at him out of the hood was that of a young man with round cheeks and sparkling eyes. He was chuckling with glee. Piay recognised him – one of Akkan's acolytes.

Before Piay could move, the acolyte whipped out his hand, unfurling his fingers as he did. A cloud of white dust swept out. Piay felt it fill his nose and his mouth as he drew breath, prickling his throat as if he was being stabbed by copper needles.

An instant later, he felt the world around him twist and he realised he was falling back. The stars and that orb of Khonsu filled his entire vision.

Myssa dug her toes into the shifting sand. She shivered as the chill night wind curled around her simple dress of plain grey, undyed linen, turning her skin to gooseflesh. On her tongue she tasted the acrid smoke from the burning tents, and she could hear the cries of the terrified labourers.

Her command had been to keep casualties to a minimum. The Hyksos warriors would move forward on their powerful horses, driving out the labourers with the flats of their blades. Some men might fall beneath the onrushing hooves – that could not be avoided – but none were to be cut down. She saw no purpose in a massacre.

All had gone as planned.

Myssa looked to where Piay lay prone on the sand. She told herself she felt nothing. That was not entirely true, though. That strange emotion which she couldn't quite identify lurked in the very depths of her.

There was no reason why she should feel anything at all. Piay had been her captor, her oppressor. She heard the Cobra's whispers rustle through her head. Piay could not be trusted. He cared nothing for her. If she ever dared voice her fears, Piay would whip her and beat her until she understood her lowly position. She could never let that happen again.

So why had she not killed him, as the Cobra insisted? He had shown her the poison he had selected from his jars and pouches. It would be a simple enough task, and the threat Piay posed to their success would be eliminated.

She'd refused. The deaths of the guards at the palace still haunted her. At first, she'd told herself that she didn't care who died so she could achieve her ends, but that wasn't true. For all that the Cobra had tried to persuade her to let him kill the man who claimed to have been her lover, she could never quite bring herself to give the order.

Now she told herself that was of no consequence. He posed no danger, and he meant nothing to her.

Myssa forced herself to drag her attention away from the drugged, motionless body and to look up the vast wall of stone to the summit of the pyramid and the glimmering stars beyond. The Cobra and his acolytes had told her all she needed to know. She had the Eye of Horus and the Disc of Ra in her pouch at her side.

She was ready to unlock the mystery that lay within.

The baboon bounded out of the trees and squatted on a slab of granite. The air was suddenly thick with its musk, a smell so pungent that Piay's nostrils flared. The beast threw its head back and unleashed a rolling chattering that burst into a series of barks. In the forest a sound erupted as if a thousand wings were flapping, but Piay saw no birds soar up from the high branches.

Once the greeting was done, the creature lowered its head and stared directly at Piay. Those eyes crackled with an unsettling intelligence that was more suited to man than beast, the black centres glinting with the pale reflection of the moon, though it was day and no moon hung overhead.

'You are a messenger from Khonsu,' Piay breathed.

The baboon howled at the moon and listened to Khonsu's response. The god acted through them, and always had.

'Am I dead?' Piay asked. 'Are you welcoming me to the afterlife? Will I sit at the feet of Khonsu?'

The beast continued to stare.

'What message do you have for me?'

'Wake!' The baboon roared the word.

Piay's heart thumped in shock to hear it.

'Wake! Seth is coming!'

Piay's eyelids fluttered and a ruddy light flooded his vision.

'The gods have smiled . . .'

Ankhu's voice drifted from somewhere nearby as Piay blinked until his sight cleared. He was lying under a shelter, a cool breeze billowing the grimy cloth above him. The shadows were long, and everything was painted with the crimson glow of the setting sun.

The scribe leaned over him and mopped his brow with a dirty strip of cloth.

'We thought you were dead.'

Hannu loomed over Piay. His assistant scowled as if he was sorry that he had somehow survived, but Piay heard the concern in his voice.

'How long has passed?' Piay croaked.

'Most of a day.'

Ankhu leaned over him, searching his eyes for anything that might be of concern.

'We found you lying at the foot of the monument in a sleep like death,' Hannu said. 'If it was up to Adon, you'd already have been prepared for the afterlife. It was Ankhu who insisted that there was still some spark in you.'

Piay pushed himself up on his elbow. Every part of him ached. Deep in his head, though, he could still hear that baboon's roar.

'You must recover,' Ankhu said, trying to push Piay back down.

'No. We cannot rest, not even for a moment. Seth is coming.'

'Seth?' Ankhu said.

Piay told the story of what had happened to him, his words tumbling over one another.

'In my vision, I was warned by Khonsu,' he concluded, 'and that can only mean one thing – Myssa has already ventured into the Pyramid of Khufu and found what she was looking for.'

'The lookouts saw nothing,' Hannu said.

'I should have listened to you,' Piay said. 'I should never have tried to fool Myssa. Now we've just got to try to catch up.' He looked at Ankhu. 'You said you knew where the hidden entrance was . . .'

'I know roughly where it is.'

'Then let's go and find it.'

The dying sun had turned the western desert to a patchwork of red sand and pools of shadow. The camp was still – no song, no aromas of cooking food – and in that light it seemed that a dismal atmosphere had settled heavily over the remaining tents.

The three men clambered up the crumbling stones of the monument, then Ankhu paused, looked around and started pointing to places where the entrance could be, while Hannu and Piay scrambled from one possible site to another. At first, they found nothing but solid, immovable masonry. But then they came to a slab that half-covered a hole leading into the pyramid.

Ankhu sighed. 'The slab has been moved.'

'Myssa has been inside,' Piay said. 'She made no attempt to cover her tracks. Why should she? She has what she wants and now she has gone.' He looked towards that red slash across the horizon. The dark seemed to be drawing in too fast. 'She was cleverer than all of us.'

'Then it is over,' Hannu said. 'We have lost.'

Piay pushed his chin up. 'I won't accept that. And Myssa did make one mistake . . . I don't know why, but she let me live.'

'So what can we do?' Hannu asked. 'We don't know what Myssa found, or where Imhotep's signs will lead her next.'

Piay heard the baboon's roar again.

'Well, we can't give up now. There has to be a way. Khonsu wouldn't have come to me if it was hopeless.'

Ankhu sat down on the rough stone beside Piay and looked towards the western horizon.

'If you have truly been chosen by the gods, then you must have a special strength. One that may not be visible to those around you,' the scribe added with a smile.

Hannu grabbed a fragment of stone and hurled it out across the void.

'Would recklessness be a strength?'

Piay pondered.

'Bravado in the face of all reason,' Hannu continued.

'And a silver tongue,' Ankhu added, still smiling.

Piay raised a finger. 'All right, I know, those things are weaknesses. But I am who I am, and Khonsu has seen fit to give me this role. So all I can do is be reckless for one last time, a final gamble, with all that I have left as a wager.'

'So, what do you have left?' Hannu asked.

'My life. That's it.'

Only a thin band of red wavered on the horizon.

'I can't outwit Myssa,' Piay continued in a low voice, 'but I can confront her, face to face. Speak to her as a man who loved her, and get her to speak to me as a woman who once loved me.'

Hannu's silence told him what his assistant thought of this plan.

'We can still catch them,' Piay pressed. 'The trail across the waste will be easy to follow. And they won't have gone too far from here. Myssa still needs to be close to the pyramid.'

'How do you know that? What if she's solved the whole riddle?'

Piay gave a wry smile. 'Hannu, the prize is the power to be one with the gods and change the world forever. If Myssa had already found it, don't you think we'd all know by now? Look around . . . do you see any great changes?'

'Fine – the puzzle still needs completing. But suppose you track her down . . . Then what? The two of us against a whole company of Hyksos?'

'No, this is just between me and Myssa.'

Ankhu turned to Piay, the lines in his face growing starker in the thin light.

'You're certain this is the path you choose?'

'I've tried hating Myssa. I've tried telling myself that she means nothing to me. But the truth is, I can't abandon her now, even if it costs me my life. And . . .' Piay paused and gave a mirthless little laugh. 'I know that this sounds crazy, but I think she's in danger.'

'Wait,' Hannu said. 'That woman's got a small army of Hyksos and you're all by yourself . . . and she's the one in danger? Have you completely lost your mind?'

'No, I mean it . . . Listen, Myssa tried to persuade me that she was in control of the people around her, and that she'd never bow down to any man. But I still think the Cobra is using her, even if she won't admit it. And if he reckons she's found the answer to Imhotep's puzzle in the pyramid, then the Cobra won't need her any longer. Her time is running out.'

'That is what drives you on this final desperate attempt to stop Imhotep's secrets falling into the wrong hands?' the scribe said. 'Not preventing the rise of Seth upon this world and the return of the Hyksos?'

Piay looked into the older man's face, but he felt that if he spoke he would choke upon his words. He had never felt so desperate in his life.

Yet instead of berating him, Ankhu only nodded. 'I understand.'

The three men clambered back down the side of the monument in the moonlight. When they reached the ground, Hannu muttered that he would go in search of some bread and a water hide for Piay to take with him.

Ankhu stripped off his robe and the scarf that was tied around his head.

'Wear these,' he said. 'If you are seen from a distance, they will think you a desert wanderer and leave you alone.'

Piay pulled the garment over his head and wrapped the scarf tight.

'I'm in your debt.'

'If I have to walk back to Memphis naked, I will make sure that debt is paid in full,' Ankhu said with a chuckle.

He wandered away towards the camp, still chuckling, his body as wrinkled as a dried fig.

Piay strode back to his shelter and sat down cross-legged, waiting for Hannu to return. In the dark and the stillness, his thoughts drifted to Myssa and he felt a yearning deep in his heart.

Closing his eyes, he cast his mind back and was once again lost in the lush pleasures of her kiss. Her warm body pressed against him, her breasts heaving against his chest. That moment when they had first embraced would be etched in his mind forever.

It had been in that lonely land of the great apes, a short walk from a secluded beach, on the edge of the vast steaming jungle. He could still feel the moisture misting his skin, still breathe in the heavy scents of the hot vegetation and—

Suddenly a taut line lashed across his throat, and Piay felt himself yanked back. Thrashing, he clawed at the constriction, feeling the roughness of a hide rope biting into his flesh. Strong hands wrenched it tighter still.

His heels kicked out against the ground but found no purchase. Powerful hands dragged him further back until he was pressed hard against a bare chest. His nostrils flared at the sharp reek of sweat.

The noose was so tight Piay could not stab his fingers beneath it to attempt to loosen it. Pain lanced through his neck and shoulders from where it cut into his flesh. When he lashed out in a desperate, flailing attempt to break his captor's grip, he could not reach whoever was behind him.

His lungs ached from the lack of air.

Darkness swelled around the edges of his vision.

Then Piay felt a jolt and the pressure around his neck loosened. A body crashed into the sand as the hide rope fell away. Piay collapsed, sucking in huge lungfuls of air.

Rolling over, he looked back at his attacker. Adon was sprawled on the ground, dazed, the hide rope still trailing from one hand.

Hannu loomed over him. His sword was in his hand, and it seemed that he had cracked the hilt against the taskmaster's skull.

As Adon recovered, he tried to force himself up. Hannu stepped over him and stabbed his blade towards the prone man's chest. The tip bit into the flesh and a bubble of blood burst.

'What is this?' Hannu snarled.

'Don't hurt me,' Adon babbled. 'I bear no grudge.'

'No grudge?' Piay rubbed the stinging sensation away from his raw neck. 'You tried to kill me!'

'Speak,' Hannu snapped at Adon, 'or I'll kill you.'

The taskmaster looked from Hannu to Piay and back.

'Zahur and Lord Harrar ordered me to commit this act once you had given up all that you knew of where the gold was buried.'

'You knew it was gold?' Piay said.

Adon nodded. 'They promised me a fine reward if I did their bidding.'

Hannu lifted his blade and stepped back. 'Run from this place as fast as your legs will carry you. If you see my face again, it will be the last thing you glimpse.'

The taskmaster did not need to be told twice. He scrambled out of the shelter and his pounding footsteps disappeared into the night.

Piay slumped back on one elbow in relief, still rubbing his neck.

'Harrar and Zahur were always going to want our imaginary gold for themselves.'

'The two of them could be brothers,' Hannu spat. 'So much in common, and none of it good.'

'I won't forget this,' Piay said. 'If I ever get back to Memphis, then Harrar and Zahur should be very afraid.'

'There's still time to change your mind about Myssa.'

Piay shook his head. 'I can't. This is my only hope of saving her. And it's not just about her, whatever Ankhu said. This is my only hope of stopping the Cobra and saving Egypt, too.'

Hannu sheathed his sword. 'All right, your mind's made up.' His voice was quiet, his face lost to shadow. 'I'll pray to the gods that you survive. And if you don't—'

'Don't say another word,' Piay interrupted. 'I won't even think about failure. I've got no choice. I have to win – whatever the cost.' And then he smiled at Hannu. 'But even if you can't help me getting in, you can definitely help me getting out.'

'Ah . . . right,' Hannu said. 'That old trick.'

'Yes,' Piay said. 'That one.'

The moon floated on the black surface of the still lake. The wind had fallen and the palms had ceased their rustling. All was peaceful across the oasis.

Myssa stood in the entrance to her tent and looked out across the camp. She breathed in the heavy musk of the horses and the sharp, fruity tang of their dung, listening to the stamp of their hooves.

Not far away, a fire glowed through the tight jumble of tents. The gruff voices of the warriors drifted with the smell of the woodsmoke as they refought the brutal battles of the Hyksos retreat from the Lower Kingdom. They eagerly imagined new glories once they had uncovered the prize for which they were searching, the spells that would renew the vigour of the Hyksos and allow them once again to rule this land.

Myssa paid no mind to their fantasies. These were not her people; this was not her land. With the gold that came with Imhotep's spells, she would buy a passage back to her home in the hot south and return to the life she knew. She would rebuild her village, bring back her scattered people, make them strong enough to resist any attack by the hated slavers. There was nothing to keep her in Egypt.

Except . . .

Myssa pushed aside that stray thought. Unsettling emotions seemed to assail her more and more these days, and she had no notion from where they were rising. But she woke each morning with a feeling that something was missing. What it was, she could not tell, but it was a thirst she could never seem to assuage.

She would not let it stand in her way, though; of that, at least, she was certain.

Sparks swirled up as a sod of straw and dried dung was tossed on the fire. Myssa looked around the small camp. The acolytes would be in their tents, poring over their scrolls. Where the Cobra was, she had no idea. Tallus was a law unto himself, disappearing into the desert to conduct his strange rituals to Seth whenever the mood took him.

Since Akkan's demise, he had continued to play the part of humble advisor, but Myssa was sure that he was simply biding his time. Tallus had his own aims. What they were, precisely, Myssa could not say. She just knew that he could not be trusted.

She stepped back into her tent and let the flaps fall shut. The light from the lamp wavered as the air current shifted and the acrid smell of the oil filled the small space. Tallus no doubt thought her oblivious to his machinations. He was really not so different from the priests in the Temple of Amun in Thebes: her skin and her sex would always make her inferior in his eyes, no matter how often she proved herself as a leader. But she was watching him closely. Should he make a move against her, she would be ready. Her knife was never far from her fingers.

Myssa had lied to Tallus about what she'd discovered in the Pyramid of Khufu, telling him it would take long days to decipher it by matching the Disc of Ra to the stars above.

That would keep him at bay, at least for a while. In that time, she had to work out a way of getting back to the monuments, alone, and finishing the journey that would take her to Imhotep's prize.

Myssa sat cross-legged on the ground and pulled the leather pouch out from beneath the blanket she used to keep the chill of the night at bay. She glanced inside. The Eye of Horus and the Disc of Ra were there, and there was no reason why they should not be, for she never let these items stray from her person.

The flap of the tent shifted as if someone was about to enter. 'Who's there?' Myssa said.

The flap shifted again and a cat pushed its way inside. Myssa felt a shiver of surprise. This was the animal that had followed her out of the city of Bubastis and had attached itself to her on that journey across half the world, until, for some reason, it had abandoned her when she had seized the Eye of Horus and the Disc of Ra at the palace in Memphis.

So why was it here with her now?

The cat made itself comfortable in the circle of light thrown by the lamp. Its eyes were huge, and it stared at Myssa as if trying to communicate.

'What is it you want?' she breathed, suddenly rediscovering another suppressed emotion: she had missed her faithful companion.

'Is the goddess truly within you?' she whispered. 'The lioness who protects her cubs. Have you returned to protect me?'

Myssa sprawled on her belly and rested her head in her hands so she could stare back into those bewilderingly mysterious eyes.

The cat did not break eye contact, and Myssa felt something shift deep inside her as she sank into their depths. The whispers of Tallus' voice that had been a constant companion since she had been taken captive receded.

In its silent intensity, the cat called to a long-lost part of her.

Piay crept towards the oasis. In Ankhu's white robe and purple scarf, he would have looked like just another desert wanderer, but so far as he could tell, the Hyksos war band had not posted any guards.

Why would they? Who would dare challenge them out there in the wastes?

He cocked his head, listening to the low rumble of the voices around the campfire. The warriors were settled, perhaps drunk.

From his vantage point, he'd watched Myssa stand in the entrance to her tent. It was far enough away from where the fighting men lounged for him to attempt his plan. He laughed silently at that word. It was no plan at all – worse even than all his other plans. It was simply one final attempt to break through whatever had bewitched Myssa.

Piay felt his life repeating itself. As a small boy, he had desperately wanted to believe that his parents loved him enough to come back for him. Now he was letting the same wretched, vain hope possess him again. His whole strategy rested on a childlike faith that some part of her love for him still lay buried within Myssa – that with all his sorcery and potions, the Cobra could not forever eradicate the Myssa that was, that had been.

In every act of recklessness he had been condemned for over the years, Piay had never been this rash. But it was all he had left. And if he did not live to see the dawn, he would know in his final reckoning that he had done all he could to rescue the one who was more valuable to him than life itself.

Creeping along the edge of the camp, he made his way to the tent where Myssa slept. On the threshold, he sucked in a deep breath, steeling himself, and then he slipped through the flaps.

Myssa lay on the ground, staring into the eyes of Bast as if she was caught under another spell. Piay gaped. He had left the perplexing creature at the camp by the great monument. There was no way under the heavens that it could be here. And yet it was.

At first Myssa did not stir, but then she blinked once, twice, and broke whatever strange connection she had with the feline. When she noticed Piay, she jumped to her feet.

Myssa's face seemed thinner and more drawn. There were hollows under her cheekbones and around her eyes that he had never noticed before. But that fleeting impression vanished from his mind at the sight of the knife in her hand.

'Take one more step and you'll be dead,' she hissed.

Piay reached out his hands. 'I have no weapons. I am no threat to you.'

'Are you mad to come here unarmed? To come here at all, into the very heart of your enemy's camp?'

'Absolutely,' Piay replied. 'Driven mad by my love for you.'

Myssa sniffed. 'Love!'

Despite her contempt, her hard gaze flickered and the knife dropped a little lower. She reached down under a blanket and pulled out a pouch which she slung across her shoulder.

'You're wasting your breath.'

'Maybe, but I have to speak with you. I couldn't stay away.'

Myssa snorted. 'Your words won't work on me.' She twirled the blade. 'You're not getting your hands on the Eye or the Disc.'

Piay let his arms fall to his sides, overwhelmed by the battle raging inside him. In his heart, everything paled beside his love for Myssa. Treasure beyond imagining. The fate of Egypt. Even the battles that consumed the gods.

But more than ever, he now understood his duty.

If he allowed the power and the riches stored away by Imhotep to fall into any other hands, he would be dooming all Egypt. On the one hand was his honour, on the other his heart.

Myssa narrowed her eyes. 'There was no reason to kill you before. You weren't a threat. But all I have to do is call out and my men will come and drag you away, and this time there'll be nothing that can save you. They're brutal, the Hyksos. They'll tie you between two horses and rip you apart.'

Piay shrugged. 'Let them.'

Myssa shook her head with incredulity. 'Whatever you imagine lies between us is long gone and will never return.'

'The Cobra has you under a spell—'

'I am my own woman!'

Piay bit off his response, allowing space for her temper to cool. He could not risk their exchange being overheard.

'You are filled with more fire than any person I know, man or woman,' he began again, his voice lower but crackling with passion. 'That's not flattery, just the truth. Everything that lies within you, all the wit and the words, the passion and the kindness and the laughter, all of those things have *me* under a spell. And whatever that snake has told you, I could never see you as a slave, only as an equal.'

Piay hesitated, then gave in to the heartfelt words tumbling out of him.

'Myssa, without you I am nothing. I can't exist without you at my side. I'd plead with you to overcome whatever sorcery the

Cobra has worked on you, but in the end, this is your choice. I came here tonight to tell you how I felt, knowing that I could lose my life.' He shrugged. 'But what use is my life without you to share it with?'

Myssa's jaw dropped a little and her knife fell to her side.

'Leave now,' she said. 'You have said what you needed to say. But leave now.'

'You must choose,' Piay pressed. 'Come with me now. Whatever you hope to achieve with Imhotep's secret, together we can find some way to make it happen. But I can't allow such power to fall into any hands other than Taita's. He's the only one wise enough to use it without risking disaster.'

Piay waited for Myssa to raise the alarm. He felt relieved when she did not.

'Come with me,' he repeated, reaching out a hand.

He could see from Myssa's face that there was a battle going on inside her. Had his words touched her? He could not be sure.

Myssa shook her head. 'I don't know you. You stand before me as a stranger. I . . . I . . .' she stuttered. 'A part of me does know you, I feel that, but I do not know you,' she added, bewildered.

'You must know that your usefulness to the Cobra is nearing its end. He won't hesitate to kill you.'

Myssa's face hardened. 'If you think I don't know how the Cobra's mind works, you take me for a fool.'

'One final time – come with me now.'

'I reject you.' Myssa stepped forward and Piay flinched, thinking she was going to stab her blade into his heart. Instead, she pushed past him. 'I reject you. I don't care about the games your master plays, or the Hyksos. I walk my own path. That hidden power and the gold will buy a new life for my people. I will never again have to suffer the miseries I have endured for so long. If you stand in my way, I will consider you my enemy, whatever we might have shared before.

'Do not be here when I return,' she added, before she flew out into the night.

Piay felt his stomach twist. He had failed. He had appealed to Myssa's heart and it had been for nothing. Perhaps the Cobra's spell was too strong. Perhaps she truly believed what she said. But he could not give up. The consequences would be too terrible, for both of them . . . and for all Egypt.

He pushed out after Myssa, unsure what his next step should be.

Piay glimpsed her ahead, silhouetted against the glow rising from the campfire as she walked among the tents. He cursed under his breath. He could not follow.

As he weighed his options, Piay noticed more silhouettes moving towards Myssa from the other side of the camp. Once they neared the fire, the dancing light revealed the Cobra and three of the acolytes.

Piay crouched, peering through a gap in the tents. The Cobra tipped his staff forward so it was pointing at Myssa.

'We were coming to find you,' Tallus said. 'We have been deep in discussion since your success within the Pyramid of Khufu.'

Myssa's shoulders tensed. Like Piay, she suspected no good would come of this confrontation.

'What do you want?' she asked.

'We are close to the end of our quest,' the Cobra said, 'and we cannot afford any errors at this stage. The time has come to entrust the Eye of Horus and the Disc of Ra to our care, for safekeeping by men who can defend them with their lives.'

'They stay in my hands,' Myssa said.

Tallus took a step towards her and Myssa stepped back.

'We cannot afford any risks – not now,' he said. 'This is not a decision for you to take. Our minds are made up.'

'No.' Myssa's voice cracked.

Piay felt a burst of pride – Myssa would not be cowed by anyone – but with it came a pang of fear. The Cobra would not back down.

'I know they are in that pouch that you always carry on your shoulder. The pouch you took from the Egyptian at the palace in Memphis. The pouch I gave to him.'

Myssa took another step backwards. Piay watched her head turn slowly as she looked from the Cobra to the scribes and warriors, who had now risen to their feet around the fire.

Piay sensed what was to happen next an instant before it unfolded.

Someone lunged for the pouch on Myssa's shoulder. Her right hand slashed down. The man nearest her screamed and fell back. Piay couldn't see the blood from his position, but he knew it flowed.

Then Myssa darted away into the dark.

Piay's heart pounded. Those warriors would be on her in no time, and that would be the end of her.

He leaped to his feet and bellowed, 'Strike now! While they are disorganised!'

His ploy worked. The warriors wrenched out their swords and fell into a defensive circle around the Cobra and the scribes, their heads turning back and forth as they searched for attackers out in the night.

Piay darted away before anyone could hurry in the direction of his voice. Weaving around the edge of the camp, he called out again, before racing in the opposite direction. At least he still had his knife with him, hidden in the kilt beneath his long robes.

Stumbling in the dark, Piay's nose filled with the stink of the horses. He regretted that he hadn't paid more attention when Taita was discussing them, and had not taken up his master's offer to learn how to ride. At the time he had felt that he had more important tasks, like drinking the pharaoh's wine and seducing the women of the court.

'Idiot!' he cursed himself. But the horses might yet serve a purpose.

Piay crashed against the makeshift pen, smashing down the fence and running among the stamping, snorting beasts, clapping his hands and exhorting them to move. In no time the horses were galloping out of their enclosure.

From the direction of the fire, Piay heard cries of alarm rise up from the Hyksos warriors. Then he was racing away into the night.

Piay left the Hyksos caught between rounding up their horses and preparing for an attack that would never come. He headed away from the camp, making a clear trail in the opposite direction from the one Myssa had taken. Then he looped around, erasing his tracks as he went, and set off after her.

The sun had risen above the eastern horizon when Piay looked down from the rim of a dune and glimpsed a figure in the distance, heading across the wasteland. He skidded down the dune and drove himself forward. The Hyksos would long since have realised they had been tricked. It was only a matter of time before they would be bearing down on Myssa's trail.

Crouching, Piay wrapped Ankhu's purple scarf around the lower part of his face to keep the dust out of his nose and mouth, and tried to remain out of Myssa's sight. He ran at a crouch, taking cover behind the grey-bronze rocks that stabbed up from the ground like the fingers of some buried giant, diverting every now and then into hollows where he dipped below her eyeline, straightened up and ran faster. Piay knew how quickly Myssa could travel across even the roughest terrain. But, to his surprise, when he caught further glimpses of her, Piay saw that he was closing fast. Myssa was barely managing to walk, let alone run.

As he came closer still, Piay saw the reason for her slow progress. Somehow Myssa had lost a sandal, and her foot was bloody from racing across sharp-edged stones. She was limping. Perhaps the pain also explained something else that was troubling him: *How has she let me get so close without even seeming to notice?*

Piay dashed out from behind his final scrap of cover. Now Myssa noticed him. She reached for her knife and turned to face him, but her movements were slow and her grip weak. It was easy to knock the knife from her hand and then grasp her wrists before she could hit him.

Myssa's skin was hot to the touch – far hotter than it should have been, particularly given the pace at which she'd been going.

'I am not here to harm you, only help,' Piay said. 'Look back.'

Myssa glanced past his shoulder. She blinked, as if finding it hard to clear her vision. In the distance a cloud of dust billowed. The Cobra and his men were coming.

'If they catch us, our lives are over, you know that.'

Unfurling his fingers from her wrists, Piay stepped back and picked up Myssa's knife. He offered it to her.

'I am not here to harm you,' he repeated as she took it from his hand.

'We won't be able to outrun them,' Myssa said.

Piay glanced back at the dust cloud and did a quick mental calculation.

'Sit down,' he said. 'Let's do something about that foot.'

'We don't have time.'

'It's worth it if you can move faster.'

He tore a strip from the bottom of his robe to use as a bandage.

'Hope old Ankhu doesn't mind!' he said with a light laugh, trying to lift Myssa's spirits.

He'd never seen her so downcast. And now he looked at her in the daylight, he saw that his impression of her back at the oasis had been accurate. She had lost weight, and with it some of the strength and vigour he had always associated with her.

'When did you last have a good meal?' Piay asked, as he got down on his knees and took Myssa's cut foot in his hands.

She looked at him blankly, as if she had not even thought of food in an age. Suddenly she shivered convulsively, almost pulling her foot from his hands.

'What's the matter, my love?' Piay said. 'Are you sick? A fever, maybe?' That might explain why she looked so unwell. Then another thought struck him and he asked, 'Has the tomb done this to you?'

Myssa shook her head. 'No . . . not that. It's just, I haven't . . . I mean Tallus hasn't . . . Ah . . .' Her words petered out as if her mind could not form them.

'Of course, it's that bastard sorcerer,' Piay said, as he tied the fabric tight around her foot. 'I should have guessed.'

He checked the finished bandage, then lifted Myssa to her feet and draped one of her arms across his shoulder. Glancing up at the position of the sun, Piay calculated the right direction and pointed.

'That way.'

Myssa didn't question him. Piay led her down into gullies cut out of the dry desert by ancient waters, doing his best to hide their tracks by using all the skills he had long ago been taught by Taita.

The bandage hadn't worked. Though Piay tried all he could to ease her pain, Myssa was limping on her wounded foot. The time had been wasted.

'I'll carry you,' Piay said, lifting her onto his back.

Myssa wrapped her arms around his shoulder and he felt a shiver at her closeness. He breathed in her musk and felt her hair against his cheek and her breath against the back of his neck.

'There is no hope, not now,' Myssa said.

As he picked up his stride, Piay replied, 'There is always hope.'

He was able to move faster when he carried Myssa than he had done when he was slowed by her walking. But even so, the dust cloud at their backs had been drawing inexorably nearer. Now Piay felt sure he could hear the beat of the Hyksos' hooves.

Then Piay heard another sound, this time from ahead. He grinned.

'What is it?' Myssa asked.

'Hope.'

He prayed he was right.

Renewing his effort, Piay pushed on, racing towards the beat of marching feet that he could hear in front of them. Soon after he glimpsed what he had hoped for – the Blue Crocodile Guards, with Hannu among them, marching along the bearing Piay had indicated to Hannu before dispatching him to Memphis.

Piay hailed the approaching force and soon he and Myssa were standing among the finest fighting men in all Egypt. The cloud of dust was still approaching, but it would stop soon enough. The Hyksos would not risk a fight with the guards.

'You survived, then,' Hannu growled.

'The gods favour the brave,' Piay replied, adding, 'and fools.'

Hannu nodded before eyeing Myssa. 'Are you with us?'

Myssa narrowed her eyes. 'Expect no gratitude. I will not tell you what I discovered in the Pyramid of Khufu, not even under duress.'

Piay eased the pouch from her shoulder. She didn't resist – she knew it was pointless. Instead, she raised her chin in defiance and looked towards the horizon.

'We would never force you to do anything,' Piay said. 'We will discover the pyramid's secrets ourselves.'

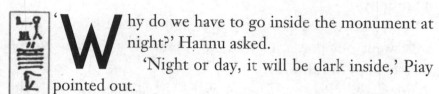

'Why do we have to go inside the monument at night?' Hannu asked.

'Night or day, it will be dark inside,' Piay pointed out.

'Night is different.'

The mountain of stone soared up ahead, a majestic sight silhouetted against the spray of milky stars. Now the labourers at the camp had ended their work for the day, all was at peace, though their toils had been only half-hearted since Adon the taskmaster had mysteriously disappeared.

Piay studied the vast monument, letting its awesome presence settle on him. At night it seemed to hold even greater power, as if the wonder of the almost unimaginable passage of time since its construction was magnified by starlight.

'We can't afford to wait, you know that,' Piay said. 'Now that the Eye of Horus and Disc of Ra are back in our possession, the Sons of Apis will once again see us as enemies.'

'Don't forget the Cobra,' Hannu muttered. 'He won't hold back, not now that he's so close to his prize.'

Ankhu stepped out of the shadows of the Valley Temple, which would once have greeted Khufu's priests as they made preparations to receive the royal body. Piay had heard the scribe's rhythmic chanting roll out from the open courtyard in the centre of the temple. Spells of protection, Piay hoped.

'Everything is ready,' the scribe said, his voice heavy with foreboding. 'I have told you all that you need to know of the tunnels and chambers within the tomb. Are you prepared for what lies ahead?'

'Yes,' Piay replied.

'No,' Hannu said.

'Heed my warning,' Ankhu said. 'Do not venture into the lowest region of the pyramid. Go up.'

Piay eyed Hannu, still wondering if he could trust Ankhu's intentions.

Ankhu muttered another prayer and then he stepped aside and swept out one arm, ushering them on a journey to the threshold of the afterlife.

For a while Piay and Hannu walked in silence, with only the sizzle of their torches to accompany them.

'Myssa will not thank you for making her a captive,' Hannu said, speaking as a means of distracting his mind and keeping the fears that lurked there at bay.

'The Blue Crocodile Guards will treat her like a queen, at least,' Piay said. 'Left unguarded, she would be away like an ibis on the wing.'

And I would never see her again, he thought.

Was he wrong to deny Myssa her freedom? It was certainly going to make it harder to win back her affections.

'You're still planning to give her the blue lotus pellets your father gave you?'

'When we return to Memphis and it's easier to watch over her.'

Piay dreamed of holding Myssa in his arms again, of everything being as it once was. He would never take her for granted again.

An angry shout rang out from the labourers' camp. Another voice roared in opposition. A fight was brewing.

Hannu looked towards the jumble of shelters.

'Things haven't gone well while you've been away.'

'The men were bound to lose their discipline without Adon to crack his whip.'

'It is more than that. The caravan bringing supplies from Memphis has not arrived for two days now. There are empty bellies, and a hungry man is an angry man.'

Piay sighed. 'I can't say I am surprised. Feeding mouths is not a priority for Zahur or Harrar. I can just imagine them deciding to stop the caravans.'

'Or it could be corrupt merchants and officials, taking the money that was meant to be spent on supplies and keeping it for themselves instead.'

'Maybe the mule-drivers had heard about the Hyksos' attack, and refused to come out here,' Piay said. 'No point worrying about that now. Just concentrate on the task in hand.'

To their left, the ghostly outlines of the mastabas appeared out of the dark, the mud-brick buildings that would have been the final resting place of dignitaries during Khufu's time. Beyond them, a line of three smaller pyramids crouched like children in the shadow of a stern father.

By one of the mastabas, Bast was waiting for them. Piay shook his head.

'That cat!'

'Leave it be. Cats come and go.'

'Not like this one,' Piay muttered.

He eyed Bast as he passed, but she only licked her paw and began grooming herself. He hoped it was an omen of a successful night to come. The lioness goddess watched over her own.

They passed through the Mortuary Temple, where Khufu's cult would have drained the blood of beasts in his name. The black basalt flooring under their feet seemed as if the night sky had been brought down to earth.

And then they were standing at the foot of that towering wall of stone.

'One thing you should remember – Myssa returned to the land of the living . . . and we are following in her footsteps.'

They clambered up the crumbling rows of blocks until they reached the entrance Ankhu had shown them. Piay dragged back the covering stone. He looked up at the stars, searching for the Four Sons of Horus, and then he stepped over the threshold into the unknown.

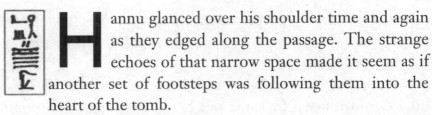annu glanced over his shoulder time and again as they edged along the passage. The strange echoes of that narrow space made it seem as if another set of footsteps was following them into the heart of the tomb.

Never had Piay been in such a disorientating place. His own whispers floated back to him from the dark ahead, as if he was standing there, waiting for himself to arrive. The stone pressed in hard on either side, choking the spirit so that Piay felt as if he were in his own grave. He breathed in air so dry it burned his throat. All he could smell was the dusty odour of stone.

Ankhu had warned them that the place was a labyrinth. But it was the other warning that still troubled him: the scribe's insistence that Piay should not descend deep into the bedrock beneath the pyramid where, by all accounts, an unfinished chamber waited. It was a trap, Ankhu had said, and Piay would never return if he visited that place. The only way was up. But that advice seemed to be the opposite of what Imhotep intended. Piay wondered once again if Ankhu was trying to deflect them from where the next sign lay or, worse, send them to their doom so that he could claim the reward.

'Myssa's footprints,' Hannu said.

He lowered the torch so Piay could see the tracks in the dust.

'Then we follow them,' Piay replied.

As they pushed on in the wavering pale gold light of the torches, Piay took whatever small comforts he could. Everywhere he looked there were signs of the robbers who had broken into the tomb in times long gone – tunnels carved through the vast blocks of stone of the original construction, side passages to avoid the many obstructions the original builders had put in place to keep the king's riches safe.

No old bones littered that place. No blood had seeped into the stone. Those robbers had, like Myssa, escaped with their lives. That, at least, was some small comfort.

'Hold it,' Hannu raised a hand to bring Piay to a halt.

When he waved his torch, the dark flew away from the sputtering flames to reveal a junction with a passage descending into the gloom and another ascending.

'That way to the trap that Ankhu warned us about,' Piay said, pointing down.

'Or the way to the truth,' Hannu said.

'Which way do Myssa's footprints go?'

'They've vanished. The dust is thinner here. Hang on . . .'

Hannu took a few more paces forward and got down on his haunches to look at the passage floor. He turned his head back to look up at Piay.

'More prints, and they're heading up,' he said. 'But these aren't Myssa's. They're larger . . . a man.'

'Then someone else was in here.'

'Or still is.'

Piay's eyes darted back and forth from the footprints in the rising passage to the tunnel leading down into the dark. Should he trust Ankhu or not, knowing full well this could be a matter of life and death?

He turned the decision over in his head, then told himself to rely on his instinct.

'We go up.'

As they moved upwards, Piay took one last glance back down the tunnel into the depths, and wished he hadn't. Something appeared to be waiting there, just beyond the edge of the torchlight – a dark bulk, hunched in readiness.

Just your imagination, he told himself.

But he could not forget what the texts said waited in the next stage of the journey through the underworld: a monstrous serpent that threatened to dismember whoever dared venture there.

'Pick up your step,' he said to Hannu, trying to keep his voice steady and bright. 'No point wasting time. The sooner we're done, the sooner we can return to the land of the living.'

Piay's lips puckered in that arid air and the dust tasted bitter on his tongue. When he breathed in, he felt that dryness seep deep into his lungs. The light did not seem bright enough to keep the dark at bay.

His heart thumped faster as he thought of the mountain of stone above his head, pressing down upon him. And there he was, crushed in such a narrow passage that his shoulders almost brushed both walls and he had to stoop to avoid bumping his head on the low ceiling.

Was this how it would feel in his own tomb at the end of his days? Would he finally meet the gods themselves when they guided his soul through the afterlife?

His skin tingled and he ground to a halt. In the bubble of light from his torch, he half-turned, his shoulders dragging across the bare stone. He could not tell if it was his imagination, but he felt convinced he had heard something – something that sounded like nails being dragged along the wall.

A chill settled deep inside him. Piay cocked his head, straining to listen, though a part of him did not want to know if anyone was there. He could not throw off the vision of that thing swathed by the gloom in the descending passage.

The silence swallowed him, so intense he felt like he was drowning in it. The more he forced himself to listen, the more the blood pounded in his head, making it impossible for him to hear anything.

Finally, Piay could not bear to wait there any longer. He turned back, and only then did he realise he was alone.

Lost to his own thoughts, Hannu must have pushed on ahead.

Cursing his friend for moving so fast, Piay clawed his way up the slope into the gloom. His knuckles ached from gripping the torch so hard; he was afraid that if he dropped it the light would vanish and the dark would rush in to claim him.

His ragged breathing echoed in that suffocating space.

Piay began to wonder if Ankhu's information had been wrong – after all, the scribe had not been within the great monument himself, and was only passing on stories that had been handed down through the generations.

What if these passages were designed to confuse the unwary, like the ones that existed beneath Djoser's pyramid? He could be trapped there until he drew his last breath.

The torchlight flickered past the constricting space to reveal the vast, steeply ascending passageway that Ankhu said led to the tomb where Khufu's mummy would have been laid to rest. But in front of him was a much narrower horizontal passage to a smaller chamber. That was where he would need to explore first.

And still no sign of Hannu, not even the scrape of a leather sole upon stone.

Crouching down, Piay pushed himself into the small passage. His mouth was numb now from the bitter dust, and he felt as if his throat had constricted so that it was no wider than his little finger. He could not seem to draw in enough air to fill his lungs.

Piay scrambled on into the gloom. The light barely reached an arm's length ahead of him.

Finally, he crawled out into the small chamber. The golden glow rushed up the walls to the ceiling, and for the first time in what seemed like an age he could stand upright.

The room was bare. Perhaps once it would have been filled to the brim with everything the king needed to sustain him in the afterlife, but the space did not seem large enough to contain such sumptuous riches.

Creeping into the centre of the chamber, Piay looked around. *Where should I begin?*

Once again he thought of Imhotep, and Taita, and he tried to imagine what his master would have done if he was preparing a ritual path to test the wisdom of those who came after him.

The more Piay thought, the more his head ached. He wished Myssa was there – even Ankhu. And then he remembered what the scribe had said about Imhotep drawing the connection between the heavens and the earth. Was that why the scribe had urged him to take the upper path, that pointed towards the sky and the home of the gods, rather than the path that led away from it?

Swinging up the torch, he swept the light across the low ceiling. Pulling the Eye of Horus from the pouch, Piay steadied it in front of the brand until the pure white light blasted out.

Fiery tracings blazed across the stone and his heart leaped. His reasoning had been correct once again. Perhaps he was not as dull-witted as he thought.

The etching revealed the bed-shaped symbol *pt* – sky or heaven. Piay frowned. What could this mean? The sky, as everyone knew, was an ocean across which the dead sailed to the afterlife.

Piay searched on, and the shifting glow revealed another symbol beneath that one. It was a single stroke – *I*. One.

One step had been taken along Imhotep's path into the eternal dark. Piay sucked in a wheezing gulp of that tainted air, trying to stay calm.

'Turn you not around.'

Piay's heart hammered. The voice had been barely more than a whisper just behind his left shoulder. His hand crept to the knife hidden in his kilt.

'Turn you not around. You must not look upon my visage.'

The voice was like the desert breeze stirring the sand on a moonlit night. The tone was not unkind or threatening, Piay thought.

'Khonsu?' he murmured.

'There is great danger for you here. You must not tarry any longer than you need to, for if you do, you will be lost forever.'

Piay felt his thoughts shift in an odd way, as they did when he had swilled too much wine.

Then he heard the god whisper, 'What part you play in these unfolding events will decide the way of all things. You must not fail.'

Once again, Piay thought of a great struggle taking place among the gods, acted out upon the earth with agents of the deities' choosing. He had accepted his role as Khonsu's emissary in these matters. He had thought Seth had chosen Akkan, but now it seemed the Cobra was the one to whom he should really have been paying attention.

Yet there was something in those hoarse words that troubled him. The outcome of this war seemed to be hanging in the balance. Could it really be that his own actions would echo forever?

Piay felt a breath on the back of his neck.

'When the time comes, only water will keep the fire at bay.'

'What does that mean?' Piay breathed.

He waited for what seemed an age, but no reply came. Steeling himself, he glanced back into the darkness. The presence that had been there had departed.

There was no time to waste. Piay scrambled back into the cramped passage and hauled his way along until he reached the junction.

The torch crackled lower. It was slowly burning itself out. Yet there was still enough light to see by. The ascending passageway from this point was grander than any other he had seen, the magnificence no doubt designed to catch the breath on the approach to the king's tomb. Piay raised the brand higher and marvelled at a vaulted roof of such fine workmanship that it reminded him of the temple in Thebes. Yet this one had been constructed a thousand years ago.

A cough bubbled up, and then another. Piay tried to stifle them, in case he alerted some other denizen of the dark, but the dust had reached deep into his chest.

As the echoes died away, he felt sure he heard the sound of footsteps behind him.

Piay hurled himself up the passageway, his free hand clutching at the wall to pull himself on.

At the summit of the passage, he stared down a short corridor. A few steps further on, he slipped into the chamber that had been set aside for the king's mummy. Like the smaller chamber, it was bare except for a large stone sarcophagus with the lid cracked and half slid off.

Piay breathed in to steady himself, and then leaned over the gap. To his relief, the brand's dancing light showed that the sarcophagus was empty. Those grave robbers must have even stolen Khufu's mummy, though what good that would do them, he had no idea. Were they not afraid of being cursed? Or was it, as Ankhu had suggested, that no remains had ever been interred? Could this entire edifice have just been part of Imhotep's plan to reach across the ages?

Piay turned in an arc, letting the glow kiss the walls. Blocks of granite lined the chamber, which was coldly austere in its design. Fine particles of dust floated in the shimmering light. But the torch was dimming rapidly.

He cocked his head to listen, and once he was satisfied that the footsteps had not followed him, he lowered the torch to illuminate the flagstones.

Fresh footprints ended just inside the entrance, next to his own trail. Hannu had been in there, by the looks of it.

Once again, Piay brought the Eye of Horus and the brand close to the stone over his head. This time he found the mark *II* first – the second of Imhotep's signs. Above it, the brilliant light revealed two engraved stars and above them the ankh, the key of life.

There was no time to muse on the meaning – that would come later, when they had found safety.

The glow of the torch had shrunk down to a small globe of light, gradually turning ruddy.

The dark started to close in.

Piay's heart beat faster still and his thoughts slid back and forth. In that delirium, he felt sure he could hear the footsteps approaching again, heavy and methodical, this time accompanied by the sound of a body dragging itself along the wall and the rasping of breath, like a bull preparing to attack.

Piay felt the first sparks of panic lick into a flame inside him. But he knew what he had to do.

He crushed the torch against the wall, extinguishing it in a shower of sparks. The all-consuming dark engulfed him.

Feeling around, Piay's fingers caught on the edge of the sar-cophagus. His legs trembled in a blaze of dread.

Heaving himself up, he slid under the half-removed lid and into the sarcophagus.

In that confined space, Piay thought he might go mad. He was lying in a grave, half-expecting Khufu to descend on him in fury. At the very least, he would be cursed.

Whatever was in the dark stepped into the chamber.

Piay heard footsteps thump upon the flagstones and he felt sure the very sarcophagus shook. He clamped a hand over his mouth to stifle any sound of his breath.

The intruder's own breath rasped louder, the rumble of something immense and powerful. The footsteps boomed towards the sarcophagus.

The air took on the earthy musk of some beast Piay didn't recognise, like a carcass rotting in the hot desert sun. Piay sensed the creature was beside him now, searching for him. He couldn't resist peeking out through the gap in the lid.

Red eyes burned in the dark. Though the beast-head was lost in the gloom, in that instant Piay knew Seth was there, the god of disorder and violence.

Seth prowled around the sarcophagus, close enough to drag Piay out of his hiding place and rend him limb from limb, close enough to fling him into the underworld.

Piay screwed his eyes shut, so that all he knew was the bang of blood in his head. Gripping onto the stone, he waited for the ending that was surely about to come.

An age seemed to pass, an unbearable agony of waiting. But when Piay breathed in he realised that the reek had faded, and he could no longer sense the presence of the god.

Finally, he cracked open his eyelids a little and saw the dark had turned grey and was growing lighter.

'Hannu,' Piay muttered.

Easing himself out of the sarcophagus, he dropped to the floor. A bubble of light was floating along the passageway – a torch drawing closer. Just as Piay was about to cry out, he heard a metallic scraping. A blade was being drawn along the stone wall. The step was heavy, steady, without his assistant's shuffling limp.

This was not Hannu.

Piay snatched out his sword just in time. A figure lurched into the chamber and Piay felt horror course through him. It had the shape of a man and carried a vicious-looking knife, but where its head should have been a nest of horned vipers churned. The milky-scaled bodies thrashed, ghostly in the half-light, and their jaws snapped wide to reveal venom-dripping fangs.

Here was the next test – the terror that lurked in the underworld, come to cut him to pieces with the long knife it gripped in its right hand.

The creature surged forward, whipping the cruel blade above its head.

Piay focused on that seething mass of serpents for only an instant. If he gave in to the terror it would destroy him in an instant.

Hurling himself to one side, Piay crashed against one wall. The knife carved down into the space he had just vacated.

The hissing of the snakes echoed so loud it filled that cramped space, drowning out even his ragged breathing.

The serpent-man whirled, bringing up the blade again, but Piay was already moving. There was little space to manoeuvre. Somehow, he threw himself on the other side of the sarcophagus as the knife slashed a finger's width away from his neck.

As the creature rounded the stone box to catch him, Piay pulled himself up onto the lid and hacked his sword down into that writhing clump of pale serpents. His ears rang as the hissing became a screech.

Piay hacked again and again until the nest of horned vipers flew from the shoulders and skidded across the floor. The forms stilled instantly.

Staggering back to the wall, Piay scrubbed a trembling hand across his sweating brow. Had he done enough? Did more horrors await?

Even as the thought passed through his head, he heard more footsteps approaching, but these were smaller and shuffling. Another light neared.

'Where are you?' a muffled voice boomed.

This time it was Hannu. His assistant rushed over and thrust the torch aloft so he could inspect his master. Hannu now had a scarf tied across his mouth and nose.

'Hurry up or you'll be doomed,' Hannu insisted. He wrenched Piay's scarf free. 'Tie this across your face.'

'Seth was here. And a thing . . . with a head of snakes—'

'This is no time for talk. We've got to get out of here.'

Piay thought of Khonsu's words: that if he tarried too long, he would be lost forever.

Fumbling, he wrapped the scarf across his mouth and nose. He grabbed Hannu's arm and dragged him around the sarcophagus.

'Look! The thing that attacked me.'

'Thing? That is one of the Sons of Apis.'

'No . . .'

Piay glanced down and saw Hannu was right. The torso was dappled with tattoos, as was the head. Of the horned vipers there was no sign.

Piay gaped. This made no sense. How could he be mistaken?

Hannu rammed a hand into the small of his back and propelled him towards the passageway.

Then Piay was scrambling out and down that grand gallery, and down and down until he glimpsed a rosy square ahead of him. He heaved himself out of the hole and onto the side of the pyramid.

Before him, the sun hovered on the horizon, the land glowed pink and purple and the river sparkled.

The entire night had passed in the depths of that cursed place.

Only when Piay had stripped the scarf from his face and was lying back across the stones of the pyramid did he realise how much he had been affected by his journey deep into the heart of the great monument.

As the rising sun drove the last of the dread from his bones and his breathing subsided, he felt his thoughts settle back into a steady rhythm. They had been off-kilter for a long time, he realised.

Piay glanced at Hannu, who squatted beside him, studying his every movement.

'What happened to you?' Piay asked.

'I went on ahead. When I realised you weren't behind me I came back to find you, but by that time my thoughts had been turned around.'

'What do you mean?'

'Ankhu told us the subterranean chamber was a trap. He was right, in a way. The entire monument is a trap.'

Piay pushed himself up on his elbows, baffled.

'The dust of ages that covers the floor . . .' Hannu continued. 'It isn't just dust. You know the stuff the Sons of Apis have in their hands? Well, it's been left on the floors of all those passages and chambers. You saw what it did in the palace at Thebes.'

Now Piay understood what had happened to him. He remembered the bitter taste on his tongue, the numbness in his mouth, the choking sensation and the way his fears had run away with him. Whatever he had witnessed there had been a vision caused by that strange dust, twisting his thoughts. He had believed he would see the serpent from the underworld, and so he had.

'How long has it lain there, do you think?'

Hannu shook his head. 'Since the days the monument was built? Or perhaps the Sons of Apis crept in when they realised what people like us, and Akkan – and Myssa, come to that – were up to, and spread it all around as a final protection for the secret of Imhotep. One thing I know – any grave robbers who went in there would have fled the place in terror once that bad magic had worked its spell upon them.'

Piay slumped back, looking up at the sky as it turned from pink to pale blue. Were Khonsu and Seth mere imaginings conjured up by the dust he inhaled? He could not believe that. They had seemed so real. And yet perhaps it was so.

'Myssa was unwell yesterday morning,' Piay said. 'She blamed Tallus . . . but maybe it was her journey into the monument.'

'I'd be happy to be proved wrong about her,' Hannu replied. 'I felt my own thoughts twisting when I stepped into the king's chamber. So I wrapped the scarf across my mouth and nose. That seemed to help. But let's ask Myssa herself.'

The two men clambered down the stones and trudged to where the Blue Crocodile Guards had made their camp. Myssa's condition had improved as the previous day had gone on, but now she seemed shivery and distracted, wincing occasionally as if in pain. And she still looked drawn and weak.

She cast a baleful eye at Piay and Hannu when they stepped into her tent, but said nothing.

Once Piay had explained his experience in the monument, he asked her if she had been troubled by visions or fears.

'Not from the pyramid,' she replied. 'I wore a scarf across my face.'

'Why?'

'I did not wish to breathe in the dust of the dead.'

'You seem unwell again this morning. Maybe it's being close to the pyramid.'

'It's got nothing to with the damned pyramid!'

Inspiration suddenly struck Piay. 'A women's sickness, perhaps?'

Myssa closed her eyes and sighed at the idiocy of men.

'No. Not the pyramid, not my moon. It's something else, but it's getting better, and I think it will pass in time. Now, does that satisfy you?'

'Enough to stop me asking you about it again.'

'Good,' Myssa said. 'So . . . your journey into the tomb. Did you find Imhotep's signs?'

Piay nodded.

'Huh . . . Then you're not quite so stupid, after all.'

As Ankhu listened to Piay's story, his eyes sparkled with wonder and a smile of amazement crept across his lips.

'I feel in awe of the mind of the Great Architect,' he murmured.

The scribe was sitting cross-legged under a shelter on the edge of the work camp, where he had been waiting patiently for Piay and Hannu to return.

'You have no understanding of what you have discovered?' Ankhu asked.

Piay shrugged. 'The symbol for the heavens. Two stars. The Key of Life. These things are clear. The riddle lies in the stars – but which stars?'

Angry voices rang out from the middle of the camp. Once again, the caravan containing supplies from Memphis had not arrived. The men had long since downed tools and the first of them were already marching away in the direction of Memphis. Even as Piay watched, others followed those who had set out for the city. They, in turn, inspired even more men to do the same.

It won't be long before the camp is deserted, thought Piay.

'Excuse me, young man, I'm trying to explain something!' Ankhu snapped.

'Oh, I'm sorry, I was watching the diggers. They're all leaving.'

'Good – fewer ignorant brutes getting in our way. Now, look at this . . .' Ankhu pointed at the Disc. 'Two stars together – the most important stars in the heavens.'

'One star looks much like another,' Hannu muttered.

The scribe crawled out from the shelter and beckoned for the other two to follow him. The wind whisked clouds of ochre dust across the waste from the west, but the gusts died out before they reached the monument glowing in the morning sun.

Ankhu shielded his eyes against the glare and pointed to the Pyramid of Khufu, then the two smaller pyramids beyond it.

'As above, so below,' he said. 'We have spoken before about how these three monuments reflect the three stars in the night sky – Alnitak, Alnilam and Mintaka – only in reverse, as if reflected in a bronze mirror. The ancients knew that our earth was a reflection of the heavens, and did all that was in their power to connect the two.'

'That's three stars,' Hannu grumbled.

Ankhu narrowed his eyes at him. 'I am teaching you a lesson here. You would do well to heed my words.'

'My assistant apologises,' Piay said. 'Continue.'

'The Pyramid of Khufu is connected to the sky above in more ways than one.' He traced one finger through the air, marking the slope of the monument. 'Were we to stand here at night, we would see the angles of the pyramid point directly to two stars, Mizar and Kochab. They are known as the Indestruct-ible Stars, so-called because they never seem to set. And that is where heaven lies, and the afterlife—'

'Ah! The Key of Life,' Piay exclaimed.

Ankhu smiled at him as if he was looking at a precocious child.

'In the weeks before the Great Flood, the sun's rays would break through the clouds at such an angle that it would provide a stairway to those heavens for the king to ascend, where he could spend his time among the Indestructible Stars. To the priests, from even the earliest days, those stars have been of the greatest importance.'

Piay ushered Ankhu back under the shelter and, when they were sitting where they could not be seen, he pulled the Disc of Ra out of the pouch.

'Show me,' he said.

The scribe twisted the moving discs until a symbol for two stars appeared in one of the windows. When he looked into the second window, he smiled.

Ankhu turned the Disc to Piay. The window showed a crouching lion staring at the rising sun.

'Now you have the sign directing you to the next part of Imhotep's road, perhaps the last part,' Ankhu said. 'The Sphinx.'

iay had been adamant.

'I'm going back in tonight. Got to finish the job.'

'Not a chance,' Hannu had told him. 'Anyone who tries to take on Imhotep's challenges will have to be at their strongest, most alert best. And you, my friend, are not even close. So, we're going back to the palace. You are going to get some food inside you. Get a good rest. Then, in a couple of nights, maybe we go back. Maybe.'

The fact that Piay was in no state to mount any kind of resistance to Hannu merely underlined how weak he was. He was only able to walk at his wounded comrade's limited speed as they began the journey back to Memphis.

While Piay and Hannu led the way, Myssa was walking beside Ankhu. They were surrounded by soldiers, there to keep the old man safe and the young woman captive. Piay hated making Myssa his prisoner. After the miseries she had suffered as a slave, he knew the pain that this would make her feel.

But if Myssa was resenting her treatment, she didn't show it. On the contrary, she seemed, if anything, a little stronger than before, and was talking to Ankhu with an animation that had been missing since their escape from the Hyksos camp.

Piay went to her and asked, 'How are you doing?'

'The control that Tallus had over me is fading.'

Myssa's tone was matter-of-fact, rather than warm, but Piay's heart leaped, nonetheless.

'It's still very soon since he had his claws in you. We should wait, just to be certain.'

Myssa nodded. 'Yes, we should wait.'

Suddenly Hannu shouted, 'Over there!'

Piay followed the direction in which Hannu was pointing and saw vultures, lots of them, circling lazily in the sky. He walked back up the line to Hannu and said, 'We'd better check that out.'

'I reckon I know what we're going to find.'

Ten minutes' march revealed the answer. The birds watching from on high were just a fraction of those feasting on the ground. They had almost stripped the flesh from the bones of five men and an equal number of mules that had been taking five carts in the direction of the great monuments.

'So, it wasn't the governor, or corrupt officials, or cowardly mule-drivers that stopped the supplies,' Piay said. 'Someone stole it – look, the carts are completely empty.'

'I swear, my men had no part in this,' Myssa said.

'And all the Shrikes in these parts died at Akkan's camp,' Hannu said.

'Which,' Piay said, 'leaves just one possibility.' He turned his head towards the guards' commander and told him to march on. Then he looked back at Hannu and Myssa and said, 'Don't worry. I'll deal with it.'

By the time the travellers made their way through the gate into Memphis the sun was at its highest point. A gentle breeze cooled the streets, catching the fading peppery scent of cinnamon from the empty spice warehouses. An old man perched on a stool in the shade by his door, waving away the fat flies that droned in clouds from the middens. He nodded to Piay as the soldiers trooped by.

'I half-expected the city to be burned to the ground,' Piay said.

He sensed a rumbling discontent in the sullen faces and the restrained conversation, like black clouds blowing in at sea, but there was not that simmering intensity he had felt shortly before they had departed for the monuments.

'Maybe your fake treasure plan wasn't that bad after all,' Hannu said. 'At least the people got enough food to take the edge off their hunger.' He grinned at Piay. 'There's a thought – perhaps you should persuade Taita to install you as governor.'

Piay snorted. 'Governor? Can you imagine me listening to endless talk of taxes and trade and repairs to crumbling walls? No, I know where my strengths lie, and it usually involves a sword.'

'And wine and—' Hannu bit off the word 'women'. Piay was a changed man now; they both knew that.

When they reached the palace, the air was filled with soothing scents of jasmine and the sun winked off the ripples on the surface of the pool. As the Blue Crocodile Guards prepared to march to the garrison, Piay stepped up to Myssa.

'I want only the best for you, and I'll do everything I can to make that happen,' he said. 'But we should both be careful, in case the Cobra's whispers return.'

'I understand.'

'You will be given a chamber in the palace, your old chamber, and you will be treated well. You will have the freedom to wander where you want.'

'After what happened that night?'

'You were bewitched by the Cobra. It wasn't really you doing that.'

Myssa looked at him. 'Are you sure?'

Piay did not know how to reply, but then he looked down and saw that Bast was walking beside them.

'Well, she likes you again,' he said, with a relieved but nervous smile. 'That has to be a good sign.'

They reached a wing of the palace used for bedchambers. Myssa looked at the building. In front of them, a flight of stone steps led to an upper storey.

'I . . . I don't know where to go,' she said. 'My memory's not quite . . .'

'Don't you worry,' Piay reassured her. 'I know the way.'

'Oh . . . So . . . it was like that between us?'

'What we shared was stronger than you can imagine. The Cobra tried to steal that from both of us.'

They walked into the chamber and Bast trotted straight to the bed, jumped up onto it and settled herself down on the bedding. Myssa glanced down at her cat and frowned.

'The way she's lying there . . . it seems familiar.'

'This was always her favourite place,' Piay said.

They were both standing up, a couple of paces apart. He longed to cross the space between them, take her in his arms and . . .

Myssa frowned. 'There have been times when I felt I almost knew you, and about us . . . Just flashes of memory, fragments of feeling . . . like a dream that vanishes the moment you awaken . . .' Her voice trailed off and she shook her head, as if the task of remembering was too great.

Piay absently dipped a hand into the pouch where he kept the blue lotus pellets his father had given him. As he rolled them around in his fingers, he remembered the instructions Asil had given him to break the spell. He pulled the pellets out of the pouch and held them in his clenched hand.

'There's something I need to confess to you,' Piay said.

'What sort of thing?'

'Something I planned to do . . .' Piay opened his hand. 'These are blue lotus pellets.'

Myssa started, and stepped away from him. 'No, you can't do that to me! Not now . . . when I'm trying so, so hard . . .'

Piay had no idea what she was talking about. He closed his fist around the pellets and held out his other hand in supplication.

'Wait . . . Please . . . let me finish what I want to say.'

Myssa looked at him with a suspicion, even hostility that seemed to undo all the good things that had been starting to happen between them.

'My father gave me these pellets. He said that if I gave them to you and spoke to you as the Cobra must have done . . .'

Piay could see that his words were only making Myssa even more tense. At any moment she might scream at him to get out, and all would be lost.

'Please,' he begged her again, 'I swear that there's no harm in what I'm going to say. Because, you see, I was planning to do that, and try to reverse all the spells he'd cast on you . . . But I'm not going to do that. Just watch.'

Piay strode to the window and threw the pellets out into the garden. Then he turned back to Myssa and said, 'There – all gone. I was wrong to even think of doing anything to you. That would make me no better than the Cobra. He twisted your mind one way, I'd be twisting it another. But you would have no say in either of them, and that would be totally, utterly wrong. You must make your own choice, one way or another. And whatever that choice is, I swear to you that I will accept it.'

Myssa looked calmer now, but still far from happy.

'You know that I've been ill?' she said.

'Yes.'

'It's because I haven't been taking the lotus potion Tallus used to give me.'

'Oh . . .' Piay frowned. 'Why would you feel worse when you don't take it than when you do?'

'I don't know. It just makes you feel wonderful, and then you feel terrible without it, so you want more . . . and then you become its prisoner.'

'Which you, of all people, could not bear.'

Myssa nodded. 'If you had tried to feed me those pellets, I would have killed you. But you didn't do that – and you were also honest with me, even though you must have known that your words would not please me.'

'I had no choice.'

Myssa smiled, 'Very well then, Piay of Thebes . . .' There was a faint hint of a smile as she said those words, as if the formality of his full name might one day become a private joke between them. 'I am going to stay here and consult with my wise cat. We will consider you, she and I.'

So there was still a glimmer of hope. Piay had to restrain himself from cheering.

'But,' Myssa said, 'I am making no promises. So, don't go boasting to that hairy little friend of yours just yet.'

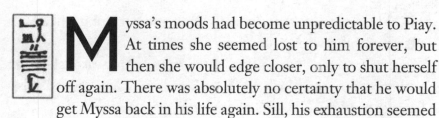

yssa's moods had become unpredictable to Piay. At times she seemed lost to him forever, but then she would edge closer, only to shut herself off again. There was absolutely no certainty that he would get Myssa back in his life again. Sill, his exhaustion seemed to have disappeared and there was a spring in his step as he left the palace. He stopped off at a now-familiar tavern, discovered what he needed to know, and then headed towards the quarter of Memphis where the very poorest people lived.

The streets there were narrow and shadowy, but still sweltering in the heat of the day. Most of the homes were little more than one-room hovels, constructed from crumbling mud bricks only one layer thick and unpainted. Through the doorways, Piay glimpsed nothing more than a bed, a bench, a few pots and tools for grinding wheat. The air choked with the reek of human waste from the middens that almost dwarfed the shacks.

With every step into this poverty and degradation, Piay's good mood dissipated. Finally, he came to a cramped square where a crowd had gathered, spilling out into the side streets. Men and women called out to whoever stood in the centre of the throng, waving what poor possessions they had – old, damaged items of jewellery, pots that looked like they had been handed down the generations, rusty tools, and the carcasses of birds that must have been hunted along the banks of the river.

Looking around, Piay spied his father standing to one side, watching the proceedings. Muscular men stood either side of him, as they always seemed to do in public, their arms folded, their eyes searching the crowd for any hint of trouble.

When Asil saw Piay, he beamed and pushed his way through the crowd.

'I went to your home and they said you would be here,' Piay said.

Asil heard the less than friendly tone and cocked his head.

'Is something wrong, my son?'

At the centre of the square, a tall man with a broken nose clambered onto the block and in a slow, loud voice began to list what was available: bread, cheese, beer.

'But not much, not much. Make your offer!'

'There's no more need for pretence, Father,' Piay said. 'I know what you are.'

Asil frowned. 'I don't understand, my son.'

'You belong to the Guild of Thieves. And since you seem to be the only man apart from Zahur who walks around Memphis with his own troop of guards, I'd say you might just be the leader of the guild.'

Asil's face hardened, his eyes flashing. Though he tried to force his puzzled, little-old-man smile back onto his face, Piay saw the truth revealed. In that instant, Asil looked years younger, a hard man used to facing down enemies.

'You're mistaken—'

'Don't lie to me. I'm your son. I've got a right to the truth.'

Asil's mouth was a slash among the wrinkles. 'We all do what we must to survive. I told you that.'

'Survival, yes. But profiting from the misery of others? That is a different matter.' Piay glanced towards the square, where the broken-nosed man was waving a flatbread while the crowd bartered away what little they owned to feed their bellies. 'Your men stole the food from the caravans delivering supplies to the labourers at the great monuments. They murdered the mule-drivers. And now you're taking all the food that should have been given to the poor and you're selling it to them instead – to profit only yourself.'

'You're soft, boy.' The lilting tone in Asil's voice had long gone, as if it had never existed. 'You've had it too easy with Taita and all that palace life. Don't judge me until you've suffered like I've suffered.'

'You know nothing about my life,' Piay said. 'As for Taita, he taught me about sacrifice, duty, and one thing above all – honour. No remotely honourable man would ever profit from the misery of the poor.'

Asil's eyes blazed. 'You're saying I am not honourable?' He caught himself and looked away, struggling to find the mask that had served him so well. 'My son, let us not argue, not now when we have found each other after so long.'

Piay studied his father with new eyes. This was not a man reduced to crime by hardship. It was his nature to take advantage of other people, rather than to work hard for himself.

'Let's set aside our differences,' Asil said. 'Join with me. Together we can achieve great things. We are blood, after all, and blood is the most important thing.'

Piay shook his head. 'No . . . A man's actions count more than his blood, and I hope and pray that I will be judged to have been a good man when I stand before Osiris.'

The old man's mouth twitched into a sneer. 'A good man, eh? A better man than me, you mean.'

Piay said nothing.

'Very well.' Asil surveyed him with narrow eyes. 'Then let us do business. You owe me two debts – one for telling you the location of the Shrikes, the other for providing you with the blue lotus you needed to win back your woman.'

Piay shook his head. 'I have no need for the blue lotus now.'

'Whether you use them or not is your choice. Nevertheless, they have been provided and a price will have to be paid.'

'I'll pay no money to common criminals.'

Asil looked at Piay. 'Let me teach you a lesson about the real world, boy. What I did for you was no small thing. The men who gave me that potion do not easily forget a debt. So now you owe them as well as me. But . . .' Asil smiled. 'I have a way in which you can satisfy your debts to both them and me. So . . . you have been digging for lost treasure. Just give me half of everything that you find and all your problems will be solved.'

'Or what?'

Piay felt the muscles in his shoulders tighten. He did not like to be told what to do, and he did not like to be threatened, by anyone, not even his father.

Asil shook his head, feigning a show of sympathy that was so transparent it was laughable.

'If you travel down that road, I cannot protect you, my son. I cannot protect your sullen little friend. And I cannot protect the woman you love.'

Before Piay could respond, Asil turned and pushed back through the crowd to discover what profit he had made from that day's misery.

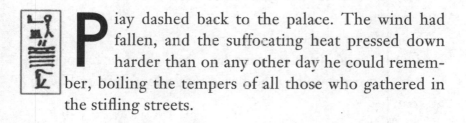 iay strode away from the stink of the middens. He heard more loud voices ringing out across the city, this time from the direction of the western gate. Puzzled, he walked towards the source of the noise, among a growing throng of Memphis citizens, all wanting to find out what was going on.

Along the street to the gate, Piay saw the diggers from the great monument, still streaked with the dust and sweat of their labours. Their kilts were filthy and they swung their mallets and chisels as if they were cracking rocks. On the long walk back to the city, their simmering anger had clearly burned deep into their hearts. Their faces were twisted, their fists bunched as they punched the air.

'Zahur lied to us!' one shouted. 'He promised us food in payment for our work, but none was sent.'

'Zahur cannot be trusted!' another roared. 'We are nothing to him, none of us.'

'The time has come!' another bellowed. 'We must let him know our displeasure.'

'The time has come,' a fourth one echoed.

And then all the people gathered around them took up the cry: 'The time has come!'

P iay dashed back to the palace. The wind had fallen, and the suffocating heat pressed down harder than on any other day he could remember, boiling the tempers of all those who gathered in the stifling streets.

As he raced through the gate, Piay ordered the guards to bar it behind him. In the hall of the palace, Zahur and Harrar sipped wine, laughing together.

Harrar scowled when he saw Piay.

'I would have thought you would have learned your lesson. Have you come to make more false accusations?'

'Muster the garrison, every man,' Piay said.

Zahur's eyes widened in terror. 'What is happening?'

'The labourers have returned from the great monuments. They're hungry, and angry, and they're blaming you for their problems. And there are crowds of people listening to them and believing them.'

'But that was not our fault!' Zahur protested.

'Maybe not this time,' Piay said, 'but the people don't know that. There's already been one riot. This is going to be much worse.'

'We can throw open our stores.' Harrar jumped up from his winged chair. 'All the food we have will surely placate them.'

'Don't you understand? It's too late. They're coming for you – for all of us – so get ready to defend the palace. Every man at your disposal, the slaves, too. Arm them with anything that can be used. If we can just hold out for a few days, there may be hope.'

Piay sprinted towards the door.

'Where are you going?' Harrar cried. 'We need you!'

'You had no use for me when you told Adon the taskmaster to choke the life out of me.'

Piay turned a cold gaze on both men and then he ran out.

At the garrison he found Hannu sipping beer.

'The slaves are bringing us wine from the kitchens,' Hannu said cheerily.

'No time for that now.'

Hannu's face darkened when he heard what was happening.

'I am not prepared to die here alongside Zahur or Harrar,' he spat.

'You won't have to,' Piay said.

Piay hailed the captain of the Blue Crocodile Guards and said, 'Lord Taita has gone back to Thebes, but the army's still north of here, finishing off the Hyksos. Hannu, I want you to go down to the docks, right now, while you can still get out of the palace. Get a boat, any boat, steal one if you have to, and head north. You've got to get them to send a force south, at least a regiment, to come to our rescue. Captain, can you spare six men to go with him as an escort?'

'Of course,' the commander said.

'Thank you. Tell them not to wear uniform, or they'll never get across the city. Now, Hannu, if anyone questions the need for this, tell them the truth. Memphis is facing total anarchy. This will be the first great test of Pharaoh's rule across the Lower Kingdom. The army has to restore order here, or none of the battles they've won will count for anything.'

Once the captain had hurried away to make the arrangements, Hannu grabbed Piay's arm and said, 'Come with me. If you wait any longer, you'll never get out of here alive.'

'I can't leave,' Piay said, shaking his arm free. 'I've got to go back to the monuments and follow the trail to the Sphinx.'

'How in Ra's name are you going to do that?'

'If we can just hold out till nightfall, Myssa and I can sneak out of here under cover of darkness. It's not like we haven't done that before.'

'But the whole place could be surrounded.'

'Yes, it could . . . but not by soldiers who know how to keep watch. These are untrained civilians. Half of them will be drunk. None of them will know how to organise a proper watch. Lots will just go home for the night. Do you seriously think that Myssa and I can't get past them?'

Hannu's look told Piay that that was exactly what he thought, but he bit his tongue and instead said, 'Well then, I wish you luck . . . and I hope this isn't the last time you tell me your latest mad plan.'

'It won't be, count on that.'

The commander came back into the chamber.

'My men are ready,' he said.

'Then go,' Piay said. 'Now – while you still can.'

He watched Hannu leave, then offered up a silent prayer: 'Please, Lord Khonsu, just keep the palace secure till nightfall.'

Now only the gods could decide their fate.

The bronze hills far to the west wavered in the heat haze. Within the city, the towering white walls of the Temple of Ptah glowed so brightly they dazzled the eye, and the fronds of the date palms along the canal hung limp in the dead air. On days like this, the citizens of Memphis would normally be sheltering in any shade they could find, praying for nightfall. Now every street throbbed with thousands of people, all of them pressing towards the palace with rage in their hearts.

Piay looked out of the window across the baking rooftops, watching the mob's steady progress. His ears rang from the din, and within the grounds the soldiers could barely hear the commands barked at them. Every man and woman in the city seemed to be roaring their fury.

'They would not dare break into the palace.'

Piay turned to see Zahur standing in the doorway to his chamber. His entire body trembled as if he had a fever. He had dressed in his finest robe, embroidered with gold thread and studded with jewels upon his chest. Piay thought him mad to show off his wealth so blatantly.

Perhaps Zahur thought that his finery conferred some authority upon him. Did he dream that the rebellious citizens of Memphis would fall to their knees when they stood before him, and see the error of their ways? Plainly he had never been hungry for a day in his life, or he would know that starving people had no thoughts but relieving the ache in their empty bellies.

'They are Egyptians!' Zahur said, when Piay did not answer. 'They live by the principles of the great goddess Ma'at! Honesty. Loyalty. Order. That is the only way to keep chaos at bay!'

'Do you still not understand what life in this city is like?' Piay growled. 'Don't you hear the babies crying for food that never comes . . . or the pleas of the old folk, too weak to lift themselves from their beds . . . or the desperation of husbands watching their wives waste away?'

'You cannot blame me for that!'

'You rule the city – who else is to blame?' Piay turned back to the window. 'But my opinion means nothing. The gods will make the final judgement.'

Behind him, Zahur began to sob. Piay imagined those jowls shuddering, slick with tears that had come too late.

'They must show obedience to Pharaoh!' the governor wailed.

'There are no pharaohs here,' Piay said, 'not yet. There are only the citizens . . . and you.'

Zahur scurried from the room, and Piay focused his attention once again on the army of the dispossessed as they drew closer to the palace. Against the white walls of the grand buildings, the great tide of humanity surged forward, and Piay wondered whether any walls – or any fighting men – would be strong enough to withstand it.

'Come on, Hannu,' he muttered to himself, 'just get to that boat.'

But he had a terrible feeling that it was already too late to call the army for help.

Piay hurried from the chamber and searched all the rooms until he finally found Harrar cowering in the kitchens. Unlike Zahur, the nobleman was wearing a stained kilt that looked as if it had once belonged to one of the slaves. He was taking the opposite route to Zahur: setting his grandeur aside and hoping that the angry mob would ignore him if he looked like a lowly toiler in the hot kitchens.

But one look at Harrar's soft, clean hands, and one sniff of his perfumed skin, would be enough to dispel any idea that he was a common working man.

'You've got to go out and meet the citizens when they arrive,' Piay said. 'Tell them their demands have been heard. Put every scrap of food in the palace storerooms onto carts and send it out to them. They're starving. If you do something about that, it may calm the situation.'

'Are you mad?' Harrar blustered. 'I am not taking one step outside the gates under any circumstances.'

'That's the only hope we have of calming the situation.'

'If anyone should do it, it is Zahur.'

'Zahur is a lost cause. His nerves have gone completely. In any case, the people see him as the cause of their problems. They don't know you, or blame you as much.'

'No! I will not risk my own neck! This is not my problem!'

'Pharaoh sent you to—'

'Pharaoh did not send me to die!'

Piay could see there was no point trying to convince Harrar. His mind was made up, his cowardice confirmed.

The most powerful men in Memphis had abandoned the city and their own people, too.

The sun was setting, but the air still boiled. Sweat soaked the band of Piay's white kilt as he watched purple shadows pool around the sycamore trees. Would the oppressive heat never pass?

He breathed in the rich scent of the yellow roses clumped around the pool. The gardens had been designed as an oasis of peace. No more. A never-ending roar thundered over the entire compound, like that of a ravenous beast stirred from sleep.

Around the gardens, men stood like sentinels at the head of their lengthening shadows. Everyone there was bracing themselves for what was to come. There were a few members of the Blue Crocodile Guards keeping watch atop the walls on either side of the palace gate. Small clusters of palace guards and frightened slaves, armed with whatever weapons they could muster, were dotted around the perimeter in case anyone tried to breach the walls.

The rest of the Blue Crocodile Guards, the palace guards and their respective commanders were waiting in the middle of the garden, ready to rush to where they were needed if the walls were breached.

They are pathetically few in number, Piay thought as he slowly turned, surveying the defences. He prayed they would not be needed.

He had sent Myssa and Ankhu to the latter's house in the corner of the compound. If the worst should happen, and the palace were invaded, the little building might just go unnoticed as the attackers headed for the main palace buildings and all the food, drink and loot they contained.

'Aren't you giving me anything with which to defend myself?' Ankhu protested, when Piay told him where to go. 'I've not survived this long without knowing how to look after myself, you know.'

'My knife alone will not be enough,' Myssa said.

'All right then,' Piay said. 'Come with me.'

He led them to the palace armoury and gave them a sword each and a bundle of spears.

'I'll be there with you,' he said. 'If the time comes.'

'Not if, but when it comes, dear boy,' Ankhu said. 'I felt the mood of the city as we walked through it this morning. They won't stop at the gates.'

Piay had seen Myssa and Ankhu safely installed in the house. Then he returned to the garden and spent the last of the daylight talking to the guards' commanders and encouraging their troops. Then he went to all the defenders scattered along the wall, offering up words of encouragement, ensuring that they had food and water to sustain them.

'You don't have to do this,' the guards captain said, as the sun finally set beyond the western horizon. 'No one would blame you if you just saved yourself.'

'Well, I'm still hoping to do that.' Piay grinned. 'But in the meantime, there are people here who are frightened and need someone to keep their spirits up, and we both know Harrar and Zahur have no intention of doing that. So . . .'

Piay shrugged. The guards captain said nothing. They both knew how bad things were. What more needed to be said?

The moon of Khonsu filled the garden with silver-grey light. The crowd that now surrounded the palace had pressed up against the walls, but no attack had been made.

Piay dared to feel just a little bit more optimistic. He turned to the captain of the Blue Crocodile Guards and said, 'With any luck, the men out there may just become bored, hungry and thirsty enough to decide that their beds are better places to spend the night.'

Before the captain could reply, Piay felt the ground beneath his feet tremble. He stooped and picked up a jagged piece of worked stone from a mason's yard.

'Watch out! Raise your shields!' Piay shouted, but it was too late. Stones flew over the walls on every side, raining down from the sky, thumping into the hard ground, bouncing off the sycamore trees, splashing in the pool.

One missile smashed against a soldier's head, caving in his skull. His legs folded under him as if they were made of papyrus, and he sprawled across the ground, spilling blood and brains.

'Take cover!' the captain yelled, diving behind the trunk of a sycamore tree.

Piay landed beside him an instant later.

'Someone planned this!' he shouted, over the shouts and cries of pain of men all around him.

Piay saw another guardsman on the wall spin as a projectile hit him and topple backwards over the crenellations. The crowd below roared its approval.

'I'm going to find out who's leading them,' Piay said.

He dashed out from behind the tree and sprinted as fast as he could to the steps that led up to the battlements beside the gate, ignoring the projectiles falling all around him. There were even arrows embedding themselves in the ground now, alongside the stones and bricks.

Piay hurtled up to the walkway that ran around the inside of the walls and crouched down, leaving as little of his head exposed as he could while he looked out across the crowd.

Men everywhere were brandishing torches.

They're going to burn this place to the ground, Piay thought.

For now, though, the light of the flames only served to illuminate the crowd. And it wasn't hard to find what he was looking for.

The Cobra towered over those around him. Beside him were faces that Piay recognised. They might be dressed as city folk, but they were the Hyksos warriors who had fought under Akkan – an island of calm amid the heaving, shouting, stone-throwing mayhem. As Piay watched, the Cobra moved among his men, talking to them one at a time, pointing out where they should go next. He could command the entire crowd, Piay thought, without the people of Memphis ever realising who was really in charge.

The common folk might be longing for food and a chance to avenge the men who had oppressed them, but amid the havoc, the Cobra would concentrate on recapturing the Eye of Horus, the Disc of Ra and, above all, Myssa. She had been inside the pyramid. She, like Piay, knew where Imhotep's trail led next.

Tallus raised his right arm, and then brought it down. At once, a group of eight men, standing directly in front of the palace gates, formed into two orderly lines of four. The Hyksos warriors bent down as one, and when they stood again, they were holding a wooden battering ram, fashioned from a tree trunk. Piay ducked back behind the wall as a band of men with bows came forward to fire more arrows up at the walls.

Around him, the slaves and soldiers scattered along the battlements were doing the same – they, too, had seen the bowmen moving into position and none of them would dare expose themselves. The men on the battering ram could go about their work undisturbed.

The ram smashed against the gate. The wood splintered and bowed, but the bar across the gate held.

Piay ran back down the steps, shouting at the guards to follow. When they reached the ground, they ran to their commander, who was lining up his men, and those of the palace guard, to meet the invaders.

'Return to the garrison!' Piay shouted.

'We can hold them off for a little while.'

'There's no point. You've got no chance out here in the open. You'll all be killed, and what good will that do? Just get as many people as you can inside the garrison and hold out there.'

'What about you?'

'I'm getting out another way.'

Before the captain could say another word, Piay was dashing for Ankhu's house. Behind him, he heard the ram beating on the gates – two, three, four more times.

A tremendous crack reverberated across the palace grounds. The gate shattered into pieces and the army of citizens flooded in with a roar, sweeping across the grounds like the unstoppable rush of Mother Nile during the season of floods.

Piay sought cover behind a sycamore, just a few paces from Ankhu's door, and took one last look at the invaders. Two of the henchmen who always accompanied his father were leading the charge, whipping their arms in the air and bellowing to urge the other rebels into a frenzy.

Piay was certain that his father would not be far behind. The Guild of Thieves would be free to loot the palace while Tallus and the Hyksos went after the means of solving Imhotep's riddle.

Asil can use Zahur's gold to pay off my debts, Piay thought, grimacing at the irony of it all.

Then he turned and, still unseen by any of the onrushing horde, dashed to Ankhu's house. The scribe let him in and Piay was pleased to see he had been sensible enough not to light any torches – the fewer eyes that were drawn to this corner of the palace compound, the better.

'Give me a hand with this,' Piay said, pointing to a heavy wooden chest.

Ankhu and Myssa helped him to shove it – and every other piece of furniture they could find – up against the door to barricade it. Then they closed the shutters over the ground-floor windows.

'Upstairs,' Piay ordered. 'Get upstairs.'

As Ankhu and Myssa made their way upstairs, to Ankhu's observatory chamber, Piay began to look around for anything he could use to defend himself. Seconds later a terrible, high-pitched scream cut through the noise of the invasion. Piay knew that sound could only mean one thing.

'They've found Zahur,' he said quietly to himself.

Asil, the father of Piay and master of the Guild of Thieves, gave the young man who normally served as the guard at his door a hearty slap on the back. 'Your dad'll be proud of you.'

The young man held a bloody cleaver in his hand – he and Asil were staring down at Zahur's severed head where it sat in front of them on the limestone flagstones of the garden room. The governor's wide-open eyes conveyed a look of surprise – even outrage – at what had been done to him. His plump lips hung open to reveal a set of tiny brown teeth, and his jowls were like melted candle wax.

Zahur's body, dismembered by the knives and hatchets of hate-filled citizens, was scattered around the room like joints of meat in a butcher's market.

Another throat-rending scream echoed across the palace. Three members of the Guild of Thieves burst from the direction of the kitchens, laughing. They were dragging Harrar, who was howling in terror.

His disguise had not helped him.

The criminals shoved the nobleman to his knees in the centre of the room. Harrar cowered as his eyes registered that he was staring at the head of his old co-conspirator. Then he lowered his forehead to the stone, prostrating himself, begging for mercy, his body racking with sobs.

'This is the man who denied you food, along with Zahur,' one of the thieves shouted at the crowd of rioters who had forced their way into the chamber. 'There will be no justice while he lives. Our hunger will never be assuaged. What shall we do with him?'

The crowd hung back for a moment, their faces fixed as they stared at the prone man, and then, as one, they fell upon him.

'Not bad work, for beginners,' Asil remarked to one of his gang as Harrar's screams fell silent.

The men who had ripped him apart stepped away from the body, covered in blood.

'Right, lads,' Asil said. 'Let's see what we can find – and if you see anyone carrying anything valuable, just, ah . . . advise them to hand it over.'

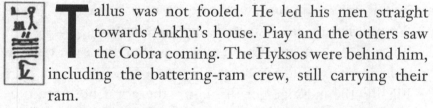

Tallus was not fooled. He led his men straight towards Ankhu's house. Piay and the others saw the Cobra coming. The Hyksos were behind him, including the battering-ram crew, still carrying their ram.

Seconds later the first thunderous hammer of the tree trunk against the front door echoed around the house.

'Get out!' Piay shouted up the stairs at the other two. 'Get out through the window. Go . . .! Go!'

Again, the ram hit the door. It buckled and the impact pushed the hastily assembled pieces of furniture back across the floor: no more than the width of two or three fingers, but the makeshift barricade was not going to delay the Cobra's men for long.

Piay turned back to face the door and picked up an ancient spear that he had found wrapped up in an oil-stained carpet under the stairs. There were three more in easy reach.

'I'll try to slow them down.'

The third impact of the ram smashed the planking of the door, and now the Hyksos were clearly visible on the other side. Hands were pulling at the wood. Piay threw a spear into the hole they had made and heard a scream of pain. He was caught up in the battle now, thinking of nothing but the next man he had to beat.

'One down . . .' he muttered.

'You stupid, headstrong young fool!' Ankhu shouted, making his way down the stairs.

A Hyksos warrior was prising the planks apart and forcing his way in. Piay threw another spear, but the door shifted and the spear tip hit wood, rather than human flesh.

'Can't you see? You're the chosen one!' Ankhu said as Piay cursed his misfortune. 'You go! I've lived long enough . . . and Egypt needs you.'

The Hyksos were clambering through the door now, and over what was left of the furniture on the other side.

Piay threw a third spear and hit the Hyksos in the chest, but as he fell, others appeared in the doorway.

'I'm not letting an old man do my fighting.'

'Please!' Ankhu was almost sobbing. 'For the sake of your people, go!'

Finally, the message got through – there was no more time to argue. Against all his instincts, Piay grabbed his final spear and fled, leaving Ankhu to face the Hyksos alone. When he got to the top of the stairs, Piay found the observatory empty. He dashed to the window but could see no sign of Myssa outside.

Piay heard feet on the stone stairs and the guttural curses of the Hyksos. Once again, he fought his instincts. He did not follow Myssa out of the window, but instead turned to face the Hyksos. This time he did not throw his spear, but held it as he crouched, ready to keep his attackers and their swords at bay.

The first of the warriors charged into the room. Two others were close behind.

Piay jabbed his spear.

The men fanned out, making it harder for Piay to deal with any one of them without exposing himself to the other two. Another pair of Hyksos arrived. One of them was the Cobra.

Five against one, Piay thought. *Tough, but not impossible.*

He readied himself for the fight. But then the looks on the faces of the Hyksos changed from hungry anticipation of a swift kill to alarm – panic, even.

Piay realised that they were not looking at him, but past him. He turned his head, just for an instant, to follow their gaze . . . and looked straight into the eyes of the leader of the Sons of Apis.

The tattooed man swung up the palm of his right hand and blew the heap of white dust upon it into Piay's face.

Piay staggered, the particles searing his nose and mouth. He thought he heard the Cobra shouting out in alarm, but then the darkness rushed in until there was only the grinning visage of the cult's leader, and then nothing at all.

The moon blurred and the stars streaked by. Myssa floated on her back, hands carrying her aloft as she looked up at the sable sky. The powder the cultist had blown into her face had heightened her senses and stolen her strength, but it had not thrown her into the depths of her dreams, as it had done with Piay. Perhaps she was numb to its effects because of the concoction with which the Cobra had been dosing her for so long.

Where am I being taken? she wondered. *If the Sons of Apis meant to kill me, they could have done so at the palace. So, what other purpose do they have in mind?*

The edges of rooftops whisked by on the fringes of her vision. She felt her direction shift, and she floated between two columns. A limestone portico came into view, glowing in the light of a torch.

Myssa glimpsed the mark of the bull on one of the pillars as she swept into the shadowed interior, and realised that she must be in the Temple of Apis. She heard a loud, grinding noise and then felt herself tilted, feet first, on a downward trajectory. Her skin prickled at a sudden chill. She breathed in dank, still air as suddenly her entire field of vision was filled with damp stones passing just above her. So, now she knew she was in a tunnel, but to where?

Footsteps scraped on stone, and then the echoes faded and Myssa realised they had moved into a larger space. She could hear the sizzle of torches. Ruddy light washed over the ceiling, pushing the shadows away to the corners.

Myssa felt herself lowered until she was standing, albeit unsteadily, on her feet. The effects of the dust had worn off a little now, and she was able to take in the glow of the torches and the glistening walls, slick with moisture. Ahead of her, the Sons of Apis gathered, tattoos stark against flesh the colour of bone, heads bowed slightly as they watched her with baleful eyes from under hooded brows. Behind them, a statue of Apis crouched upon a plinth in its attacking pose.

Myssa was not alone. Craning her neck round, she glimpsed Piay slumped against a pillar, his eyes flickering back to life, and beyond him the Cobra, lying flat out on the floor, his breathing ragged.

The leader of the Sons of Apis stepped forward and Myssa shivered as his gaze fell upon her, weighed her, judged her, before moving on to the others.

'The cult of the Sons of Apis was founded by the Great Architect an age ago to test those who would walk the road to his final reward. The trials would make the unworthy fall by the wayside.'

The leader's soft, clear voice seemed to fill the air without the slightest effort.

'You are the first in all that long march across the days to have reached the threshold of the afterlife, and the end of the Great Architect's quest. You have been tested and you have proved yourself worthy to proceed. Three of you have the strength and the wisdom desired by the Great Architect, and so three of you now must undertake the final trial. That is my verdict.'

The eyes in the skull face scanned the three people before him.

'But only one of you can seize the power and the riches that must be used to rescue Egypt from the peril it faces. Only one can be victorious.'

Myssa stiffened. The Sons of Apis intended to pit the three of them against one another, that was clear from the leader's words.

Then let this challenge commence, she thought.

She was not afraid. The dream of taking Imhotep's reward and using it to rebuild her devastated home, that had started as a spark – the smallest of notions – now consumed her mind and her heart.

Piay had been right when he suggested that she had not been eating. Somehow, the lotus had seemed like the only nourishment she had needed. The battle to rid it from her body had left her weaker. Her foot had still not healed. Her hunger gnawed at her belly.

But none of that mattered. Her thoughts were clear, her emotions certain.

To restore her people, to reverse the events that had scattered them to the four winds and to protect them from the ravages of the slavers – that was worth any battle and any sacrifice. And she still had strength enough to do whatever was required to achieve it.

'Now the only way is forward,' the leader continued. 'If you choose not to meet this trial, you will be put to death and you will take Imhotep's secrets to the grave. Do you understand?'

'I understand,' Myssa said in a clear voice. 'I am ready. Take me to the trial.'

On the edge of her vision, she felt Piay jerk his head in her direction, but she did not meet his eyes.

'Very well,' the leader of the Sons of Apis said. He strode in front of Myssa and commanded, 'Hold out your hand.'

Puzzled, she raised her left palm. The cultist swept his own hand across it and Myssa felt a sharp pain. She cried out, recoiling and folding her fingers into a fist. The leader moved on to Piay, who had managed to get to his feet.

As Piay cursed, Myssa unfolded her fingers and inspected her palm. A thin bloody line stretched across her flesh.

Once he had finished with the Cobra, the tattooed man stepped back in front of them and raised his palm. Now Myssa could see a thick gold ring on his middle finger, with a small hook upon it. The tip was stained red.

'Now you will die,' he said, 'and only one of you will be reborn.'

Myssa winced. She felt fire burning through her hand.

'What have you done?' Piay croaked, as if he already knew the answer.

'We are learned in the wisdom of potions and spells, secrets and mysteries even older than the works of the Great Architect.' The leader lowered his hand. 'In your veins now flows a poison made from the venom of the horned viper. In the hours to come, it will burn its way through your body and steal your life.'

'This is madness!' the Cobra boomed.

Myssa watched Tallus' face and for the first time saw it twisted with fear. She snorted, pleased.

'The one who is victorious in the Great Architect's trial will receive an elixir that will cleanse them of the venom,' the leader continued. 'As the chosen one, they will be exalted. The Sons of Apis will answer only to them, and under their command we will ensure Imhotep's vision is delivered.' He paused, looking from one face to another. 'The other two will die an agonising death.'

A clever plan, Myssa thought, as she fought not to give in to cold dread.

There would be no joining forces, no trying to escape to return for the prize another day. You were victorious or you died.

Myssa heard a moan and looked round. Piay had sagged forward, his head bowed as if the stones of that temple were crushing down upon his shoulders. He was not afraid for his own life, she knew that. No, his agony came from the realisation that any hope of winning her back had died the instant the venom had entered their blood. They could never be together, even if the stars aligned, even if she ever recalled the strength of feeling he so frequently and fervently described.

Surely Piay would now, at last, accept that the Sons of Apis had torn them both apart irrevocably. Only one of them could live, and by doing so they would consign the other to death.

The darkness fell once again upon Piay, and when he awoke he was standing beneath the stars and his head was filled with the cries, the shouts and the whispers of the dead. He heard the men who had died under his command in the fields outside Thebes, his mother, whose face he could no longer see, the farmer he had condemned to die, and the long parade of those who had fallen before his blade.

In this life, death was never far away. And now his own was closer than it had ever been. But that was not the worst of it. Everything paled beside the devastation that threatened to tear him apart. He cast a sideways glance at Myssa, then snatched his gaze away. He could not bear to look at her. He felt overcome by a feeling of loss greater than anything he had experienced in his life.

When they had first spoken with Taita, that night after the great battle before the walls of Thebes, Piay had imagined that he and Myssa would work together, hand in hand, their hearts entwined from the start of the quest to its conclusion. Even in the past few days, he had dared to hope that all their troubles would finally be overcome. No longer. Death was coming for one of them, no matter what he did.

With a languid movement, the leader of the Sons of Apis raised one tattooed arm and pointed. Piay followed the direction of that finger.

The Sphinx stared back.

The monument was a poor echo of what it had been in its glory days. Yet even now a majesty burned deep within it, with the stars hanging above it and the moon catching it in stark relief of silver and shadow.

Piay closed his eyes, letting the dry desert breeze lick his skin. With it floated the scent of the cooling rocks and sand. He pushed himself up. His veins burned with the viper's venom and his head felt as if it had been stuffed with papyrus, but he shook it free and looked around.

The Sons of Apis were statues across the moon-washed sands. The wind whipped around them, stirring whorls of dust at their feet. They were so still and unblinking that Piay could not tell if they were praying or in some kind of trance, but they all looked directly towards the Sphinx.

Only the leader watched Piay. The whites of his eyes stared from shadow-shrouded hollows, shifting as he drank in every detail. For some reason, almost as if someone else had thought of it, Piay remembered his hidden knife. He patted his kilt, just below the belt. The knife was gone, and when he looked up it was sitting in the leader's open right palm. There would be no unfair advantages in this contest.

Now the Cobra stepped forward a pace, eyes fixed on the Sphinx. Tremors rippled through the muscles of his face. He knew his potions, and was aware that the poison was draining his life by degrees. Through his own misery, Piay felt a pang of cruel pleasure that a man who had used his potions to cause so much pain now suffered in the same way.

The leader of the Sons of Apis pointed past the Sphinx to the horizon.

'The sun dies in the west each night. The west is where the afterlife lies. The east is where the sun rises. That is the home of birth and renewal. On this line that divides the two, you will decide which of those fates lies ahead for you.'

Piay glanced towards the monument. The Sphinx was staring directly towards the east, at the point where the sun rose.

'One final test,' the leader continued. 'One final test to decide.'

Tallus' black robe seemed to swallow all the moonlight. He shoved aside his terror and said in a commanding voice, 'I am ready.'

Myssa's face hardened with determination. Piay felt a deep warmth at the strength he saw there, and then another wave of grief. If he was to save Egypt, Myssa must die. If he sacrificed himself for the woman he loved, he would doom his entire nation. There was no good choice.

Piay shook himself. He could not afford to be paralysed. Pushing aside his emotions, he prayed to Khonsu that he would be guided on the right path. He must not weaken, not now.

'Follow me.'

The leader of the Sons of Apis strode away, past his statue-like followers, to a place where the ground had been disturbed. Sand and rocks were heaped around a freshly dug hole.

Piay walked to the edge and peered in. A square stone had been revealed. The moonlight picked out an engraving of the Eye of Horus. He shook his head at the irony of it. There really had been a treasure hidden in these sands, after all.

'Beneath that door lies the Passage to the Gods,' the leader said. 'You must pass through it to reach your destination, the Temple of Birth and Renewal, which lies beneath the paws of the Sphinx.'

Piay looked across the stretch of ground to the monument. It wouldn't be too far to go. But, even so, his thoughts flew back to the shaft near Khem, the chamber and water-duct beneath it, and the terrors they had contained.

'As above, so below,' the leader intoned.

Two of his followers slipped hooked rods of bronze into slots on either side of the doorway and heaved the slab off its resting place. A blast of dank air rolled out of the black space that had been revealed.

'You are already dead,' the Cobra said to Piay and Myssa. 'Seth beats in my heart. His fire burns in my limbs. He whispers in my head. He will give me the strength I need to be victorious. You test yourself against a god, and that is a battle a mere mortal can never win. When Imhotep's legacy is revealed, I will be the one who summons Seth to earth. A new age will dawn, the Age of Seth, and the Hyksos will rule all before them.'

The Cobra paused to draw breath.

'Well,' Piay said, 'if you happen to see your god, I have a word of advice.'

The Cobra looked at Piay in surprise, plainly unsure whether he was being serious.

'Talk less,' Piay added. 'Seth strikes me as the kind that's easily bored.'

For an instant, he wondered whether an expression of something perilously close to amusement had flickered across the face of the leader of the Sons of Apis, but then he reached out an arm towards the dark shaft.

'This quest is also a rite, and the wisdom of Imhotep will only be revealed when the ritual is complete. Every step you have taken has been through death, and towards death, but now you must learn that death always walks behind you. See here.'

He swept his hand behind him and Piay turned to see what he was pointing towards. Far away, on the edge of the canal where moonlight shimmered across the black water, a shadowy figure stood motionless.

'Who is that?' Myssa breathed.

For a reason he couldn't explain, Piay felt a cold dread build deep in his stomach. As if obeying a silent summons, the figure began to walk towards them, the steps slow and steady.

As the figure neared, the moon picked out the features and Piay saw that it was Akkan.

The Child-Killer walked with stiff movements, torso rigid, arms hanging by his sides, and as he neared, Piay choked at the reek of rot caught on the breeze.

Akkan's face was corpse white, the skin mottled with decomposition, and though he stared ahead, he did not seem to see. Now Piay understood what the cult leader had meant the night when he had taken the Child-Killer captive: 'There are worse things than death.'

Akkan was dead, yet somehow also still alive. The Sons of Apis were masters of secret, ancient knowledge, and with their potions and incantations they had captured the Child-Killer on the very threshold, still caught in the grip of mortal suffering, with no promise of the joy of the afterlife. This was to be his eternal punishment.

The leader of the Sons of Apis held out his hand.

'Behold Death in Life.'

Step by step, the dreaded Hyksos captain advanced, relentless, merciless.

'Do not slow down,' the leader said with a cold smile. 'As in life, you must stay one step ahead of death. The Child-Killer will keep coming, and if you falter he will claim you.'

Piay spun back to the door in the sand. Only a short drop led to the bottom of the hole, where he could just make out flagstones in the thin light.

Grasping the edge of the doorway, Piay lowered himself into the dark.

The passage was lined in granite, as smooth and clean as the day the stone was laid a thousand years before. Piay felt dank, chill air swamp him, rushing into his nose and his throat, and he shivered: water lay somewhere ahead. In the shaft of moonlight that fell through the doorway above him, he looked around. The way was wide enough for five people to walk shoulder to shoulder, and sloped gently downwards away from the doorway in the direction of the Sphinx. Ahead, the impenetrable dark swam.

First Myssa, then the Cobra dropped into the passage.

'Take one step closer to me and I will claw out your eyes,' Myssa hissed at the sorcerer.

'Victory lies only with Seth.'

As Tallus swept off into the dark, Myssa turned to Piay and said, 'You should know the truth about me . . . about us.'

Piay shook his head. 'This is not the time—'

'It is the time!' Myssa's eyes flashed. 'Now, on the brink of death, for your sake, you must be clear-headed and accept the truth. All the things that have happened to me have changed me . . . forever! I am not the woman you knew. I do not love you. I cannot remember what that love felt like. To me, it seems like another form of captivity. If I am to be truly free, I have to be free of you, too.'

'No!'

'Yes. I walked in your shadow. Perhaps out of adoration, I don't know. But I will never be a slave again.'

Myssa reached out and touched Piay's arm, a hint of warmth after the harshness of her words.

'If we once were friends, now we must be enemies,' Myssa said, and her voice was soft – kind, even – as she pleaded with him. 'Think only of love and you will doom yourself. If you want to die, so be it, but don't delude yourself that some good will come from it. Be strong. Fight hard, and let the gods decide who will be victorious. That is now the only way.'

Without waiting for a reply, she turned and loped away into the dark.

Her foot's still bothering her, Piay thought, seeing her uneven gait. He despaired at what she had said, but she was right – this was not the time to give in to emotion. Only a clear head would help him now.

Pushing aside his feelings, Piay turned his mind, as calmly as he could manage, to the poison coursing through him and the thing that had been Akkan at his back. His immediate instinct was to rush on like the Cobra, to reach the life-giving potion first, but if the shaft at Khem had shown anything, it was that all kinds of perils could lie ahead in the dark.

Was that what the Sons of Apis hoped? Fear of death made men reckless, and rash actions would not be the sign of the wisdom Imhotep required.

Piay edged into the dark, trailing his fingers along the wall for guidance. After a few steps, he glanced back and wished he hadn't.

In the shaft of moonlight plunging through the entrance to the tunnel, a figure dropped down, just a shadow against the pale illumination. Akkan stepped forward, his footsteps echoing at their backs.

The dark swallowed them.

With each step, Piay felt ahead. His blood thumped in his temple; one misstep could reveal a yawning abyss.

Echoes: Myssa's footsteps, and the Cobra's, all of them creeping away from death towards death. Behind him, the thump of Akkan's feet never ceased.

Piay's nostrils flared as the atmosphere grew suddenly more musty. An instant later he splashed into water. Daggers of cold stabbed into his shin bones.

To his right, Myssa cried out in shock. She, too, had entered the water. He strained, but he could hear no sound from the Cobra. That threat was coiled up somewhere else, away in the dark.

Piay gulped in chill air, adjusting to the discovery. He eased one foot forward and realised the passage floor continued to slope down into the water.

A rasp of breath whispered out behind him. That was the Cobra, waiting, no doubt, for Piay to risk his own life investigating what lay ahead.

This was the first of the final challenges that led to the ultimate judgement of Osiris. The dead had to prove to the gods that their hearts were good, that they were not weighed down by spite or fear, pride, greed or hatred. Imhotep must have fashioned this last stage of his great puzzle to echo the same judgement. Only a good person could pass through these last few doors to win the Great Architect's ultimate reward.

Piay prayed that he was both wise and good. If he was not, only death awaited.

Determined, he waded into the water. He shuddered as the numbing cold crawled up to his thighs, his waist and finally his chest. He waded forward a step further and gave a gasp of pain and surprise as he bumped into a wall of smooth granite.

Piay slipped his hands back and forth across the chilly surface, his fingertips stubbing against first one side wall, then the other. The entire passage was blocked. There was no way forward.

Piay turned to look behind him, his heart pounding. Though he could see nothing in that vast ocean of dark, he sensed the Child-Killer drawing closer.

Now the spiritual challenge was clear. The only way was down. He would need to show that he believed he had lived a good life and so was unafraid of death, for he would not be able to see what terrors awaited him in the dark beneath.

Piay muttered another prayer to Khonsu, begging for him to guide him, then ducked below the surface. Down he went into that endless dark, the cold burning into every fibre of his being. The terrors of his experience in the shaft at Khem rushed back to him.

All he had was his sense of touch. Piay scrabbled along the foot of the wall until his numb fingers slipped into a hole. Up he thrust, to suck in a gasp of air, and then pulled himself back down to the bottom.

Three small holes were set in the wall. As he felt around, Piay realised one was shaped like a square, one like a circle and one an arch. He imagined that only one of the holes led to a tunnel that would pass beyond this gate. The other two would be traps, perhaps travelling so far that it would be impossible to make his way back before his breath ran out, or containing shifting slabs that would close behind him.

But which one should he choose?

Piay burst from the water again, his breath ragged. In the dark, his hearing seemed magnified. He could hear the slap of Akkan's sandals on the stone floor, unbearably close now. Nearby, the breathing of Myssa and the Cobra was strained with the fear they both must have been feeling. They seemed to be crouched in the shallows, waiting to learn what he had discovered.

Piay waded in the direction of Myssa. When he sensed she was close, he whispered, 'Any contest between us should wait. If we work together now, we may at least cling onto our lives to survive this test.'

Though he was speaking as quietly as he could, the acoustics of that space magnified every syllable. Wherever the Cobra was, he would certainly hear everything.

Myssa sighed, as if frustrated at Piay's determination to act with her, rather than against her.

'Hurry,' he urged. 'Akkan draws closer with every breath you take.'

That jolted her to a decision.

'Very well,' she muttered.

Piay described the entrances to the three tunnels.

'Which is the right one?' he asked.

Myssa thought for a moment, then said, 'The arch – Imhotep always valued its secret strength.'

Piay did not wait to debate the issue any further. He sucked in a huge breath of air, and once his lungs were full, he thrust himself back beneath the surface of the water.

Steadying his mounting fear, he hauled himself into the arched tunnel, using the walls to propel himself forward. It was even narrower than the sarcophagus he had sheltered in within the Pyramid of Khufu, and he felt claustrophobia tug his wits towards panic.

Then, with lungs burning, his fingers first sensed empty space, then curled back against the wall at the end of the tunnel. Piay pulled himself forward one last time. He kicked out of the narrow space, then placed his feet on the stone beneath him and leaped for the surface.

Clawing his way out of the water, Piay collapsed onto cool stone. The musty air tasted sweeter than any he had breathed in his life.

There was no time to rest, no time for further thought or reflection. Piay heaved himself up on shaky legs.

Behind him the water splashed and he heard the slap of feet on the stone. It was Myssa, by the sound of it. He felt a rush of relief that she was still alive.

'Thank you for—' he began.

'Don't thank me,' Myssa snapped in reply. 'I'm doing this for my people, not for you.'

As the echoes of her words died away, Piay heard more splashing. The Cobra had followed the path he had discovered.

That's the last time he steals any help from me, Piay thought, stumbling on into the darkness with Myssa close at his heels.

A choking odour of bitter fruit surrounded Piay. He winced as it stung the back of his throat. A few steps further and the atmosphere became so thick, he felt his head swim.

Piay cracked his foot against something. Reaching down, he closed his fingers around a rod-shaped object with a soft tip that felt like layers of mouldering linen.

As he imagined the shape in the dark, his thoughts leaped and he snatched his flint out of his soaking pouch. He struck it several times until a spark flared. After the endless dark, his eyes burned from the glare.

Behind him, Myssa cried out in surprise.

Piay struck the flint again, and this time the fabric caught and flames licked up. Beside him, Piay saw a slim rope dipped in some kind of dark tar-like substance. He raised the torch to see where the rope led and found another torch set into the wall. So, the rope was an oversized, upside-down candlewick.

Piay put the flame of his torch to the wick. At once it fizzed with sparks, then the flame caught hold properly, raced up the rope and ignited the torch on the wall. Piay just had time to spot the rope that ran horizontally away from that torch when it, too, burst into flames. A few seconds later another torch was lit, and then another, and on it went, again and again. In the blink of an eye, the whole tunnel was filled with a light that burned so brightly that Piay's eyes, now accustomed to the dark, were blinded. He blinked hard, cleared his vision and looked around.

Ahead of them, a channel had been carved through the floor. It was filled with some dark liquid that gleamed in the blazing light.

Piay glanced at Myssa. She was as drenched as he was, her sodden dress clinging to her body, her hair lank around her face. Droplets glimmered like jewels on her dark skin and the torchlight danced in her eyes. Piay's breath caught in his throat.

This woman is not your lover, he told himself, forcing himself to confront the truth. *She is your enemy*.

Piay's vision suddenly blurred. When he blinked it clear, he felt a growing ache throughout his entire frame that seemed to be draining the very life-force from him. The viper venom was beginning to overwhelm him.

He looked into Myssa's eyes and saw her lids growing heavy. She was suffering, too. How long did they have left? Neither of them could know for certain, but he felt sure the end was near.

Tearing his attention away from Myssa, Piay kneeled beside the channel and sniffed. Now he knew where the smell was coming from. It was filled with olive oil.

His curiosity piqued, Piay edged forward, holding the torch high. A little further the wash of light plucked out three signs carved into the stone floor, each one set a spear's length apart. Piay bowed over them. One was a crook and flail, one the sun, and the third an ibis.

'What do you see here?' Piay breathed.

Myssa did not reply.

She's your enemy, Piay repeated to himself.

Very well, he would think for himself alone. There were lines etched into the stone, moving ahead from each sign. He would follow them.

As Piay stepped forward, Myssa went with him, and he heard the slap of wet feet behind them both. The Cobra was hanging back, staying cloaked in the shadows beyond the glow from the torch. The desire to lead the way was long gone. Now he was content to let the others take risks, so that he might learn and profit from their misfortunes.

The fruity odour swelled as Piay and Myssa tracked along the lines until they both choked on its reek. Finally, they edged to a halt. The stone flags ended before a vast lake of oil. There were no more torches on the walls to illuminate the entire scene. The flames of Piay's hand-held brand painted a wash of amber across the surface, but not far enough to see to the far side.

Piay looked from side to side.

'There are no paths across this.' Despite himself, and in the face of all he knew, he still hoped that he and Myssa might somehow find a way to work together – to be together. 'And how deep is it? If we try to wade across we could drown.'

'Imhotep would not have made it that easy,' Myssa said, grudgingly.

A sharp sliver of hope cut through the toxins that were slowly overwhelming Piay's body. When he trekked back to the three symbols engraved in the floor, Myssa followed him.

Piay looked from the brand to the channel carving through the stone.

'We use the torch to light the oil.'

This time he kept his voice so low that only Myssa could hear. Her reply was equally quiet.

'But that will set the lake ablaze, with no path to the other side.'

Piay glanced back. 'Exactly. The soul must face the Lake of Fire on the journey through the afterlife. Imhotep wants the oil to burn.' He waved the torch towards the symbols. 'If there is a way across, then it's hidden here.'

'Crook and flail . . . the sun . . . ibis,' Myssa murmured. Sweat trickled down her brow.

'Oh . . .'

Piay sighed in anger at his own slowness. Myssa was a foreigner. Even with her intelligence, she could be forgiven for not spotting something very Egyptian.

'They're the symbols of gods,' he said. 'The crook and flail is Osiris. The sun is Ra. And the ibis is Thoth.'

'I did not need to be told that,' Myssa said.

Piay heard the anger in her voice, but there was no time for emotion. He started thinking aloud.

'All right, then – one of them leads to a way through the Lake of Fire. But which one? The underworld belongs to Osiris, so that would be the likely choice. Thoth records the verdict of the heart-weighing ceremony . . . and . . .'

Myssa tapped her foot impatiently towards the sun symbol.

'That one.'

'Ra is not important here—'

'Imhotep was the high priest of Ra at Heliopolis,' Myssa said, dismissively. 'He valued Ra above all others. That would have been his choice.' More because she wanted to win the argument, than from any desire to help him, she pointed to the channel of oil. 'Light it.'

There was no time for any further debate. Sweeping the torch down, Piay plunged it into the viscous liquid. Flames roared up and raced along the channel.

Ahead, the orange light swelled until the Passage of the Gods reverberated with a roar like a beast in the throes of fury. A scorching wind smashed along the tunnel, crashing over Piay and Myssa. Piay cursed as his skin seared and choking fumes filled his lungs.

The Lake of Fire blazed across the chamber.

Piay reeled from the roasting heat and threw an arm across his face to protect himself.

Myssa shielded her eyes and squinted into the flames.

'How do we get through that?' she shouted.

'Imhotep is testing our faith!' Piay shouted back, knowing that the Cobra could not possibly hear him. 'Show faith in the gods to guide our way!'

Through the haze of the poison coursing through him, he remembered the voice that had whispered to him in the Pyramid of Khufu.

'When the time comes, only water will keep the fire at bay.'

Piay leaned in to Myssa. 'Will you trust me?'

She nodded, reluctantly. They both knew that, even now, he could not bring himself to hurt her.

'Take off your dress,' Piay said.

Myssa frowned but did as he said.

Once she stood naked before him, her body gleaming in the firelight, Piay snatched the dress from her and raced back along the passage.

At the pool of black water reaching across the tunnel, he skidded to a halt and crouched. Grasping the linen of Myssa's dress in both hands, he ripped it in two. Without pause, he dunked the material into the pool.

The water cooled his hot skin, and the dank odour pushed aside the choking reek of burning oil. Piay thrust the remnants of the dress up and down, soaking them thoroughly.

As he began to withdraw them, bubbles broke on the surface.

Piay stared, puzzled. A hand burst from the pool, the white flesh mouldering. Fingers as hard as bronze clamped around his wrist.

Piay cursed in shock. In his addled state, he had forgotten the death that stalked at their backs.

Convulsing, he tried to rip himself free, but the rotting hand only gripped him tighter. Slowly, it began to pull Piay down towards the black water.

Piay tossed the dress aside and jabbed the fingers of his free hand behind the Child-Killer's grasp. Even as he edged closer to the pool, he thrust all his strength into those fingers and prised. Akkan was strong, perhaps even stronger than he had been in life. As Piay's arm slipped into the water, he forced enough of a gap to twist his hand free.

Piay flew backwards, sprawling across the flagstones.

In the flickering light, Akkan's head pushed up out of the water, first the rotting skin on his crown, then those dead, milky eyes.

Piay felt the cold clutch at his heart. In that silent figure rising from the depths, he could see only death given human form.

Jumping to his feet, Piay snatched up the cloth and pounded towards the light. The Cobra loomed in his path, but Piay barged past him and tossed one half of the sodden dress to Myssa.

'Wrap this around you as best you can,' he shouted over the roaring of the inferno.

Myssa heard the urgency in his voice and immediately complied.

Overhearing their plan, Tallus spun around, no doubt with the intention of soaking his own robe, but after only a few steps the sorcerer skidded to a halt and scrabbled backwards on his heels. Piay didn't look round. The Cobra had clearly seen Akkan rising from the depths. There was no way back now, no way to the pool, and no way forward for the Cobra.

Piay flashed a glance at Myssa. She nodded that she was ready, and they darted forward together along the line stretching out from the symbol of the sun.

Without missing a step, Piay tossed half the drenched cloth across himself and bowed his head into the scorching heat.

The flames were a liquid wall of gold and crimson, the roaring so loud it drowned out all other sound. Piay could see no way through. Faith was all he had: in the gods, in Imhotep, in Myssa.

He felt a pang of fear as the overheated air rushed into his lungs, but he threw himself on. To slow his step, even for an instant, would be disastrous.

The inferno swallowed him. At the moment when Piay thought he might plunge into the burning oil, he felt his feet pound on something solid: a stone path across the Lake of Fire. It would have been hidden beneath the surface of the oil, but the fire had already burned off enough of the liquid to reveal it.

Piay didn't dare to look back to see if Myssa was behind him. His exposed legs burned and the sodden cloth steamed.

When the air became too hot to breathe and barbs of agony stabbed deep inside him, Piay felt certain he was doomed. But then he stumbled past the last of the conflagration into the other side of the chamber, careering across the flagstones until the air cooled a little.

He looked up, gasping for air, to see Myssa crouched beside him, mopping her own skin. Their eyes met, and she smiled in relief that they had both survived. In that instant, Piay saw the face that he had known before she had succumbed to the Cobra's potion.

That warmth faded as Myssa looked past him. Piay followed her gaze. A long chamber stretched ahead, shimmering in the light from the Lake of Fire. On either side were looming statues, representations of the forty-two mummified beings who would carry out the final judgement of the soul in the afterlife. Piay glimpsed the Swallower of Shades, the Bone-breaker and the Eater of Entrails. Beyond them, in the centre of the hall, was a statue of a baboon – Thoth in his animal form.

Finally, against the far wall there stood a gigantic throne on which perched a statue of Osiris, the judge and the lord of the underworld. Piay shuddered as he looked up at the green-painted face – the colour of rebirth – topped by the tall *atef* crown with the curling ostrich feathers on either side. The figure was mummified to the neck and clutched the crook and the flail against its chest.

Three circular holes had been cut in the stone dais on which the throne was set. Piay stared at what had to be the final test, but he could see no distinguishing features near any of the holes. They were set in the dais at different heights: one near the floor, one level with Piay's waist, and one that came to halfway up his chest.

Myssa looked at Piay. Her gaze was steady. Her eyes neither asked for his help, nor offered any of hers. She was simply acknowledging what they both knew. This was the moment when one of them would win . . . and the other one would be condemned to death.

As Piay hurried forward to examine the holes, his feet kicked up a cloud of white dust. Before he could stop himself, he breathed in and winced at the bitter taste of one of the Sons of Apis' potions.

With the viper venom coursing through him, and the dust burning the path to his lungs, Piay felt as if the world was spinning away from him.

When his vision finally cleared, he gasped.

The gods had been summoned.

On one side loomed the enormous figure of Khonsu, the moon-disc atop his head, staring with a cold fury as he brandished the *was*-sceptre.

On the other side of the hall loomed the beast-headed Seth. His hatred burned as hot as the desert sands that were his home. So terrible was his visage that Piay wrenched his head away, but his skin still prickled from the seething sense of evil contained in the towering figure.

Khonsu and Seth stared each other down. This was the final phase of the battle that had raged between the two gods through their chosen agents upon the earth. In front of the gods, Piay felt insignificant, but he knew the outcome of this struggle now rested with him.

Pushing aside his terror, he dashed to the three holes. Each was large enough to take a single arm, and when he peered into their depths, the wavering light that reached that far revealed what looked like a loop of a dark metal.

Piay shook his head. Darkness was closing around the edge of his vision and his heart appeared to be slowing, his limbs growing more leaden with each fading beat. The venom was eating its way through what remained of him.

As his fingers wavered over the middle hole, Myssa grasped his shoulders and hauled him back. When he spun round, Piay saw her eyes were blazing.

The truce between them was over. The battle for who would live and who would die had begun. Suddenly a booming wail like that of a wounded bull elephant erupted from the direction of the Lake of Fire. The Cobra burst from the conflagration with his arms across his face. Flames leaped from his hair and surged up his robes. Piay breathed in the meaty odour of cooking flesh.

Howling, Tallus tore off his burning robe. His desperate attempt to cross the Lake of Fire had all but destroyed him. Half of his mane had been scorched away, and his skin was blackened and charred. One eye was entirely closed by a red curtain of burned, swollen flesh. His legs trembled, close to buckling, and only force of will kept him erect.

'Seth will not let me die!' he bellowed, his words ringing off the granite.

In an instant, the Cobra took in the statue of Osiris and the three holes in the dais and made his calculation. Swinging his arm, he smashed the back of his hand across Myssa's face. She flew across the stone floor and sprawled there, dazed.

Piay hesitated, unsure of whether to run to Myssa or try to stop Tallus. Before he could move, the Cobra had leaped forward and rammed his hand into the hole that was at chest height.

A grin spread across his scorched face. Victory was his.

Piay felt a queasy despair rush through him. How could he have failed? He had been one step away from claiming Imhotep's prize.

'For Seth!' the Cobra roared.

With a snap of his wrist, he twisted the handle at the base of the hole. A sharp click resounded from the depths. From the stone dais, a deep grinding reverberated.

Yet no opening appeared.

The Cobra's victorious grin faded and his charred face twisted with bafflement. Piay watched his expression turn to worry, and then his eyes widened and he wrenched back and forth with increasingly furious movements.

The Cobra's hand would not come free. Whatever had shifted within the dais had locked him fast.

Spitting curses, Tallus threw himself this way and that. He pressed one foot against the dais and heaved back with all his strength. Still he could not loosen himself. Blood trickled down his forearm, droplets splattering to the flagstones around his feet.

On the edge of his vision, Piay glimpsed a shadow moving through the now-dying flames of the burning lake.

The Cobra had been badly burned, but his injuries were as nothing compared to what Akkan had suffered. Smoke curled from his blackened skin; his hair had been burned away, as had his ears, eyelids and most of his nose. The Child-Killer lurched towards the Cobra, who still thrashed in a futile attempt to tear himself free. Blood pooled around his feet now. Gripped with terror, the sorcerer craned his neck back at that vision of death drawing towards him and screamed, throwing himself into even greater wildness, all to no avail.

To either side, the gods looked on, immortal spectators at a very human contest of life and death.

Akkan clamped his hands on the Cobra's neck and squeezed, the fingers digging deep as he slowly crushed the life from his former aide.

Piay didn't wait to see more. He sensed Myssa starting to shift behind him. Now he had to make a choice between the two remaining holes.

He blinked once, twice, trying to force away the encroaching darkness of the venom, and then he had it. Here was Imhotep's final spiritual test. A worthy man would approach humbly. He would come with head bowed on hands and knees, prostrate before the glory of the gods.

Myssa was clawing herself up on trembling arms. She was still half-stunned from the Cobra's assault, but more than that, it was the poison that was stealing her strength.

Before Myssa could make her move, Piay hurled himself forward and jabbed his hand into the lowest hole. His fingers closed around cold metal and he twisted. He clamped his eyes shut, fearing he would suffer the same fate as Tallus, but this time he felt the stones shift. A slab slid up and cool air drifted out from a dark square behind the dais, just big enough to crawl through.

As Piay dropped to his belly and slithered into the unknown, he could not resist one final glance.

Myssa stared at him, her dark eyes moist with despair. Piay felt his heart break when he saw the torment there. She knew that he had consigned her to death.

Crushed by the terrible emotion he had seen on her face, Piay turned away and dragged himself towards the ultimate revelation that would solve a thousand-year-old-mystery.

The slab slammed down the instant Piay crawled through the hole, the echo thundering across a space filled with a swimming darkness.

Piay imagined Myssa on the other side of that cold stone, her life ebbing away as the venom consumed her essence. He felt as if he had been stabbed, but he could not give in to wretchedness. His own life was hanging by a thread, and his only hope of rescuing her was to rescue himself first.

Staggering to his feet, Piay swayed on shaking legs. The fire in his veins was creeping inexorably towards his heart.

Through that vast stone door, the Cobra's howl reverberated as Akkan the Child-Killer dragged the life from him. Piay cared little for the torments he was enduring. Now only one thought burned in his mind.

He felt around for what he had glimpsed as he crawled through from the Hall of Judgement, and his fingers closed on another of the linen-topped torches. He struck his flint and a flame curled up.

Light raced across the walls of a granite-encased space that echoed the coffin chamber in the Pyramid of Khufu. 'As above, so below,' the leader of the Sons of Apis had said, and those words now seemed so much clearer.

Piay's skin prickled at the chill air. He breathed in the lingering ghost of a sweet scent like incense. In awe, he turned the brand to reveal more of the space and as he did his breath caught in his throat.

On every space along the walls the *medu netjer* – the gods' words – were painted in colours as brilliant as the day they were applied a millennium before. Here were the spells that so many had killed to find.

Whether it was the trace effects of the dust he had inhaled, or the tightening clutch of the viper venom, Piay felt certain he could feel a cold power radiating from those terrifying incantations. They seemed to be whispering in the depths of his head.

Piay wrenched his attention away before he was lost to them. He thrust the torch higher, and the dark unfurled to reveal a granite sarcophagus like the one in which he had hidden in the Pyramid of Khufu. But this one was still sealed. No adornment marked its smooth surface, no sign at all that it contained any king. Small statues, a goblet and some other ritual objects stood beside it.

It can only be the tomb of Imhotep himself, lost for an age, Piay thought. The Great Architect had set his plan in motion one thousand years before, and when he died, he had been buried at the very heart of it.

Piay bowed his head in reverence. He let the gravity of this moment settle on him until the pain from the venom cut even deeper and snapped him out of his reverie. He was growing delirious. His thoughts were drifting as death neared.

In desperation, Piay hurled himself towards the ritual objects. His fingers closed on the ornately carved golden handle of a knife and, still fearful that there might, even now, be one last enemy to overcome, he slipped it into the waist-band of his kilt.

The darkness around his vision edged closer. Now he felt as though he was peering along a tunnel that seemed to be slowly disappearing. The beat of his heart slowed until it was like the gentle lapping of the water in the shallows of the Nile.

Waving the torch over his head, Piay glimpsed what he needed most: a doorway on the other side of the chamber that opened on to another passage sloping upwards. The way back to the world of the living. He muttered a prayer to Khonsu, hoping beyond hope that there was still time for him, and staggered on. Soon he caught sight of a shaft of silver moonlight breaking through at the end of the tunnel.

Piay grasped the lintel of a small doorway in the passage ceiling and heaved himself up into the cool night air. The lush scent of the fertile river valley pushed the last of the reek of burning oil from his nose. Around him, heaps of freshly dug sand and shards of rock tumbled away from the tunnel entrance. Ahead, the Pyramid of Khufu soared up to the stars, limned in ivory by the moon.

Piay rocked from side to side as his legs threatened to give way. His heartbeat had become a distant whisper.

Through hazy eyes, Piay saw the Sons of Apis were waiting. The leader bowed his head, and his followers dropped to their knees and pressed their foreheads against the sand.

'You have been found worthy,' the leader said, keeping his head down in deference as he made his way towards Piay. 'You are the exalted one, predicted by Imhotep.' He raised a small hide pouch to Piay's lips. 'Just one brief draught and the potion of the viper venom will be driven from your body. Here you are reborn into your new life.'

Piay tasted the sweetness of honey, but behind it lay something bitter, like the skin of a melon. His lips puckered and he felt his throat burning as the liquid slid down. Then, as if a spell had been uttered, the darkness around his vision began to retreat. He could feel that his full strength would take some time to return, but he did not have time to wait for it. For now he saw his opportunity.

The Sons of Apis regarded him as their master. The antidote to the venom was almost in his grasp. Hope surged through him. It wasn't too late. He could still save Myssa.

Piay grabbed the ritual gold dagger from his kilt and levelled it at the leader of the Sons of Apis.

'Give me the potion – now.'

 The Sons of Apis had long wondered what the moment when the Riddle of the Stars was finally solved would be like. But nowhere in their myriad speculations had anyone considered the possibility that the Chosen One might undermine his own achievement and threaten the prize for which he had fought, by trying to rescue one of his vanquished competitors. Nor, for that matter, had they envisaged that the competitor in question would be a woman. So, now the leader of the Sons of Apis was faced with an unforeseen conflict between his sworn loyalty to the Chosen One, whoever that might be, and his first oaths to protect and uphold the testament of the Great Architect.

Now the leader looked at the desperate young man, standing in front of him with a knife in his hands, and knew at once that there could only ever be one choice: no one could be allowed to threaten the blessings that Imhotep's spells could bestow on the people of Egypt.

He stepped towards Piay.

'Do not even think of going back for her.'

'Do not forget – I am the exalted one. You answer to me!'

The leader sighed.

The young man was tall and strong, in the very prime of his physical powers, and yet, even now, there was so much that he did not understand.

'I have to go back!' Piay insisted. 'I can't let her die!'

'She is already dead. You are not responsible for her death.'

'No!' Piay cried, falling to his knees, his head on his chest. This was his moment of supreme victory, yet his despair was crushing. 'No! It cannot be!'

'You won a contest and shall have the prize. She lost and paid the penalty. You, the Kushite and the Hyksos all agreed to the same terms, in full knowledge of what those terms were, and what consequences they entailed. You proved yourself the worthy winner. Myssa the Kushite was young and strong, but the viper's venom is stronger.'

The leader stepped forward, placed a hand under Piay's chin and lifted it, so that their eyes met.

'Listen to me,' he said, his command a kindly one.

He withdrew his hand. Piay kept his head up.

'Tell me,' the leader said, 'did Lord Taita teach you by means of questions, drawing knowledge out of you, and leading you to your own conclusions?'

Piay nodded in agreement.

'Very well, then,' the leader said. 'I will do the same, and I will begin with this simple enquiry. Do you respect Lord Taita?'

Piay nodded again, as if that were so obvious that he was surprised even to be asked.

'Because he is your teacher and your master?' the leader asked.

Piay nodded once more.

'And what was the task he set you?'

'To solve the Riddle of the Stars . . .' Piay replied.

'And what would that accomplish?'

'It would bring peace and prosperity to Egypt . . . and perhaps even a communion with the gods.'

The leader nodded. 'Indeed . . . So, now I ask you the same question, about another. Did you respect Myssa the Kushite?'

Piay winced at the past tense. He could not bring himself to use it yet about Myssa. He still bore some desperate, irrational hope of a miracle.

'Of course, I love her—'

'That is not quite the same thing. I want to know whether you respected her right to make her own decisions.'

'Yes . . . She made it very clear to me that this was the one thing that mattered more to her than anything. Including me.'

'Very well. And when she chose, as you chose, to go in search of the Riddle of the Stars, what were the terms that I set out? How many would win, and how many would die?'

'One would win. Two would die.'

'You agreed to those terms?'

'Yes.'

'Of your own free will?'

'Yes.'

'Did she also agree to those terms, of her own free will?'

The leader waited for an answer, but the word *yes* seemed to stick in Piay's throat. He just nodded and gave a murmur of assent.

'Was she not the first to hold out her hand and take the poison?'

'Yes,' Piay said, angrily. 'You're right, I admit it, she knew what she was doing!'

The leader's inquisition continued, as calmly as before. 'And when you first went down to face the tasks that Imhotep had set, what did she say to you?'

Piay groaned. 'She said that she did not love me – that love felt like a form of slavery to her, and that I should set my love aside and be her enemy. And then . . . Then we should let the gods decide.'

The leader knew that answer to be honest, for nothing had happened in the entire Passage of the Gods that the Sons of Apis had not seen and heard. That Piay of Thebes could answer so honestly, even when his answer undermined him, was a point in his favour.

'Tell me,' the leader asked, 'was that the first time that she had made it plain that she did not want to be tied to you? That her hopes and ambitions lay elsewhere?'

Once again, Piay told the truth. 'No, she kept telling me that it was over between us.'

'Yet you would not listen. You would not believe her. Even when she had told you not to try to help her, you did so, more than once, didn't you?'

'Yes, I just . . . I couldn't just stand there and let her lose.'

The leader remained entirely calm, methodical, like a mathematician working through a logical sequence to solve the problem in front of him.

'But that was exactly what she said you should do,' he pointed out. 'Be her enemy, and let the gods decide. You have just said as much, yourself. Yet, from the moment you entered the Passage of the Gods, you were doing neither of those things. You insisted on acting as if you were still a couple, taking every step together . . . even though Myssa had made it plain that she did not want you to do that . . . even though you had earlier sworn to let her make a free choice. Was that showing respect to her?'

The leader looked at Piay, almost daring him to give any answer but the right one.

'No, it was not.'

'And were you showing respect to your master when you risked the mission with which he had entrusted you, because of your own personal feelings?'

Piay shook his head.

'And what of Imhotep and the gods? Were you respecting them by trying to bring two people to the end of the journey, rather than one, as they had, for the past thousand years, intended?'

Again, Piay could not even say *No* for shame at his impiety.

Now, the leader allowed a slightly greater degree of animation to enter his voice, just as that mathematician might have become a little more excited as his solution came into view.

'Only at the very last moment did you finally act for yourself alone, and understand that you should humble yourself and go down on your knees,' he said. 'Only then did you save yourself . . . and obey the rules of the challenge, the command of your master and the wishes of the one you say you love.'

'I failed her . . .'

'Do not punish yourself.' The leader placed a hand on Piay's shoulder. His voice was kind again as he said, 'You have done something extraordinary. You have succeeded where, for an entire millennium, all other men have failed. And when you did wrong, it was only because you have a good heart. There are many worse faults for a man to have, just as there are many worse things than death . . .'

The leader saw the puzzled look on Piay's face and asked, 'Would you really want to live forever, to see everyone you love die, and never be able to join them in the afterworld? Would you not long for release?'

The leader could sense the realisation dawning in the young man's mind.

'Yes, I am speaking from experience,' he said. 'When you referred to the Sons of Apis as ghost-warriors, you were not so far from the truth. We have existed as long as we have been needed. Now that you have fulfilled the prophecies of Imhotep, we can be released. Believe me, you have our deepest gratitude for that.'

'But Myssa—'

'Was fated to die, as you were fated to survive. Even if you had rescued her, we would not have let her live. We could never have allowed her to take the secrets of this place away to her own land, and place the gods of Egypt at the service of other men. As you mourn her, console yourself with the thought that Myssa may have lost her family in life, but now she can be with them in death. Is that not a blessing?'

Piay nodded. 'Yes . . . If she could be with them again, she would think she was blessed.'

'Everything that is truly worth having comes at a price. You have accomplished something that will benefit your people for centuries to come. In so doing, you have lost the woman you loved. That is the price that you and she have paid. But there will be other women whom you love as much as you loved Myssa.'

'I can't imagine that.'

'And yet it is so . . .'

The leader paused as he saw Piay casting his eyes around him, as if searching his surroundings for something he had lost.

'What are you looking for?' he asked

'I don't know, really . . .' Piay frowned. 'Just . . . something different . . . some sign that the spells are working.' He gave a wry laugh. 'And treasure . . . All the treasure that we were hoping to find.'

'The spells will work – but slowly. And there will treasure, but not as you, or the others, have imagined. My lord Imhotep wanted a better land for his people. If he had left storehouses filled with gold and jewels, that would merely start men fighting again. And what good would that do? But peace, and good harvests, and a land free from invaders . . . Are those things not better than gold?'

Piay thought of the greed in Harrar's and Zahur's eyes when he had told them that he was digging for treasure, and the terrible effects of poverty and hunger on the people of Memphis.

'Yes, they are . . . much better,' he said.

'Very well, then, your work and mine are both done. You must go to Thebes to carry news of what you have accomplished to Lord Taita. Our last duty will be to guard the Hall of Spells until you and he return. Now, go to your master, and be thankful, for you have a long life and many adventures yet to come. And—'

'Wait,' Piay said, and the leader could see a new sense of animation within him: an idea coming to his mind and a plan beginning to form.

'As you wish . . . We are at your command.'

'Then I am going to give you an order. Make it possible for me to get back into the temple, where Myssa is lying. If I cannot save her . . . If she is . . .' The leader watched as Piay forced himself to say the word *dead*, and went on, 'Then, it makes no difference if I go to her. I am still the only survivor.'

'That is true,' the leader said. 'But you are the Chosen One. If you die before the spells can be cast, then they die with you. Akkan is still there. He was not poisoned. He is still Death in Life.'

For the first time, the leader saw the warrior spirit in Piay's eyes.

'Can he be killed?'

'Yes . . . but not easily. You know for yourself how much he has already survived. Still, it is possible to finish him.'

'Good,' Piay said. 'Then that is what I will do. So, I have given my order – now you must obey it.'

'Indeed,' the leader agreed. And then, for the first time in an age, he felt something close to a sense of mischief as he added, 'But first I must ask a favour of you, Chosen One. The knife you are holding is sacred. It cannot be sullied by blood, and certainly not by the body of Akkan. If you go back to the temple, you will have to go without it.'

Piay could not believe what he had just heard. Even now, the leader of the Sons of Apis was trying to frustrate him. And to make it worse, there was a smile on his tattooed face.

'I insist! I absolutely must . . .' Piay began, but then he saw the hand extended towards him, and a knife lay on its open palm.

'Your friend,' the leader said. 'A far sharper, more piercing weapon, being bronze. And . . .' He shrugged. 'More apt, perhaps, since it was given to you by your master, who sent you on this quest, and named by your woman. May your love for her give you strength. Now . . . go.'

Piay nodded. He took the knife; another of the Sons of Apis handed him a burning torch, and then he made his way back to Imhotep's burial chamber. He paused for just a second to look around at the spells upon the walls. In them lay the hope of peace, justice and a better life for all the people of Egypt. If he failed now, he would be failing them, too. But if he did not go back into the temple, he would be failing Myssa.

Piay walked towards the square of deep, black shadow that marked the short tunnel to the temple. When he reached it, and looked in, he saw nothing but blackness. It was still blocked at the far end. But the Sons of Apis were not tricksters. If the leader had let him return, then he would also clear his way.

Just as he was about to climb into the tunnel, holding his torch out in front of him, Piay realised that the Lake of Fire would surely not have burned itself out. In that case, the temple would be illuminated, so he would not need the torch. Surely, he would be better off with both hands free. But what if the flames had vanished as quickly as they had appeared and he was about to blunder into total darkness? Was this yet another test?

Piay did not stop to debate the matter. He put the torch on the granite floor, ready for him to pick up on the way out. Then he got down on his knees and crawled into the tunnel. And as he made his way through it, his mind was filled with the same words, repeated again and again, so that he did not give in to temptation.

Don't look at Myssa. Kill Akkan first.

Piay crawled on. The end must surely be near. He held out a hand in front of him and kept going forward, just a little way, until his fingers touched the cold granite slab that blocked the way. An instant later, the slab slid back up into the wall.

Piay emerged into the temple and was confronted with a vision of the Land of the Dead. But this was no place of peace, more a land of eternal torment. The Lake of Fire was still burning, but only just, and its last flames emitted a half-light that cast the clouds of smoke, the walls and the statues of the gods in demonic shades of red, grey and black.

Immediately beside Piay, as he emerged into this hideous world, the body of Tallus hung from the hand that was trapped in the topmost hole. The Cobra's head sagged to one side on a shattered neck. His stomach had been sliced open and the tattered, glistening remnants of his guts trailed down his naked torso and across the flagstones.

Then, as he got to his feet, Piay saw the remains of the man who had been Akkan. The gaping maw of his mouth was covered in blood.

He had feasted on Tallus' innards, and now he was stalking towards Myssa on stiff legs, hands reaching for her body.

She was curled across the stone floor, her head resting on her bent right arm. Her face looked so peaceful that it was as if she had fallen asleep and might wake up at any moment. Even though he knew it was impossible, still Piay's heart leaped at the hope that somehow, even now, she might have survived.

Akkan stood directly over Myssa, looking down at her as if deciding where to strike first. Then he reached down, grabbed her hand and began to pull her body up off the floor.

Her body did not respond. Her eyes did not open. That last cruel flicker of hope was extinguished.

'No!' screamed Piay.

He dashed towards the monstrous figure, the dagger clenched in his fist.

Akkan turned his head at the sound and let go of Myssa's arm. Her body dropped to the floor like a little girl's discarded doll, as Piay plunged his blade into the Child-Killer's chest, right up to the hilt, then pulled it out, ready to strike again.

But Akkan did not even flinch. Instead, he lunged, wrapping his huge arms around Piay and hauling him off his feet. Their two heads were face to face and Piay gagged at the nauseating stench of Akkan's rotting flesh, coughing the air from his lungs as his chest was constricted. He could not breathe.

Piay flew into a frenzy, driving the dagger again and again into the Child-Killer's neck. Still, Akkan seemed to feel no pain.

Piay's vision was closing in, his strength was fading, his whole body was screaming for air. He summoned all his remaining energy and struck again, three times.

They were the last blows he could muster. His grip loosened. His knife fell to the floor.

And then, quite suddenly, Akkan's neck gave way; his head sagged to one side.

Piay was on the brink of total oblivion. His senses were numbed, his mind dulled, and it took him a moment to realise that he could breathe again. He sucked the smoky air deep into his chest and coughed so violently that he did not see Akkan fall. But when his breathing calmed and he wiped the tears from his eyes, the massive body was lying beside Myssa on the temple floor.

The sight of the two of them side by side was more than Piay could bear. He stepped over Akkan's lifeless form, then bent down, lifted Myssa and carried her away from the remains of the men who had ruined her life. Then he lowered her, very gently, to the floor.

Myssa's face was as lovely as ever, but the spark had gone from her eyes and the warmth from her body. New tears blurred Piay's vision, gentle at first, until a dam burst inside him and he was racked by desperate sobs at the loss of such a glorious life. He tried to control himself with the thought that Myssa deserved better than this unmanly display, and slowly the storm inside him blew itself out.

Piay calmed himself. He wiped his eyes and his nose with his forearm. Then he gave a half-laugh and said, 'Look, my love . . . your goddess has come to see you.'

Bast walked up to Myssa's body, licked her shoulder three times, then sat back, wrapped her tail around herself and examined Piay expectantly.

'You want me to say something, don't you?' he murmured, as he looked into eyes that somehow still looked green, even in the red haze of smoke. 'All right . . .'

Piay paused as he tried to compose himself, then a very clear, coherent thought entered his mind. He looked at the cat, almost seeking its approval, then said, 'I'm going to make two vows to you, Myssa, my true love. The first is that I am going to take you back to your own land, so that you can be with your people for all eternity. And my second vow is . . .'

Piay had to stop as he felt the tears rising once again. He fought them back as he repeated, 'My second vow is that from now on, till the day I die, I will do everything I can to honour your legacy and make sure that your death was not in vain. I will be a better man, the kind you always deserved. I will try to do good. I will fight as hard as I can to stop other women suffering as you did. I swear by all the gods that I will be worthy of your love . . . and of your sacrifice.'

Piay looked at Bast. The all-knowing cat looked back and then, apparently satisfied with what she had heard, she unwrapped her tail, got to her feet and started trotting off towards the tunnel. Piay took the hint. He picked up Myssa's body, cradled her in his arms and said, 'Come on, my darling, it's time I took you home.'

DISCOVER
THE ANCIENT EGYPTIAN
ADVENTURES

Set in the land of the ancient Pharaohs, Wilbur Smith's bestselling series vividly brings Ancient Egypt to life. Following the beloved Taita, Smith's most iconic hero, this is an unmissable series from the Master of Adventure fiction.

RIVER GOD
THE SEVENTH SCROLL
WARLOCK
THE QUEST
DESERT GOD
PHARAOH

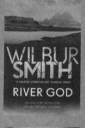

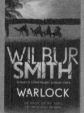

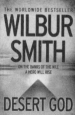

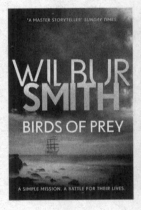

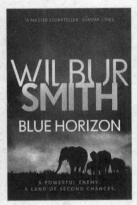

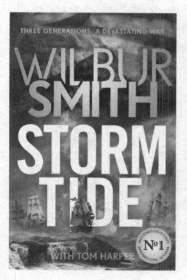

**THE STUNNING CONCLUSION TO THE ASSEGAI
SEQUENCE OF THE COURTNEY SERIES**

LEGACY OF WAR

The war is over, Hitler is dead – and yet his evil
legacy lives on. Former Special Operations Executive,
Saffron Courtney, and her beloved husband, Gerhard,
only just survived the brutal conflict, but Gerhard's
Nazi brother, Konrad, is still free and determined to
regain power. As a dangerous game of cat-and-
mouse develops, a plot against the couple begins to
stir. One that will have ramifications
throughout Europe . . .

Further afield in Kenya, the last outcrop of the
colonial empire is feeling the stirrings of rebellion.
As the situation becomes violent, and the Courtney
family home is under threat, Saffron's father, Leon
Courtney, finds himself caught between two powerful
sides – and a battle for the freedom of a country.

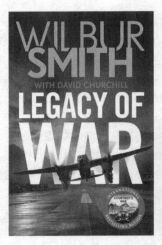

The thrilling conclusion to the
Assegai sequence. *Legacy of
War* is a nail-biting story of
courage, rebellion and war.

AVAILABLE NOW

 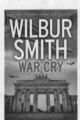 

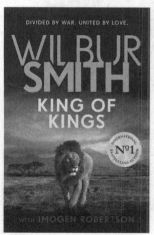

UNLEASH THE
ULTIMATE PREDATOR IN . . .

Share the adventure with a new generation in this
brand new series for children aged 10+, featuring
Ralph and Robyn Ballantyne!

AVAILABLE NOW